DAOIST ENIGMA

MODERN PATRIARCH

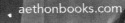

aethonbooks.com

MODERN PATRIARCH
©2024 DAOIST ENIGMA

Aethon Books
www.aethonbooks.com

Print and eBook design and formatting by Josh Hayes.

Published by Aethon Books LLC.

Aethon Books is not responsible for websites (or their content) that are not owned by the publisher.

ALSO BY DAOIST ENIGMA

MODERN PATRIARCH

Modern Patriarch

Modern Patriarch 2

Check out the entire series here! (Tap or scan)

1

PATRIARCH V. HEAVEN

YAO SHEN ROARED DEFIANTLY toward the heavens, his protective formations long shattered, precious soul armor disintegrated to nothingness, and regal robes tattered beyond repair. Blood gushed out from the holes, drenching the originally azure robes a crimson red.

The heavens rumbled loudly in response, the intention behind its gesture clear— he was not qualified to become a Soul Emperor. His nascent soul was of average quality, his Dao a mishmash of concepts cobbled together to barely form a coherent domain. Yao Shen was not a talented *cultivator* – a practitioner who seeks enlightenment over the profound Natural Laws that govern the realm of Eliria; his spiritual roots were too impure, his heritage too muddled, his cultivation speed too average. Even his own Sect had never expected him to cross beyond the threshold of the foundation establishment stage.

A hundred years later, he was the patriarch: A bona fide, Peak-Stage Nascent Soul Cultivator— one of merely four in the entire Azlak Plains. And now, he would become a Soul Emperor.

"I am not qualified," Yao Shen roared, spraying out a mouthful of red blood moments later. "For two hundred years, those are the words I have heard countless times— from my fellow core disciples, from the sect elders, and even from the only man I have revered in this lifetime, my late master!"

A wave of weakness washed over him, followed by another fit of hacking coughs, but he remained standing.

"But when have I let that stop me?" Yao Shen asked as he broke out into a bloodied sly grin.

The heavens thunderously rumbled, and bolts of thick blue lightning transformed into a brilliant, bright red that spoke of tremendous, terrifying power— the power to destroy everything it touched, to reduce anything to nothingness.

"Oh, mighty Heavenly Dao! Whether I live or die, bear witness to the synthesis of a lifetime of cultivation!" Yao Shen roared, and the landscape around him began to change. The dried patch of land was replaced by a dazzling golden wheat field, rays of sunlight tearing past the tribulation clouds and landing upon the fields. Transparent silhouettes of Faceless farmers dressed in grey clothing manifested around Yao Shen, harvesting the wheat by hand— they were not cultivators, merely mortals. At the center of the wheat field, a small, dainty wooden house rested, adding to the scenic natural beauty of the rustic landscape.

This was his domain— his will imposing order over the Natural Law, reshaping the world in his image. This was a law that could not be defied, only broken.

Yao Shen calmly walked forward and plucked a stalk of wheat from the fertile farmland, strolling over and depositing it in a basket fastened on one of the illusory farmer's backs.

The red lightning could not bear the affront to the Heavenly Dao any longer and it viciously crashed down on him the next instant— with an intent to obliterate him and his puny domain that dared tarnish heaven's prestige.

Yao Shen ignored the lightning strike, focusing his attention entirely on harvesting stalks of wheat.

The red lightning paused mid-air, simply hovering in the air as if it had been frozen in place. Yao Shen had done nothing; The Heavenly Dao in itself had chosen to withhold the tribulation.

"The mortal farmer takes months to accomplish what a cultivator can do in a day. He is denied Qi by the heavens, deemed unworthy for reasons beyond the understanding of man— mortal and cultivator alike. A cultivator's fate is determined at birth— his bloodline, spiritual roots, and talent determine how far he will go on the path of ascension. The mortal farmer and the impure cultivator may be different in many ways, but they are united in one truth." Yao Shen deposited three stalks of wheat into another farmer's basket.

"The heavens may have taken much from them both," Yao Shen looked at the skies, his gaze serene as the clouds, "but it cannot take the human heart."

The red lightning crashed down the next instant, but Yao Shen just laughed heartily, despite his near-fatal injuries. It headed right for him, ruthlessly smiting him down without giving him an opportunity to react. Yao Shen's body burst into flames before scattering into nothingness, the entire sequence taking place too quickly for the spectators to even begin to process it.

"Both the mortal farmer and the impure cultivator," Yao Shen continued as the silhouette of a nearby farmer morphed into a spitting image of Yao before gaining a solid, tangible form, "are united in their perseverance, their determination, their will— to prove the mighty heavens wrong!" Yao Shen roared mightily and was met with another red lightning strike blasting him to smithereens.

"You can kill me as many times as you wish," Yao Shen mockingly gazed at the heavens, as another farmer morphed into his spitting image, "but what you are fighting against is not me, but the will of countless mortals and cultivators alike— their defiant spirits! Kill one, and another will take his place. Kill a thousand, and ten thousand more will rebel! Tell me, do you dare!?" Yao Shen screamed toward the heavens, a glint of madness shining in his eyes.

The phantoms around Yao Shen all looked toward the skies along with him, and soon where there were originally ten phantoms, there stood a hundred. They all morphed into the likeness of Yao Shen, staring at the heavens with the same glint in their eyes.

"Do you dare!?"

"Do you dare!?"

"Do you dare!?"

"Do you dare!?" a hundred voices all screamed in unison, resulting in a cry of defiance far more powerful than any war cry. This was a display of the true power of the Human Dao, one of the *Esoteric Daos*— those that could not be sought after, only experienced.

The red lightning receded, turning back into a light blue color, and the next moment, the clouds dissipated. An ancient hymn resounded in the surroundings, and golden scriptures from the sacred text circled around Yao Shen. Above him, a phantom image of a radiant wheat field with farmers milling about manifested, a projection so large that it could be viewed from thousands of kilometers away. A wave of golden light crashed down from the heavens, but this time, Yao Shen made no attempt to resist. His severe wounds were healed instantly, and Qi rushed toward him from all directions, ripples felt across the Azlak Plains as the entire region's Qi was monopolized by one cultivator alone, if only for an instant.

The process of ascension began.

2

THE MODERN SECT

YAO SHEN'S consciousness began to fade, but he did not channel his Qi in an attempt to resist the foreign influence weighing down upon his soul. There was no reason for him to do so; after all, he had expected this. A Soul Emperor was one who had earned full command over his soul. Each soul only received ten chances to reach Soul Emperor or, simply put, ten full life cycles, before the soul is irreparably shattered. With every life cycle, the potential for ascension was irrevocably diminished by a slight margin.

Thus, it was not a surprise to Yao Shen that he was only on his second cycle of reincarnation. As the memories started flooding back, though, Yao Shen, who was in a dream-like state, felt chills crawl up his spine, feeling shock so intense that words alone were not sufficient to convey the breadth of his disbelief.

He dreamt… of a world.

And at that moment, Yao Shen realized that the world he lived in was not his own. He was an otherworldly existence, a soul that had managed to sneak past the heavenly web guarding the planet of Eliria. An *anomaly*, an *aberration*, that snuck into the cycle of reincarnation.

Yao Shen felt like keeling over and vomiting, his hands trembling in the astral state he found himself. He perceived himself as shadowy silhouette floating in the vast expanse of space, a concept he did not even know existed up until a few seconds ago.

He dreamt of a world... of mortals.

A world where the Heavenly Dao did not exist A world where mortals were simultaneously both the weakest and the strongest existence on their planet, vexingly enough. For without access to the *breath of the world,* what the cultivators of Eliria knew as *Qi* and spiritual roots to cycle that Qi and empower the body, all the humans of this world had left was their intellect. So that was what they did: honed their intelligence to a point where their weapons could slay beasts, or animals as they had termed them —animals that were faster, stronger and far more deadlier than the human body ... with *shocking* ease.

A world that destroyed his conceptions, his understanding, and ironically, his very world view. Mortals were supposed to be weak, hapless existences that served cultivators. He had never thought of them like that, but most cultivators did. Yet these same mortals were capable of using a Dao that required not murder and bloodshed, but *understanding* and *rational thinking*, to make the impossible possible.

As a Soul Emperor, he could level an entire town, or even a large city or sect by himself alone. But the weapons these mortals had developed were potent enough to level their entire planet, leaving not even ash behind.

But with these powerful weapons... instead of waging war, they brokered peace. On this world, Earth, Yao Shen was not a warrior. He was just a person, like any other. A merchant, or rather a businessman, that worked for a 'company.' He had a wife, who he deeply cherished, two children that he would grow to adore, and a peaceful life where he contributed to the community he lived in before dying a natural death. A peaceful death, surrounded by those he loved right until the end.

"*Weak*," was what Yao Shen should have been thinking. The mortal version of him was clearly soft, easily trusting, and naïve. He did not train his body or learn martial arts to defend himself and his family. However, despite waiting and waiting, no attack came. His sect, or rather, 'office' brothers and sisters, did not betray him. No assassins were sent to his house to eliminate him, and no one coveted his position enough to try and destroy him.

"*Weak*," was what Yao Shen should have thought, so why then, for the second time in his entire lifetime, was he crying?

How many people had he killed to climb to the position of Patriarch? How many cultivators had he eliminated, to protect his so-called 'face,' the reputation that he prided so much? He had done so in order to progress his cultivation much as any other cultivator would, without an iota of hesitation. What had he received in return? *More* power. *More* resources. *More* territory.

All logical spoils of conquest.

Why then, did it hurt so much? All the wealth, resources, and incomparable, absolute power within the Azlak Plains could be his for the taking with the flick of his finger, so why did he feel that he was... *happier* in his previous life, as a normal, hapless mortal?

He had brought shame to the people of Earth, for they would no doubt see his present self as a monster. The will of a Soul Emperor, however, is not to be underestimated. To others, it might be a tribulation, but for Yao Shen, who had climbed up all the way up from an ordinary, talentless cultivator to Patriarch, it would take a lot more than that to break his will.

However, his paradigm had shifted, and try as he might, Pandora's Box could not be sealed. Another term from his old world that he'd used without thinking, simply because it was the first thing that came to his mind. He remembered the time when, at the peak of his arrogance, he struck down a disciple of a rival sect for rudely gesturing at him as he was walking with his fellow Heavenly Sky Sect disciples.

He had defended his prestige, just like his sect had taught him. At that point, when he stared at those shocked eyes, he felt nothing but arrogance and pride. Now, he only felt disgust and revulsion. Perhaps a weaker man would not be able to live with these terrible sins. But every world should be viewed with its own paradigm; his actions were wrong and terrible, resembling those of his early ancestors on Earth, those he had read about in *'history books.'*

That did not justify his sins, but the cultivators of Eliria accepted his actions, for they were simply the norm prevalent in society.

His death would serve no purpose, but to reinstate another despot like him, perhaps even more cruel.

His Dao Heart was shaken by these revelations, but it would not shatter. However, even if he discounted the morality aspect of the moment, there was a question that had to be considered.

Was Eliria's approach the correct one? Why then, was their food bland and uninspired compared to the styles of cuisine he'd sampled on Earth? Why then, were the only sources of entertainment they had access to tournaments, duels, and other competitions much like their forefathers had? Why then, were all cultivators mindless zombies who spent year after year, decade after decade, becoming stronger, and then using that power to kill instead of build?

The answer was simple.

They were wrong, and their approach was flawed because they didn't know any better.

"So be it," Yao Shen muttered, and the illusion around him shattered, his Dao Heart reborn with a crystalline clear determination. He became the Sect Leader, not only out of a desire to repay the sect and the efforts of his late master, but to transform his sect into a behemoth, one whose reputation was so hallowed that their name would even be well-known to foreign continents, so fearsome that nobody would dare to raise a hand on his disciples unless they were seeking death.

Now, his determination was reborn anew, and this time, there was no doubt in his heart. For this was the only correct path.

He would start by renaming his sect. It was time to cause a storm in this bloodthirsty world, and this time, his weapon would not be murder, but something even more *potent* — civilization.

It was time for the Modern Sect to make its debut.

3

MIRACLE

YAO SHEN'S eyes snapped open just in time to gaze at the receding tribulation clouds. It all made sense now. Those who sought the esoteric Human Dao by pretending to show kindness or even living amongst mortals to prove the 'nobility' cresting in their hearts, some demonic cultivators even going so far as kidnapping mortals for experimentation, could never attain it, not even in a thousand years.

Why did he sympathize with the plight of mortals as a powerful cultivator? A person can never fully deny the impact their environment has on them, not without access to outside information or perhaps a mortal who left a lasting impact on them, changing their worldview.... but Yao Shen had none of these experiences. Then why did he respect mortals, when he had no qualms about killing his fellow cultivators?

Because he had lived as one, if only a lifetime ago. The mind may forget, but the soul remembers. Was there truly anyone more qualified to study Human Dao than him, who knew the true potential of mortals? No, such a derogatory term was no longer necessary Yao Shen could only wistfully wonder how different Eliria's landscape would have been if, instead of valuing martial prowess as the sole criterion for an individual's worth, they had valued inventiveness and ingenuity equally. Then, perhaps, the humans born without the ability to cultivate would not grow up believing themselves inferior to the 'chosen ones.'

The true potential of humanity. Somewhere out there in the stars, perhaps galaxies away, was a planet named Earth. One day, Yao Shen would like to return.

He felt the nearby Qi submitting to his control, but for weaker threats, he no longer required it. His physical body alone was enough to tear through a Peak Core Formation Cultivator's defenses. His two Nascent Souls, after going through the process of compression and refinement with each strike of tribulation thunder he withstood and a final refinement directly from the Heavenly Dao, had been fused into one, single soul that *exceeded* a Peak Nascent Soul Cultivator's soul potency by a hundred times.

He had not just ascended to Soul Emperor, but achieved perfection. The esoteric Human Dao invited the greatest punishment from the Heavenly Dao, the red lightning that had attacked him earlier being the *Divine Lightning of Extermination*, bearing the full power of a soul attack at the level of an early-stage Soul Emperor.

Had he not revealed his Human Dao Domain, the tribulation would have continued on as normal, but he would no longer be able to progress in the pursuit of Human Dao... his Dao Heart forever incomplete due to his own cowardice. Yao Shen was not a reckless man, merely a *talentless* one. If he had continued to attempt it the normal way, his *patchwork rotating domain* that was a combination of Minor Daos would have shattered to pieces, and he himself would have miserably perished.

Soul Cultivation had never been his specialty, but due to the sheer volume of his soul, he could overwhelm any Nascent Soul Cultivator with his divine sense alone, a feat that he doubted that many Soul Emperors could match.

His divine sense was currently in *'passive mode,'* in Earth's terms. He was not focused on scanning for anything particular in his surroundings, but everything in a distance of a hundred li was being monitored for any threats.

His divine sense was far more responsive than before, allowing Yao Shen to detect eight silhouettes fast approaching in his direction, including two especially powerful presences that unmistakably belonged to his rival sect leaders, who approached with solemn footsteps, knowing that *every subsequent step could be their last.* If the Heavenly Dao did not strictly forbid interference during the tribulation, even when it desperately wished to kill the cultivator in question, he had no doubt they would have interfered. Then again, if it did allow interference, there would hardly be any cultivator who succeeded.

If there was one thing Yao Shen appreciated about Eliria over Earth, then it was the fact that there were no cowards among cultivators. Cruel, *yes.* Despotic, *indeed.* Vicious barbarians? *Fair.* But no true patriarch would choose to flee and abandon their sect when death came knocking at their doorsteps. If fighting was possible, then they would fight until both sides were bloodied and hurting. If the gap was unfathomable, then they would offer up their lives and hope the other party was merciful to their descendants.

For a cultivator, shattering one's own Dao Heart by fleeing was a proposition worse than death.

"Patriarch! You succeeded!" Three inner disciples knelt on the floor in reverence, speaking the same words in unison with an indescribable joy in their voices, trailed by Elder Han, who was at a loss for words from the jumble of shock and disbelief he felt, his hands quivering.

"Indeed." Yao Shen nodded and then gave a wide, toothy grin that was unbecoming of his stature.

His disciples blanched at that gesture, their faces going white from fear, and the female disciple even took two steps back.

"P-P-Patriarch…. Please calm yourself," the young girl, who couldn't be more than sixteen years old, pleaded.

Yao Shen gave her a questioning look, before realizing that… he didn't really smile. *Ever.* Except for that one time he'd gone out looking for vengeance.

Sighing wearily, Yao buried a pang of guilt in the corner of his heart, before he replied, "Relax, child. I am in a very pleasant mood today."

He walked over and patted her on the shoulder before walking past the group of disciples and toward the two aged men with stern, poised faces, who stared at him with ferocity in their gazes.

He took one step forward, and for them, death grew closer. They flinched not.

Soon, he was face to face with them, two core disciples from each rival sect shivering in fear behind their respective leader's backs, almost on the verge of fainting.

"Patriarch Kang Long. Patriarch Lei Weiyuan," Yao Shen began, his words calm and pleasant to the ear, as if he were offering greetings to two old friends.

"Patriarch Yao Shen," Patriarch Kang Long replied in return, followed by Patriarch Lei Weiyuan, who solemnly repeated the same greeting, his mind clearly distracted by the more pressing issue at hand.

"I am here to kill you both. You will not run?" Yao Shen asked with curiosity, though his tone bore no real doubt or hesitation, only a bone-chilling certainty.

"You two, get out of here," Patriarch Kang Long commanded, followed by a long, weary sigh. The two disciples behind him belonging to the Sacred Flame Palace and the Divine Mountain Sect sprinted away without any hesitation, knowing that they had no power to interfere in the confrontation that was about to ensue.

To the large congregation that was watching the spectacle from a safer distance, it appeared as if the disciples of the Heavenly Sky Sect's two rivals were frantically fleeing for their lives.

"Our old lives are already considered forfeit. Patriarch Yao Shen, we are all members of the righteous path. Let the blood debt incurred over the centuries be resolved with our deaths. The elders of our respective sects may have had our *differences,* but Nascent Soul Cultivators are still a priceless force against the demons that cannot be lost, " he implored, though the absolute calm with which he made his request was very uncharacteristic of a man prepared to forsake his life for his sect.

The next instant, two of Yao Shen's oldest foes moved to bow to him in unison.

Two firm hands were placed on both their shoulders, locking both the Patriarchs in place.

"Raise your heads, Patriarch Long! Patriarch Weiyuan!" Yao Shen's voice boomed out, causing the two Patriarchs to look up at him with confused expressions on their faces.

"What do you mean, Patriarch Shen?" Kang Long questioned, his face paling a little as he immediately assumed the worst. Their lives, which they had already resolved to sacrifice, would not alone suffice as atonement.

"If I was the same person I was before my ascension..." Yao Shen began, his expression calm as he watched dangerous lights flash in the two Patriarchs' desperate gazes. "I would have killed you both. For decades, you have *conspired against my sect, killed my disciples* as mine have yours and even gone as far as to have an *elder assassinated...* your crimes are simply too many to count. I should kill you as you stand, along with all the vile elders that were behind these crimes against my Heavenly Sky Sect. Perhaps for no other reason than the irrefutable fact that you would do the same if our situations were reversed, in a heartbeat."

Yao Shen's voice cracked a little as decades of frustration and enmity were sounded out.

"*Indeed,*" Patriarch Kang Long replied, staring back into his eyes without any falsity or deceit. He would have killed Yao Shen and would have lost no sleep over it.

"Then why haven't you?" Patriarch Lei Weiyuan asked, perplexed by Yao Shen's change in demeanor.

"The histories of our sects can be traced back thousands of years. Hundreds of sects once ruled over this ancient land, but after the great calamity, only our three sects survived in the entire Azlak Plains. Tell me, do the both of you remember why we fight? Why do our sects, generation after generation, take pride in killing each other's disciples, the seeds of our future?" Yao Shen asked slowly, deliberating on each word.

"Our sect records show—" Still unable to discern Yao Shen's intentions, Kang Long tried to answer the question truthfully.

"Not the sect records!" Yao Shen snapped angrily, pointing a finger at Kang Long's chest. "Do you personally remember? Were you there when the original grievance took place? The Azlak Plains have been in conflict for the past thousand years, fighting over grievances of old fossils that have long since rotted in the ground! Tell me, Patriarch Kang Long, can you truly verify the authenticity of events that occurred generations before you were born? Thousands of years ago?" Yao Shen furiously roared at them, taking both Patriarchs by complete surprise.

Beads of sweat rolled down their forehead as they pondered upon his words, the insinuations striking at their hearts more viciously than tribulation lightning ever could. They were sharp, cunning leaders who understood that it was possible for the sect records to have been doctored far before their time. Cultivators did not prize maintaining historical records even half as much as they did scrolls containing powerful techniques, legacies, pill recipes, and anything else that could lead them toward greater martial strength.

Tattered old records written in obsolete script... was that truly all that rested at the inception of their conflict?

"Does the reason matter when the flames of hatred have been reignited every subsequent generation?" Patriarch Lei Weiyuan asked, for after a point, it had become less about the original conflict and more about resources and sect interests.

"Ah, yes. *Conflict*. Is that not how we justify gambling the lives of our disciples each time a new inheritance ground is discovered? Sure, we may not ask them outright, but all of us are aware of what happens when two disciples of rival sects encounter each other without the oversight of elders. Conflict separates the wheat from the chaff, hones the disciples' combat instincts and acts as a way to distribute the resources of the Azlak Plains without resorting to open warfare. Tell me, Patriarch Kang Long, did you not just say that we are cultivators of the righteous path?" Yao Shen's words were spoken in a self-deprecating tone, but the two Patriarchs were too high strung to catch the nuance in his tone.

"I did," Kang Long responded plainly, seeing no issue with his statement. Perhaps it could be considered cruel by some, but Yao Shen was Patriarch, and it was the Patriarch's role and obligation to choose the route that resulted in the least blood spilt without compromising the interests of the sect. The choices they made, whether that be the Patriarch of the Heavenly Sky Sect or the Divine Mountain Palace, were the ones that *needed* to be made.

"Sure, we do not practice any arts that require blood sacrifice. We do not kill mortals to advance our cultivation base and hone our techniques. But, Patriarch Kang Long, is that your definition of righteous? Not sacrificing mortals? The demonic path fights among themselves like we do. The demonic path sacrifices their disciples like we do. The demonic path's greed is insatiable like ours is! Then, Patriarch, what is the difference between heartless animals who have abandoned their humanity, and us?"

"That is…. That is simply the way things have always been!" Patriarch Kang Long rebutted, not willing to admit why he felt the need to defend an accusation that was effectively leveled at them all. For if the Patriarch's decisions had been wrong…. what of the lives willingly sacrificed under his command?

"What if I offered an alternative?" Yao Shen smiled, causing both the Patriarchs to flinch in unison. But Yao Shen had made no threatening movements, seemingly content to remain rooted to the spot and offer them a friendly smile.

"An… alternative…?" Patriarch Kang Long muttered under his breath as the possibilities flashed through his mind, before a look of utter shock spread across his features. There could only be one reason why Yao Shen would consider sparing them in lieu of the threat they posed. To confirm his suspicions, Kang Long turned his gaze to his fellow Patriarch. Patriarch Lei Weiyuan's expression was solemn, clearly weighed down by Yao Shen's resounding statement.

"You mean…?" Lei Weiyuan muttered, his eyes flashing with realization as he reached the same conclusion Kang Long had.

"A unified Azlak Plains," Yao Shen spoke with conviction as he gazed at the sky, knowing that somewhere out there in the vastness of the expanse was a planet that defied all expectations—a planet that gave him the courage to do the same.

"Impossible," Patriarch Kang Long blurted out.

"The hatred of centuries cannot be washed away so easily," Lei Weiyuan lamented, the sadness in his tone audible.

"That would be true, Patriarch Lei Weiyuan. After all, a Soul Emperor, no matter how powerful, cannot fight all the Nascent Soul experts of three sects. That would be true, at least, if I were a normal Soul Emperor." Yao Shen's grin grew wider and this time, a flicker of the old, vicious Yao Shen could be seen within.

Yao Shen released fifty percent of his True Soul's pressure, distributing it equally among the two Patriarchs. Their pupils dilated in horror as they remained rooted to the spot by a true, all-consuming terror that crashed down upon their Nascent Souls. A fight amongst equals was the last thing a cultivator feared, for it implied that they had ample chances to either exploit an opening or retreat. But this... this was a veritable nightmare. A single forced step in any direction and their souls would shatter into nothingness.

This was... the gap shouldn't be this exaggerated. The gap *couldn't* be this exaggerated.

Yao Shen withdrew the pressure he was exuding, causing the two elders to break out into hacking coughs... perhaps more out of the psychological toll inflicted upon them instead of any real harm.

"I... would rather die... than be enslaved! And the same stands true for my disciples!" Lei Weiyuan roared, while Kang Long's resolved glare clearly mirrored the former's emotions.

"Patriarchs, Patriarchs, you misunderstand my intentions. What I seek to create here is not a sect that you are coerced into joining, but one you wish to offer your loyalty to! Before absolute power, all tricks are meaningless. There is no one left to oppose me in the Azlak Plains, so I will unite it, " Yao Shen boldly stated as the two Patriarchs stared at him as if he were a lunatic, but they would be lying if they said that their old, shriveled hearts did not beat just a tad faster.

"You wish to create a utopia, one which I have a hard time believing can exist," Lei Weiyuan muttered, even though the outcome was favorable to him. Such a thing was simply unthinkable in the world of cultivation, and Yao Shen himself was no saint!

"All I require is an *oath of first betrayal* from you two, and all the elders in your sects. The new sect that I create shall be named after none of our Sects, and the law shall apply to everyone equally, regardless of which sect they originated from. For there will be only one sect, The Modern Sect! And we shall accomplish what none of our ancestors dared to dream of! After thousands of years of obscurity, the Azlak Plains shall once again be united, and rise together!" Yao Shen's voice was carried forth with an unshakeable confidence, moving the two Patriarchs' hearts. This was a proposition that sounded too good to be true, but Yao Shen was powerful enough to instantly destroy them all! Was there any use in lying to dead men?

"What did you see? What can a man *possibly* see... to change this much?" Kang Long could no longer hold back the curiosity that was eating away at him, asking a question that was most definitely a taboo among cultivators.

Yao Shen broke out into a wolfish grin, sending chills down their spines before he replied,

"A miracle."

4

OFFICIAL EDICTS

YAO SHEN WALKED FORWARD toward the congregation of spectators, largely hailing from his own sect at this point, with the two Patriarchs in tow– much to the abject shock of the onlookers, who could not puzzle out the specifics of the bizarre situation that was unfolding before their eyes.

There was still a small group of about fifty disciples from the two rival sects that courageously, or perhaps stupidly, depending on one's perspective, stood their ground—with their weapons drawn. A trickle of red and brown in a sea of azure robes, they knew that they were likely to meet their end here but valiantly refused to budge; this was their *pride*, their *loyalty*, their *respect* to the sect that had given them everything they owned and had learned.

Yao Shen walked in front, followed by the two Patriarchs, who walked a step behind him, flanking his either side, in a slightly acquiescent manner, reminiscent of the way sect guardians trailed behind the venerable elders of the sect.

He raised his open palm in the air, causing the hushed whispers, the uneasy glances and the confused gazes to cease all at once.

"You all, regardless of which sect you hail from, must undoubtedly be wondering why I trust Patriarchs Lei and Kang with my unguarded back. No doubt, a question has sprung in your mind—how could Patriarch Yao Shen, who barely managed to ascend to Nascent Soul, reach the Soul Emperor level? Why has he not struck down the other two patriarchs now that he is effectively invincible?" Yao Shen began his explanation, his tone solemn as he captured the complete attention of the crowd gathered before him.

No one dared to voice their doubts out loud, but the doubt in their gazes was evident for all to see, even in the eyes of the venerable Elder Han, who was only elder from the Heavenly Sky Sect that was present.

"Only now can I reveal a plan that was set in motion decades ago," Yao Shen wistfully sighed, as if he were about to narrate a grand tale he had been longing to share. His memories of Earth had not only taught him about modern values, ethics and development but also touched upon the art of warfare. That, in part, had made him realize how truly profound the teachings of Earth were and how backward Eliria could be in certain comparisons— to subdue the enemy without fighting was truly a magnificent Dao.

"For a thousand years, our righteous path sects have been trapped in a cycle of in-fighting, clawing at each other's throats with the viciousness of rabid beasts. Yet, no one seems to remember the reason why this dispute started, why the remaining three sects of the Azlak Plains continue to stagnate. Once upon a time, the very mention of our three sects brought fear into the hearts of foreign cultivators, so much so that even a Qi-Refinement novice carrying our sect's identification would be offered respect deserving of a core formation cultivator. But now? Look at us now!" Yao Shen's voice boomed out loudly, stunning the spectating disciples.

Was there truly such a time? Did their sect really use to be that powerful? Then what happened, for things to go so wrong?

"A few decades ago, we three patriarchs came together and pondered upon this same question. We combed through sect records, scouring numerous tomes and scrolls in search of the true historical records of the past thousand years, conducting divination to verify its contents and even going as far as to awaken our reserve elders and ask them to verify the facts. I can no longer conceal the truth from you, for we reached a startling conclusion!" Yao Shen exclaimed, while the other two Patriarchs tried their best to keep their mouths shut and expressions placid. When did they come together? Who would awaken their reserve elders to ask historical questions? Wasn't that courting death? What nonsense was this?

Many of the disciples felt their breaths seize and their hearts go cold. As a Human Dao practitioner, Yao Shen could imbue his Dao into his words. It wouldn't do much except amplify the effect of his meaning, making them feel the emotions of 'tension,' 'shock' and 'anger' Yao Shen pretended to feel when he 'stumbled' upon the revelation.

"It was the demonic sect! Demonic sect spies!" Yao Shen screamed out loud with the feigned rage of a masterful orator, stunning everyone in attendance including the two Patriarchs.

Stunned gasps could be heard, disciples looking around at each other with distrust in their eyes. The fact that someone they trained, ate, and slept with could be a demonic sect spy was frightening, knowing the sheer cruelty they were capable of, especially when dealing with cultivators from the righteous path.

"Why has the dispute between our sects persisted for a thousand years? We are all righteous path brothers and sisters that share the same ideologies and our approach to cultivation are similar. Then *why* are there always cries for war, murder, and bloodshed? I shall tell you why! Because every time we press for peace, these spies fabricate an incident that once again forces us to resort to violence!"

Silence reigned for a few seconds, the bombshell revelation stunning the crowd into shock.

"Kill the demonic sect dogs!" an azure-robed disciple whispered under his breath, his inflammatory words overheard by a male disciple in his immediate vicinity.

"Kill the demonic sect dogs!" the male disciple next to him furiously exclaimed, clearly not having the same reservations as his sect mate. Soon, an entire chant had begun, with the disciples of the two rival sects joining in as well, carried into it by the crowd's fervor. To know that a third party had been maliciously hiding in the shadows and profiting from their conflict tarnished the pride of any cultivator, to be used and misled in such a demeaning manner.

Patriarch Yao raised his right hand in the air, causing the chants to reluctantly die down.

"While this may be true, this does not change the animosity our three sets have accrued over generations. The demonic sect has truly played us well, for now even though we are made aware of their treachery, the ties of past hatred tear us apart, making us unable to unite as one," Yao Shen's voice was low, his expression dark, as he clenched his fists in anger.

The azure-robed disciples' expressions hardened as they recalled years of conflict, espionage, assassinations, and even betrayal, all but the youngest among them. The red-and-brown-robed disciples went pale upon witnessing Patriarch Yao's muted but terrifying anger, clenching their weapons until their knuckles went white.

"But they underestimate the righteous path's wisdom and resolve!" Patriarch Yao pronounced, his voice charging forth with renewed vigor, startling all the cultivators in attendance, even the two Patriarchs standing behind him— though the old foxes did well to conceal their surprise.

All the cultivators in attendance watched on with bated breath, clearly able to perceive the tension in the air. What path would Patriarch Yao Shen choose? War? Or...

"Disciples. Guardians. Elders. I address those from all three sects, including my own. Record my edict and present it to your elders when you return to your sects, knowing that this is the collective will of all three Patriarchs. I hereby proclaim that I, Yao Shen, Patriarch of the Heavenly Sky Sect..." He paused, using a small strand of divine sense to prod Patriarch Lei Weiyuan.

Intuitively understanding his intentions, he coughed lightly in an attempt to mask the momentary hesitation that flashed across his face before he firmed his resolve. "I, Lei Weiyuan of the Sacred Flame Palace..."

Finally, Patriarch Kang Long spoke up, able to ascertain the shared perception of the audience and choosing to project collective strength over divisive weakness. "I, Patriarch Kang Long of the Divine Mountain Sect..."

"Hereby proclaim the creation, foundation, and establishment of the Modern Sect, under which all the disciples, guardians, elders, and even reserve elders of the Heavenly Sky Sect, Sacred Flame Palace and the Divine Mountain Sect, shall unite under one banner, under one name and shall shake heaven and earth for the next hundred generations!" Yao Shen's voice rang out with aplomb, moving the hearts of many disciples. Many of them were no longer able to maintain composure under such a shocking announcement. Loud gasps, sharp, heavy breathing, and even undignified murmurs echoed in the background, but Yao Shen paid them no heed.

"I, Grand Patriarch Yao Shen of the Modern Sect, hereby pass my first official edict," Yao Shen's voice was calm and collected, but the disciples in azure robes immediately ceased their conversations and knelt down upon one knee. The disciples of the other two sects seemed conflicted, but upon seeing the confident expressions of their patriarchs standing next to Yao Shen, the doubt and fear in their hearts receded. After all, they were willing to die for their sects under the command of the Patriarch; why would they not trust them now? They, too, chose to kneel.

A bead of sweat rolled down Kang Long's forehead, as he knew that the moment of truth had arrived. If Yao Shen had made fools of them or had tricked him, he would fight back in search of vengeance and die a martyr even at the cost of going down as a blasted fool of a Patriarch in the sect records, who was played by the treacherous Patriarch of the Heavenly Sky Sect.

"The Modern Sect will have one cardinal principle that will forever stand above all others. When one joins the Modern Sect, their past allegiances are forgotten. The disciples of the Heavenly Sky Sect shall be treated no differently from those of the Sacred Flame Palace or the Divine Mountain Sect. Even further, no disciple shall be given preferential treatment over the other on the basis of their background. Even my own son or daughter would not be given a core disciple position if they do not deserve it! The cardinal principle of the Modern Sect is only one: fairness! Talent and determination will be the only factor for advancement, whether you come from an impoverished mortal family or a legacy bloodline of cultivators! I, Yao Shen, guarantee it on my honor as a Soul Emperor cultivator!"

This time, Yao Shen's announcement was met with complete silence. He did not miss the looks of hunger ignited in the weaker disciples that stood at the back, their natural inclination to blend into the crowd and hope that they were not noticed—and consequently, targeted. He also noticed the stark difference; the proud looks of young cultivators wearing enchantments worth over a hundred years of their labor as Qi Formation cultivators. He noticed the sickly expression on Elder Han's face, who looked like he was having a mortal affliction, called a 'stroke' back on Earth. He looked at the looks of relief that erupted on the two rival Patriarchs' faces, knowing that Yao was unlikely to go back on his word as a Soul Emperor. Of course, there was no physical restriction binding him, but his honor instead. And honor was a very valuable currency in the world of cultivators, at times even more so than resources or wealth.

"I, Grand Patriarch Yao Shen of the Modern Sect, hereby pass my second official edict," he proclaimed once again, and this time, some of the disciples kneeled immediately, while others had conflicted expressions on their faces as they bent the knee.

"The Grand Tribunal of Heavenly Justice shall be established to address the grievances and the wrongs previously committed upon you by members of the Modern Sect. I, Grand Patriarch Yao Shen, along with Earth Patriarch of the Modern Sect, Kang Long, and Flame Patriarch of the Modern Sect, Lei Weiyuan, shall each send one Qi Formation clone to head the tribunal, and we shall investigate the matter thoroughly. If your claims are valid, the Grand Tribunal of Heavenly Justice shall order the offender to pay reparations. If you believe that no number of reparations can absolve the sinner of his crime, then you shall have the right to challenge the offender to a blood duel, to the death, contingent upon our approval." His voice rained down upon them like heavenly pronouncement, the imposing words Grand Tribunal of Heavenly Justice ringing in their minds. While they did not quite understand its meaning, the term 'blood duel' seemed to entice vigorous nods in agreement. After all, if the Patriarch expected them to simply forget decades of hatred without any repayment, it would be impossible for them to accept.

Of course, Yao Shen still reserved veto rights for himself. Modernization was ideal, but he was Yao Shen, Patriarch of the Heavenly Sky Sect far longer than he had been a denizen of Earth. He would do things the right way, but if someone were to propose one of his disciples for a blood duel... well, there was no such thing as absolute fairness.

"Finally..." Yao Shen proclaimed, a faint smirk tugging at the corners of his mouth. "...I hereby challenge all elders of the Modern Sect to a friendly duel tomorrow, at the break of dawn upon the site of my ascension. You may now disperse and carry my words back to your respective sects." He allowed them passage, and the disciples rushed back to their sects to deliver this heaven-toppling piece of news.

A few minutes later, only four people remained at the site, the remaining cultivators long having cleared the area as per Yao Shen's command. He, the Earth Patriarch, the Flame Patriarch, and Elder Han.

"You have until tomorrow, at the break of dawn, to convince the elders. If they remain unconvinced, tell them to attend the duel tomorrow so that they can witness the immensity of heaven and earth for themselves. If they try to run... Well, I suspect that you already know. The moment I succeeded, the encirclement already began and I have yet to call it off. Any elder who tries to run will be killed. Any guardian who tries to run shall be imprisoned. As for the disciples, if they choose to leave the Azlak Plains, I will not stop them. But any resources in their possession will be seized. Now leave and return as the Earth and Flame Patriarchs of the Modern Sect. I have already extended to you the limits of my kindness. Do *not* test me any further."

5

ELDER HAN

THE ROLLING PLAINS stretched out into the distance, vibrant green tall grass rustling under the presence of a strong gust of wind. Only two men remained standing on a patch of blackened, scorched earth, the grass long having vaporized under the fury of heavenly lightning— Elder Han and Yao Shen.

"P-Patriarch... no, *Grand Patriarch*, was there really such an agreement between our sects?" The aged man's expression was one of disbelief, his azure robes bearing the insignia of the Heavenly Sky Sect etched onto his chest with threads derived from a golden silkworm, indicating his veritable status as an elder.

Yao Shen focused his divine sense, envisioning a dome that encompassed both him and Elder Han before projecting it outwards. His newly acquired Soul Emperor level divine sense would ensure that the specifics of the conversation would remain privy to only their ears only and any interference or encroachment would be detected well in advance .

"Naturally not, Elder Han," Yao Shen replied with a light laugh, amusement twinkling in his mischievous gaze. "I am sure Zhou Hui will be devastated when he receives word of my unexpected success; that I, Yao Shen, now stand unrivalled in the entire Azlak Plains," he added with a boisterous laugh, for even he himself had not been certain of success, knowing the heavenly retribution his Human Dao Domain would summon would be ferocious beyond belief.

"Grand Patriarch…" Elder Han tried to interject, but Yao Shen cut him off.

"It is fine, Elder Han. You were not the only one that cast aspersions upon my chances of success. As a Nascent Soul Cultivator, I was powerful, yes. I could defeat Zhou Hui, indeed. However, that spoke more to my obsession and ingenuity rather than raw skill. If my talent limited me from reaching mastery in any one Dao, then I would achieve minor success in ten. If ten were not enough, then I would achieve minor success in a hundred! That resolve allowed me to reach today's heights. Frenzied training on the verge of life and death let me become the man I am today. But was it enough?" Yao Shen imbued a hundred years of pain, jealousy, anger, frustration and even resolve into his words, lacking even a hint of falsity or deception.

Elder Han grimaced, but inwardly, he was moved by Yao Shen's determination. As Patriarch, Yao Shen was an inspiration to even the weakest, most talentless cultivator in the sect, though his existence served as a blot on the reputation of legacy disciples and ancient families that had existed since the sect's foundation. He shook his head with a weary sigh, knowing that, ultimately, even if Yao Shen managed to imbue even a hundred Minor Daos into his domain, the Heavenly Dao's lightning would shatter a lifetime's effort in a matter of seconds.

Indeed, Yao Shen could defeat Zhou Hui in a fair battle, but that had more to do with his ingenuity and resolve. Yao Shen's Patchwork Domain was indeed a fascinating accomplishment in its own right, cycling between combinations of elements depending upon the type of opponent he was facing. Fire-Water-Earth-Wind combined to form the *Domain of Four Elements*, which he could immediately switch out for the Minor Daos of Mist-Water-Wind-Shadow to form the *Domain of Illusory Shadows*. They were not separate domains, but part of a larger whole that had ingeniously formed a rotation system. A domain that incorporated all the elements under Yao Shen's command, but only actively utilized four at a time.

Ultimately, however, it spoke more to the decline of the Hui family than Yao Shen's prowess as a cultivator. Of course, Elder Han did not look down upon Yao Shen's abilities, but with the inheritances, techniques, powerful pills and resources the Hui family had amassed over the years, even after most of it had been exhausted over their long existence, should have been enough for him to defeat the Grand Patriarch.

"Indeed." Yao Shen nodded when he saw Elder Han wistfully shake his head. "Had it been Zhou Hui who applied for ascension, the Council of Elders would have declined his request. There is no shame in admitting that Zhou Hui's potential is higher than mine, not to mention that my very existence is a polarizing one. They ultimately had faith that Zhou Hui would surpass me, and my death would let the legacy families breathe freely again."

Elder Han remained silent, a bead of sweat trickling down his forehead. While he did not belong to one of the legacy families, he was greatly indebted to the 'Zhu' family for providing him with valuable resources and elixirs early on in his cultivation.

"But all that is in the past, Elder Han." Yao Shen brightly smiled, giving Elder Han's shoulder a light pat. "As the first Soul Emperor born in the Azlak Plains since the *Era of Turmoil*, I am not lacking in determination, ingenuity, and now, I can truly say that my talent eclipses Zhou Hui, that no cultivator born in the Azlak Plains can even begin to compare. Are you not curious, Elder Han, to what heights such a leader may take this land to?"

"Grand Patriarch, I apologize if this question comes across as rude but... what was that mystical Dao you used to subdue heavenly lightning? I do not know what omen the red lightning bears, but I could clearly sense that my soul would not be able to bear even a sliver of that horrifying energy." Elder Han finally asked the question that had been plaguing him since Yao Shen ascended. Had Yao truly concealed himself so deeply? But why? And now that he had the power to devastate the Sacred Flame Palace and the Divine Mountain Sect, why did he instead invite them to a new sect as if past transgressions were forgotten? He, more than anyone else, understood Patriarch Yao's ability to hold a grudge in his heart, recalling how Yao had levelled a small subordinate sect for far more trivial reasons than the offenses of the Sacred Flame Palace and the Divine Mountain Sect. Although no lives were lost on that day, a learning ground that hundreds of disciples had come to consider home was incinerated, leaving not even the building's foundations behind.

A righteous path sect could never harm those that had taken refuge under their banner, but even then... Yao Shen's display had left the subordinate sects so intimidated that they hadn't dared to conspire against the main sect in decades now, since that fateful day.

Was this really the same Yao Shen that inspired fear and despair in the hearts of the Heavenly Sky Sect's enemies or had he been possessed by a demon!?

"I am sure you already have your conjectures, Elder Han. Peer through the sect records and you shall receive your answer. Now let us head back to the sect. I am sure the Council will be awaiting our presence. This is one meeting you do not want to miss."

6

STRATAGEM

YAO SHEN effortlessly flew through the sky, his speed limited to allow Elder Han to keep pace with himself. His mood was complex— five parts ponderous, three parts melancholic and two parts uncertain. The path he had set the Heavenly Sky Sect on could not be reversed, or the weight behind his words as the leader, the Patriarch, would no longer hold any meaning. Edicts, once issued, could no longer be retracted nearly as easily. It was not a matter of martial strength, but of prestige, of *face*— even a cultivator as powerful as himself could not suppress the will of the Azlak Plains by himself.

Still, he was now a Soul Emperor, a fact that he still found hard to believe. Although, if his accomplishment was viewed from a broader lens, perhaps it would not seem as impressive; The stages of cultivation were divided into five major tiers and it had taken Yao Shen everything he had just to reach the second.

The Physical or, as it was more commonly known, the Mortal tier was the first step in every cultivator's journey. The metamorphosis from a normal human to something… different. An evolution to a higher state of being that was achieved through taking the ambient Qi from the environment and using it to strengthen one's physical aspects.

It was also a distinction many young cultivators failed to make; as much as they wished to believe in the opposite, the truth of the matter was that cultivators did not borrow Qi from the world but *took* it instead. If the heavens wished to bestow Qi onto man, they would not send tribulation thundering down from the skies.

Cultivators were an existence that stood in defiance of the natural order. They took from the heavens and offered nothing in return, surpassing the mortal lifespan and defying the ravages of time until their dying breath.

Perhaps no cultivator in existence had managed to surpass time, but that wasn't enough to keep them from trying.

The Mortal tier had three stages that Yao Shen had already conquered, namely the 'Qi Refinement,' 'Foundation Building,' and the 'Core Formation' tiers. Refining the physical body, remodeling the body as a vessel to bear greater concentrations of Qi, expanding one's Qi channels, or meridians as they were referred to on Eliria, and evolving the 'Dantian.'

The metaphysical center of a cultivator's Qi reserve and the spiritual organ that heavily determined a cultivator's talent was known as a Dantian in Eliria—a source of great joy and anguish for both cultivators and mortals alike. Those born without a Dantian did not possess the ability to cultivate. Many had tried to overturn this cruel fate, but to date, Yao Shen had not heard of a single attempt succeeding. Even those born with a Dantian often found themselves resentful of the heavens, much like Yao Shen himself, who had found himself, in his younger years, ruefully wondering why Zhou Hui possessed a Dantian naturally attuned to the fire element to an astonishing degree whilst his own Dantian, despite tirelessly training and spending countless hours meditating upon the Dao, refused to develop a strong element affinity.

. . .

The Second Tier of Cultivation, namely the 'Soul' tier, was a natural progression after the physical body was refined to an acceptable degree. It was also the tier that Yao Shen had attained after over a century of cultivation; a tier that most cultivators would *never* be able to attain.

Refining the soul was the natural progression after the physical body had reached an acceptable standard. Although the focus was not completely shifted from the latter, if one wished to progress further, it was crucial to empower the soul to be able to bear larger concentrations of Qi. After all, one could not expect to draw in ambient Qi from the atmosphere without any limitations or consequences. Qi Deviation was the consequence of the body and soul losing control over the Qi cycling through the physical body and the metaphysical Dantian; an outcome that left the most intrepid of cultivators shuddering at the mere thought.

The Nascent Soul stage required a cultivator to take the ultimate risk; shattering their core, that is, the physical manifestation of their cultivation in order to transcend the limits of the fleshly body and step into the realm of soul cultivation.

Every living being had a soul, but only after reaching the fourth stage of cultivation and condensing a Nascent Soul could one actually perceive it. The newly synthesized soul was akin to a newborn child, but Nascent Souls were reservoirs of incredible power; the gulf between the Mortal and the Soul tiers so vast that there were very few instances in history of the former defeating the latter, if they could even be believed.

Yao Shen's time in the Nascent Soul stage had been spent refining his Daos, studying the interactions between multiple Minor Daos and eventually synthesizing the Patchwork Domain that had allowed him to defeat Zhou Hui.

But that hadn't been enough.

Only when Yao Shen had accepted that he simply did not have an affinity for any Major Dao; that no amount of training, no amount of Minor Dao Domain combinations would ever amount to the sheer potency of a Major Dao... Only when his inquiry took a different shape did a new path reveal itself.

It was ironic how a journey he'd taken to self-reflect upon his responsibilities as Patriarch and his bitterness at the Heavenly Dao for denying him the capability to ascend did he find a Dao far more archaic and potent than any ordinary Major Dao.

Although Yao Shen didn't know it back then, what he had been searching for was inner peace. The fifth stage of cultivation, Soul Emperor, was the stage Yao Shen had finally attained after two long centuries of cultivation. His hopes, his dreams and his ambitions had been shattered and reforged many times across this tumultuous journey, but in the end, it had been his perseverance and tenacity that had illuminated a path for him when he had found himself trapped in the depths of despair.

It had been a disappointing day, that one. His attempts toward grasping the Minor Dao of Sound had been met with abject failure. His obsession with comprehending new Minor Daos and integrating them into his Patchwork Domain had reached an unhealthy level, to the point where it was affecting Yao's ability to fulfill his duties as Patriarch.

It was with those considerations in mind that Yao Shen had decided to take a sabbatical from his responsibilities, leaving the sect in search of something that he believed to be long since lost to him; to reconnect with his mortal roots and rekindle his bonds with whom he once used to be.

Yao Shen had only hoped that living among mortals would teach him the values of patience and virtue that a cultivator's life had made him forget, not having even once imagined that it would lead to him mastering an Esoteric Dao. To the disciples of the Heavenly Sky Sect, the significance of Yao Shen's ascension was perhaps not evident at the outset. However, the elders were well-attuned to the wider state of the world beyond the confines of their lands and thus understood that the birth of a Soul Emperor in the Azlak Plains would shake the geopolitical landscape of their continent.

The last of the seven major continents on Eliria, the continent of Ionea, was also considered the weakest. The other six continents were rumored to be led by multiple Fourth-Tier Cultivators whilst the highest known stage attained by the cultivators of Ionea stopped at the Third. For largely unknown reasons, Ionea had seemingly suffered the greatest losses during the series of wars that embroiled all the seven continents in a sea of blood, a time period that the cultivators of today had dubbed the '*Era of Turmoil.*' The Third-Tier – a tier that Yao Shen was only a single Stage away from. The elusive Soul Paragon Stage, of which he knew far too little about to have any confidence in ascending to was also the final Stage of the Second-Tier.

In the far eastern corner of Ionea lay the small, forgotten Azlak Plains, protected from the horrors of the coastal region and the risk of foreign invaders by an ancient formation that had defended the entirety of Ionea from the harshness of the outside world for thousands of years.

To the far north lay the impenetrable *Dwarven Mountain Range*, their famed defenses the result of generations upon generations of Dwarves dedicating their lives to constructing and refining layered formations that were ingeniously designed to empower themselves by harnessing the natural Earth Qi and aura of the mountains. Another reason why the road to cultivation had been unkind to Yao Shen was his race, as a human. The Dwarves possessed a natural attunement to Earth Qi, making it rare to find one who could not attain one of the numerous Minor Daos of

Earth within their lifespans. That did not mean that all Dwarves could reach the coveted Nascent Soul level, but core formation was not a hard feat for them. An affinity to Earth, however, was also a shackle, for many Dwarves failed to break free from their reliance upon a single element and limited their potential in that manner.

The West was dominated by dozens of righteous path sects, the terrain oscillating wildly between a land of wintry frost to a desert full of endless, roiling sands; the environment attuned to the preference of the dominant sect in the region.

The center was a land full of horrors and mystery, inheritances and traps, the home and the territory of the demonic sects on Ionea, the battlefield where the grand war that defined the Era of Turmoil was fought, where the blood of tens of thousands of peak cultivators was shed and dozens if not hundreds of clans and sects alike were extinguished for all of eternity— the *Bloodsoul Forest.* Dark Elves, Vampires, the Undead Alliance and even human cultivators that were practitioners of the blood, soul, and other forbidden paths—were only a sampling of the terrors that lay within.

To the south were their greatest allies, the True Elves, the children of the forest. The Elves belonged to neither the righteous path nor the demonic path, maintaining a principle of neutrality through strength.

However, that had not always been the case.

Past agreements had been forged with humanity's righteous path, and for a moment in time, the two races had prospered in unison. Together, not only were they a force to be reckoned with, but they had actually managed to suppress the Bloodsoul Forest's influence and slay many heinous cultivators with their combined might. However, the hypocrisy of the righteous path in letting the True Elves down in the time of their need and their incessant clamor for resources ultimately caused the alliance to fall apart.

Although their moral inclinations were similar, the True Elves were blessed with superior lifespans to both humans and Dwarves, albeit at the cost of a far more limited birth rate. The Dwarves outnumbered the Elves ten to one, while humans outnumbered Dwarves a thousand to one, easily at that.

Inherently living for hundreds of years from birth and being blessed with attunements to *nature* itself, including the elements of earth, water, fire, and wind amongst others made it easy to understand why the concept of human greed was so foreign to them. Although the Dwarves might surpass them in their understanding of a single element, namely earth, their versatility was what made them so incredibly formidable and also the reason why the Dark Elves hated their distant cousins with such ferocity.

The reason why such a mighty force had chosen to ally with the puny Azlak Plains, of all regions, was an odd one. Perhaps calling it an alliance in itself was a misnomer. The True Elves were and continued to be largely unconcerned with the ones in charge of Azlak Plains' governance, their interests being limited to the preservation of spiritual beasts and plants within the geographical bounds of the region.

For one could find many young Elves roaming the Azlak Plains in search of aspects of nature; serving to attune new Minor Daos and hone existing ones. It was not hard to conclude that due to Elvenhold's closed off borders, certain Minor Daos could no longer be attuned within their territory, making it necessary for Young Elves to traverse to the plains, specifically in the depths of the Nayun Forest, in order to master these elusive Daos.

It was for this reason that the East, or more specifically, the five major righteous path sects that maintained their hegemony over the Eastern region, could not exert their influence over the Azlak Plains in a more overt manner. It was the Eastern Righteous Path Alliance that held back the bulk of the demonic sect's influence at bay for the Azlak Plains, and normally, such protection would come with an equally heavy price.

However, the presence of Elvenhold meant that the East could not wantonly plunder the Azlak Plains resources, greatly reducing the territory's value in their calculating gazes.

The Azlak Plains was still required to send their strongest cultivators for regional defense if the situation devolved into all-out war, but the pact that had been formed after the Era of Turmoil by the major powers of Ionea was not easily broken.

After all, both sides had lost simply too much due to the conflict. Their inheritances stood incomplete, incredibly valuable resources and techniques lost in the chaos of the war and the very chronology of events that took place in that era maligned by conflicting accounts.

Each of the major Eastern powers had one Soul Paragon that served as the guarantor of their safety, at the very least. Up until now, Azlak Plains had not been considered a major power of the East, but with multiple Nascent Soul Cultivators that had reached the limits of their stage, their position was not a negligible one either. With Yao Shen, a Soul Emperor who could possibly ascend to the Soul Paragon stage, the East simply wasn't in a position to ignore them any longer.

In the end, the True Elves of Elvenhold were not currently an ally the Azlak Plains could rely upon. Their relationship was a conditional one and their neutrality was not something that was easily broken; it would take half of the Azlak Plains to be charred to ash before they would interfere. They might be a deterrent, but they were also the cage that bound their actions, placing limits upon how Yao Shen and his sect could enjoy the resources within their own territory.

On the other hand, the demonic sects' influence might be

diluted due to the bulwark the Eastern Sects had inadvertently formed for the Azlak Plains, but that did not mean that they had no presence in Yao Shen's lands.

Although they could not mobilize the strength to strike at one of the three hegemonic sects of the Azlak Plains, that did not stop them from targeting mortal villages without the ability to defend themselves and conducting heinous rituals that required blood sacrifice.

Their countermeasures had improved over the years, but the fact was that it was simply too easy for a cultivator with the intent to destroy mortal holdings. Villages and mortal holdings had continuously moved closer to one of the sects, but some were stubborn in their ways or simply refused to believe the claims of cultivators even when recording stones were used to show them the aftermath of the devastation.

Although the True Elves did not condone the behavior of the demonic path and their moral compass was more closely synchronized to the righteous path's, ultimately, no matter how repulsive it was, the death of mortals remained a solely 'human' issue. At some level, Yao Shen wondered if they valued fleeting human lives with far lesser importance than they did their own long-winding ones.

Perhaps that wasn't an entirely fair assessment.

After all, the Elves weren't spared the demonic path's cruelty either. Elvenhold was mighty and isolated from the outside world, but that was precisely why the demonic sects *had* to test their strength. Each year, a few young Elves that had ventured outside their land for their own missions would be killed, which would prompt a brutal retaliation that often left thousands of undead guarding the periphery of the Bloodsoul Forest dead.

Thousands dead would normally be a severe loss for any force, but the demons did not care about such superfluous losses, continuously testing their response time, power, and growth.

And the day when they judged Elvenhold to have weakened sufficiently would also be the day when they launched their true offensive. This was the demonic path, lacking neither in cruelty nor in cunning.

Each major Ionean power, namely the True Elves, the Dwarves, the Righteous Path of the West, and the Demonic Sect Alliance, had at least one Third-Tier cultivator. The East had no Third-Tier cultivator, but the Pact and the *legacy constructs* inherited from the Era of Turmoil and their alliance with the Western Righteous Path Alliance prevented the demonic sect from overstepping their boundaries.

The continent of Ionea was a powder keg that could be lit afire at any given moment, but it had attained balance in its own twisted way.

And that was without factoring in the three mysterious races into the equation— the *Ancient Dragons*, the *Fae-Blessed* and..... the third unknown race, all records of their existence intentionally purged from their sect records, but their existence acknowledged.

This was the grand stage Yao Shen had inherited from his predecessor and now, after two hundred long years of cultivation, he finally possessed the strength to influence matters on the scale of Ionea, if only barely.

Should he perhaps approach the reclusive True Elves, known for their fascination with the arts and try to draw their atten—

"Grand Patriarch?" Elder Han's voice cut off his train of thought abruptly, but Yao Shen was not irritated in the slightest.

For they had arrived at their destination.

7

SHADOW

YAO SHEN DID NOT NEED his divine sense to detect the presence of cultivators ahead as a Human Dao practitioner, but all that was visible to the naked eye was lush planes stretching out into the distance, light azure clouds overlooking the grassy lands. What once struck him as mundane now seemed peaceful, making Yao Shen wonder just how much his past life's memories had managed to impact his personality in such a short period of time.

Well, the term 'Human Dao Practitioner' was accurate, yet at the same time, wildly untrue. The Esoteric Daos were truly both fascinating and utterly bizarre at the same time, for Yao Shen would dare not call himself an expert despite being the only one to awaken the aforementioned Dao since, perhaps, the Era of Turmoil, for the aspects of third-stage practitioners were not entirely unknown to him.

It was closer to the 'Dao of Sapient Beings,' or rather, the Dao that represented the will of the sapient beings. He was certain that his human domain could not be recreated if he were to use a lesser spiritual beast as its core, but if it was a beast emperor whose image he channeled, well, it would still fail, but for different reasons. The resonance he felt with the mortal farmer was not an emotion that could be falsified, nor a concept that could be faked. The Heavenly Blessing he had received upon ascending to Soul Emperor had given him many insights and knowledge upon the true nature of his Human Dao, but it had not advanced his understanding of the mysterious *'Dao Path'* that held the key to ascending to Soul Paragon, possibly indicating that the rumors he had based his knowledge upon had been false.

Without further ado, Yao Shen gently landed upon the ground with Elder Han accompanying him, landing a few steps behind Yao out of deference. He began walking forward with a relaxed expression on his face, smiling as he gazed at the azure sky. How ironic it was, for the Patriarch of the Heavenly Sky Sect to have incurred the wrath of the heavens, he thought with amusement flickering in his eyes.

He had always disliked the ways of the heavens— *unfeeling, uncaring, ruthless* and *unchanging* in its ways, but he had not really realized how abnormal his views were until much later in his cultivation journey. He would not say that all cultivators revered the heavens, but most held a trace of reverence for the heavens that was engraved into their very soul— for the ways of the heavens may be cruel, but its power was not to be disputed. And power was respected in Eliria; that much he knew held true about all seven continents.

The sect formation bore down upon them, but Yao Shen continued walking forward as he felt himself make contact. It was like walking through a viscous bubble, but the sensation only lasted for a second before they reached the other side.

The loud cacophony of the outer sect made its way into his ears, a smile creeping on his face as he realized that he was back home. Finally, he let his divine sense expand, switching it from passive to active mode as he took in the sights and smells. Dozens of young disciples milled about, through the crowded streets that had been smoothed over by Earth-aspected cultivators and then paved over with flat, even rocks whose dimensions were both perfect and entirely identical. Sure, they did not have gravel roads and concrete houses, but any skilled workman would be floored at the master craftsmanship that had gone into the tiling. In a world of superhumans, though, it was a feature that barely went by noticed. The Dao Impartment Hall, Medical Pavilion, Sky Exchange Hall, and the various legacy family pavilions did not escape his divine sense, as young cultivators full of energy bounded forward with dreams of ascension.

His focus shifted to the Ascension Stage, realizing that a fight was about to commence.

"Patriarch!" A disciple's loud voice rang in his ears as she bowed at a ninety-degree angle, her cry stunning the disciples around him. Their gazes focused in the direction the disciple was bowing, resulting in stunned gasps, sharp breaths of air and visible shock.

"The Patriarch has returned!" a disciple shouted in incredulous joy, even though the other disciples had already notified their fellow batchmates in advance and his success in ascending to the Soul Emperor Stage was a hot topic of discussion— even if they had no idea what it meant or represented.

"The Patriarch has succeeded! The Patriarch is mighty!" another disciple roared, with perhaps a little too much jubilation and a violation of protocol. Not that Yao Shen minded, for today was a day of celebration and jubilation.

"The Patriarch is mighty!" the rest of the disciples, almost in unison, proclaimed, before bowing down with reverent expressions on their faces. Yao Shen did not blame them, for to these young cultivators, he was no different than a celebrity back on Earth. Usually, he would choose to fly directly toward the inner sect, his duty seldom giving him time to interact with outer sect disciples.

"At ease, children. Pay me no heed. I only wish to take a light stroll before returning to my duties." Yao Shen smiled and nodded at the disciples before continuing to walk forward upon the paved road. The disciples hurriedly made way for him and separated on his either side, but the reverence in their expressions was unchanged. A few, though, had the cheek to gaze upon him with ambition in their eyes, knowing that even if the Patriarch took the slightest interest in them, their lives would be changed forever, and that stood true even for the legacy disciples now that he was a Soul Emperor.

Elder Han walked silently behind him, his own fame shadowed by Yao Shen. Finally extricating himself from the mob of disciples, his attention was attracted by the Outer Exchange, a place where any outer disciple of the Sect was allowed to rent a stall and hawk their wares.

"Come, Elder Han. Walk alongside me. It has been a while since I have visited the Outer Exchange," Yao Shen requested more than commanded, but as Patriarch, that distinction meant little, whether he liked it or not.

Elder Han tried to hide the confusion he felt at the Patriarch's actions, although he hid it well. The Council of Elders would undoubtedly be rankled when they realized he was fooling around in the outer sect, but Yao Shen was more inclined to enjoy the sights, smells, and sounds he had previously taken for granted. As a Human Dao Cultivator, the very action of experiencing the lives of sapient beings was cultivation, and it could not be trained or brute-forced like he had with many other Minor Daos.

The strong sense of spice wafted over from the Outer Exchange, piquing his attention. His divine sense traced the origin, a small stall run by a young girl likely no older than fifteen. Her silky black hair, green eyes and unblemished features were nothing out of ordinary in the cultivation world, as she stirred a large cauldron with her tiny hands, but the motion was completely effortless. Two disciples sat on wooden stools, their expressions satisfied as they enjoyed the warm soup, whilst Yao Shen's gaze flickered to the four vacant seats adjacent to them.

Intrigued, he headed for the stall, with Elder Han walking alongside him. He did notice the gazes of the disciples falling upon him, but none lingered too long, the disciples likely already having been warned by the Foundation Establishment Guardians not to disturb them. He seated himself upon the stool without making a noise, and Elder Han complied, not considering a wooden stool beneath his station, one of the reasons why he was good company. A legacy elder would no doubt have made his displeasure clear at being in the presence of outer disciples, let alone eating alongside them.

"Two bowls," Yao Shen calmly asked, a natural confidence flowing into his words even when he did not intend to impose himself upon the surrounding disciples. A two-hundred-year-old persona was not so easily disavowed, after all.

The young disciple looked up, her hands almost fumbling the oversized ladle she was clutching on to as she stuttered over her words, like she had seen a ghost, "P-P-Patriarch...."

Yao Shen almost felt guilty, seeing the girl's spooked expression. Drawing upon his reserves of Human Dao, he envisioned a few memories from his time upon Earth and projected the emotion of 'comfort.'

"It's okay. We are just here to enjoy the sights of the outer sects." His voice's pitch and temperament seemed to change, but it would manifest differently for every person and Yao Shen himself did not know how. It was only one of the aspects the heavenly blessing had taught him, making Yao Shen himself curious of the effects.

Elder Han felt a chill down his spine as he heard Yao Shen

speak to the young disciple, his hands trembling as he gazed at the Patriarch with an expression of abject shock. His mortal father had passed over a hundred years ago, but Yao Shen's voice was identical to his father, the words bringing him warmth and unearthing memories that he had long forgotten. The world of cultivation had transformed him from a mortal merchant's son to a figure that struck terror into the hearts of the Heavenly Sky Sect's foes, but why... why...

Why, even after a hundred years, did the memory of his rotund, cheerful father embracing him tightly before he left for his sect bring a single, solitary tear to his eye?

"Elder Han?" Yao Shen asked, both confused and slightly concerned. "Are you alright?"

"Hmm...? Yes, Patriarch." Elder Han snapped out of a daze as he hurriedly wiped the tear from his eye, before looking up at the sky. "It must be raining outside," he added, undoubtedly flustered as he probed with his divine sense to be sure that no one else detected that disgraceful scene.

"Indeed, it must be," Yao Shen added seriously, his head bobbing in agreement, even though the thought of rain getting past the sect formation was laughable. A cultivator's pride was a delicate thing, one often more greatly valued than their very life itself— thus certain situations needed to be managed by a deft touch.

"Yes, Patriarch. It is an honor to serve you," the young girl finally replied with a bright smile on her face, intriguing Yao Shen. He had no doubt that it was his actions that prompted such a strong reaction from Elder Han, while it seemed to have rid the girl of her insecurities, at least for a short period of time. The act of projecting emotions was a harmless one, as it only highlighted the certain emotion Yao Shen had selected, and even then, it could not control their actions. But to be able to influence a Nascent

Soul Cultivator when he had just used it so casually.... Human Dao was truly terrifying.

Two bowls were placed in front of them a second later, the other two customers already having hastily departed after leaving payment. To eat alongside the Patriarch and an elder was an intimidating prospect for most, let alone two Qi Formation cultivators, so he did not stop them.

Yao Shen's divine sense detected a disturbance behind him, observing as the shadows his back was casting beginning to roil and shift before they formed the vague silhouette of a human, whose features got clearer by the minute. A woman dressed in pitch black robes materialized behind Yao Shen and Elder Han, but neither of them were alarmed by her arrival. The shadows cast by their backs abandoned them, forming a cloak around the woman's back that only served to further intimidate the disciples around her. Her white hair shimmered under the sunlight, her violet eyes staring at Yao Shen's back whilst her face remained emotionless. She appeared to be in her early twenties, her short, lithe frame concealing the ferocious strength contained within. Her right hand rested upon a sheathed dagger, her eyes suspiciously flashing as she took in the surroundings and every face in the vicinity.

"Shadow," Yao Shen acknowledged, but the seemingly young girl ignored him as she walked to his side and scooped a mouthful of soup from his bowl with his spoon before cautiously sipping it.

"It is not poisoned," she calmly stated, pulling out a fresh spoon from her void storage and gently placing it back into the bowl before retreating a few steps and maintaining a watchful eye on the surroundings.

Yao Shen just sighed.

8

MUSINGS

Y<small>AO</small> S<small>HEN</small>'<small>S</small> mouth twitched slightly as he accepted the new spoon Shadow had procured for him without comment. The light golden soup awaited him, imbued with nothing but the lowest ranking of herbs, a few mortal spices and a dash of finely chopped vegetables, soaking in and adding depth to the flavor.

He savored the mouthful of soup, a contented expression forming on his face. The soup was no more than the sum of its parts, and Yao Shen was a man who had sampled many delicacies across his two-hundred-year journey in Eliria. Yet, the simplicity of the soup, the warmth of the liquid flowing down his throat provided him... It evoked memories of his wife's cooking, making up for what it lacked in fine ingredients and chef's skill that his palate was accustomed to with... heart.

Seven decades' worth of memories were not something that he could recollect and sort immediately, but now that he had success-fully ascended, he knew that all would come back with time. A flicker of amusement bubbled up in his heart at the thought of thinking of his wife's cooking as lacking, but he was not quite sure why. He did not mean it as an insult, after all; to use nothing but the mundane to create the magical was a blessing.

Perhaps the young girl in front of him yet lacked a love for the culinary arts, and in a world where the strong could impose their will over the weak, that was understandable. But Yao Shen had seen many disciples, and the passion gleaming in her eye did not go unnoticed. If her passion persisted, then perhaps she would be helpful in his plans of 'modernization,' but that was a distant thought.

As for Shadow… just thinking about her made Yao Shen want to sigh. She was his first, and eldest true disciple, and she went by many titles. Her existence probably made him an even bigger eyesore in the eyes of the legacy families, for one independent powerhouse had already stretched their patience thin.

Yao Shen was no prodigy, and it was his ability to accept his own lack of talent that had let him progress this far. Shadow on the other hand, was a true, bona fide genius. A prodigy among prodigies, a scion blessed by the heavens. One would wonder why Yao Shen would take such a gifted individual under his wing, one that was the very antithesis of his existence, but Shadow's past was complicated, to say the least. She was an orphan that Yao Shen had found on his travels, born with *Pure Shadow Spiritual Roots*— implying a 90% or higher purity percentage. This was one of Yao Shen's most closely guarded secrets, and he had killed to keep it a secret.

Of course, others perhaps suspected the truth— but their speculations were only that, and Shadow had never displayed talent beyond 65% purity. Shadow Spiritual Roots, or for that matter, any single element spiritual roots were one of the most coveted bloodline inheritances, and it showed why.

Age eight, early-stage Qi formation. Age fifteen, late-stage Qi formation. Age twenty-one, early-stage foundation establishment. Age twenty-five, mid-stage foundation establishment. Age twenty-eight, high-stage foundation establishment. Age twenty-nine, peak-stage foundation establishment. Age thirty-eight, early-stage core formation. Age forty-five, peak-stage core formation.

He did not know when she would cross the barrier, but the thought of having a Nascent Soul Cultivator a quarter of his age was a frightening concept even for Yao Shen. He had reached the coveted stage only after a century of struggle, but for Shadow, it was almost as easy as breathing.

But her growth, as much as it brought pride and prestige to the sect and his own reputation, tore away at his heart. Without his memories from Earth, he would never be able to understand why, or perhaps even dismiss the thought outright. Eliria was far too rigid and conservative in its ways, but now the reason seemed so obvious that the depths of his own *obliviousness* astounded him.

A part of him still found it hard to accept, a resistance welling up from the values and ideals the world around him had instilled in him, but he would not deny it any longer. He had come to think of Shadow as his own daughter, and her behavior concerned him. Stung at him. Frustrated him to no end.

As a cultivator, controlling one's emotions was a paramount concern. Those who lived as long as him could not be lacking in intelligence, strength or resourcefulness, or their journey would have never taken them that far. But when Yao Shen recalled the day he had discovered Shadow, an unfamiliar rage bubbled up in his gut. It was a foreign sensation for Yao Shen, one who had trained himself to dull his emotions and assess matters with cold rationality— for this rage eluded him, and any attempt to cage it only intensified it. Cold, vicious rage that would destroy the world if he let it out, one that promised murder and vengeance.

It was then that he realized that this rage was not entirely his own, or rather, its origin lay in the memories he had inherited from his past life. Yao Shen was stunned, shocked that his previous self, a harmless businessman who had never known combat, could bear such fury in his heart. His fist clenched tightly, and for a moment, Yao Shen wished to tear through the Bloodsoul Forest and lay devastation to all that crossed his path.

A few seconds later, rationality and experience prevailed, the anger once again contained. He did not wish to further deliberate upon the matter and his movements were concealed enough that no one, barring Elder Han, detected his brief instability. He, wisely, chose not to comment upon the subject.

The events of that day had left an indelible mark upon Shadow, and sadly, the effects manifested by the events of that day were only encouraged, and even revered in a society of cultivators. Shadow did not care about interacting with her fellow peers, and neither did she particularly care about cultivation. It was only a tool for her, a means to an end— one that let her kill as many Demonic Cultivators as she could, her methods getting increasingly refined over the years. Even then, she was the number one core disciple cultivator, a fact that had brought him great pride now tasting like bitter ash in his mouth.

Shadow only cared about one thing, and that was protecting him. She had called him a *'naïve old fool'* and then swore to protect him from those who sought to harm him or exploit his kindness. It was a ridiculous notion, and he was likely the only Soul Emperor with a Core Formation bodyguard. She even went as far as to taste his food, even though the art of blending poisons that could affect Nascent Soul Cultivators had been long lost in the Era of Turmoil, let alone a Soul Emperor. Even if one existed, it would have to evade the full scrutiny of his divine sense, not to mention the political consequences the existence of such a poison would cause.

That was not what bothered him, though. Shadow seemed to be determined to die before him, if it came to that, and that tore at him far more than anything in the world could. He had tried many approaches to change her perspective, even going as far as to forbid her from guarding him once. He had only wished that he had his memories from Earth back then, for that had been a grave mistake. Once he barred her, she grew listless, like a wilted flower. What little interest she showed in other pursuits evaporated without a trace, and even her cultivation started to regress. Terrified that he would create a heart demon for Shadow, he had immediately rescinded his statement and profusely apologized to her.

Thankfully, she was back to 'normal' a few days later, but it did not change the fact that Yao Shen had failed, left without any cards to play. Earth's wisdom had a terminology for such an affliction, but alas, it carried no way to cure her. Shadow may have lived for close to five decades, but emotionally, she was no older than two, for most of her time spent had been spent cultivating and fighting.

Had she not witnessed his true Dao Domain, and had Yao Shen not greatly exaggerated his chances of success, she would have never let him go in the first place. Shadow would never display her true emotions in public, but he knew that the past day must have been nerve-wracking for her. He had many contingency plans in place in the event of his death, but when he saw Shadow's face, he instantly knew that she had been crying— and it had occurred to him how ascension was such a selfish act. Lost in his musings, Yao Shen had only just now realized that the bowl of soup had long since finished. Turning his head to Elder Han, he nodded, sending a message to him with his divine sense. The young chef would be compensated handsomely for the meal, and it would be seen to it that no one dared to appropriate the wealth from her possession.

"That was excellent," Yao Shen spoke loudly, his attention catching the attention of nearby disciples trying to act natural as they eavesdropped. He had a feeling that this little stall was going to explode in popularity, if the girl continued to run it. In a way, it was a little test of her business acumen and inclination toward the culinary arts. Perhaps she would surprise him.

"Thank you for your patronage, Patriarch. This little one does not deserve such praise," the young girl replied with a gentle bow, her words spoken with the utmost confidence and respect.

Yao Shen nodded, as Elder Han placed a pouch on the table and said his thanks. A foundation establishment guardian jogged over, no doubt having received a command from Elder Han, and began to explain the situation to the young girl, assuring her that her newfound wealth would not cause her trouble. Such details were important to ensure that gifts did not become curses, and Yao Shen would not miss such a crucial detail.

Yao Shen and Elder Han had already resumed their walk through the Outer Exchange, with Shadow walking behind them and giving intimidating glares to anyone whose body language hinted at a desire to approach.

He knew, though, that his moment of tranquility could not last much longer. It was time to confront the Council of Elders, and then prepare for tomorrow's battle. Regardless of how the meeting went, he had a feeling that it would be interesting, to say the least.

9

CONFRONTATION

"I SUPPOSE it is time to return, Elder Han." Yao Shen clasped his hands behind his back and sighed. They had reached the end of the Outer Exchange, and unsurprisingly, no further stall could truly attract his attention. He could feign interest in poorly forged swords, weak spiritual herbs and supposedly 'rare ores' peddled by the more daring disciples, but a single sweep of his divine sense had already indicated that there was nothing that could hold his interest.

"Shall we go by foot?" Elder Han chose to politely ask, some caution leaking into his voice. Yao Shen's display of strength had been impressive, but it was not a 'novel' concept. Elder Han was well aware that there existed individuals far stronger than himself in the continent of Ionea, and even though it was shocking to bear the brunt of the Patriarch's power, it did not shake his Dao Heart. As a cultivator who originated from mortal roots, if the concept of stronger existences than himself roaming the Azlak Plains had fazed him, he would never have progressed to this stage.

But the power Yao Shen had displayed earlier… that was an entirely unfamiliar concept to him. Had he himself not been influenced by the power and witnessed its serene purity, he would be inclined to think that the patriarch was dabbling in the demonic arts. For the act of influencing another's emotions in itself was not unfamiliar to cultivators, many forbidden demonic arts could even control another person's mind.

However, while the demonic arts were vile, tainted, and required time, effort and sacrifice to reach completion, the Patriarch's actions were casual and unhurried. Moreover, not once did the power try to influence his mind into doing something he did not wish to— the memories were his own, but the tone and inflection of the Patriarch's voice unmistakably that of his father. It was as if the mysterious concept the Patriarch had employed wished to gently coax him to remember the safety and comfort he felt in the embrace of his father's arms as an infant, not out of maliciousness but... *kindness*? *Empathy?* He was utterly unsure regarding this matter, barring just one thing: the Patriarch had become an unfathomable character, and he would be lying if he claimed that it did not unsettle him.

"No, there is no need. Shadow?" Yao Shen shook his head before turning around and offering his right hand to Shadow. As a late-stage core formation cultivator, Shadow still needed to rely upon an artifact to achieve flight.

Realizing his intentions, Shadow seemed to lightly flinch as she averted her gaze and pretended to scan for threats in an attempt to hide the light blush forming on her face. A few seconds passed before she gingerly accepted his hand, a slight smile forming on her face before she hurriedly concealed it with a mask of indifference.

Yao Shen started floating a foot above the ground, and the next second, a strong gust of wind started forming around Shadow, raising her to his level. Elder Han nodded, choosing to float next to him and wait.

Maintaining a firm grip over Shadow's hand, he channeled his Qi and they began to ascend higher until they cleared the tallest building in the outer sect by a fair margin. Then, Yao Shen propelled them forward, their sect robes fluttering in the wind. A cursory divine sense sweep made Yao Shen chuckle in amusement, as many disciples pointed toward the sky and exclaimed words of astonishment and congratulations.

Yao Shen limited his speed to the threshold of a mid-stage core formation expert to ensure that Shadow felt no discomfort. He found flying a fairly pleasurable excursion, the wind resistance no more than a cool, pleasant breeze for a Nascent Soul expert, let alone a Soul Emperor.

A few minutes later, he began a gentle descent, landing with such control that even a mortal would have no cause to complain, let alone a cultivator. They were now situated at the very edge of outer sect territory, confronted with a set of ancient azure double-doors that exuded a sense of oppression and heaviness, blocking their path forward. A majestic flood dragon was carved onto each of the door's surfaces with impeccable attention to detail, so much so that if one were to gaze for too long, they would find it difficult to distinguish it from reality, and the doors far eclipsed them in size, as if they were made for twenty-foot giants instead of humans.

Ten middle-aged men in azure robes stood in single file, their expressions stern and uncompromising as they glared at the newcomers— each wielding a peak-stage core formation spear artifact. The Elite Guardians of the Heavenly Sky Sect were not a force to be trifled with, each of them seasoned core formation experts that were trained in combination techniques from an early age. When they attacked as one, holding back an early-stage Nascent Soul expert was an easy task and killing one was not entirely impossible.

"Patriarch!" they announced in unison, but they did not bow to him, not even the slightest. Their duty was not one that allowed them to lose sight of their targets, even now constantly scanning the crowd to make sure no one used the opening of the gates as an opportunity to sneak in.

"At ease," Yao Shen acknowledged, and the cultivators stepped aside with a practiced motion and allowed them to pass.

Yao Shen released his grip on Shadow's hand, walking past the Elite Guardians without exchanging any further words. Shadow and Elder Han walked at his side, but neither of them tried to interact with the Elite Guardians either, the latter merely nodding in acknowledgement.

A few seconds later, Yao Shen stood in front of the azure gates, the flood dragons' gaze intimidatingly landing down upon him. They were peak-nascent soul constructs, embedded with the fragmented soul of an adult flood dragon, one of the few surviving artifacts that had survived the Era of Turmoil. One glance at it and Yao Shen could tell that it was the work of a Soul Emperor, or perhaps an even higher level of existence. The art of imbuing souls in artifacts had been long lost to time, and although many attempts had been made to study the constructs in the sect's possession, they were like cavemen trying to derive the laws of physics, lacking the tools, wisdom and guidance. Yao Shen, Elder Han and Shadow lightly flared their Qi, and he could feel the gaze of the flood dragons intensify as it recorded their Qi signature and compared it with the records.

Then, as abruptly as it began, the attention upon them dissipated. The gates began to rumble, the very earth trembling beneath their feet as it slowly creaked open. The gates were not part of a larger installation or structure like one would expect, but instead integrated directly into the inner sect's protective formation. A dome of azure energy separated the inner sect from the outer sect, shielding it not only from foreign attacks, but also blocking any attempt to pry. Thus, for the outer sect disciples, the inner sect was forever shrouded by a veil of mystery— it served as to both protect from espionage and motivate the disciples harder if they wished to experience the true heavenly sky sect.

The doors finally opened, leading to misty clouds blocking both normal sight and divine sense. That, however, would not stop the perception of a Soul Emperor. His divine sense swept past the restriction, covering the entire inner sect in a matter of seconds. Only when he was convinced that there was no ambush prepared for him did he withdraw it, his expression remaining stoic. Yao Shen was not naïve; he knew very well how the legacy families carefully guarded their power base. An ambush would be an act of grave foolishness, however; while he was certain to escape unscathed, the same could not be said of Shadow.

"Proceed," Yao Shen muttered, his words intended for Shadow as he stepped forward into the entrance without further hesitation. Shadow walked in lockstep with him as Yao Shen felt the layer of soft, moist clouds harmlessly brush off against his skin— if anything, the sensation left a wind and mist practitioner like himself refreshed.

The next moment, Yao Shen took his first step into the inner sect territory. The first thing he noticed was the spike in Qi density, the disparity so intense that it was like comparing a barren desert with riverside territory. The inner sect was only a third in size compared to the sprawling outer sect, which in part contributed to maintaining the Qi density— but that was far from the only reason. Here lay the true foundation of the Heavenly Sky Sect, one of the three survivors in the Azlak Plains since ancient times— having come close to annihilation many times, their formations broken, treasuries looted and ancient knowledge forever lost. Despite all that, they had still survived the Era of Turmoil and stood strong today, even if as a mere shadow of its past glory.

Finally, he focused his gaze on the lone figure standing at the inner sect entrance, whom he had long detected with his divine sense. His sworn rival, Zhou Hui, Patriarch of the Hui Family, stood fifteen meters away, cautiously observing him with a solemn expression on his face.

Yao Shen grinned.

10

PATRIARCH V. ZHOU HUI

"ELDER HAN, Shadow, please go on ahead." A small smile continued to rest on Yao Shen's face as he withdrew a small, circular violet-blue token that was covered in a complex web of inscriptions, holding it out in Shadow's direction.

Shadow pocketed the token with practiced ease, but did not immediately leave. Her gaze narrowed upon Zhou Hui with a scorching focus, memorizing every aspect, every detail of his visage before she turned her gaze to Yao Shen.

They made eye contact, and Shadow lightly nodded to him before she began walking, Elder Han falling in lockstep beside her. They walked past Zhou Hui without any interruption, for the Hui Family Patriarch's attention had never left Yao Shen from the moment they had stepped into the inner sect premises.

Yao Shen split an insignificant part of his divine sense to trail Shadow and make sure she reached his chambers without interruptions, though now that he was within the inner sect's territory, he had little cause to fear for her safety. The optimal period and positioning for an ambush had already passed.

"Old friend." Yao Shen finally decided to take the initiative, his tone warm and cheerful as he locked eyes with the Hui Family

Patriarch. His divine sense spread out at the same time, before focusing on Zhou Hui's solitary figure. Beneath his azure robes, which were emblazoned with not one, but two insignias— one belonging to the Heavenly Sky Sect, stitched with the threads extracted from a golden silkworm, and the other stitched with silvery-white threads that bore the mark of the Hui Family—he concealed a full set of light armor that Yao Shen immediately identified at the Peak Nascent Soul level. But that was only the beginning of his show of wealth, for Yao Shen detected three rings worn on each hand, every one emanating an ancient aura barring the last, which he placed as a spatial ring.

A sheathed sword rested at his waist, but Zhou's hands remained clasped behind his back as he silently observed Yao Shen.

"Sapience," Zhou Hui finally spoke, uttering naught but one word— his tone, even now that Yao Shen had far surpassed him, radiating confidence and aplomb. "You wield the power of the Esoteric, that which cannot be sought after, only understood," he continued, for it was not a question but a statement.

"Indeed." Yao Shen nodded lightly, not surprised that the Hui Family managed to trace the origins of his Major Dao in such a short period of time.

"The wind around you stills in abeyance, waiting for your command. You have reached Major Understanding in the Dao of the Wind," Zhou Hui continued, exposing one of the three elements Yao Shen had chosen to receive heavenly assistance in improving without batting an eye.

"Perceptive." Yao Shen smiled even wider, but inwardly it served as a reminder. Zhao Hui might not command the elements like his ancestors had once been able to, but he had made up for his shortcomings with intelligence and resourcefulness. Even now, he remained a worthy rival.

"Very well, then. Humor me, Yao Shen." Zhou Hui's words

were carried forth by the wind as he slowly unsheathed his ancestral blade, *Skyraiser*. The translucent green blade thrummed with power, and the moment it was fully released, strong gales of wind whipped outwards in all directions. An illusory, blurred figure of a reptilian creature with four wings manifested behind him, as Zhou Hui tightly clenched his teeth and wrestled for control over the artifact spirit. A Pseudo Soul Emperor blade was not something a Nascent Soul Cultivator could use for long, but it would cause no lasting harm.

Yao Shen materialized a generic Early Stage Nascent Soul blade from his spatial ring, curiously staring at the artifact spirit that had materialized behind Zhou Hui. Yao Shen had long memorized the contents of every bestiary the sect had access to, and the four-winged creature matched none of the entries.

"Domain of Endless Blades." Zhou Hui muttered the words aloud for Yao Shen's benefit, since this was the equivalent of a 'friendly duel' in the world of cultivators. The next second, Yao Shen felt himself lose control over the wind that surrounded him, snatched away from him to form a sphere of wind that encapsulated Yao.

Zhou Hui had imposed his will over the natural law of the world, marking it as his territory. Within his domain, Yao Shen was a foreign entity that would be heavily suppressed, the laws of the wind refuting his control. Zhou Hui raised his sword and slashed in Yao's direction, releasing his wind-attuned Qi. A hair-raisingly sharp wind blade empowered by the *Skyraiser* exploded with momentum, and Zhou Hui's domain mirrored his actions—dozens upon dozens of wind blades were released from the interior of the wind sphere's membrane, from widely unpredictable angles.

Yao Shen's divine sense exploded outwards, forming a zone of absolute perception within Zhou Hui's domain, completely disregarding the suppression. Each blade's trajectory was already visualized in his mind as he evaded the wind blades with frenzied, erratic movements. Those that were clustered too close for comfort, he contested control over—Zhou Hui no longer had any advantage over him since they both shared a major understanding over wind, and he was at a higher level of existence. Without much suspense, he tore away control from Zhou Hui and dissipated the wind blades into a harmless gust of wind.

Zhou Hui had undoubtedly known that his attack would fail, but it had been a distraction from the very beginning. The few moments Yao Shen required to evade his attacks, he used to close the distance between them. The illusory beast behind Zhou Hui roared, and the green glow within intensified. Wind coiled and sharpened around the blade until it was almost a physical object, the very physical manifestation of '*sharpness.*'

"Human Dao Domain: A Slice of Heaven." Yao Shen smiled, and the landscape around him began to change— A dazzling golden wheat field now stood in place of the ruthless wind sphere, rays of sunlight cascading past the clouds that had not been there a few seconds ago and landing upon the fields. Transparent silhouettes of Faceless farmers dressed in grey clothing manifested around Yao Shen, harvesting the wheat by hand— they were not cultivators, but mere mortals. At the edge of the wheat field, a small, dainty wooden house rested, adding to the scenic natural beauty of the rustic landscape.

Yao Shen had not needed to break Zhou Hui's domain since he had abandoned it of his own volition the moment his attack failed. Zhou Hui had been testing him since their duel began, probing his abilities and forcing him to display novel methods— trying to decipher the unknown was in his nature, and Yao Shen did not hold that against him.

But if that were the case, he would present Zhou Hui with a test of his own. Yao Shen no longer restricted his own senses, and the world exploded in color. He peered upon the inner sect, but only detected roiling clouds of vapor-like energies, painted in as many hues as there were emotions— red, yellow, white, orange, indigo, violet, gray, everything that came in between, and then more. Yao Shen willed it, and a small portion of the chaotic energies were funneled in his direction. He carefully absorbed the energies, replenishing his dwindling Human Dao reserves— not out of scarcity, for where there were sapient beings there were traces of Human Dao, but out of self-preservation. Once the energy entered his Soul Lake, it turned into a transient, milky white energy that peacefully rested at one end of the Soul Lake.

Yao Shen drew upon it, focusing on the concept of "Protect" as the core concept and the ancillary concepts of the human senses: "Sight," "Sound," "Smell" and "Touch." The next instant, he was shrouded in a layer of Human Dao, unworried for his own safety since he was invulnerable in this state— at least against a Nascent Soul Practitioner.

The world faded away as Yao Shen recalled decades-old memories, back when he was only a normal elder of the Heavenly Sky Sect. A young Shadow clung to his robes, digging her head into them each time an inner disciple drew near. He remembered the first time he'd brought her to the *Skytree*, recalling the expression of childlike glee that was reflected on her face when she gazed upon the ancient tree— letting her forget about the childhood that was robbed from her, if only for an instant.

And he remembered the desire he held in his heart, the desire to protect that innocent smile. He could die. The sect could be torn asunder, ripped to shreds. But Shadow.... Shadow could not die. She was not allowed to die, not before him, and preferably not after him.

"Protect," Yao Shen muttered aloud.

. . .

Zhou Hui felt the wind upon his back, aiding his cause by propelling him with speed that was at the very limits of his endurance. He felt Yao Shen's odd domain manifest around him, but he wasn't worried, for the disciples that had reported to him had claimed that it had no offensive ability. He knew better than to rely upon the claims of disciples, but all the records of the Human Dao he had studied in the brief time he had before Yao Shen arrived indicated that it was the weakest Esoteric Dao by far, and had no means of attack, so he was inclined to give some credence to their claims. The fact that Yao Shen's Human Domain possessed no oppression aura only added to this theory, unless he was being intentionally misled.

He knew that this was his last chance at gathering information, for he was waging two wars at the same time: one, against the rebellious artifact spirit that kept trying to refute his control, and the other against an opponent that he no longer understood. Zhou Hui could accept that he was no longer Yao Shen's match, but what he refused to accept was the massive, gaping hole in his intelligence that had led to this outcome, and he would do his utmost to rectify it.

So he channeled his wind-attuned Qi into the artifact left by his ancestors, which Skyraiser promptly amplified— almost doubling the strength of the attack in potency. Zhou Hui had reached within striking distance of Yao Shen, and was on the verge of lashing out with the most powerful attack of his life when the unthinkable happened.

Yao Shen... was gone. In his place stood his son, Wen Hui, who looked back at him with a blank expression on his face. Zhou Hui was a perceptive man, and the realization was almost instantaneous— this had to be one of Yao Shen's abilities. Zhou Hui had cultivated for almost the same time as Yao Shen and had experienced many illusory Daos and techniques firsthand.

But the person that stood in front of him— all his senses, the senses of a father over the Patriarch of the Hui Family, told him that it was undoubtedly his son that stood in front of him. A desire to protect him welled up from the deepest corners of his heart, a suggestion more than a compulsion...

Zhou Hui knew that it was a trick, a ploy, and if this were a real battle, he would die if he did not swing his blade...

He knew... He knew and yet...

His Qi dissipated and the blade reverted to an inert state, mere inches away from his 'son's' neck.

The next second, the illusion shattered and Yao Shen stood in front of him, the tip of his blade held against Zhou Hui's throat.

"A test for a test, old friend." Yao Shen had a wide grin on his face, but there was neither pride nor condescension on his visage but instead...*Approval?*

"A test?" Zhou Hui asked as a wave of shame and revulsion washed over him. Skyraiser was sheathed with a flash of motion, but Zhou Hui himself clenched his fists as he reflected upon his loss. He had known it was an illusion, a paltry damned trick from the beginning. His scouts were not wrong: Human Dao truly did not have any offensive methods, only illusions and deception.

"I failed." Zhou Hui gritted his teeth and accepted his loss with the dignity of a Patriarch, swearing that he would never allow himself to show such weakness again.

"Failed?" Yao Shen questioned, and then burst out into a light laugh. Zhou Hui felt his temper flare; he had already been defeated but to tarnish his honor like this... Until he tilted his gaze upward and saw Yao Shen's look of admiration. He was starting to think that Yao Shen and he himself were operating on entirely different metrics.

"You are not as ruthless as you believe yourself to be, Brother Hui. That is why you succeeded." Yao Shen leaned closer to his ear before lightly whispering, "Send Wen Hui along with your best artificers to the tower, and I promise to help forge the best protective artifact that I can."

Yao Shen then patted Zhou Hui twice on the shoulder before walking away and breaking into another laugh.

His old rival was calculating, and could be ruthless when the situation demanded it, but Yao Shen was glad to know that he was not entirely lost, that Eliria's jaws had not completely sunk into his throat and corrupted him beyond repair.

Zhou Hui, meanwhile, remained rooted to the spot— his facial expressions constantly shifting, no longer reflecting the dignity or poise of the Hui Family Patriarch.

Was that... Was that really Yao Shen, his *sworn rival*?

The world had truly gone mad.

11

FACELESS

YAO SHEN ASCERTAINED Shadow's location via the thread of divine sense he had split off earlier, marking her position near the center of the inner sect. Even from this distance, the eight-story ivory tower that jutted into the skies was clearly visible to the naked eye, representing one of the landmarks of the Heavenly Sky Sect— Silveni's Heirloom, a rather peculiar name for a majestic construct that served, partly, as the Patriarch's residence.

However, most disciples referred to it as 'The Sky Tower,' or simply, 'The Tower,' its true name deliberately concealed from them. Only Yao Shen, the elders, and the higher ranked guardians were aware of the implications behind the name 'Silveni' — for even though it was far before their time, the fragmented records from before the Era of Turmoil spoke highly of the House of Silveni, a highly skilled line of cultivators specializing in the art of forging true constructs.

Silveni's Heirloom was the only remnant left of such an illustrious and influential House that it only deepened Yao Shen's suspicion related to the events surrounding the Era of Turmoil, but his prudent side had always maintained a tight hold over that curiosity. Safe to say, it was no mere ordinary tower, but a Soul Emperor level construct that had flight and defensive capabilities.

Shadow stood outside the tower with Elder Han at her side, who had likely been observing their sparring session intently with his divine sense and had instructed Shadow to wait. Yao Shen's figure blurred as he flew forward with the speed of a Mid-Nascent Soul Cultivator. Disciples were forbidden from flying within the inner sect premises, but as Patriarch, such trivial restrictions did not apply to him.

A few moments later, Yao Shen's silhouette hovered over Elder Han and Shadow, his hands clasped behind his back as he gently drifted down, lightly landing in front of them. His divine sense had reverted to passive mode, and he detected Zhou Hui flying toward the tower at a modest speed— his intention clearly to avoid him until they were before the Council of Elders.

His actions amused Yao Shen, but he did not further wish to disturb the Hui Family Patriarch's equilibrium. He willed his divine sense into his storage ring and withdrew a small, circular token that was identical in size to the one he had given Shadow, but the similarities stopped there. Dense fractals that were barely visible to the naked eye covered the surface of the golden token, a small wisp of translucent light flickering at the center. He approached the thick, mottled set of double doors that were embedded into the tower's structure, and a circular slit opened on the side.

Yao Shen walked forward and inserted the Master Control Token, one of three in existence, into the slit. The doors started rumbling, and then slowly creaked open— the sheer weight and density of the material felt through the vibrations of the soft earth beneath them, taking half a minute to completely open.

The House of Silveni was quite ingenious in their design of the Master Control Token, reminding Yao Shen that Planet Earth was not alone in their ingenuity. Three Master Control tokens existed at any given time, and the one in Yao Shen's possession, much like the other two, was both soul-bound to him and managed to isolate a sliver of his divine sense without it losing integrity, the process a mystery to him.

That implied that if Yao Shen died, the insignificant part of his soul embedded into it would shatter the Master Control Token internally. If he was compromised, he could mentally order his divine sense to implode, and the token would crumple under the pressure instantly. And the moment it was destroyed, a new one could be formed by Silveni's Heirloom almost instantaneously, resulting in an almost negligible risk of the construct falling into enemy hands.

The door finally opened, and they were greeted by four individuals dressed in unassuming gray robes, each one wearing a mask that bore a simple depiction of a spiritual beast's outline. Their gloves and leggings covered almost every inch of their skin, and the mask's eye slits periodically changed the color of their irises, the process seemingly random.

They were the Faceless, and they guarded that which could not be revealed, operated in lands the sect could not openly enter and bore the burden of the darkness so the Heavenly Sky Sect could shine in glory. Yao Shen's memories from Earth had taught him much about the profundities of espionage. Though his past self's knowledge on the subject was rudimentary at best, it was still enough to bring him great surprise.

The Faceless, though, were not a force to be underestimated. They had no face, no past and no expense was spared in their martial training— they could infiltrate a demonic sect that posed a threat to their sect claiming to be rogue cultivators looking to convert to the demonic path, and they would trip no alarms.

"Patriarch Yao Shen, Elder Han. The Council awaits your presence," the man, or woman, that had short black hair identical in length to his or her other compatriots, spoke in a garbled voice that continuously oscillated in pitch and tone, an expensive arti-fact being used to achieve the effect.

Yao Shen felt a twinge of pity as he saw the young woman's expressionless face behind the mask, the mask unable to shield her features from the divine sense of a Soul Emperor. The Face-less had existed long before his rule, and loath as he was to admit it, their existence saved the lives of hundreds of cultivators, and thousands of mortals, if not more. He would see to it that arrange-ments were made to ensure better working conditions, but it was a pity there existed no equivalent of a 'psychologist' in the world of cultivation.

This was a matter that had many lives at stake, and thus it was not a decision that could be taken lightly. But he would ponder upon it, so for now, he crushed whatever pity he felt with his resolve and spoke:

"Very well. Lead the way, Sixty-Eight," Yao Shen gently commanded with a light smile on his face. Their faces turned tense, but they regained composure remarkably quickly—news traveled fast, and it was no surprise that the Faceless, who dealt in the world of classified information, were aware of his ascension. Thus, his being able to see through their disguises was not entirely unexpected, but surprising nevertheless.

"Follow me." The masked woman nodded and turned around before Yao Shen's gaze could linger upon her, but not quickly enough. Her lips twitched a few times before they morphed into a half-smile, exhaling a deep breath of air that she did not know she had been holding.

Perhaps Faceless Sixty-Eight herself did not understand those emotions, but to Yao Shen, who had removed the limiter on his senses and switched to his 'human sight,' it was more than obvious.

Her cover had been exposed, and even the artifact that could shield them from the prying of a Peak Nascent Soul Cultivator did not manage to prevent the intrusion. Of course, it had no offensive or defensive capabilities, and a Nascent Soul Cultivator could just rip the mask off their face and they would have no means to resist — but such a thing would be tantamount to a betrayal of the sect, and had never happened in the past hundreds of years.

She was ... *happy?* Relieved even, for now there was someone could *finally* pierce the veil.

There was one person in the world who saw her for who she truly was, the true face inherited from her mortal mother and father, whose faces she was too young to coherently recall.

For one who had been trained to become a ghost her entire life, she was seen.

That was enough.

12

COUNCIL

THE GROUND FLOOR of Silveni's Heirloom was lavished with a display of wealth— peak core formation artifacts with unconventional and bizarre effects rested behind crystal displays, affixed to the circular wall of the tower. A small lacquered wooden plaque rested below each display, with a brief note detailing the artifact's effects. Naturally, they were not suitable for use in real combat, but it spoke to the Heavenly Sky Sect's storied heritage that they could use peak core formation artifacts as mere conversation pieces.

Dire Wolf fur carpeted the tower's floor, known for its silken texture and airy feel while being surprisingly springy at the same time. Yao Shen's foot sank a little into the ground with every step he took, but the material reverted to its original form a few seconds later— an imitation of stepping on a cloud cultivator's domain. Plush divans were neatly spaced out across the floor, offering seating for individuals as well as groups. A bowl of freshly sourced spiritual fruits was placed next to each divan, and the seating arrangement for groups each had a rare Nieven Orb placed in the center, named after the game's Elvish creator. It was a favorite pastime of some of the older elders, a game that involved controlling small constructs via divine sense and battling each other. It sounded simple in theory, but in reality, the constructs were designed specifically to resist the intrusion of divine sense. If the potency of the divine sense exceeded the threshold of the construct, it would fall apart. Essentially, it was a test of pure control that even brought a challenge to the Elders, who had repurposed a few sets for their entertainment.

Faceless Sixty-Eight led them to a flight of steps at the tower's periphery, the ancient structure showing no sign of decay or wear even after thousands of years had passed— some of it had to do with regular maintenance, but Silveni's Heirloom had its own self-repair capabilities. Faceless Sixty-Eight then stepped aside, having bought enough time to recompose herself. The smile on her face was gone, replaced with the focused, calm gaze of a trained operative— her face largely expressionless. Perhaps she feared being reprimanded if she let her true emotions slip, and Yao Shen found that to be a travesty...one that he intended to rectify. He gave her a slight nod, which she took as a dismissal, turning around to return to her post. The rules mandated that one must always remain within the line of sight of a Faceless within the perimeter of the tower, but as Patriarch, he could waive that requirement for Shadow and Elder Han.

Yao Shen proceeded to ascend the steps with the dignity of a Patriarch— his back held straight and taut, arms held firmly at his sides, each of his motions controlled and deliberate. Yao Shen's pace was unhurried, but not relaxed, and Elder Han had already slowed to match him while Shadow trailed behind the two men. There was no particular emotion expressed on his face, but his sharp, penetrating gaze conveyed all that was needed to be said. It was important to remind the Elders that he was the one in control — now, more so than ever.

A solitary Faceless stood guard at the top of the staircase, his presence largely ornamental— for here lay the strongest beings that existed within the Heavenly Sky Sect, the few chosen among thousands of disciples and hundreds of thousands of mortals that successfully managed to reach the coveted second stage, transcending the limits of the physical body.

The Faceless stepped aside without needing to be prompted, waiting for Yao Shen and Elder Han to step past him or herself before announcing in a garbled, distorted voice, "Soul Emperor Yao Shen, Patriarch of the Heavenly Sky Sect, has arrived!"

"Nascent Soul Ye Han, Dao Repository Hall Elder has arrived!" the Faceless once again announced loudly.

Yao Shen immediately felt multiple gazes land upon him as he gazed back at the congregation. An elongated table stretched across the center of the tower's first floor, constructed out of a dark ebony wood with streaks of purple running across its surface. Six wooden chairs constructed of the same purplish-ebony wood were equidistantly placed across the long side of the table on either side, two of which were presently empty. At the northern end of the table was a chair, that at first glance did not seem markedly different from the others— only upon close examination would one realize that the violet streaks cut far deeper than the others, and even faintly pulsed every few seconds, the purple hue deepening before reverting to normalcy.

Elder Han finally separated from under his wing, making his way to one of the corner seats that placed him furthest away from Yao Shen— not intentionally, of course, but Elder Han was neither a scion of legacy families, nor was he particularly powerful, so it was only a given.

Yao Shen continued to ignore the gazes directed his way, walking toward the northern end of the table and seating himself on the hardwood chair. Almost immediately, Yao Shen felt a strong pulse of vitality course through his body, the sensation akin to a long, refreshing bath and a long night's sleep somehow melded into one. Considering that two of the members of the

Council were past the three-hundred-year mark, Eocava wood furniture was always a welcome choice. Shadow remained standing by his side, much like the other core disciples— all handsome young men and women, standing beside their masters or, for the legacy families, their relatives.

He continued to remain silent, the tense atmosphere in the room all but palpable. Yao Shen was tempted to switch to 'human sight,' but he chose to wait to do so until their final member arrived. Zhou Hui's son, Wen Hui, stood next to his father's empty chair— and Yao Shen did not need human sight to tell that he was afraid of him.

To a lesser extent, all of the legacy families' held a mélange of fear and caution toward him, to varying degrees. After all, the thorn in their side, the *houseless* vagrant that had used his misshapen domain to climb to the position of Patriarch, who had already been written off. His decision to ascend both mocked and ridiculed among their circles...for none of their Houses had managed to achieve such a feat in the past thousand years, so how could Yao Shen achieve such a thing, lacking even a Major Dao? The mere thought was the very definition of insanity.

Now that very Yao Shen, who should have been a distant memory, had returned as a *Soul Emperor* who wielded the power of the Esoteric Daos.

How were they supposed to react?

"Nascent Soul Zhou Hui, Patriarch of the Hui Family, Elder of the Enforcement Hall, has arrived," the Faceless announced, as Zhou Hui walked in with a solemn expression on his face, Skyraiser no longer seen upon his person. The Faceless shut the door after the final member had arrived, then activated the perception-shielding wards.

"The meeting may commence," the Faceless announced before relegating himself to an unassuming position next to the door.

Yao Shen lightly smiled as he activated his human sight— the world exploded in color, and it took Yao Shen a second to acclimatize to his new sight. All eyes were now focused upon him, waiting for the first words he would speak after achieving ascension.

The first thing that surprised Yao Shen was the sheer breadth of emotions that the core disciples projected upon the world— fear, joy, anger, pride, disgust, confusion, shock, and amusement —oscillating from one to the next as they tried to calm their thoughts. Such a thing was only to be expected, given the sheltered lives they had lived— for the legacy disciples, their family had always acted as an umbrella that shielded them from the wind and the rain, their safety assured in knowing that no bigger predator other than their own uncles and aunts had its gaze upon the lush fields of Azlak Plains.

Yao Shen had shattered that illusion, shattered their worldview, and partly, perhaps even fractured their belief in the indomitability of the legacy families. On the other hand, the disciples who came from humble beginnings but had climbed all the way to attract an unaffiliated elder's attention, of whom there were only four, projected powerful emotions onto the world because of jealousy and an undercurrent of anger, at the privilege, the nepotism and the humiliation they had suffered. Now that *one of them* was a Soul Emperor, they were delighted and amused, even eager, to see how he would suppress the holier-than-thou legacy families.

His attention shifted from the disciples to the elders, slightly surprised how *little* emotions the elders allowed themselves to show. A trickle of curiosity, a trace of shock, a bout of confusion — they had prepared for his arrival in the little time they had, and they had prepared well. It mattered not if they used an artifact to achieve the effect, for this was the real foundation of the legacy families: resources and the knowledge to employ them.

"Sect brothers and sisters…" Yao Shen finally spoke, and the next second, every gaze in the room was upon him with scouring intensity— each aspect of his tone, body language, and even micro-expressions being closely watched.

"….I, Yao Shen, Patriarch of the Heavenly Sky Sect, shall unify the Azlak Plains under the banner of the *Modern Sect*."

The emotions in the hall erupted with such intensity that not even Yao Shen could keep track of all the hues and the colors.

Hearing it through the mouth of a fellow disciple was one thing, but for Yao Shen to boldly state his desires instead of proposing a motion before the Council of Elders was an entirely different matter. A Patriarch's word was his bond, and a statement once claimed could not be retracted without losing all credibility with the sect and its disciples. This implied one of two things:

Either Yao Shen would convince the Council of Elders, or the outcome could be decidedly less….*pleasant.* The disciples' hearts hammered in their chests, for they had all heard about Yao Shen's reputation—their Patriarch knew how to hold a grudge and none of them wished to make an enemy out of him.

13

TEN NAMES

Silence. Absolute, deafening silence enveloped the Council of Elders chamber. The core disciples' faces had already turned ashen, and Yao Shen had stopped trying to make sense of the chaotic, jumbled cloud of emotions enveloping them. Well, of course, besides one exception. Shadow was sure to have heard of Yao Shen's outlandish desires to unite the Azlak Plains under one banner, but her face remained impassive— not once had she asked a single question about his plans, from the beginning to the end.

Finally, one of the Elders could take it no longer.

"Outrageous!" Wenyan Ren, Patriarch of the Ren Family, Elder of the Forging Hall, roared angrily, his fist slamming upon the Eocava wood table with a loud bang. The table quivered under the pressure, but the Eocava Tree was a Nascent Soul level resource— a casual blow from the Ren Patriarch was not enough to cause any real damage. Surely enough, the table's surface stabilized a few seconds later, but the Ren Patriarch's rash actions allowed Yao Shen to get a glimpse of the dark obsidian armor he wore under his Earthen robes— *The Earthflame Guardian*, a Pseudo Soul Emperor defensive artifact that had great resistances to the elements of Earth, Fire and Wind, its robust exterior offering supreme protection against even Peak Nascent Soul blades.

Of course, Yao Shen had already detected the armor with a sweep of his divine sense earlier on, and he had not been surprised in the slightest. Each of the legacy family heads had arrived only after thorough preparations— carrying one Pseudo Soul Emperor level artifact upon their person, barring only one exception: Zhou Hui.

"Now, now, Brother Wenyan, let us not be so brash," a soft, gentle voice interjected before Yao Shen had the opportunity to respond, preventing the situation from escalating any further. Meili Zhu, Matriarch of the Zhu Family and Elder of the Skyless Hall, turned to gaze in Yao Shen's direction, offering him an apologetic smile as she bobbed her head downward to show deference to his authority.

Yao Shen's expression remained inscrutable as he observed her coy act, paying close attention to the black feathered fan in her left hand that she used to conceal the lower half of her face— Meili Zhu liked to play the part of a shy, young mortal maiden in public, her short black hair, dark brown eyes, slender, fit body and flawless skin preserved through the use of vitality pills made her look like a woman in her mid-thirties, even though her actual age had crossed three hundred years. Every elder had picked up their fair share of eccentricities across their long lifespans, but Yao Shen found Meili's act too targeted and deliberate to be attributed as such. It reminded him of those 'public relations' firms back on Earth, cleaning up a celebrity's image and perception among the populace for a hefty price.

As if such trivialities would let them forget that she was Meili Zhu, Master of the Faceless and Major Practitioner of the Dao of Darkness. The black fan she held in her left hand was a Pseudo Soul Emperor offensive artifact, each feather's spine concealing a needle bearing such sharpness that it could puncture through his body instantly—Soul Emperor or not. The master artifact let her control the feathers at will, the connection forged through the artifact spirit and not easily detectable, let alone shattered. Had the art of blending true poisons not been lost to time, Yao Shen would not call it an exaggeration to say that Meili Zhu was capable of assassinating Early Stage Soul Emperors with ease.

"Patriarch Yao." She finally decided to continue speaking, since Yao Shen had shown no indication that he was going to respond. "When I heard of your desire to unify the Azlak Plains, I *will* admit that I was quite enthralled by the idea. However, at the time, I had believed that your promises to the Divine Mountain Sect and the Sacred Flame Place were part of a greater scheme, that this little one could not see through. Now that you have professed a desire to act upon the creation of this..." Meili Zhu paused, as she once again reflected upon the mysterious name Yao Shen had chosen, but her mind came up blank.

"...Modern Sect, as you have termed it. I must ask you, Patriarch Yao. What is it that prompted such an *unconventional* decision?" Meili Zhu chose her words carefully, not wishing to antagonize him unless absolutely necessary.

"Indeed!" An aged man dressed in jade green robes lightly thumped the table in agreement, his actions attracting the attention of other elders. He was Zhiquang Yi, Patriarch of the Yi Family and Elder of the Alchemy Hall, the second elder who had crossed the three hundred-year-old mark among those present.

"Aye." The next one to thump in agreement was Wenyan Ren.

"As the one who proposed the motion, I am inclined to agree." Meili Zhu once again dipped her head slightly as an apology, after which she proceeded to lightly tap the table with her free hand. By rephrasing her question as a motion, she had invoked the authority of the Council and wished to use its power to compel Yao Shen to give her an answer instead of evading the question.

"I, Dongmei Xue, Matriarch of the Xue Family and Elder of the Healing Hall, agree."

"I, Liewei Hu, Patriarch of the Hu Family and Elder of the Wind Distribution Hall, agree."

"I, Jie Tang, Patriarch of the Tang Family and Elder of the Divine Might Hall, agree."

"I, Jiayi Song, Matriarch of the Song Family and Elder of the Skytree Dao Hall, agree."

"Enough," Yao Shen's calm voice echoed out in the chamber. "The motion passes with a majority vote," he acceded with grace, honoring the agreement he had with the Council.

"However," Yao Shen added, and in that instant, his human sight detected the spike of emotion, a small cloud of 'concern' forming around Meili Zhu before it dissipated in the next instant. The Nascent Soul Cultivator had not lived three centuries for nothing, her instincts frighteningly sharp. "To answer your question, I must question Zhou Hui, Elder of the Enforcement Hall. Is that acceptable to the Council?"

"Yes," Wenyan Ren replied, and soon, every member of the legacy family nodded in agreement, including Zhou Hui, who seemed more curious than worried, and Meili Zhu, who was the last one to assent.

"Very well. Elder Zhou Hui, do you agree to truthfully answer all questions proposed to you before the Council of Elders?" Yao Shen asked, a serious expression on his face while he *smiled* inwardly— Meili Zhu was cautious, and her instincts had not failed her. But even then, she could think of no justification to deny such a simple request.

"I do," Zhou Hui replied with composure, a burst of curiosity escaping past whatever measures he had prepared to isolate and contain his emotions.

"I will not stand on ceremony then. Your fellow legacy elders may not have come seeking conflict, but they stand sufficiently prepared for one. Zhou Hui, you, instead, have effectively come unarmed. Why?" Yao Shen proposed the question, and immediately, the gaze of everyone in the hall, including Wen Hui, his son, fell upon him.

Zhou Hui locked eyes with Yao Shen, his eyes shining bright with intelligence and wisdom, before he broke into a light, self-deprecating laugh.

"Yao Shen, as the Enforcement Hall Elder, it is my sworn duty to root out any internal threats that threaten the stability of our Heavenly Sky Sect. As part of my duties, as I am sure all present in this hall are aware, I like to understand the capabilities and limitations of those who have the capability to threaten it. I believed that I understood the extent of your power, but I was *gravely* mistaken, and for that, I would like to apologize to all present. Hubris and conceit prevented me from accurately assessing the situation, and it is a mistake that shall not be repeated twice," Elder Zhou Hui explained, a certain gravitas in his voice that compelled attention, making him the center focus of the entire Council.

"And yet, you are willing to rely on that very same judgment to walk unarmed into a meeting that may end in conflict?" Yao Shen countered, his words lacking judgment or derision but instead, intrigue.

Zhou Hui smiled, and then answered, "Brother Yao, you have spent two hundred years of your life contributing to the glory of the Heavenly Sky Sect— such bonds are not so easily broken, and while you and I may have had our fair share of disagreements in our heyday, the sect itself has not mistreated you and neither have you ever given me a cause to doubt your loyalty. Unless every word, every action, every step you have taken in the last two hundred years was part of a larger deception, I do not believe that you are here to spill blood upon the sacred halls where your master had once presided."

Yao Shen silently observed Zhou Hui, slightly moved by his impassioned words. Truly, his rival was not only powerful in his own right, but also an unparalleled orator that backed his words with actions— if Skyraiser was sheathed upon his waist, they would hardly have had the same impact.

"You believe that I am acting in the best interests of the sect?" Yao Shen asked him without equivocation, and Zhou Hui would have to answer very carefully— if he answered in affirmative, then his relation with the other legacy families would sour, but if he answered with a denial, then his earlier words would lose all credibility.

"I believe that you *think* you are acting in the best interests of the sect, Yao Shen, which is why I hold great curiosity with regard to your purported objectives." Zhou Hui parried the verbal offensive without difficulty, as silence once again enveloped the hall.

"A final question, then, Zhou Hui. As Elder of the Enforcement Hall, do you regulate the activities of the eight legacy families?" Yao Shen concluded with the question he had really wished to ask from the very beginning.

"No. As you are well aware, the rules of the Enforcement Hall state that the legacy families shall have the responsibility to regulate their own members," Zhou Hui answered, his eyes narrowing in thought.

"Thank you, Zhou Hui. That will be all," Yao Shen gave him a nod, and then pulled out a sheaf of bamboo papers from his spatial ring, gingerly placing them upon the table. The attention of the attendees congregated upon the papers, but as far as their divine sense could tell, there wasn't anything special about them — they were just a mundane, mortal resource.

"This," Yao Shen gestured toward the sheaf of papers before

continuing, "is a list of all inner disciples that are not aligned with any house. Shadow, please choose any ten names at random from this list." Yao Shen had all but needed to request, and Shadow stepped forward.

A minute later, she recited ten names from memory, all selected from different pages in accordance with his instructions.

"Perfect. Thank you, Shadow. I need you to summon these disciples and bring them to the council meeting. Can you do that?"

Shadow nodded.

"If anyone, and by that, I mean *anyone* at all, tries to impede your quest, then you are authorized to use my crest and authority to declare them a *demonic sect spy* and order their detention. Is that understood?"

"Yes, Patriarch," she replied as the shadows started enveloping her, forming a cloak around her back. She moved toward the exit, a portion of his divine sense splitting off and trailing her from behind to ensure her safety.

Now, all he needed to do was wait.

"Patriarch, may I know what the purpose of summoning these children is?" Meili Zhu asked, her facial expression inscrutable as ever, but Yao Shen could guess at her emotions—she did not like the direction this meeting was proceeding, that much he was certain of.

"You wanted an answer, did you not? You need only wait, and you shall have it."

14

CONFRONTATION II

THE CONVERSATION in the hall stalled after Shadow's departure, but it was well evident to Yao Shen that the legacy family heads covertly communicated with their divine sense— their queries most likely directed to Meili Zhu and Zhiquang Yi, the two most aged and experienced among them. Wenyan Ren, Patriarch of the Ren Family, continuously clenched and unclenched his left fist underneath the Eocava wood table in an attempt to control his burgeoning fury— the forgemaster infamous for his vicious outbursts and fits of rage.

The preparations the Ren Patriarch had made to isolate his emotions were beginning to fail him, as a small, roiling cloud of 'anger' formed around him, expanding and contracting in size as the Ren Patriarch attempted to rein it in. Perhaps Wenyan Ren himself was not certain about the cause of his outburst, the trigger for his 'anger management issues' as psychologists from Earth would likely describe it, but to Yao Shen, it was clear as crystal.

His entire life, Wenyan Ren had been taught about the superiority of the legacy families, their inherited right to rule derived from their noble bloodline, powerful inheritance techniques, and their mighty ancestors who had navigated the Heavenly Sky Sect through the Era of Turmoil— for they were one of the three survivors of the ancient conflict that resulted in the destruction of dozens upon dozens of glorious Azlak Plain sects, the death toll of such an epic battle too fearsome to even imagine.

Now, thousands of years later, the so-called 'legacy families,' despite all the advantages vested in them from birth, could not even produce a single Soul Emperor. Yet, an *outsider*, a *talentless vagrant*, who came from an unremarkable mortal village, born to unassuming mortal parents that had long since perished, managed to reach the fabled stage and achieved ascension. Wenyan Ren could perhaps accept that, if Yao Shen was a talented son of the heavens, but he, as an Elder of the Heavenly Sky Sect knew, more than anyone, that the thought of calling Yao Shen talented was simply *laughable*.

The heavens had made their disfavor for Yao Shen evident, and no one in the sect, not even his own master, had expected him to reach the Nascent Soul stage. *Yet, he did.* The legacy families were surprised by his achievement, but had never been truly alarmed— they had considered him to be an insignificant elder that they could control, much like the present Elder Han. *Yet, he challenged Zhou Hui for the position of Patriarch and won.* Defiance was ingrained into his nature, into his very bloodline— Yao Shen was a cultivator who rose from rabble to become the Patriarch of the Heavenly Sky Sect, not because he was a talented scion of the heavens or a legacy family patriarch, no, the truth was far simpler. Yao Shen was a cultivator that was not content with the future the heavens had ordained for him, and sought to defy fate's bindings with every fiber of his existence, *even if it came at the price of his life.*

He was the very antithesis of everything the legacy families represented, his very existence a living, breathing reminder of their failure, their continuing decline and an even deeper possibility that Wenyan Ren would never acknowledge— the terrifying possibility that their insistence to rely upon the traditions inherited from ancient times *was* the real reason for their decline.

And Wenyan Ren hated him for it.

"Shadow, First Disciple of Patriarch Yao Shen, has returned in furtherance of the Council's command," the garbled voice of the Faceless echoed out across the hall as Shadow stepped into the hall, followed by ten inner disciples that obediently trailed behind her in single file, their sight obscured by thick shadows as they relied only upon their natural sense of balance and hearing to conform to her instructions—which, for a cultivator, was enough.

Shadow's gaze turned to the Faceless, and she nodded once toward them. The Faceless nodded back as their Darkness Qi flared and enveloped the entirety of their body— allowing them to vanish in plain sight, at least in the eyes of the inner disciples. The existence of the Faceless was not acknowledged, and not revealed unless absolutely necessary— thus making such precautions standard procedure.

Her gaze shifted to Yao Shen, who nodded in the affirmative. The shadows that were pooling around the disciples' eyes began to fade, retreating back to form a cloak upon their master's back. Yao Shen focused his human sight with absolute concentration as the disciples' sight was restored.

The young disciples found themselves in the hallowed hall of the Council of Elders, facing twelve of the mightiest beings that existed in the Azlak Plains— a force that would be well-respected, even revered, wherever they ventured upon the continent of Ionea.

Their emotions flared with far greater intensity than the core disciples', but Yao Shen stretched his soul's perception to the very limits as he kept track of each and every single hue, each one representing a different fragmented emotion that sometimes combined together to form a complete whole.

'Awe' radiated from a majority of disciples, with such radiance that it almost obscured his senses, followed by a strong cloud of silvery white hues that combined together to form a sincere, deep 'respect' as they realized who they were in the presence of.

The inner disciples, who were at varying stages of foundation establishment, bowed deeply and would continue to bow with their lowered heads, for Yao Shen felt a burst of 'confusion' — they were unsure why they were summoned, seeming almost at a loss.

"At ease," Yao Shen muttered, and 'relief' bubbled up in their hearts as they straightened themselves and awaited the Council's commands.

"You have been summoned before the Council of Elders. Understand that you are to answer any question the Council poses to you truthfully and to the best of your knowledge." Yao Shen had an intention to explain the rules to the inner disciples, but he was well aware that anything he said would be interpreted as a command by the disciples.

"Yes, Patriarch," they replied in near-perfect unison, a dense cloud of 'reverence' forming around them indicating that they had heard news of his ascension.

"Good." Yao Shen nodded, and then continued, "Do any of you know why you have been summoned to the Council of Elders?"

A cloud of anxiety formed among some of the disciples, but it lacked any real density. That indicated that they had nothing to fear, or at least felt like they had done nothing that would incur the Council's wrath.

A minute later, all of the disciples had replied in the negative. This question was only for the benefit of the Council, to show them that the selection process was truly random.

"Very well. Shadow, please announce the names of all elders present for the benefit of these children," Yao Shen commanded, at the same time using his divine sense to send a message to Shadow, which was only one word: *'Slowly.'*

Yao Shen's earlier observation had not received the results he had hoped, but layering and masking emotions was not impossible— if his fears were true, which he was convinced they were, the truth would soon reveal itself— either with this batch of the disciples, or the next.

The elders, even those who were not affiliated with the legacy families, gave him odd looks. After all, what need was there to introduce them to a bunch of juniors? What gave them a right to such a treatment?

But they would not interfere with the process; otherwise, Yao Shen could simply claim that he had tried to give them an answer but failed due to their interruption.

Yao Shen, however, did not care what the elders thought. His attention was fully focused on the disciples, examining each of them carefully. Six names along with their titles were announced, and there was no reaction.

"Dongmei Xue, Matriarch of the Xue Family and Elder of the Healing Hall," Shadow impassively announced, and the truth finally revealed itself.

The reaction came from a young girl, a mid-stage foundation establishment cultivator roughly around thirty-two years of age with sky-blue irises, light golden-blonde hair with pale white skin, who averted her gaze as soon as that name was mentioned. Her round, bright eyes brimmed with innocence, however, the emotions that coursed through her mind were anything but.

Fragments of emotions swirled together in a chaotic cloud that had half submerged her in an instant: 'self-loathing,' 'indignance,' 'remorse', 'regret.' 'frustration,' 'grief,' 'trauma,' all fused together to form a complete emotion that was far more powerful than the sum of its parts— hatred, in its most pure, unadulterated form, hatred that threatened to consume her whole. Hatred, that undoubtedly concealed a story behind it—one that would never otherwise reach his ears, due to the difference in their positions.

"Stop," Yao Shen's voice echoed out, and the attention in the room focused on him. "You," he pointed at the blonde-haired girl, "step forward."

"Yes, Patriarch," the girl managed to croak out in time, shocked out of her inner thoughts— had she done something wrong?

"Shadow, direct the other disciples to the lower floor and have them wait there until they are needed," Yao Shen commanded, and Shadow proceeded to lead them out of the room. Soon, there was only the Council, Yao Shen and the blonde-haired girl who was lightly trembling from the uncertainty.

Yao Shen withdrew an object from his storage ring, his actions immediately attracting the attention of the other elders.

A rectangular token was held in his right hand, carved from golden jadeite with the words "Shen" inscribed upon its surface on both sides.

"Do you know what this is?" Yao Shen asked her politely. The elders had been perplexed by Yao Shen's actions earlier, but now they were absolutely flabbergasted.

"N-n-no, Patriarch. Am I in trouble?" The mid-foundation establishment cultivator was no different from a child in the eyes of anyone present, and she felt so out of her depth that she did not know how to react.

"I am Soul Emperor Yao Shen, Master of the Esoteric Human Dao, Master of three Major Elemental Daos, Patriarch of the Heavenly Sky Sect and the strongest cultivator in the entire Azlak Plains. This is a token of honorary discipleship. If you accept it, then you will be free to use the sect's resources in my name and request me for guidance, your mortal family's security will be ensured until their natural death, and in the event of an unnatural death befalls you, I, Yao Shen, will personally investigate the matter until the killer is found, and then I will avenge your death. I offer this to you, upon one condition." Yao Shen's voice was solemn, as he pulled out another item from his inventory. A recording stone, of the highest grade available in the sect.

The disciple's hands started trembling from shock, her eyes widening as she breathed heavily— the golden token in Yao Shen's hands was something that core disciples would kill for, let alone an insignificant inner disciple like her. No one, not even in the middle of a battlefield, would be willing to attack her, for the fear of a Soul Emperor's retaliation. To be able to receive the Patriarch's guidance…

"P-Patriarch, m-may I know the condition?" the young girl asked hesitantly, feeling guilty about not immediately accepting the offer.

"You must answer a question. A question that will forever mark you as an enemy of the legacy families, and in case of my untimely death, mark you as a target for retribution. If you are not willing, leave now and no one in this room shall speak of this matter again. That much, I assure you." Drawing upon his reserves of Human Dao, he envisioned moments in his life when he was pitted against unfair odds but still managed to prevail because he remained calm and rational, rational and objective, before projecting the "emotion" of calmness in his words.

His Human Dao projection was not meant to influence the girl's decision, but instead give her clarity of thought to not let his authority influence her decision. For better or worse, it would permanently alter the course of her own life.

A minute passed in silence, before the girl nodded calmly, a glint of intelligence shining in her eye. "I accept. Please ask the question, Patriarch."

Yao Shen nodded, channeling his Qi into the recording stone before locking eyes with her. She gazed back at him fearlessly, and Yao Shen stealthily enveloped her in a cocoon of his divine sense— this way, if any of the other elders tried to whisper into her ears, they would be met with an unpleasant surprise.

"Very well. Then tell me, Yanyue Meng. Why do you hate that woman?" Yao Shen asked as he pointed his finger directly at Dongmei Xue, Matriarch of the Xue Family, who somehow managed to look both furious and wronged at the same time.

15

YANYUE

THE YOUNG FOUNDATION ESTABLISHMENT DISCIPLE, Yanyue Meng, should have been *horror stricken* when Patriarch Yao Shen called upon her to testify against the Matriarch of the Xue Family, an existence so far removed from her own meager power and status in the Heavenly Sky Sect that, under normal circumstances, their paths were unlikely to ever cross.

Dongmei Xue, Major Practitioner of the Dao of Water, was an existence whose distinguished repute stretched far beyond the walls of their Heavenly Sky Sect. The few disciples fortunate enough to personally receive her care claimed that no wound or injury was below her ability to heal, as long as it was not outright fatal. It would then surprise one, as it had surprised Yanyue Meng, when she had discovered that it was not the ability that formed the cornerstone for her fame— her Water Dao Domain, *The Immortal*, was a perfect representation of the arrogance and pride of the legacy families, and as loath as Yanyue was to admit it, even her hatred for the woman did not preclude her appreciation for her skill, which stood at the very pinnacle of the Dao of Water.

The Immortal Domain was as simple in application as it was *domineering*— any wound or injury that Dongmei Xue suffered within the bounds of her domain would be healed nigh instantly to perfection, regardless of its lethality. It did not matter if half her body was disintegrated from the elemental strike of an enemy cultivator or even if her head was completely severed from her body— as long as the integrity of her Nascent Soul was not compromised, her water element would heal the damage and restore her body to optimal condition without fault.

Had it not been for the complexity of the path she had chosen, many believed that there would be a third peak stage Nascent Soul Cultivator in the Heavenly Sky Sect, but alas, who could truly be certain about these matters. For Yanyue, who was both suited and had attuned her Qi to the water element, it would not be a lie to say that Dongmei Xue was the goal she aspired to reach by the end of her cultivation journey.

However, as she gazed into Patriarch's eyes, she felt no fear at the thought of confronting Dongmei Xue. Her thoughts flowed with such clarity that Yanyue felt like she had snapped out of a trance— up until that moment, she had not truly realized how much being in the presence of the Council of Elders and the Patriarch had been affecting her. Her heart no longer beat a click faster with every scrutinizing gaze that fell upon her; the queasy knot in her stomach, as insecurities gnawed at her from the inside, unfurled in one smooth motion.

Many connections that Yanyue would not otherwise have made threaded together in her mind as she instantly understood that this mysterious energy the Patriarch had imparted to her had to do with the Esoteric Human Dao that he had mentioned as a part of his long list of titles and accomplishments. She had also understood his intentions, but that hardly required much deliberation— Yanyue, a mere mid-stage formation establishment cultivator—had nothing of value to give to the Patriarch and neither did she have any knowledge that warranted his attention. The only possible value she could provide to the new ruler of the

Azlak Plains was recalling and sharing her account of the series of injustices she had been forced to suffer after entering the Heavenly Sky Sect— which she would have gladly explained to the Council earlier on without need or want of remuneration, if she had the slightest hint of faith in their ability to regulate one of their own, not to mention the impossibility of getting an audience in the first place.

The origin of the calmness flowing through her expression, thoughts and body language came from experience that was not her own, but it nevertheless reassured her to know that one of such wisdom stood behind her. The heavens could collapse, and Dongmei Xue could perhaps choose to end her puny life in the next second in but a single strike— but Yanyue would remain unmoved, like the Ancient Skytree that had existed far before the Era of Turmoil, and continued to stand rooted at the very same spot until this day. It was not apathy or misplaced confidence that guided her decision, but an understanding that terrorizing her own thoughts with scenarios of negative consequences would only hinder her judgment. Of course, understanding was one thing, and imbibing that concept into her actions and judgment an entirely different matter. She was not naive enough to believe that she could accomplish such a feat without Yao Shen's assistance.

So she accepted the opportunity of a lifetime, and now she had nothing to lose by divulging the thoughts and memories she had shoveled into the deepest corner of her mind out of a desire for self-preservation. The legacy families already knew of her, and of the hatred that she carried within her heart for them— so she would let them hear the truth.

The memories came flooding back to her mind as she braced herself against the waves of regret, self-deprecation and anger that washed over her in cycles, gritting her teeth and forcing herself to raise her head up and face the council members. She felt a warm dampness accumulating near the inner corner of her eyes, feeling a pang of shame rise in her chest when she realized that she had started crying— but the emotion of calm once again surged, swatting aside all shame as she faced the Council with two warm streaks running across her face.

"Patriarch Yao Shen," she addressed, her voice sounding much more vulnerable and smaller than she'd have liked it to, but her tone at least managed to stay even throughout.

Yao Shen tapped his index finger against the Eocava wood table a single time to acknowledge her address, not wanting to interrupt her story by raising his voice. The recording stone was active, and Yao Shen did not wish to make it feel like an interrogation, so he remained silent.

"I..." Yanyue uttered, pausing to take a deep breath as she seemed to grasp for the right words. "I come from a mortal village that is situated three hundred li away from our sect, at the border of the Grand Sealing Formation. Spiritual Beasts do not dare to approach the formation's periphery, and demonic sects have little reason to venture that far out east— making our small village a safe place to live. The sealing formation's presence siphoned at the vitality of the land and the ambient Qi in the surroundings, but we had always had enough to survive," she explained, a reminiscent look on her face as she thought back upon simpler times.

"Our village was under the protection of one of the subordinate sects of the Heavenly Sky Sect, and a few months after my thirteenth birthday, I met my first cultivator— a young man dressed immaculately in azure robes flew across the sky upon a flying sword, and few words could describe that experience. I had heard of the tales, of course— of mighty cultivators that can uproot mountains with the swipe of a hand and fly upon their divine swords to slay the evil that plagued our lands, but to see it in front of my eyes... It was *different,* in ways that I cannot explain, and in that moment, I was almost certain that it was the path I wished to pursue in this lifetime." Yao Shen saw the spark in her eyes, one that all those who stepped on the path of cultivation shared. A calling that spoke to them from the moment they witnessed another harnessing the laws of the natural world, until it became a yearning, and eventually, an obsession.

"My prayers were answered, as few visited these barren lands without purpose— he had indeed come on behalf of the Heavenly Sky Sect, to test if there were any mortal children with enough latent talent to be admitted into the sect. I, naturally, passed his test with ease. However, there was one other that passed the test along with me." Yanyue's voice abruptly cut off, as fresh, hot tears started streaming down her eyes.

"*My sister*," she whispered under her breath, her expression wavering as the emotions of regret and self-loathing clashed against the undercurrent of 'calmness' shielding her, the latter barely eking out another victory— but only by the slimmest of margins.

"What happened?" Yao Shen finally asked, choosing to provide direction to their conversation— he did not wish for his newest disciple to dwell upon these memories for too long, for he saw how it tore at her from the inside.

Yanyue sniffled, Yao Shen's voice providing a welcome distraction that she could direct her attention to. Marshaling her resolve, she cleared her mind and focused only upon the question that had been posed to her— she would not let her own *weakness* be what prevented the truth from coming out.

"My sister was not as talented as I, but it was originally rare enough for a mortal family to produce one with the potential to step upon the path of cultivation, let alone two, sisters at that. Mother and Father were overjoyed when the cultivator had announced the results, knowing that their two beloved daughters would experience much more in their lives, go on to accomplish far nobler purposes— and they too could rest easy, for the Sect would provide for their parents until the end of their mortal lives, lavishing them with mortal wealth. She joined the outer sect's Dao Impartment Hall, where she would end up attuning Wind Qi, while I joined the inner sect's Skytree Dao Hall, attuning Water Qi as my chosen element," Yanyue explained, wondering how her parents would feel if they realized that the world of cultivators was just as narrow-minded and selfish as the mortal world, if not more. They were no race of noble saviors like in the fables recited to her as a child had depicted them to be, that illusion shattered the day she had learned of the treachery of the legacy families.

"In the outer sect, my sister was pressed to keep pace with her peers as we grew older, but she clung to the desire to cultivate with every fiber of her being— and to ask her to cease her pursuit of the Dao would destroy her, much like it would myself. One could not simply return to their mundane life after bending and shaping the natural elements to one's will, and so I never had the courage to ask her to. I had been blessed with a strong affinity for water, so I would train myself in the healing arts. As my sister's explorations in search for natural inspiration got riskier, the missions she took for the sect harder, I would stay by her side and make sure that she returned." Yanyue's expression turned increasingly crestfallen, so much so that Yao Shen had no difficulty in guessing at the eventual outcome.

"So I approached the Healing Hall for guidance," she said, each of her words spoken slowly and with purpose. "I was young back then, no more than a peak-stage Qi Establishment Cultivator — young, naive and stupid. The Healing Hall directed me to purchase a healing technique from the Dao Repository Hall, but when I asked for its cost, I was perplexed— it would cost a Foundation Establishment Disciple years, perhaps decades, before she would be able to purchase the technique, let alone a Qi Establishment Cultivator. It was only later, when a woman bearing the mark of the Xue family approached me, did I understand the situation. She wished for me to pledge my silent allegiance to the

Xue Family, and serve her family's interests for the next eighty years in exchange for the healing technique. I, in a moment of misplaced pride and foolishness... *refused,*" Yanyue gazed at Yao Shen, or rather more accurately, the recording stone within his hands, her expression frail and vulnerable.

"Within a week, the Xue family destroyed my reputation within the inner sect, spreading rumors that I had abandoned a fellow disciple to his death when faced with a spiritual beast, claiming that I used my healing techniques to torture outer sect disciples, among other such insidious claims— they made sure that no inner sect disciple would accompany me on missions outside the sect, offer me assistance or even *interact with me.* That made it impossible for me to take the missions that offered higher rewards, making it even harder for me to support my sister. My sister only took larger risks, until a few years later when she lay bleeding in my arms, the horn of a dead spiritual beast embedded in her chest."

"All I wanted..... All I *ever* wanted, was to be able to heal her. Was that truly such..... *a great ask*?" she asked as the strength left her body and she collapsed to the ground, her question addressed to the Matriarch of the Xue Family without any malice or anger within...just exhaustion.

Just exhaustion.

A chilly silence enveloped the hall as Zhou Hui gazed at the young disciple lying upon the floor with trembling hands. Elder of the Enforcement Hall, he was supposed to be the Elder of the Enforcement Hall... yet such deep corruption and rot had infested one of the eight pillars of the sect right under his nose. He had known that the legacy families took certain *liberties* with their positions, but from the very beginning of the education he had received, he was taught not to take any actions that would negatively impact the harmony and cooperation between the legacy families.

Where was the honor? Where was the dignity of the legacy families?

The hall was silent, except for Yao Shen, who continued to tap upon the Eocava wood table with his index finger, the time between each tap uniform. His expression was inscrutable, but when Zhou Hui gazed upon him, a vague feeling of crisis enveloped his entire body that sent chills up his spine.

Tap, Tap, Tap, the sound continued to echo out, in the backdrop of a lightly sobbing Yanyue.

"Yao Shen! You bring this disciple before the Council of Elders and fill this sacred hall with her slanderous lies! Your actions bring shame to your late master's honor!" Wenyan Ren angrily roared as the chair he was seated upon flew backwards, his earthen robes discarded to reveal the dark obsidian armor— The Earthflame Guardian—beneath. A large obsidian warhammer was drawn from his spatial ring, the two-handed weapon held with a single, gauntleted arm without any struggle.

The room instantly divided into two sides— on the right were the seven legacy family heads, each with their Pseudo Soul Emperor level artifact in hand or worn upon their bodies, while on the left were the three elders unaffiliated with any family. Elder Han remained seated, as if he wished for all parties involved to forget that he existed, while Zhou Hui's expression seemed as pale as a ghost as he remained sitting in a state of shock.

Yao Shen had not moved from his original spot on the table, as if the actions of the parties involved held no meaning to him.

Tap, Tap, Tap, the sound echoed out again, far too repetitive to have no meaning at all.

Finally, Yao Shen spoke.

"You seem to have misunderstood," Yao Shen spoke, his voice

distant and detached, as if the events that had transpired had no relation to him.

"Misunderstood what?" Dongmei Xue sharply countered. "You tarnish the image of my Xue family within these sacred halls and use a recording stone to record your slander so that you can steal my Xue family's resources. What is there to misunderstand?" she asked in the form of a wronged scream, her theatrics so impressive that perhaps even she herself was convinced that the real victim here was her.

"My Human Dao has no offensive means, so you do not believe it to be a threat. *You are correct.* I may have achieved mastery in three Major Daos, but I have had no time to consolidate my gains. Your understanding of the Major Daos are natural, earned, whereas mine are imparted by the heavens. You believe there is an irrefutable difference between the natural and the imparted, that with your Pseudo Soul Emperor artifacts you can contest my control over the elements. *Once again, you are correct.* But what you underestimate is not I, *Yao Shen*, but the very resolve of the Heavens— *to extinguish my soul, scatter my ashes and erase all traces of my cultivation.*" His piece said, Yao Shen relaxed his control over his facial expressions, the trembling rage he felt smoldering deep within his irises no longer concealed.

He did not shift from his position, and neither did he unleash his domain. All Yao Shen did was tap his finger lightly upon the table, and his divine sense— the external manifestation of his soul, engulfed the seven elders that had attracted his fury.

Instantly, a seven-layered shield manifested around each of the legacy family heads, the ancient rings they wore upon their hands glowing with power. The outer six layers were formed out of a translucent grayish energy, while the innermost layer glowed with a radiant golden energy that spoke of its superiority.

His divine sense bore down upon each of the elders, leaving

light cracks upon the exterior of the outermost shield that was quickly repairing itself.

"Yao Shen, you underestimate the foundation of our legacy families! Did you really think that we would not be prepared for the soul suppression of a Soul Emperor?" Wenyan Ren mocked with a gleeful expression on his face, not surprised that the shields had held against Yao Shen's Soul attack.

"If that is all the strength you possess, then it is truly a little disappointing," Dongmei Xue coldly snorted, before adding, "Don't waste your divine sense any further, it is a waste of both our time and yours. Have that girl recant her statement, hand over the recording stone and make sure she never appears in front of me again, and this matter can be considered forgotten," she added, not truly wanting to have irreconcilable enmity with a cultivator as extreme as Yao Shen. If he wanted the girl, he could have her; her Water-Light Dual Spiritual roots were only at a meager thirty-four percent purity, after all.

"These are a set of artifacts forged by true soul emperors at the pinnacle of their power, Yao Shen. No matter how possibly strong your soul is, it cannot match the potency of these rings, created through the combined efforts of our ancestors. Agree to Dongmei's demands, and this matter can be considered forgotten. You are not someone we wish to make an enemy out of." Meili Zhu's sweet voice tried to mediate between the two parties, but she too held supreme confidence in her ancestors, as was the nature of legacy families.

"That was a tenth," Yao Shen replied simply, his voice cold and unamused.

Wenyan Ren stood there in incomprehension as Yao Shen's statement echoed in his mind, as he tried to decipher if there was a hidden meaning, or even a cipher hidden within those words. But no matter which approach he took, the only logical answer kept slapping him back in his face. His eyes widened in disbelief as his hands started trembling lightly, for he did not consider Yao Shen to be a cultivator who bluffed about his abilities.

Yao Shen tapped his finger against the Eocava wood table, and the strength of his divine sense immediately doubled— from ten times that of a Peak Nascent Soul Cultivators, to twenty times.

The seventh layer of the shields protecting the legacy family heads exploded at once, countless ephemeral shards falling upon the ground and sinking within, not leaving a trace behind.

"Yao Shen, stop!" Zhou Hui's imploring voice echoed in the background, but Yao Shen paid him no heed.

He tapped a third time, and the sixth layer exploded.

Fourth time, fifth layer.

Fifth time, the fourth, third and second layers all exploded at the same time.

Finally, Yao Shen tapped a sixth time, and cracks started appearing on the golden shields, the aghast Patriarchs and Matriarchs watching as the rings on their hands shattered one after the other with horror reflecting in their eyes.

He was surprised that the golden shield managed to bear sixty times the pressure of a peak Nascent Soul Cultivator, but ultimately, it did not matter.

Yao Shen tapped a seventh time, and the golden shields exploded in all directions like the shattering of a sun, golden sparks flying like small meteors in all directions. The seven legacy family heads crumpled to the ground at the same time, a pressure equivalent to seventy times that of a peak Nascent Soul Cultivator weighing down upon them like an elephant's leg holding a mortal in place— an immutable, irresistible force that the limitations of their physical existence could not defy.

Their eyes were wide with terror as they did not dare to move a single inch, fearing that the force would come crashing down upon them and not even a trace of their souls would be left behind.

"Do not be so agitated, Brother Hui," Yao Shen replied to his rival, who held a generic nascent soul blade against his throat but did not complete the strike, only holding it as an empty defiance, a symbolic gesture that was powerful in its own right. "I am not here to kill anyone today," he said, as he moved the tip of the blade away from his neck with his index finger, and walked past Zhou Hui, who did not stop him.

"But there will be consequences," he added, almost as an afterthought, as his soul's pressure continued to bear upon the legacy family heads' Nascent Souls. As long as they did not try to move or escape, they would be unharmed. Yao Shen, however, did not care about them, as he walked toward the poor, trembling girl who had lost a sister due to the corruption that ran deep within the sect. The Healing Hall was a place to train and raise healers, a crucial resource for any sect that faced multiple external threats. To cripple or hobble the growth of a promising healer for personal gain was one of the most *gross transgressions* one could commit, and had killing Dongmei Xue not been the one of the triggers for a civil war, he would have likely gone through with it.

But that was alright, for his new disciple had enough motivation and resolve when it came to dealing with that particular matter.

He walked over to his new disciple, who was curled up in a ball as she sobbed lightly, her head digging into her knees as she hid her face from the world.

He offered his hand to the young disciple, who, perhaps out of deference to his authority, promptly accepted it. He raised her back onto her feet, but to his surprise, she wrapped her arms around his back and started loudly crying into his chest. Her entire time in the Heavenly Sky Sect had been one long cycle of running from one nightmare to the next, and she had grown increasingly isolated after the one person who made suffering through the injustice bearable had perished right in front of her eyes.

After so long, someone had finally *noticed* her pain. Someone was willing to show kindness to her, and even going as far as to offer her protection. A solitary man who was willing to bear the wrath of the legacy families alone, even when he himself claimed that he was not infallible.

Such kindness....was almost too heavy to bear.

Yao Shen was stunned for a solid moment, not used to such displays of emotion considering his first disciple was, of all people, Shadow. Recalling his memories from Earth, he accepted the hug, his hands moving awkwardly as he wrapped them around her back, and softly spoke, "It's going to be alright."

"Everything is going to be alright."

16

NEGOTIATIONS

YAO SHEN patiently waited until his grieving disciple regained composure, maintaining the awkward hug for one long minute before she hurriedly pulled away with a panicked expression her face— in her moment of weakness, she had completely forgotten that she was in presence of the Council of Elders, whom she had just become sworn enemies with. She now followed a singular path, having gambled everything on Patriarch Yao Shen's reputation and strength. If he were to perish, she had no qualms about the calamity that would befall her— the legacy families did not react well to those tarnished their honor, and she had gone far, *far* beyond their bottom line.

The feeling of calmness had already left her, the effects of what she had hypothesized to be the Patriarch's Human Dao worn out without leaving a trace. The sheer *audacity* of belligerent actions was starting to sink in, but even so, she could not bring herself to feel the slightest trace of regret. Not only that, but when she saw the heads of the prestigious legacy families lying sprawled across the floor, their usually stern and proud faces flushed red from resisting Patriarch's soul encroachment, an unfamiliar sensation started to well up in her heart, one that had always been a laughable dream for her: *vengeance*. She may not have entirely avenged her sister's death, but in her mind, she had never even considered the possibility that a mid-foundation establishment disciple could bring harm to a legacy family led by a Nascent Soul Cultivator.

She felt good. Delighted, even.

Was this how it was to feel alive?

If so, she had missed the sensation.

Yao Shen, of course, noticed the mélange of emotions rising from his new disciple. A cloud of 'relief' floated around her like a gentle guardian, shielding her from the rapidly shrinking cloud of 'hatred' that slowly evolving into a smaller, far less threatening cloud of 'vengeance,' or so he interpreted the emotion fragments, unassumingly lurking in the background as they waited for a chance to strike.

For now, at least, Yanyue's mental state seemed to have stabilized. The new desire for vengeance in her heart was far from unwarranted, and it would help her tread farther on the road of cultivation. As much as Yao Shen wished to change the ways of Azlak Plains, and eventually Ionea, he had never allowed himself to forget that the sole reason he could *even* hold such radical ambitions was not because of the memories he had inherited, but the *power* he held and represented.

Yao Shen would not stop Yanyue from seeking vengeance if she truly wished for it— she was his disciple, and her choices were her own to make. But he would not let vengeance consume her mind, body and desires, like hatred had. Instead, he would help her channel it, focus it, toward one singular goal— surpassing Dongmei Xue.

Truly, in effect, if he wished to kill Dongmei Xue, there was little that she could do to stop him. But Yao Shen was a Major Dao Practitioner in the Elements of Earth, Wind and Fire, the three elements he had chosen to ascend as a boon for reaching the

Soul Emperor stage and none of them were particularly suited to the art of healing. Dongmei Xue might have been lacking in conscience, but there was no viable replacement available at her level, and many promising disciples, guardians and even elders had received life-saving treatment from her. One could imagine the favors she could call upon, and the goodwill the elite of the Heavenly Sky Sect held for her.

Dongmei Xue had positioned herself in a politically invulnerable situation, which was why Yao Shen had such limited control and insight over the activities of the Healing Hall back when he led the sect as a Nascent Soul Cultivator. Killing her now would mean that the cycle of vengeance would start anew, and the Xue Family's loyalists would either rebel against his authority, bide their time or even worse— seek refuge in the demonic path sects.

But, even if he disregarded all those consequences and decided to eliminate a possible future enemy right now, would the sect that remained still be the 'modern sect' he wished to create? If he wished to create a sect that was ruled through fear and tyranny, he could accomplish it right now— with a mere tap of his finger. No, this was the true challenge of the task he had set out to accomplish and neither force nor diplomacy would alone achieve his goals.

His aim from the very beginning was to first cow them with force, and then offer the legacy family elders an opportunity they would be foolish to refuse. This would be their first and only warning: those who adapted to the modern sect would thrive, but if anyone dared to make a move on him or his disciples— there would be no second chance.

Yao Shen traced Shadow's location through the strand of divine sense he had split off, ordering her to return to the Council Hall. A minute later, the shadows in the room started shifting and coalescing at one point, forming the vague silhouette of a woman. Shadow appeared next to Yanyue with a wary expression on her face, hand resting upon her dagger as she examined the girl and her proximity to Yao Shen.

Yanyue stumbled back in shock, her expression turning pale as she stared at the mesmerizing silver-haired woman whose presence had completely slipped past her perception until the last second.

"Shadow..." Yao Shen protested with a sigh, but then just shook his head. "This is your new junior sister, Yanyue. She will be staying in the tower along with us for the foreseeable future, so please make the arrangements."

Shadow just stood there, rooted to the spot for one long minute before she turned her gaze to Yanyue with curiosity in her eyes, that morphed into a *perplexed* expression before she just nodded once in her direction.

Then, in an act that both surprised Yanyue and Yao Shen, she offered her open palm in the former's direction. Yanyue seemed uncertain, but she gingerly clasped her hand around Shadow's own, almost as if she feared being attacked if she didn't.

A light blush appeared on Shadow's face as she hurriedly shifted her gaze away, awkwardly dragging Yanyue to the second floor of the tower. Was that... 'excitement' he detected? The auspicious green cloud had half enveloped Shadow, but she soon disappeared out of his sight and human sense could not detect emotions through divine sense.

Once they were gone, Yao Shen released the soul suppression upon the elders, who regained composure with surprising speed. Back on their feet in an instant, they distanced themselves from Yao Shen like terrified prey in the presence of an apex predator, their horror openly worn on their faces.

"Now, now, there's no need to be like that," Yao Shen chided with a light smile on his face, but to the Council of Elders, it was no different from a demon's bloodthirsty grin staring down at them.

"Since the disciples have left, we can finally discuss benefits and the *consequences* as well." Yao Shen continued to smile, the three unaffiliated elders standing behind him respectfully, now that they had witnessed his might firsthand.

"Benefits?" Meili Zhu's voice still retained a cheery quality to it, betraying no resentment at the events that had just transpired in her voice. They were all members of the righteous path present in attendance, and while the legacy families knew it was in their best interests to assure each other's continued survival; they also had different surnames and their true loyalty would always lie with their own respective families.

"Indeed. Please, do have a seat." Yao Shen chose to play the gracious host, and the other elders except Dongmei Xue seemed inclined to at least hear him out without any further protest. Though he was sure that the legacy family heads had already informed the reserve elders of the events that had transpired in this room and dealing with them was going to be far more troublesome than the Council.

Dongmei Xue's face grew increasingly pale at the thought of the consequences Yao Shen had mentioned, but everyone in the room was tactful enough to understand that Yao Shen's words were not an offer, but a command.

The Xue family patriarch was the last one to be seated, plunging the room into a period of silence.

"Firstly," Yao Shen spoke, and he could feel the nervous tension on the room focused upon his each and every word— any one of the cultivators in attendance was one of the peak powers of the Azlak Plains, yet Yao Shen could kill them without even offering them a chance to resist.

"For ones as long lived and cunning as yourselves, you all are surprisingly short-sighted in nature. Tell me, Meili, have you been indoctrinated to such an extent that you believe your legacy bloodline to be a superior form of humanity?" Yao Shen asked her, only receiving a calm shake of the head that implied a clear 'No.'

"Then why do you not see the value of the gift I have given the legacy families? Your wisdom exceeds that of any other here in attendance, including myself. Why are you not able to see the truth?" Yao Shen asked, and he could immediately feel a sliver of confusion that was shared amongst all the legacy family elders in attendance.

"Forgive me, Patriarch. This one is not as talented as you believe her to be," Meili Zhu replied with a low bob of her head, though under his human sight, she just seemed confused instead of embarrassed or angered.

"Out of ten disciples from the inner sect that I chose at random, one turned out to conceal such a tragic tale and a burning hatred for the legacy families. You are *completely misguided* if you believe that I, or my poor disciple is the one you are fighting against. Even if I were to die tomorrow, I would still be assured of the destruction of your proud legacy families. Truly, your arrogance knows no bounds," Yao Shen explained, and then he broke out into a laugh that seemed endlessly amused at a joke only he seemed to understand.

"Patriarch, please explain," Meili Zhu's expression turned grim, because she knew that Yao Shen was not one to bluff or exaggerate about such matters.

"I was born talentless to mortal parents and yet I managed to achieve the coveted Soul Emperor stage in merely two centuries, which continues to elude your families. Now imagine another like myself, whose talent the legacy families choose to oppress instead of flourish, humiliate instead of praise, berate instead of train. Your disciples are drunk on inherited power, and they are known to abuse it. Imagine, just take a second and *imagine,* what such a person may choose to do if he reaches the Soul Emperor stage." Yao Shen paused, to allow his words to sink in, before continuing:

"You fight not against an individual... but instead, the collective will of humanity that yearns for *freedom*. You wish to force promising disciples into indentured service, and in doing so, you challenge the nature of *Human Dao itself.* A fight that you are bound to lose." Yao Shen calmly his knocked his hand lightly upon the table for emphasis, though from the shocked expressions on the faces of the elders, his statement already had more than the intended effect.

"Is there truly such a thing?" Zhou Hui questioned, not out of malice but purely curiosity.

"It is my understanding of the Human Dao that led me to this conclusion. Whether you choose to believe me or not, that is up to you," Yao Shen replied, his words spoken without falsity. The other elements he had mastered, be it Earth, Fire or Wind could be manipulated in a variety of ways, imbued in artifacts, formations, talismans and even pills, but Human Dao was an exception.

That was the reason why, when Yao Shen projected emotions such as 'comfort' back in the outer sect, it had affected both the young girl chef and Elder Han— he merely projected it outward, its destination for itself to choose. Any attempt to imbibe artifacts, formations or constructs with Human Dao would be met with failure, for the element simply refused to be caged, refused to have its freedom denied.

Yao Shen had studied his previous world's history in surprising depth, the subject a matter of fascination for him in his previous life. And throughout history, there was one scene that repeated itself time after time again— 'humans' fought for their freedom, fighting against others of their kind that wished to deprive them of it.

Yao Shen was almost convinced that the 'Human Dao' was inextricable from freedom, the two concepts having a natural synergy with each other. Maybe it was his own bias clouding his judgment, but Yao Shen's gut told him that he was on the right track— for most humans had almost an instinctual desire for freedom that seemed to be encoded in their very bloodlines, while the Elves, on the other hand, seemed to be content under the rule of their Monarchy, very few internal wars fought across their long period of existence.

Yao Shen sighed inwardly, knowing that while the legacy family elders in attendance understood the logic behind their words, a distant threat was not enough for them to change their ways. Or that, at least, was what his 'human sight' indicated, the emotional response largely muted after the initial shock from his bold claims faded away. It seemed that the only thing his impassioned speech had served to accomplish was throwing the wily old foxes off their tempo, allowing him a greater leeway in the negotiations soon to follow.

"You asked me why I wished to found the Modern Sect," Yao Shen's words were now focused, but not intimidating or threatening. Only a negotiator that was uncertain in his skills would resort to such banal measures. "I now give you my answer. It is because I am a Human Dao Practitioner, and I have concluded that your archaic ways will bring ruin upon us all. Is that reason enough?" He addressed the elders, who had concealed all traces of resistance they felt at Yao Shen's arbitrary claims.

There was silence.

"I understand that without any evidence to back up my claims, you have little reason to believe anything I say. But I am not the first to violate the sacred trust that existed between the House of the Patriarch and the legacy families. It was Dongmei Xue who went behind my back and terrorized promising healers until they capitulated to her demands, a disgrace that she will have to answer for not only to me, but the reserve elders as well. And I daresay that she was not the first among you who indulged in such activities." Yao Shen's words were calm, but it sent shivers down the legacy elders' spines.

"What do you propose, Patriarch?" Dongmei Xue gritted her teeth and politely asked, inwardly relieved that Yao Shen was perceptive enough to realize that she was not acting alone in conducting this scheme of hers.

"I offer you all two options. The first is simple— I will ask no questions, and your reputation shall not be tarnished even in the slightest. Cancel all such existing agreements you have with disciples and reimburse them generously for the hardship your actions have brought them. You may hand over a report to the Faceless, who shall deliver it to me if you wish to retain your anonymity." Yao Shen spoke after much thought; drawing from his memories of Earth's authorities utilizing a 'no questions asked' policy to great effect.

"As for the second option, well, I am sure that you understand the frightening interrogative capabilities of my Human Dao. I promise to investigate until I have unearthed every last one of your little secrets, and let the truth come to light for our entire Heavenly Sky Sect to see," Yao Shen gave them a courteous smile, but inwardly, he was greatly amused, for in his human sight, small traces of 'panic,' 'worry' and 'regret' manifested around the elders, before they managed to forcibly suppress it.

"That is acceptable," Zhou Hui's stern voice echoed out loudly in the Council Hall, an undercurrent of anger detectable in his words as his gaze shifted from one legacy family head to the next. "I also hereby declare that the legacy families' affairs shall be subject to the Enforcement Hall's oversight from this moment onward."

Yao Shen's smile grew even wider, realizing how nice it was to have an ally among the Council of Elders. It was not that Zhou Hui had never wanted to bring institutional reform to the inner functioning of the sects, but rather, he had never received the opportunity to do so without alienating himself from the Council.

Meili Zhu finally chose to speak, "Patriarch Shen, we are, of course, amenable to your terms and thank you for your generosity. But before we discuss such matters any further, may we know the structure of the new sect you wish to found?" Her words were polite, but she was hinting at the benefits that he had mentioned earlier.

"Of course. If tomorrow's events unfold smoothly, it shall have three divisions under the banner of I, Yao Shen, Grand Patriarch of the Modern Sect— the Earth Division, led by former Patriarch of the Divine Mountain Sect, Kang Long, the Flame Division, led by former Patriarch of the Sacred Flame Palace, Lei Weiyuan and finally, the Sky Division, led by *former elder of the Enforcement Hall, Zhou Hui.*" Yao Shen's announcement shook the emotions in the Council Hall, almost everyone in the hall, Zhou Hui included, flabbergasted by the revelation.

"Yao Shen, I… *what?*" Zhou Hui asked in a daze, one again pondering upon the question if this man was the rival he had known since childhood, who had robbed from him what was supposed to be the greatest day in his life— the day a scion of the Hui family was about to be appointed Patriarch, only to be challenged by a younger, far more zealous Yao Shen a few days before the crowning ceremony.

He still vividly recalled that day, even the minutest of details etched in his memories as an eternal reminder of his failure. It had been over four years since Yao Shen had stepped upon the sect premises, but extended periods of absences were not uncommon for the Second Elder of the Dao Repository Hall, who had all but delegated his responsibilities to Elder Han. Back then, he was known for his zealous pursuit of strength that bordered on insanity— Yao Shen pursued his goals with a single-minded relentlessness, a *resolve* so frighteningly and indefatigable, that even he, as his rival, had been moved. But to say that he understood his intentions, his struggle, would be a lie. Yao Shen, much like himself, had reached the peak Nascent Soul level, the end of the journey for all cultivators of the Azlak Plains, let alone Yao Shen, who was not even able to attain a single Major Dao in his lifetime.

The intoxicating power, the sheer authority he felt at his fingertips as he sat at the forefront of the Council of Elders was an unforgettable sensation that he would carry with him for as long as he lived. He was Zhou Hui, Patriarch of the Hui Family, and his entire life, he had been prepared for this very moment— he had sworn upon the graves of his ancestors to restore the Heavenly Sky Sect's old glory, and he intended to honor that vow.

It was three days.

Three days before he was appointed Patriarch of the Heavenly Sky Sect, a Faceless announced that Yao Shen, Elder of the Dao Repository Hall, had arrived. When Zhou Hui's gaze fell upon his figure, his heart almost skipped a beat. Yao Shen had arrived before the Council of Elders baring his upper body, a coarse loincloth made out of mortal materials being the only article of clothing covering his lower body, wrapped around his waist.

But the lack of decorum was not what surprised Zhou Hui. No, it was the condition of his body that left even him shocked to his very core— three long claw marks raked across his chest, a standout in the tapestry of the smaller scarred cuts, lacerations and puncture wounds that covered every inch of his upper body. His right arm bore burn marks, indicating that he had used Fire Qi to cauterize his wound—usually only done for poisonous wounds, while his left arm bore a jagged wound that stretched across its circumference, indicating that it had likely been reattached.

These were all superfluous scars that even core formation pills could remove easily, but Yao Shen had chosen to keep them— it was a statement, and a very powerful one at that.

Without speaking a single word, Yao Shen had drawn his sword and slammed it onto the Tower's floor, attracting the complete attention of Zhou Hui.

"Zhou Hui, I invoke my right to challenge under the Ritual of Succession," Yao Shen had stated simply, a challenge that had drawn much mockery and derision from the legacy families back then.

But Yao Shen's right was absolute, and thus the challenge was organized.

A fight that haunted Zhou Hui until this very day.

Yao Shen had not achieved an understanding in a Major Dao, or at least not chosen to reveal it back then. He had charged at Zhou Hui, his Patchwork Domain impressing upon the land he tread upon. The Minor Daos of Fire, Water, Earth, Wind, Mist, Shadow and a dozen other elements formed the basis of his domain, alternating between four Minor Daos in a single period of time.

Zhou Hui's expression had remained calm, his Domain of Endless Blades tearing through Yao Shen's Patchwork Domains within a minute of their formation, for it did not matter if Yao Shen's domain was offensive, defensive, illusory, healing or even supporting in nature— he would simply employ raw power to overwhelm its limit, his victory all but guaranteed.

But Yao Shen did not fall.

Zhou Hui shattered his domain with ruthless efficiency, but Yao Shen was equally stubborn in reforming another a few seconds later. Yao Shen advanced under the cover of his domain, trying to get close enough to Zhou Hui to land a strike, but each time his domain collapsed, he was forced to retreat. Since Yao Shen's domain was formed solely out of Minor Daos, his consumption was only a fraction of Zhou Hui's.

.　.　.

Another hour passed.

Yao Shen's concentration lapsed for a second as his domain collapsed, a wind blade slicing through the air and striking at his chest. Zhou Hui knew that the fight was sealed at that moment; it had to be. While the wound was not fatal, Wind Qi was violent in nature—until Yao Shen had a healer dispel it or contained it himself, it would continue to slowly tear at his internal organs, only worsening his injuries with time.

Zhou Hui would never forget the expression on Yao Shen's face as he clenched his teeth, his eyes bloodshot from the pain as he glared at him with an expression that screamed *defiance*. Flames flared to life in his free hand, and he let them flow over the wound, cauterizing it in an instant. Zhou Hui did not have the words to describe the pain Yao Shen must be feeling, but he gritted his teeth, refusing to let even a single sound out of his mouth.

Yet he remained standing.

Five hours later, Yao Shen stood in front of a pale-faced Zhou Hui, his Wind Qi reserves completely exhausted as he stared at his rival, who held a sword pointed against his chest, with utter disbelief reflecting his eyes.

He, Zhou Hui had.....unmistakably... lost.

'Why?' was the only question that echoed in his mind as he toppled over backwards. He had gone into a state of Qi Exhaustion, and this was the consequence. Zhou Hui landed with a thump, but felt no pain. His mind continued to repeat that same question in his head, a thousand different times.

'*Why* did Yao Shen have to go so far? Even when ascension was impossible, *why* did he resist so? *Why* could he simply not accept his shortcomings? *Why* could he not accept that the heavens had chosen to bless him, Zhou Hui, instead of Yao Shen?'

He had an answer to those questions now.

While Zhou Hui had reluctantly accepted his limitations and endeavored to work around them, Yao Shen had refuted them from the beginning, choosing to defy them instead by ascending to the Soul Emperor stage. Perhaps that was why Zhou Hui could never truly muster hatred for his rival. Resentment was an old companion, but never hatred— for each time he was reminded of Yao Shen's defiant visage on that day, his heaven-shaking resolve sending chills down his spine— not out of fear, but true admiration for his rival.

Two decades had passed since that historic day, one that had changed his destiny forever. Or so, at least, he had *thought*.

"Why?" Zhou Hui asked the question he was unable to two decades ago, his voice beginning to crack from emotion. "First you take it from me, and now... wish to *return* it?"

Yao Shen felt two decades of suppressed emotions bubble up and envelop Zhou Hui in a cloud so thick, his features were no longer clearly visible. Reluctantly, Yao Shen dismissed human sight, gazing back at his old rival with complex expressions reflecting in his eyes.

"Brother Hui... the legacy families may have their faults, but I was wrong to judge you unworthy merely because your roots originated from them. Within you runs the honor of the legacy families of *olden* times, and ultimately, this is one of the benefits I offer to the legacy families— Zhou Hui's major actions will be subject to my approval, but day-to-day operations of the sect and any major resolutions you wish to propose can be entrusted to one of your own," Yao Shen slowly explained, catching the interest of the legacy family heads, some of whom even sighed in veritable relief.

He continued, "Your lands and resources shall remain your own, but you will no longer have access to the sect's coffers— those will be managed by me, and Zhou Hui will have to seek approval for all major expenditures. You are free to invest in your disciples' growth if you wish to, but you will not misuse the sect's resources in order to do so. The modern sect will only judge talent, aptitude and perseverance— no longer shall nepotism be allowed to run through the ranks of the examinees, and I trust that Brother Hui, if he accepts, is competent and trustworthy enough to ensure such an outcome."

The gazes in the hall encouragingly gathered on Zhou Hui, since defiance was no longer a viable option— at least, not right now. It was not that the legacy families agreed to his demands so easily, but that not even the reserve elders could resist his wrath if Yao Shen was angered past his limits.

Zhou Hui's lips started quivering from strong emotions as he struggled to keep them at bay, bringing his right hand toward the 'water' accumulating near his tear ducts, wiping them away before they could leak out— a reminder that Sect Elders, ancient and powerful figures they might be, were still human. He understood Yao Shen well enough, and knew this was not the appointment of a figurehead— but instead, a proposal of a partnership, to combine their wisdom for the good of the Heavenly Sk-, no, the Sky Division of the Modern Sect.

It might have been in a different form than he had expected, but...

Zhou Hui had not let his ancestors down, after all.

"I accept."

17

RECOMPENSE

AFTER ZHOU HUI accepted the position of Patriarch, the atmosphere in the room had lightened by several degrees. Many of the legacy family heads in attendance had expected a far more insidious proposal, fearing that Yao Shen's grand ambitions and claims were just a guise to seize the accumulated wealth and resources of their respective Houses.

The Council meeting proceeded in a far more amiable environment, with even Wenyan Ren going to the trouble of feigning a cordial expression— his lacking theatrical skills aside, the effort was acknowledged by Yao Shen. Dongmei Xue was the only one present whose discomfort was nigh palpable, still undoubtedly pondering upon the 'consequences' that Yao Shen had yet to discuss.

The elders presented their questions upon the future direction of the Modern Sect, and Yao Shen slowly recounted the events that had transpired since his ascension as part of the explanation. His encounter with the two Patriarchs, the duel with the Elders of the Sacred Flame Palace and the Divine Mountain Sect scheduled tomorrow, at the break of dawn and the two edicts he had passed in the name of the Grand Patriarch of the Modern Sect. A few of the elders seemed amused at his antics— blaming the demonic sect for the conflict between the three righteous path sects was an unconventional move, but some of the more rising and ambitious demonic sects would only be delighted to claim credit for causing the chaos.

Yao Shen expounded upon his vision for the Modern Sect's three divisions, his ideology to further build upon existing internal structures that had been refined across hundreds of years instead of tearing everything apart and building fresh structures from the ground up, based on well-intentioned but ultimately misguided values. Yao Shen had not forgotten the most crucial difference between Earth and Eliria, the latter a society of superhumans— where one man could decide the fate of thousands by virtue of his cultivation alone. This was the reason why the legacy families' ancestors had created a system where only the strongest was allowed to become Patriarch, regardless of bloodline or talent— for when the day of reckoning came, it would be up to him to defend the sect, and neither *bloodline*, *talent n*or *comprehension* would matter if he were not strong enough.

"There are two final topics I have to discuss." Yao Shen's voice rang out in the hall, promptly drawing the attention of the elders, who reacted with some degree of surprise since all the major points of contention they had in mind had already been considered.

"Please, Grand Patriarch Yao." Meili Zhu's voice seemed even sweeter than usual, perhaps satisfied, or rather relieved, that his proposed measures were not as tyrannical as she expected, but could even be beneficial for the Zhu family if she played her cards right.

"Let us not be coy any longer, Meili." Yao Shen's tone turned grave as he scanned the expressions of the elders before continuing, "I will form a divine sense ward; please do not be alarmed."

Some of the elders seemed alarmed, wondering what matter

could possibly require the Patriarch's personal ward on top of the perception shielding wards that were built into Silveni's Heirloom, but they did not protest his caution.

Yao Shen's divine sense expanded, covering the entire circumference of the tower's first floor without effort. The next instant, he let it expand, forming a dome that stretched across the hall and carpeted the floor with a layer of divine sense— this way, any encroachment from below, above or the side would be discovered well in advance, and Yao Shen dared to say that there were few Soul Emperors that were capable of breaching his defenses without him noticing, if any at all.

Yao Shen activated his human sight to the highest degree of sensitivity, a sharp smile tugging at his lips.

"Wealth. Natural treasures. Artifacts. Cultivation resources. Your legacy families have passed their teachings from generation to generation longer than I have been in existence, thus one can only imagine the vast resources you have amassed across the ages," Yao Shen began, causing some elders to shift uncomfortably in their seats.

"But it is ultimately surprising how truly *little* importance you place upon them. Is that not true, Meili?" Yao Shen asked, and the atmosphere in the room immediately grew stifled. The three elders who were not affiliated with any legacy family had perplexed expressions on their faces, but the legacy elders, including Zhou Hui, were struggling to keep their emotions contained.

"I would be careful with your next words, Patriarch Shen." Meili Zhu's voice was no longer sickly sweet, but cold, impassive and commanding as she locked gazes with Yao Shen, her eyes narrowing in warning. "You four may leave," she commanded, her excessively polite words sending chills down the spines of the elders they were addressed to.

The elders turned their gazes to Yao Shen, who nodded once.

They started shuffling out of the hall without complaint, the events that had transpired today already providing them with enough excitement for the next two hundred years. They did not wish to be privy to any more secrets, lest they be burned from gazing too deep into the void.

"Do not mistake my intentions, Meili." Yao Shen's words and expression were relaxed, as he tried to appear as non-threatening as possible. "The West has been probing the Azlak Plains for decades now, circling the territory of our Heavenly Sky Sect—seemingly looking for nothing in particular, but persistent in their efforts even decades after. Your ancestors were impressive existences, weren't they?" Yao Shen's words caused the expression of some in the room to change drastically, but others, who had long expected such an outcome, calmly watched on.

Meili Zhu simply nodded, not offering a verbal reply.

"The inheritance of your ancestors. I am not conceited enough to believe that I can get you to divulge their location when even the West has failed in their efforts. In fact, I doubt you even know their true location, but that is beside the point. You are afraid to go to the Eastern Sects for assistance because you know that they will monopolize most of your inheritance, only leaving behind scraps in place. You need not look any further, for the solution lies seated before you." Yao Shen finally exposed the last trump card in his possession, one that he was almost certain would ensure the elders compliance in the short term.

"You mean...?" Meili Zhu lightly gasped, her eyes widening in shock as for once, she was the one that struggled to maintain composure.

"I display my loyalty to the sect in my own way, and I am known to conduct dealings fairly and with honor, as is befitting for one titled Patriarch. Perhaps if I were a regular Soul Emperor, I would not have the confidence to make such bold claims, but given my strength and versatility, I am certain of unsealing at least a few inheritances," Yao Shen replied, knowing that he had won the legacy families support in that moment— at least from the dazed expression in their eyes, it appeared to be the case.

"Even if what you say is the truth, what would it cost?" Meili Zhu countered, her voice laced with an emotion dangerously bordering on hope.

"Part of the inheritance, of course— I am a Soul Emperor with no Soul Emperor level artifacts, after all. As I mentioned earlier, I am in no position to force any of you to divulge the location, and neither do I have intention to. You may approach me of your own volition, the first Soul Emperor in centuries that has been born in the Azlak Plains that is loyal to the Heavenly Sky Sect, and we can discuss remuneration." Yao Shen concluded his spiel, offering the legacy families a lucrative choice instead of a demand, requiring that they divulge the location for the 'good of the sect.' The legacy families had concealed this particular knowledge so deeply that even the West had been rendered helpless. Who knew what long forgotten methods they employed.

'Excitement' was the one singular emotion that Yao Shen detected across the hall, coalescing around the elders in minute quantities before diminishing entirely— the concentration so sparse, it was hard to pinpoint which elder it belonged to. No further questions were asked, as it was not appropriate to do so in this forum.

"This meeting grows long, and my spirit grows weary. Dongmei?" Yao Shen's question was more rhetorical in nature, yet as etiquette decreed, Dongmei Xue responded:

"Yes, Grand Patriarch?" she asked politely, though the undercurrent of discomfort did not escape those in attendance.

"I am conflicted," Yao Shen confessed. "To punish you without punishing the others would be singling the Xue Family out, when that is clearly not my intention. On the other hand, my new disciple's tears weigh heavily upon my mind, and truly, what kind of a master would I be if I let such an egregious transgression against one of my own pass?" Yao Shen mused aloud, as Dongmei Xue watched on with a bitter expression on her face— What disciple did Yao Shen talk about? The one he had accepted on a whim, a few hours ago? This was clearly a ploy, a conspiracy designed to implicate her!

"Very well. Dongmei, I have decided," Yao Shen announced with a certain gravitas to his tone, one that did not brook disobedience.

"I shall not punish you for your transgressions, Dongmei, as I do not wish to be seen singling out the Xue Family," Yao Shen solemnly stated, but the next second, a sly smile bloomed on his face.

"Instead, I will offer you a trade." Yao Shen placed the high-grade recording stone on the table with a small thump. "This high-grade recording stone in exchange for the Xue Family's natural treasure, the Nascent Soul Grade *Heart-Cleansing Sea Pearl*."

Dongmei Xue's expression turned ashen, as the sly grin on Yao Shen's face morphed into a cruel, sadistic smirk in her mind. Instant regret flooded her mind— she truly regretted her actions because how dearly they would cost the Xue Family.

"A trade?" Dongmei asked, struggling to keep her voice even.

"Of course. There is no compulsion, and you may choose to decline if you wish to." Yao Shen smiled back at her with a tinge of vindication in his eyes, while the other legacy family elders watched the drama unfold in silence.

Dongmei Xue just sat there in a stupor for one long minute, thinking of ways to break the deadlock Yao Shen had presented her with. The reputation of the Xue family rested in one hand, while in the other was the Xue family's most prized resource— the Heart-Cleansing Sea Pearl, a natural treasure that contained extremely high purity Water Qi that could drastically increase cultivation speed and also be utilized to heal extremely potent wounds at the Nascent Soul level with frightening efficacy.

The Xue Family only had three such pearls in possession, and they could only be harvested every two hundred years.

If Dongmei Xue had been a demonic path cultivator, she would undoubtedly scoff at the choice— why give up such a priceless artifact for mere reputation? Unfortunately, she belonged to the righteous path— where reputation, or rather, *perceived reputation*, was worth more than mere cultivation resources or artifacts, at least in times of peace.

It was no secret that demonic sect disciples generally tended to be stronger than righteous path disciples at the same level, their cruel and vicious ways of cultivation often over-drafting power beyond their physical capabilities to bear. In some ways, it could be argued that the righteous path sought to actively limit their paths to power, and when the casualty reports started coming in, the central tenet that united the righteous path and gave them strength was that 'righteousness and justice' was on their side, that the demonic sects were only stronger because they had sacrificed their humanity and become abominations in the pursuit of power.

If the Xue family's reputation was slandered so in front of the entire Heavenly Sky Sect, it would not only be an eternal blot on their reputation, but their children would also no longer have the spirit of righteousness burning in their hearts, such a drastic change even having the possibility of disturbing their cultivation and causing heart demons for the ones more zealous in their belief.

Gritting her teeth, she finally forced out the words. "I accept the trade, Grand Patriarch."

"*Good*," Yao Shen replied. The thought of having Dongmei Xue herself financing the cost of his new disciple's training left a refreshing taste in his mouth. He casually tossed the recording stone in her direction, and Dongmei caught it with ease. "Have it delivered to me by the end of the day. With that, the Council meeting is considered adjourned," Yao Shen announced, lightly thumping upon the Eocava wood table. His actions were mirrored by the other elders, as they began to get up and slowly disperse from the hall. Today's events had been mentally taxing for most in attendance, and some rest would serve them well before the cycle began once again tomorrow.

18

SISTERS

THE GROUND and first floors of the Tower were accessible to the Council of Elders and the latter also served as a forum for hosting important dignitaries from both domestic and foreign sects, clans, mercantile organizations, among other institutions. However, the second floor and above was off limits to everyone except those authorized by Yao Shen, or the other two Master Control Token holders.

Yao Shen was about to leave for the second floor, having concluded the Council meeting with satisfactory results, when a familiar voice called out his name, giving him pause.

"Yao Shen." Zhou Hui walked toward Yao Shen, and even without relying upon his human sight, he could tell the difference — the Hui Family Patriarch walked with a spring in his step, chest slightly puffed out and back held straight, as if a weight had been lifted off his shoulders. Perhaps even Zhou Hui didn't realize how living under Yao Shen's shadow had affected him, making his personality more reserved and reclusive over the years — devoting himself entirely to the pursuit of Dao and his duties as the Enforcement Hall Elder.

"What is it, Brother Hui?" Yao Shen amiably asked with a light smile on his face, clearly in a good mood.

"I wish to debate upon the Sky Division's future direction, and desire to understand the vision you hold for the Modern Sect in greater detail, if this is an appropriate time." Zhou Hui did not care to modulate the exhilaration leaking into his voice, even if such an overt display of emotion was a little unbecoming for one of his stature.

"Of course, Brother Hui. Come to think of it, it has been a while since you have met the trio. Are you willing to accompany me upstairs?"

"Naturally, Brother Yao. It is a pity I don't have time to prepare gifts for them," Zhou Hui replied, but Yao Shen waved his hand.

"No matter, no matter. Come, let us proceed."

A few hours earlier….

Yanyue wore a dazed expression on her face as Shadow tugged at her wrist, leading her to the stairwell at one end of the Council Hall. 'Warmth' was an emotion that Yanyue felt with the very core of her being, as 'uncertainty,' 'confusion' and 'shock' lurked in the background— the deluge of strong emotions almost threatening to overwhelm her. There was a saying in the mortal village she hailed from that cautioned one against giving a parched man too much water in one go, and that maxim very much resonated with her in that moment.

She had heard stories about Patriarch Yao Shen's past, a young Qi formation cultivator with mortal roots lacking in both talent and background— all but destined for obscurity in the mighty Heavenly Sky Sect, where one's fate was left upon the judgment of the heavens. However, his iron will and immutable determination had not gone unnoticed— finally chosen by an elder, after eighteen long years of cultivation, as a true disciple. From there on, Patriarch Yao Shen's meteoric rise was unforgettable. Yanyue had never expected the same fortune to fall upon her lap, especially after she let her will crumble when faced with loss— she was not qualified, her accomplishments not even amounting to a tenth of Yao Shen's at the same age.

Did she really deserve such kindness? Was such warmth owed to someone who hid away from the world instead of confronting the darkness? She was just a coward, was she not? Why was she being shown kindness when others far more deserving still continued to suffer? Especially those like Yao Shen.

"You are crying," Shadow's emotionless voice roused Yanyue from the vicious cycle of self-doubt and deprecation she found herself trapped within.

Yanyue realized that she had been following Shadow blindly, having no real recollection of traversing past the halfway mark of the long flight of steps that she found herself standing upon. She turned her head to meet her new senior sister's gaze, Shadow's mesmerizing violet eyes devoid of any emotion— be it kindness or disgust, sympathy or apathy, love or hatred, there was simply nothing to be found within.

"*Why* are you crying?" Shadow asked her, but there was no judgment to be found within her question— her tone remaining as monotone as ever.

"Um, Senior Disciple, I-er, I mean I—" Yanyue fumbled and flubbed over her sentence as she struggled to find the words to explain herself without tarnishing her reputation. A soft hand landed upon her shoulder, radiating a muted burst of cold that was harmless to a cultivator of her level, but still enough to jolt her out of the overwhelmed state she was trapped in.

"Senior Sister. I am your Senior Sister, Yanyue," Shadow's voice finally exhibited a trickle of emotion as she lectured

Yanyue, patting her on the shoulder once. To Yanyue, she sounded almost *disappointed,* but she didn't trust her own judgment right now.

"Okay." Yanyue gave her an eager nod, relieved that she had been extricated from the mortifying situation she had trapped herself within.

"No." Shadow shook her head, and she *definitely* sounded disappointed this time. "Say it," she all but commanded.

"*Senior Sister...?*" Yanyue's confusedly uttered, wondering if Shadow wanted to emphasize her seniority and position in the sect.

Shadow gazed at Yanyue and then blinked twice before a heavy blush colored her cheeks, causing her to hurriedly avert her gaze.

On the other hand, Yanyue felt equally flummoxed by her senior sister's odd reactions. Was she such an embarrassment that her senior sister had to avert her gaze when she called upon her? But from her expression... that did not seem to be the case. Instead, it almost felt as if she were... *blushing?*

But that was impossible, *laughable* even. Patriarch Yao Shen had three disciples, and of them, Shadow's reputation far surpassed the other two by such a margin that they were almost incomparable. Shadow, *Bane of Demons,* was responsible for the deaths of *dozens* of demonic path cultivators that had tried to conduct blood sacrifice rituals within the territory of the Heavenly Sky Sect. Such a person was many things but could hardly be described as emotional or frivolous.

Shadow took a few more seconds to recompose herself, all traces of emotion wiped off from her face as her gaze once again landed upon Yanyue.

"*Who made you cry?*" Shadow asked, and there was a certain *intensity* to her voice that made Yanyue feel stifled, even suppressed.

She felt pressured as her senior sister demanded an answer, unsure of how to respond. Her senior sister's actions were a bit eccentric, but oddly enough, she felt Shadow's presence to be comforting. After half a minute of deliberation, she decided to answer truthfully— after all, it was not like her senior sister would do anything when she realized it was an *elder* that was responsible.

"D-Dongmei Xue, Matriarch of the Xue Family." Yanyue tried not to stutter as she replied, the name a trigger for painful and stressful memories.

"I see. Wait here," her senior sister replied, as all the shadows within the stairwell, including her own, coalesced around her to form a writhing cloak that sent shivers down Yanyue's spine. Her violet eyes were like two orbs of light that glowed within the shadows, radiating with such intensity that Yanyue feared her senior sister was about to do something radical.

She unsheathed her dagger, which served as the final alarm bell in Yanyue's mind.

"Senior Sister, um, what are you doing?" she asked, her voice coming out shriller than she had intended as a thousand thoughts swirled in her mind, all reaching one conclusion—she had to stop Shadow.

"I will punish Dongmei Xue," Shadow replied without emotion, as if fighting a renowned Nascent Soul Cultivator as a mere core formation junior was a normal occurrence.

"Senior Sister, she is a Nascent Soul expert!" Yanyue exclaimed, her expression wide with disbelief as she stared at Shadow. There was no subterfuge or trickery in her words, and no experienced cultivator would utter such words frivolously. How could someone *possibly* be this unreasonable?

"That is not your concern," Shadow replied coolly, thoroughly unintimidated by the prospects of fighting a stage above her.

Besides, it was not like she would *kill* Dongmei Xue, she only intended to make her kneel before her junior sister and apologize.

"You!" Yanyue let out a frustrated shout, catching Shadow's attention. "You just.... You *haven't* even known me for a day! Why would you dare anger a Nascent Soul expert for a.... *nobody* like me?" Yanyue vented her emotions, forgetting in that moment just who she was addressing— her own self-worth issues conflicting with the immeasurable amount of kindness she was showered with on this day, after years of grieving in silence.

Shadow tilted her head, looking down at Yanyue with a perplexed expression on her face. "You said it yourself, did you not?"

"Said what?"

"I am your senior sister, yes?" she asked again, her emotion-less voice devoid of the strong emotions Yanyue felt.

"Yes." Yanyue nodded, and she truly meant it. On any other occasion, she would feel blessed, but she could not let Shadow barge in on the Council of Elders and try to attack Dongmei Xue — the consequences would be disastrous for her, especially when it came out that she was the reason behind her actions.

"It is the senior sister's duty to protect the junior sister. You need not worry," Shadow stated simply, as if it were the most natural thing in the world.

Yanyue felt something in her heart melt, as all strength in her legs threatened to leave her.

"Senior Sister, if you go fight Dongmei Xue, Master will be angry." Yanyue gave it a final attempt, but in reality, she did not care anymore. If punishment for Shadow's actions would fall upon her head as honorary disciple, that was fine. If the Patriarch cast her out as a result of manipulating Shadow, even when she didn't have any intention or reason to, that too, was fine.

To know that someone as pure as her existed— even if it was

for a short while, she was glad, no, *honored* to call her senior sister.

"Oh," Shadow replied, her mouth agape as the shadows around her receded like a tide. She sheathed her blade the next instant and started walking forward, as if the past minute's events had not occurred in reality.

Yanyue gasped in palpable relief as the strength in her legs left her, the events of the past few hours having crossed her emotional threshold to bear shock. As a cultivator, the fall would not even leave a scratch upon her body. She just wanted to rest for a few minutes.

But she never managed to make contact with the staircase, only feeling a burst of muted cold enveloping her before she found herself staring up at two violet pupils, which reflected a slight but noticeable glimmer of concern within them.

Shadow delicately carried Yanyue in her arms, as if she was concerned any excessive strength might harm her body.

"I am unsure why, but you display symptoms of Qi Exhaustion even when your reserves are full. I shall take you to rest," Shadow explained, gently walking step by step at the speed of a mortal to ensure that she was not disturbed any further.

Yanyue felt as if she had returned to the arms of her mortal father, feeling a sense of safety and security that she would not trade for the world. *Not again.*

Before she realized it, Yanyue had fallen asleep.

19

TWO DISCIPLES

THE DOOR LEADING to the second floor of the tower slowly creaked open after Yao Shen inserted his Master Control Token. Before the contents of the room fully revealed itself, a pungent medicinal smell wafted through the opening, assailing their collective senses.

Zhou Hui grimaced lightly, as he channeled his Wind Qi— generating a small gust of wind which partly dispersed the pervasive smell—but it only seemed to return with a vengeance as the door opened in its entirety. Of course, as a Nascent Soul Cultivator, Zhou Hui could simply isolate his sense of smell, but the situation hardly warranted such an extreme measure.

In front of them lay a hall that was the very embodiment of chaos — at the center of the room rested an ancient, mottled three-legged cauldron, its original exterior long eroded by the ravages of time. Surrounding it were a series of tables, shelves and cupboards arrayed in a haphazard manner, each accommodating dozens, no, *hundreds* of crystalline jars that contained a different spiritual herb, medicinal plant or spiritual beast organ, barring one— a small, azure pill furnace unassumingly rested upon a table adjacent to the towering cauldron.

A young man floated two feet in the air, an elongated silver ladle held in his right hand that he used to stir the bubbling violet liquid that swirled within the cauldron. His sylvan green hair was tied into a neat ponytail; high cheekbones and blemish-free skin coupled with his light frame gave the impression of a well-dressed mortal scholar over that of a cultivator.

Detecting their approach, the young man shifted his position in the air so that he was facing his unannounced visitors, his focused expression breaking into a wide smile.

"Congratulations, Master. This disciple humbly greets the new Soul Emperor!" the young man exclaimed, his voice exuding pure joy and exhilaration along with a tinge of relief, but no humility was to be found within.

Yao Shen let out a light, jubilant laugh, allowing himself a moment of shared joy with his disciple, before replying with mock chiding, "Why, Xiaoli, did you think your master would fail?"

"Of course not, Master. Even before your ascension, you were unrivaled within the Azlak Plains, and now the demonic sects will quake at the mere mention of your venerable name!" Xiaoli Dai shamelessly heaped praises upon Yao Shen, the smile on his face only growing wider. He had long since known of his Master's, Yao Shen, decision to ascend to Soul Emperor, and he understood his character enough to know that Yao Shen was not one to act without sufficient preparations— even then, to reach the second stage of the Soul tier, Soul Emperor, was simply unheard of in the Azlak Plains, and Xiaoli would be lying if he claimed that he had not been worried.

He, of course, had wished to be at the site of his master's ascension, but unfortunately, it was an unwritten rule in the world of Eliria that disciples could not be present— the emotional bond between the two had the ability to shake the resolve of a cultivator, and even if the chance was slight, it was a risk that could not be taken.

"This disciple greets the Patriarch of the Han Family," Xiaoli once again greeted, his attention split between the two Patriarchs and the half-formed elixir in the cauldron that he kept stirring, leaving him too occupied to bow to the two second-tier cultivators.

"Good," Zhou Hui acknowledged the early-stage core formation disciple's greeting, choosing to honor him.

Xiaoli's expression grew thoughtful, and then a light flash of worry flashed over his face before he let out a resigned sigh. "Patriarch Hui, err," Xiaoli scratched the back of his head as if he were dealing with a particularly vexatious problem, before continuing, "... are you here for the disciple Senior Sister Shadow kidnapped?"

"*What*?" Yao Shen's flabbergasted voice echoed out in the chamber, and Zhou Hui too seemed astonished. Both of them had seen Shadow lead Yanyue to the second floor of the tower, and no one had passed them on the way up— when did Shadow get time to kidnap a disciple?

"Explain yourself," Zhou Hui requested more than demanded, but as the previous Elder of the Enforcement Hall, this was not an issue he could turn a blind eye to.

Xiaoli gazed at Yao Shen, who gave him a nod. He had already concluded that this was a misunderstanding, confident that Shadow would not do such a thing— making him more amused than anything else.

"Senior Sister Shadow walked into the alchemy floor with an unconscious disciple held in her arms. The tempo of the disciple's breathing was relaxed and she was unharmed; otherwise, I would have offered her a healing elixir. She then proceeded to the third floor." Xiaoli reiterated the sequence of events calmly, having reverted to his confident demeanor that seemed to grow even stronger.

"You didn't ask *her* why she had an unconscious disciple in her arms?" Zhou Hui asked incredulously, more bewildered than anything else.

"Patriarch Hui, please don't jest around with this little disciple. Senior Sister Shadow has never acted without noble intentions in her heart and…" Xiaoli paused for dramatic effect before continuing,"… I wish to live a long, healthy life."

Yao Shen looked on with amusement, while Zhou Hui found himself tongue-tied— after all, nothing Xiaoli had said was actually false. Shadow's reputation exceeded any core disciple in the sect by leaps and bounds, her honor and hatred for the demonic path bringing her great repute in the Heavenly Sky Sect. It made sense why Xiaoli would not be inclined to question his older sister's judgment. For all he knew, the disciple could be a demonic sect spy.

"Besides, if there is still a disciple foolish enough to provoke my elder sister, her days were probably numbered anyway." Xiaoli shrugged, his face slightly twitching as memories of his senior brother's duel with Shadow resurfaced in his mind. Of course, Xiaoli didn't actually expect Shadow to truly harm the disciple, at worst, subjecting her to a light punishment.

That last statement seemed to agitate Zhou Hui because it was a flagrant violation of the Enforcement Hall's rules and the slight disrespect Xiaoli had shown due to his casual answer irked him, but Yao Shen just placed a calming hand on his shoulder.

"Brother Hui, I think this is a misunderstanding." Yao Shen had understood everything when Xiaoli had revealed that the disciple was a girl, and he proceeded to describe Yanyue's appearance to him. Xiaoli immediately nodded, and Zhou Hui relaxed, albeit still remaining somewhat confused.

Xiaoli himself did not understand why the Patriarch seemed so well-acquainted with one whom he had believed to be a random disciple.

"Brother Yao, why would your new disciple arrive unconscious?" Zhou Hui asked with some concern, wondering if one of the Council members had done something rash.

"Do not worry, Brother Hui. If Xiaoli said that she was fine and Shadow did not raise the alarm, then there is no cause for worry. Come, let us leave him to his alchemy." Yao Shen remained calm, having his own conjectures upon the situation.

".... *Disciple*?" Xiaoli blurted out incredulously, the two Patriarchs' conversation and the implications behind it taking a few seconds to register in his mind. This time, he was the one to be shocked out of his wits.

Yao Shen lightly smiled, before replying, "Hurry up and finish your elixir so you can meet your new junior sister."

They proceeded to the entrance of the third floor, leaving behind an alchemist that was frantically trying to stir his elixir to completion.

"Brother Hui, if you would please take a few steps back," Yao Shen politely asked, and Zhou Hui had heard enough about the Grand Patriarch's second disciple to wryly smile, before he complied with the request.

The door to the third floor creaked open to reveal an astonishing sight— two earthen constructs dominated the third floor in sheer volume alone, the nine-foot tall juggernauts constructed in an exaggerated imitation of Dwarven physiology— thick, burly arms and legs, with a bulky torso, covered in layers of dense, overlapping golden fractals responsible for directing and controlling the actions of the construct.

The Dwarven Golems were late-stage core formation artifacts, a rare gift from the Dwarven Mountain Range that the sect had received a few centuries ago. Their primary function was to serve as sparring partners for core formation cultivators, also serving as a very ostentatious method for displaying the effectiveness of Dwarven-made artifacts and constructs, the latter an art that the three major sects of the Azlak Plains had lost.

The Golems moved with deceptive agility and grace for their presumed weight, but what was more surprising was the target they pursued— a bare-chested man pivoting on his left foot as the rampaging golems drew near from opposing directions, his fiery red hair jouncing in the air as he came to a sudden halt. One of the Golems finally arrived within striking distance, an earthen glow enveloping its clenched right fist as it drew it back.

Yao Shen watched calmly as the Golem's fist, which was originally a pleasing sandy brown, shifted to a muted gray, its surface transmuting until its exterior resembled hardened rock. The Golem mercilessly brought down its fist upon the unarmed man, whose hulking, muscular frame countered with an uppercut of his own, in what appeared to be laughable defiance.

A loud bang rang out as the two fists collided, followed by a shockwave that Yao Shen could feel in his bones, even if the resulting impact could not move him in the slightest. The red-haired man remained standing, his fist raised up in the sky, but the same could not be said for the Golem— its right arm was completely blown away from the impact, half its torso eviscerated from the sheer force behind the man's terrifying blow.

However, he had little time to react when the second Golem arrived in his range mere moments after he had dealt with the first, its rocky fist landing upon his exposed back with another loud bang, the resultant shockwave even stronger than before. A giant fist imprint marred the man's back, but he was not blown away by the impact as one might expect— instead, he just went sliding forward for a dozen meters while remaining upright, before the momentum propelling him fizzled out.

His figure blurred as he pivoted to face the Golem who had ambushed him from behind, stomping on the ground to send himself careening through the air in its direction. The red-haired man's intense gaze fell upon the Golem before his fist smashed down upon its head, a passing blow as he sailed past it.

The Golem's head exploded, the upper half of its body reverting to an amalgamation of topsoil and sand— the impact of the blow marginally more devastating than his previous strike.

The red-haired man landed twenty or so meters away from the Golem's remains, seemingly unbothered by the destruction of such a priceless gift. Of course, the Dwarven Golems would hardly be worthy of bearing the name of their creators if their destruction was such an easily accomplished feat.

The golden fractals that had originally been embedded into the Golem's exterior started emanating a radiant light, a majority of them scattered all over the floor, while a few still remained within the construct's body. They started floating around their respective Golem's remains, the golden light growing stronger as they linked together to form a circular formation around the Golem's remains. With each rotation the topsoil and sand amalgamation flowed back toward the Golem's remains, reforging it. Each subsequent rotation only grew faster, and around a minute later both the Golems had reverted to peak condition.

They remained rooted to the spot, as if destroying them once was the stipulation to return them to a passive, or inert state.

The red-haired man's gaze shifted to Yao Shen, and a wild grin tore at his face. The next instant, his figure blurred, as three consecutive leaps powered by a single leg's muscles covered the distance between him and Yao Shen— his clenched fist released a blow that far surpassed his previous attacks.

A loud bang rang out, followed by a strong gust of wind in Zhou Hui's direction as Yao Shen casually caught the blow in his right palm. The red-haired man grimaced as his fist connected but remained silent as he bore the backlash of the impact.

"Master," the red-haired man's boisterous voice boomed out in greeting, the joy within his voice overshadowing any pain he felt.

"Duyi," Yao Shen acknowledged, lightly smiling at his second disciple's antics.

"To think that your physical body alone has reached such a state. Truly formidable, Master," Duyi Xiong stated with a grunt as he withdrew his fist from his master's grasp and grimaced again. His knuckles were pinkish red from the impact, and his fingers were slightly swollen.

Yao Shen just chuckled lightly, tousling his second disciples' spiky hair affectionately.

"Unfilial disciple, you hear of your master's triumphant return and you dare not personally welcome him?" he asked in jest, already knowing what the answer would be.

"Hmph," Duyi grunted, disapproval clearly written on his face. "I already told Shadow and little Xiaoli to cease their need-less worrying. It is unbecoming of their stature as true disciples. Since the moment you chose to ascend, I already knew that you were guaranteed to succeed." His voice rang out with absolute certainty, not even a trace of doubt or skepticism to be found within.

Yao Shen sighed, his tone turning slightly reprimanding as he replied, "I have told you many times, Duyi, there are no absolutes in the world of cultivation."

"Yes, Master," Duyi obediently replied, but Yao Shen could make out the defiance in his eyes. His faith in Yao Shen, his master, was absolute— and one could clearly understand why this was a weakness, a chink in the armor that had to be ironed out if one intended to survive for long in the ruthless world of Eliria; for no cultivator was invincible. But at the same time, Yao Shen had already learned his lesson with Shadow, how it had severely impacted her when he *forbade* her from guarding him. Duyi's case was similar from some angles, but largely different— he looked up to him, admired him, and had founded his whole cultivation style based on the myth of indomitability that had accompanied him on his meteoric rise.

To take that away from him was difficult indeed, especially when most cultivators had a central belief, idea, or concept that let them persevere under the circumstances Eliria often threw their way.

Yao Shen nodded, choosing to drop the issue for now. "Good. Did Shadow pass by you?"

Duyi's eyes seemed to brighten up at the mention of Shadow, his mouth curling up into a light smile before he responded, "Yes, Master. I also saw our new junior sister, but she was unconscious. Shadow said it was Qi Exhaustion, but her Qi reserves seemed to be filled to the brim."

"Ah," Yao Shen replied, the puzzles finally falling into place. If it wasn't Qi Exhaustion then the girl was likely fine, the day's events just too draining on her emotional capacity to bear shock— cultivators could not truly face any lasting consequences from mortal afflictions, like a heart attack, but fainting or falling into slumber was possible if the cultivator felt that they were in a secure environment.

"Master, may I request something?" Duyi asked, his forceful request sounding like something he would do regardless of Yao Shen's response.

"Ask."

"Our new junior sister seems quite frail. May I educate her upon the joys of *body cultivation*?" Duyi asked, with a passionate gleam shining in his eyes as he flexed his rippling muscles almost subconsciously.

20

FORMATION

YAO SHEN COUGHED LIGHTLY into his fist to mask his bemused expression, as Zhou Hui valiantly fought against the smile that threatened to creep up on his face.

"You may.... *try*," Yao Shen finally replied, his voice somewhat stifled as he saw the enthusiasm reflected in Duyi's expression.

"Thank you, Master," Duyi answered with a gracious bow before Yao Shen could retract his statement, the flames of passion within his heart only burning brighter.

Yao Shen's face twitched slightly, as he held back a strong urge to sigh, while Zhou Hui seemed to be on the verge of tears from how desperately he was trying not to laugh. Yao Shen wasn't averse to the path of body cultivation, and neither did the idea of a female body cultivator rankle at his sensibilities. The issue at hand was far simpler— body cultivation was a path of *extremes*, requiring an incredible tolerance for pain, a willingness to bear physical punishment, along with extensive investment in elixirs, balms and pills whose cost no disciple was capable of shouldering alone.

One would wonder why Yao Shen's disciples' path diverged

so heavily from his own, and it was often a topic of contention among the inner disciples. Few cultivators knew that Yao Shen himself had never intended to take more than one disciple, who he would pass down his complete legacy to. He had taken Shadow as a disciple entirely by chance, and Xiaoli's discipleship had started as an asylum seeker. He had come to love the former as a daughter, making him overprotective in her training, while the latter's temperament was not suited for combat.

Only Duyi, who shared the same thirst for martial strength that had once driven Yao Shen's actions, mirroring the single-minded, crazed pursuit of ascension that had defined his journey to Soul Emperor, was suitable to inherit his legacy. Except there was one *crucial* distinction between the two, one that made all the difference. A master naturally wanted their disciples to surpass their accomplishments, and Yao Shen was no different— Duyi was *talented*, far more talented than Yao Shen had ever been, in a particularly offensive element as well.

"Do not pressure your junior sister, though, Duyi. She has had a.... *troubled* experience in the sect, and may not take kindly to your guidance," Yao Shen cautioned, though he was not too worried given Duyi's nature.

"Understood, Master," Duyi replied, a somber expression wiping away all traces of joviality on his face as his gaze hardened.

"Come, then. Let us proceed," Yao Shen walked forward as Duyi stood to the side, letting Zhou Hui pass through first before he fell in line, a step behind the two.

A minute later, they stood outside the entrance to the fourth floor, Yao Shen unlocking the entrance without further ado. A strong wave of Qi swept past them as the door creaked open, causing the ambient Qi in the stairwell to rise at a staggering rate. The three of them hurried in and Duyi manually shut the door behind them to stymie the leak.

Few outside Yao Shen and his disciples had seen the layout of the fourth floor, and for good reason— most outer and inner disciples would go green with envy at the pile of peak-purity spiritual ore stacked in the center of the floor, encased by a concentric formation comprised of two silver runic circles embedded in the tiling. The larger circle encircled the circumference of the floor, while the smaller circle was placed around the shimmering pile of ore— the formation serving a dual-fold purpose: extracting Qi from the spiritual ore and maintaining a high level of ambient Qi in the environment by releasing it periodically.

The formation let a cultivator directly absorb Qi from the environment instead of slowly siphoning it from the ore, but the costs involved in its upkeep were so steep that not even legacy family disciples enjoyed such treatment. However Yao Shen only had three disciples, and like any mortal father who had grown up lacking resources, he wished to offer the children under his wing nothing but the best.

Yao Shen's gaze shifted from the formation after taking a glance at the ore reserves, to the western part of the room where a single bed was situated. Yanyue was sleeping peacefully on the bed while Shadow was seated on a chair next to her, gently clasping her hand with both of her own to monitor her Qi flow and pulse.

Her perception detected Yao Shen's approach and she hurriedly withdrew her hands, a light blush coloring her cheeks as she averted her gaze. The sudden jerking movement caused Yanyue's eyes to snap open, groggily trying to make sense of her surroundings.

A few seconds later, Yanyue's eyes went wide with shock as she noticed the ambient Qi in the environment, sitting up on the bed before she knew it. Her instincts screamed at her to cultivate, for even a few hours of cultivation in this chamber would translate to weeks of cultivating with medium-purity spirit stones, and never had she seen such extravagance, no, *decadence,* in her life.

Thankfully, reason prevailed as Yanyue reminded herself that she was now an honorary disciple of the Patriarch, her stature and importance in the sect incomparable to before. She turned her gaze to her elder sister, who for some reason found the ceiling very enrapturing at that moment. Had she been waiting at her bedside the entire time she was unconscious?

The approaching set of footsteps attracted her attention, and Yanyue let out a mental squeal as she saw her master accompanied by one of the elders that had been present in the council meeting. She hurriedly fumbled around in bed, getting back to her feet as she anxiously tried to straighten out her rumpled robes.

"At ease, Yanyue." Yao Shen scanned Yanyue's meridians and Qi flow with his divine sense, and only when he concluded that she was fine, and it had indeed been emotional fatigue that had caused her to faint, did he smile lightly. "This will be your living quarters from now on, for as long as you are willing to stay with us," he added reassuringly, hoping that he had eased one of her anxieties.

"Thank you, Patriar...- Master." Yanyue corrected herself mid-sentence and gave Yao Shen a deep, respectful bow, partly in order to conceal the shock reflecting in her eyes. She was... *allowed* to cultivate here? For as long as she wanted? That alone was a gift that she would likely be unable to repay in this lifetime, possibly saving her *years* of cultivation in the inner sect. Had she not already broken down twice in the last twenty-four hours, perhaps this time it would have been tears of gratitude that were shed.

"Rise, child," Yao Shen gave her a light pat on the shoulder, snapping her out of her thoughts.

She straightened her back with a little more gusto, as she continuously reminded herself that she was no longer the hapless inner disciple who failed to procure even the most basic variation of the healing arts, but the disciple of the most powerful cultivator in the Azlak Plains.

"Good," Yao Shen acknowledged, and then continued, "This is your senior brother and my second disciple, Duyi Xiong."

Zhou Hui stepped to the side, and only then did Yanyue notice the hulking figure of the young man whose presence had previously been overshadowed by the two Patriarchs. Yanyue's watched as the red haired man approached, and she could not help but feel slightly intimidated— his bulky, muscular arms were easily double her own in circumference, but it was more the silent *intensity* the man radiated with every step he took, his eyes glowing with a bright passion she herself had long forgotten.

"It is nice to meet you, Junior Sister. We have much to discuss," Duyi stated, but his tone still managed to come off as friendly and encouraging.

Yanyue meekly nodded her head, wondering exactly what one had to eat to get a physique like that. The rumors were largely at odds when it came to Yao Shen's other two disciples, since they hardly made public appearances. Duyi's physique only served to further confuse her, for few cultivators found it worthwhile to train the body when the elements were more effective in almost all situations, and she found herself wondering what element he cultivated.

"Oh, Yanyue," Yao Shen added, his eyes twinkling with light mischief.

"Yes, Master?" she asked, the term of endearment and respect flowing far more naturally on her tongue.

"I have prepared a small gift that will aid you on the path of cultivation. I suspect it should be arriving soon." Yao Shen gave Yanyue a warm smile, wondering how the girl would react to being gifted a priceless Nascent Soul Natural Treasure when mere spiritual ore managed to impress her. He *almost* felt bad.

Almost.

Of course, Yao Shen was not frivolous enough to leave such a priceless treasure in the guardianship of a foundation establishment disciple, so he used his divine sense to inform Duyi and Shadow of the specifics. Shadow's expression remained unchanged, but Duyi's expression was far more entertaining— his eyes were on the verge of popping out as he stared at his new junior sister with unconcealed shock in his eyes, sizing her up and down as he pondered upon same question Yanyue had not too long ago: what did his new junior sister eat to have such earth-shattering, heaven-defying good fortune?

On the other hand, Zhou Hui felt especially stifled at the thought of Xue's Family's Heart-Cleansing Sea Pearl being referred to as a *'small'* gift...but he supposed that they had it coming.

"I am grateful for your consideration, Master," Yanyue replied graciously, entirely unaware of the true value of the gift.

"Now, I have matters of import to discuss with Patriarch Hui. We shall disturb you young ones no further," With that, Yao Shen and Zhou Hui moved to the southern end of the room, where three plush spiritual beast hide divans rested, flanked with shelfs on either side that contained scrolls, beast-hide tomes and other literary treatises on martial and elemental theory and techniques.

21

SEA PEARL

THREE HOURS PASSED as Yao Shen and Zhou Hui debated upon the direction of the soon-to-be established Modern Sect, a divine sense ward isolating the specifics of their discussion from his disciples. It was, of course, not a matter of trust, but comfort— there would be certain topics that Zhou Hui would not be willing to bring up in front of young disciples, or matters pertaining to sect secrets that his disciples were not yet qualified to know.

Zhou Hui animatedly brought up a few reforms and policy changes for discussion that surprised Yao Shen— not necessarily in ingenuity or scale, but rather in Zhou Hui's willingness to rebuke tradition. It only further gave credence to Yao Shen's belief, that perhaps the cultivators of Ionea were not as entrenched in tradition as they thought themselves to be, but simply lacked a framework through which they could implement institutional reform.

In Zhou Hui's case, he was bound by his position as Patriarch of the Hui Family, and his need to maintain amenable ties with the other Legacy Families. Yao Shen did not fault him for the teachings of his family, and indeed, presenting a united front in front of the Heavenly Sky Sect and the cultivation world was the most optimal way to secure their long-term survival and prosperity. Without Yao Shen, an absolute power at the very top of the pyramid, the reforms he was proposing now would be mere fever dreams— Meili Zhu would never stand for such a blatant transgression upon the heritage of the legacy families, and she was not an opponent Zhou Hui could openly oppose.

They were nearing the end of their discussion, the conversation having shifted to far more informal topics when Yao Shen's divine sense picked up on his second disciple's abrupt departure — Duyi left the cultivation chamber with a solemn expression on his face, a compact silver mirror held in his oversized right palm as he stepped out of his line of sight.

Yao Shen could still track him with his divine sense, but his destination, and the purpose behind it were fairly obvious— Dongmei Xue had upheld her part of their 'deal.'

"Patriarch Hui, this has been a very gainful discourse. After the establishment of the sect, perhaps we can make this a monthly occurrence." Yao Shen felt refreshed after the candid conversation, especially since the council meetings always left him feeling a little exhausted. But Yao Shen's praise had not been false— the juxtaposition between him, who had regained memories of his past life on Earth, and Zhou Hui, a denizen of Eliria through and through, had shown compatibility between the two, at least when it came to the righteous path.

"I would be glad to make our discussion a monthly occurrence, Grand Patriarch Yao," Zhou Hui amiably replied, but the implication did not escape him. Yao Shen wished to end the discussion, and Zhou Hui himself would be lying if he claimed that he was unbothered by the thought of a legacy family's prized possession falling in the hands of an outsider. "...That said, I apologize for taking up so much of your time, Grand Patriarch. I am sure that you have preparations to make for tomorrow's grand duel, and thus will take my leave now." Zhou Hui left the comfort of the divan, getting back onto his feet before giving Yao Shen a nod. Yao Shen nodded back in acknowledgement, a mutual, shared respect in their gazes, before he walked away without looking back.

A few minutes later, Duyi returned to the cultivation chamber, cupping an ornate sea-green box embellished with the silhouettes of aquatic spiritual beasts finely engraved upon the surface with both his hands. His steps were slow and measured as he approached Yao Shen, clearly afraid of damaging the contents of the box— when one was as strong as Duyi, such concerns were not entirely unfounded.

"Master," Duyi greeted as he gently placed the box on the table— immediately relieved to be rid of the responsibility. "A Faceless handed this over to me. I assume it is the *gift* we discussed earlier." He gave a brief explanation, not elaborating on the specifics.

"I see. Thank you, Duyi." Yao Shen's attention fell upon the box, immediately probing it with divine sense. Seeing that he was no longer required, Duyi returned to his fellow disciples.

Yao Shen's initial divine probe failed, but he was not surprised— Divine sense wards were only natural for such a valuable treasure, and the box did not allow the slightest hint of Water Qi to leak out— indicating that it had likely been forged with trace amounts of Zalur Stone. If he were so inclined, his divine sense could brute force its way past the wards, but that would also destroy its utility. The box was fairly valuable in its own right, and Yao Shen did not believe Dongmei Xue rash enough to employ such a crude trap— but he had not lived for two centuries without developing a healthy degree of caution.

Yao Shen formed his Human Dao Domain, startling his disciples as the golden wheat fields manifested upon the cold tiling of the floor, translucent silhouettes that represented mortal farmers silently harvesting the crop. Without further hesitation, he tugged at the lid. It offered little resistance as it popped open— a strong burst of the *purest* Water Qi Yao Shen had ever sensed blew past him, and it was merely excess Qi that the Natural Treasure had accumulated.

A small, unassuming blue orb rested in the open box, its perfectly glossy exterior reminiscent of fine marble. Yao Shen had never gotten an opportunity to witness the Xue Family's Heart Cleansing Sea Pearl for himself, so it was truly a little beyond his expectations. As he reached for the orb and held it up in the air, he almost felt sad for Dongmei Xue's loss. Casually dispelling his domain, Yao Shen absorbed a trickle of Water Qi from the pearl to test his effectiveness.

His eyes immediately widened in surprise as pure Water Qi flowed through his meridians, immediately rejuvenating every aspect of his physical body. The soft, supple nature of Water Qi brought comfort to his body, and Yao Shen's instincts told him that if he kept absorbing it, what little impurities that remained in his body would be purified. Regular contact with such pure Water Qi would undoubtedly increase one's understanding of the Dao of Water, and even had a small chance of increasing one's affinity over time.

It was not that Yao Shen's intelligence on the legacy families was lacking, but such priceless treasures almost never left their family compounds— even then Dongmei Xue would hardly let others freely inspect it. He had thought he had a grasp of the legacy families' foundation, but the Heart Cleansing Sea Pearl had made him realize that he had still underestimated the legacy families— that realization alone was perhaps, more valuable than the pearl itself.

. . .

"Yanyue, Shadow, approach," Yao Shen softly requested as he sealed the Heart Cleansing Sea Pearl with a flourish of his hand.

A dazed Yanyue trailed behind her senior sister, Shadow, whose expression remained as impassive as usual. As one attuned to the Water Element, even Yao Shen's domain could not obfuscate the spike in Water Qi she had felt moments earlier, the purity so unnaturally high that Yanyue struggled to describe the experience. She had merely taken a glimpse at the blue orb held in her master's right hand out of curiosity, not expecting an almost magnetic sense of attraction to ensnare her as the Water Qi within her thrummed in resonance— only breaking out of the trance when Yao Shen resealed the orb.

Yanyue realized that she had covered the distance across the hall and was now standing in front of her master, her mouth slightly agape as she stared at the sealed box with a mix of wonderment and caution.

"Master... what is that?" The question slipped out of Yanyue's mouth before she could second guess herself, sheer curiosity superseding any sense of propriety she felt in that moment.

Yanyue's question brought a mischievous smile on Yao Shen's face as his fingers lightly drummed on the box's surface, before he answered, "This is the reason behind the Xue Family's continued hegemony. Or at least, a part of it."

"Master?" Yanyue stuttered in disbelief, any instinctive desire she felt for the orb turning into revulsion. She could not understand how her master had a prized possession of the Xue Family in his possession, *unless...*

'"This is the gift I have prepared for you," Yao Shen replied, his words spoken with the dignity of a Patriarch— firm and domineering at the same time.

"M-Master... this... I can't accept this..." Yanyue's pupils dilated in shock as she took long, deep breaths in an attempt to calm her pacing heartbeat— the selfish yearning for the sea-blue orb once again rekindling in her chest. A cultivator could naturally sense treasures that resonated with their element, and Yanyue struggled to imagine the benefit it could bring to her cultivation— she would hardly be considered a water cultivator if she were not drawn to a natural treasure that stood at the very pinnacle of her Dao. But the Xue Family's heirloom had to be at least at the Nascent Soul level while she, a mere foundation establishment disciple, was not even qualified to know of its existence, let alone dream of monopolizing it.

"Why? Do you believe yourself to be unworthy of such consideration?" Yao Shen asked, his intention not to mortify Yanyue, but instead take measure of her resolve.

Yanyue fell silent as she pondered upon her master's question, resisting the urge to give in to her nervous tics. Yanyue would be lying if she claimed not to be overwhelmed by the situation, and a part of her wished to reply in affirmative— she was a fairly unremarkable inner disciple who had been stagnating in her cultivation for the past few years, and gifting an honorary disciple such a priceless treasure could hardly be a common occurrence. Would claiming herself worthy not be presumptuous?

Perhaps Yanyue would have done so, had she not been continuously reminding herself of her new station. She was an honorary disciple of a Soul Emperor, the most powerful existence in the Azlak Plains, and her master was unlikely to expect a self-deprecating response. Was it a test, then? Or was it a gentle nudge in her direction, prompting her to be more ambitious? More boisterous? Was she expected to be like her senior brother Duyi, who had revealed himself to be a body cultivator, of all things? Mayhap not to that extent, but Yanyue knew that her actions would reflect on her master's reputation from the moment he accepted her as a disciple.

"I do not believe myself unworthy, Master, since it is a prized possession of the Xue Family. No gift could be more fitting,"

Yanyue answered with grace, the words flowing out with ease as she drew upon her hatred of the Xue Family for strength. "However, Master, the knowledge that the Xue Family has finally been held accountable for its actions is more than enough for this disciple. I would be gratified if the treasure went to one better equipped to utilize it." Ultimately, Yanyue could not bear to accept such a valuable gift and she did not wish to appear covetous in front of her fellow disciples— the debt she had accrued to Yao Shen was already more than what she could repay in this lifetime.

Yao Shen's expression remained calm, but inwardly, he was surprised at how thoughtful Yanyue's answer was— by claiming herself worthy, she honored his own reputation as her master. By highlighting her enmity with the Xue Family, she proved that the safety and comfort of his abode had not dampened her resolve. And lastly, Yao Shen was not surprised by her refusal— not even his first disciple had received such an extravagant gift to date. But if Yanyue wished to catch up to the trio, the Sea Pearl was an opportunity she could not afford to pass up on.

"You seem to misunderstand, child." Yao Shen lightly shook his head, before continuing, "I did not seize this Heart Cleansing Sea Pearl from the Xue Family. Neither was I in a position to punish the Xue Family without creating internal strife within the sect. The *sole* reason why I have the Heart Cleansing Sea Pearl in my possession is *you.*"

"Why?" Yanyue asked, completely taken aback by the revelation. Her master, as Patriarch of the sect, would not lie to her, but she could not puzzle out how her insignificant actions could force *Dongmei Xue* to do anything.

"I merely offered her a trade— your testimony for the Xue Family's Heart Cleansing Sea Pearl. Dongmei Xue accepted," Yao Shen casually explained, stunning both Yanyue and Duyi, who was eavesdropping on their conversation.

"I…" Yanyue felt obligated to say something, but the words abandoned her at the last moment. She was torn between gratitude for her master's actions and the slight sense of betrayal that gnawed at her from the inside, but mostly, it was just confusion at why Dongmei Xue had accepted such an unfavorable trade.

"I understand why you feel conflicted, Yanyue. There is still much you do not understand about the sect's inner workings, but I have a feeling that it will not remain that way for long. Are you curious why Dongmei Xue accepted my proposal?"

Yanyue nodded.

"As you well know, a healer is an invaluable resource in any sect. In the Heavenly Sky Sect, our healing techniques are predominantly based upon the water element, its supple, nourishing nature making it ideal for regeneration and rejuvenation of the physical body. Conversely, those same properties make Water Qi far more challenging to effectively wield in combat, more potent elements like Fire and Wind easily overwhelming Water Qi in direct clashes. And as time progresses, many healers grow comfortable behind the secure walls of the sect, rewarded amply for their contributions. Dongmei Xue is an exception to that trend, as competent a fighter as she is a healer, but most, upon reaching a bottleneck, become contented with their privileged lives— knowing their protection would be prioritized in times of crisis. Do you see now why the Xue Family guards their reputation so fiercely?"

"I think I do, Master," Yanyue replied thoughtfully as she tried to look past the bias she held for the Xue Family.

"One's reputation precedes them among the righteous path, and this saying particularly rings true for the Xue Family, for its primary reliance is not martial might or a powerful cultivation technique… but rather the *goodwill* they had accrued generation after generation, carefully crafting an honorable and virtuous image within the Heavenly Sky Sect—which served as a banner for its allies to rally under. To touch the Xue Family is equivalent to offending every disciple, guardian and elder who had, or whose ancestors had, once received their life-saving treatment." Yao Shen finally divulged the reason why he was so hesitant to shed all pretenses with the Xue Family,

"But, Master, why not choose to expose the Xue Family for what they truly are?" Yanyue struggled to keep emotion out of her tone, but ultimately managed— her master had given her no reason to doubt his intentions, but she still *needed* to know why.

"Because, child, as much as I understand your desire for revenge, it was not enough. The Xue family does not offend the powerful, and the powerful are not inclined to criticize those who may, one day, decide whether they would live or die. Dongmei Xue did not wish for the Xue family's reputation to be tarnished under her rule and for that she was willing to pay the price. But that aside, even if the recording stone was enough to irreparably damage the Xue Family's reputation, Dongmei Xue could not be exiled— for there is simply no healer left in the sect who was qualified to lead the Healing Hall," Yao Shen did not withhold the truth from Yanyue, but his statement only held true for the current Heavenly Sky Sect.

"However, Yanyue, the true reason behind my actions has little to do with pragmatism," Yao Shen plucked the box from the table and held in Yanyue's direction. "I simply choose to believe in the future, while the legacy families remain fixated upon the idea of restoring their former glory. I choose to believe in *you,* Yanyue, like my master had once chosen to believe in me. If you desire to see Dongmei Xue exiled, then strive to become the alternative— the Heart Cleansing Sea Pearl alone is far from enough, but it an irreplaceable first step in your journey," Yao Shen offered, already having ascertained his disciple's resolve— choosing to phrase it as an investment as opposed to a gift, the only way he saw Yanyue accepting it without feeling burdened and providing her with a goal at the same time.

Yanyue struggled to hold back the tears as her small hands gingerly wrapped around the box, bowing deeply to Yao Shen immediately after.

22

ZIXIN REN

ONCE YANYUE ACCEPTED the Heart Cleansing Sea Pearl, Yao Shen gave her clear instructions to only use it for cultivation once a week, and that too in Shadow's presence. A Nascent Soul Natural Treasure was too potent an attraction for a mid-foundation establishment disciple, and Shadow's oversight would ensure that she did not overdraw on Water Qi and damage her meridians in the process.

Yanyue wisely chose to hand over the Sea Pearl to Shadow for safekeeping, a course of action Yao Shen would have been forced to suggest had his youngest disciple not chosen to display such impeccable restraint. Having concluded his instruction, he gave his two disciples a light nod, indicating that they were free to leave— Shadow was the first to leave, the box containing the Sea Pearl held firmly in her right hand, while Yanyue gave him a grateful bow before scurrying after her senior sister.

Not long after, Yao Shen left the fourth floor with a small smile resting upon his face, clearly satisfied with the day's progress. Merely a few hours ago, Yanyue had entered the tower lacking both a goal and a means to achieve it— while it was too early to conclude if her resolve would be able to weather the test of time, the lofty goal he had directed her toward was no longer out of her reach.

Yao Shen arrived at the fifth floor of the tower, which served as part of his personal abode. The center of the room was dominated by a clump of thick, white clouds with a soft, fluffy exterior that floated slightly above the ground. Yao Shen could feel his connection to the artifact through the divine sense brand he had left upon it— *The Cumulus*, an early Nascent Soul Stage movement artifact that was passed down to every generation's Patriarch by the Council of Elders. It offered little in the way of offensive or defensive capabilities, but even Yao Shen could not deny that it was a mode of travel befitting the Patriarch of the Heavenly Sky Sect.

These days, though, it mainly served him in the form of a comfortable bed— truly, Yao Shen had experienced many luxuries in the world of Eliria, but few could compare to the divine sensation of sleeping upon a bed shaped out of the very skies itself.

He walked over to a small wooden table that was placed next to his bedside, seating himself upon the bed before he reached for the compact silver mirror that was placed there, an exact replica of the one that had been in Duyi's possession. The malleable clouds shifted to accommodate his bulk, their impossibly soft exterior cushioning his body despite being almost weightless at the same time— a cool, soothing sensation enveloped his skin, and for a second, Yao Shen allowed himself to forget about his future concerns, simply enjoying a moment of peace.

When he opened his eyes, they glinted with a sharp, focused light. For the day's work was not over yet. Yao Shen channeled his divine sense into the silver mirror, a communication artifact, and waited. A few seconds later, a wispy grey mist started to shift underneath the mirror's surface before forming a vague outline of a man that solidified with every growing second. Color breathed into the image at the very last second, resulting in a complete, lifelike image being formed on the surface of the mirror.

A bald man with bronzed, dilapidated skin gazed back at Yao Shen with an arrogant gaze, his originally muscular physique now withered and aged, unable to withstand the ultimate test of time. Yao Shen met the man's gaze through the communication artifact, neither party deigning to be the first one to initiate the conversation— even though they were separated by dozens upon dozens of li, the intensity of Zixin Ren's, Reserve Elder of the Ren Family, was quite accurately conveyed.

Finally, Zixin Ren chose to break the stalemate by initiating the conversation. "Patriarch Shen, how can this dying old man assist you?" His voice concealed an undercurrent of dissatisfaction, but he chose to offer him an amiable smile on the surface. It was no surprise that Zixin Ren, who had been awoken after a hundred long years of slumber, was dissatisfied with Yao Shen's radical, sweeping reforms. The bitterness he would have felt when he was informed that the one who ascended to Soul Emperor was not a member of the legacy families, but instead, an outsider, was alone enough reason for him to resent both Yao Shen as well as his incompetent descendants. But Yao Shen had even gone as far as to deny the Reserve Elder vengeance by burying the hatchet with the Divine Mountain Sect and the Sacred Flame Palace, putting an end to the ancient feud— he would not be surprised if Zixin Ren and most of the other reserve elders utterly loathed him at this point.

"I request you to escort the elders of the Divine Mountain Sect and the Sacred Flame Palace to the site of my ascension. I trust that you are already aware of the specifics of my agreement with the two sects?" Yao Shen asked, choosing to maintain the facade of amicability. The reserve elders were a force that even Yao Shen was *very* hesitant to antagonize— consisting of Nascent Soul Elders from preceding generations that had near exhausted their lifespans, the reserve elders fought without consideration for life or death. Their sole purpose was to die with honor on the battle-field, and not a single one among their ranks would hesitate to detonate their cultivation bases if the situation called for it.

"Forgive my impudence, Patriarch, but this old man has had the privilege of interacting with a Soul Emperor in his lifetime. He was indeed powerful, extremely so, but to confront *two dozen* Nascent Soul Cultivators alone... are you confident?" Zixin Ren finally chose to ask the question that had been resting at the back of his mind, and for a moment opposing political interests, their clashing values, Yao Shen's decision to undermine the legacy families... *all of that faded into the background.* All that was left was a cultivator who had dedicated his life to the pursuit of Dao, curious about what separated himself from one who managed to take the next step.

"The fight will indeed be challenging..." Yao Shen was slightly taken aback by the aged cultivator's earnest question, deciding to answer truthfully, "but I *will not* lose."

Zixin Ren remained silent for a few seconds, as if he were unsure how to process his answer— before he burst out into a loud, raucous laugh, stunning Yao Shen. He continued laughing for one long minute, his lungs wheezing from the exertion, before he finally spoke, "The younger generation surpasses the old... The younger generation *truly* surpasses the old..." he chanted, his gaze coming alight with a burst of life. "So many long centuries have passed since the Era of Turmoil, and this statement *finally* holds true for our Azlak Plains again." He broke out into a cough at the end, but his gaze did not waver.

Yao Shen nodded in agreement as he understood the meaning behind Zixin Ren's words— the Azlak Plains had a storied history within the continent of Ionea, but after the Era of Turmoil, it had only suffered blow after blow, decline after decline, until it had been reduced to its present state. An unremarkable territory that partly survived upon the goodwill of the True Elves... Perhaps Yao Shen had underestimated how painful it was to live through such a decline, to see your homeland wither in front of your eyes yet be unable to change its fate.

"Prove your claims, Soul Emperor, and perhaps..." Zixin Ren's expression seemed conflicted, as he gazed at Yao Shen through the communication artifact, "... and perhaps you are worthy." He croaked out the words with great difficulty, his image dissipating the moment he uttered his final word.

Yao Shen just sat there, an expression of genuine shock reflecting on his face as he wondered if he had misheard. A few minutes later, he just shrugged and decided to sleep instead of cultivating—like Zixin Ren said, all he needed to do for now was to prove himself tomorrow, not just to the Modern Sect, but to the entirety of Ionea.

For the Azlak Plains slumbered no longer.

23

DUEL

Y<small>AO</small> S<small>HEN</small>'s eyes snapped open, his expression composed as he slowly sat up— the bed of clouds underneath him shifting to accommodate the weight. Only a few hours had passed since he had turned in for the night, but there was no trace of grogginess reflected upon his sharp features.

Without dithering any further, Yao Shen got up from the bed and moved toward the eastern side of the room, reaching for the handle of an antiquated wooden almirah. A selection of fine robes greeted his sight, arrayed in a neat row and ordered by color. His gaze lingered on a set of azure robes, an exact duplicate of the one he was presently wearing, that represented his allegiance to the Heavenly Sky Sect.

Had it been any other day, he would have donned a fresh pair of azure robes without a second thought. Perhaps he would have even chosen to make his grand entrance seated upon *Cumulus,* an artifact that symbolized the seat of the Heavenly Sky Sect's Patriarch and his indomitable might— for it was an honor bestowed only to the most powerful cultivator of each generation.

However, for better or worse, Yao Shen represented the Heavenly Sky Sect no longer. His gaze shifted to a set of satin, pure white robes, a color unadorned by the three major sects of the Azlak Plains. A part of him was instinctively drawn to the color, bearing resemblance to the transient, milky white Human Qi that swirled within his soul lake— while not a perfect representation, it would serve his purposes well.

Yao Shen channeled some Water Qi to cleanse his body before changing into the new set of robes. He walked a few steps in the direction of the wall mirror, pausing as his reflection came into sight— the satin white robes complemented Yao Shen's sharp, angular features, adding an air of disarming purity to his otherwise intimidating presence. In that moment, he knew that he had found the sect colors— for now, the unclaimed satin-white would represent his Human Dao, but one day, Yao Shen hoped that it would come to represent the *humanity* of the Modern Sect.

'Gather,' Yao Shen thought, and Cumulus rushed to his side— the floating clouds enveloping him from all directions.

'Re-form,' he commanded, and a second later, the clouds began to rapidly compress, until Yao Shen's figure emerged from within— a flowing, weightless white cloak and a pair of cloud boots concluding his outfit.

Finally, he withdrew a sheathed sword from his spatial ring and securely tied it to his waist before exiting his personal abode. On his way down, he instructed Shadow, who was the only one who chose to cultivate instead of sleeping, to stay within the tower's bounds along with her fellow disciples until his return. He did not expect anything to go awry in his brief absence, but it was always better to tread on the side of caution.

Since the last of his concerns were addressed, Yao Shen exited the tower. He was not surprised to see a small contingent comprised of Zhou Hui, Meili Zhu and Jie Tang awaiting his presence, likely chosen to accompany him as representatives of the

Heavenly Sky Sect while the others stayed behind in order to defend the Sect's interests.

After exchanging a few pleasantries, they quietly departed the sect.

The wind buffeted Yao Shen's face as his silhouette flitted across the sky, closely accompanied by the sect elders. If Zhou Hui and the others were surprised by the color he chose to wear on this historic day, they hid it well; perhaps having already expected something in a similar vein.

As they drew nearer to their destination, his thoughts inevitably wandered in the direction of the upcoming battle. There were only a few methods Yao Shen could employ against such a powerful force, and even then, it would be a complex fight— his Human Dao Domain was perfectly suited to a battle of attrition, and even though he had yet to fully incorporate his three Major Daos into his Patchwork Domain, it boasted of an entirely different level of capability now. If he alternated between the two, he would eventually attain a glacial but likely victory.

However, Yao Shen knew that such a victory would only ring hollow. The foundation of a sect was the very first entry in any sect's records, and as the challenger, his objective had always been complete and absolute domination— to let his reputation act as a deterrent against those that held nefarious intent toward their sect and serve as the binding that unified the Modern Sect.

He cut his musings short as his destination came into sight, the charred ground that bore the mark of heavenly tribulation unmistakably the site of his ascension. There were no words exchanged as they began their descent, gently landing upon the ground; opposing the congregation of cultivators dressed in red, brown and grey robes.

The aged men and women in grey robes started walking in

their direction, led by Zixin Ren, who stood at the very forefront, his expression carefree and relaxed, despite having spent the last twenty-four hours in enemy territory. They took their places at the back of their small contingent without uttering a single word, content to watch the chaos unfold for now.

"Patriarch Yao Shen," A cultivator dressed in vibrant red robes stepped forward, his expression firm and his jaw held taut from tension. "As per the agreement between our sects, the Sacred Flame Palace and the Divine Mountain Sect has arrived today to accept your challenge," Patriarch Lei Weiyuan of the Sacred Flame Palace loudly proclaimed, attracting the attention of all the elders in attendance.

Yao Shen's gaze fell upon the lone core formation guardian that stood a distance away from the elders of the two sects, a peak quality communication mirror held in his hand that was beyond anything available in the Azlak Plains.

'*Interesting,*' Yao Shen mused, forming a vague idea of the ploy the two sects were formulating.

Patriarch Kang Long of the Divine Mountain Sect stepped forth next, in solidarity with his fellow sect leader. "Patriarch Yao Shen, you shall meet the combined force of our two sects in combat without any assistance from the elders of the Heavenly Sky Sect. This duel shall be fought until one side yields or is unable to fight any longer. If you win, all the elders present from both our sects shall swear an oath of first betrayal to the Modern Sect. In the event that you lose, you will swear an oath upon your honor to grant the Divine Mountain Sect and the Sacred Flame Palace independence for the next hundred years. Are those terms amenable to you, Patriarch Yao Shen?" he asked, failing in his attempts to conceal the tension in his voice.

Yao Shen immediately understood their gambit, a last-ditch attempt to preserve their autonomy. The sects in attendance may have had deeply flawed systems, but Yao Shen had never forgotten that they were heavily skewed in favor of those in attendance. No tyrant wished to cede power, and by broadcasting this fight to what Yao Shen suspected was one of the eastern righteous path sects, they had brought his reputation into play. Once he accepted, he would not be able to renege upon the terms of the agreement without dire consequences.

"I accept." Yao Shen's voice boomed out with confidence, a small smile resting on his face as he stared down a force that alone had the ability to devastate the Azlak Plains.

The two Patriarchs, along with each of the elders present, repeated those words. Zhou Hui and the other elders retreated until they were a distant dot in the sky, while the core formation cultivator continued recording, albeit from a greater distance.

Soon, only Yao Shen and twelve elders from each sect were remaining, including Patriarchs Kang and Lei.

One of the elders stepped forward, withdrawing a large hourglass from his storage ring and placing it in the middle of the two parties. There was no explanation needed as the cultivators present focused an insignificant strand of their divine sense upon the hourglass, registering each grain of sand trickle down into its lower half.

The elders unsheathed their weapons, a collection of primarily swords, followed by sabers, spears, axes and a solitary greatbow. The elders began cycling their Qi in tandem with each other, in order to burst out with the pinnacle of their strength the moment the final grain of sand tumbled down the hourglass, and Yao Shen did not miss the protective rings, amulets and talismans they wore or carried upon their person, a single sweep of his divine sense revealing all.

The elders clearly did not intend for this to be a long, drawn out battle, and that was fine with Yao Shen. He made no attempt to draw his weapon, simply content to cycle his Qi as he mentally prepared himself for what came next.

The tension in the air grew with every passing second, their experience the only thing that allowed the elders to maintain their stoic expressions in face of a force they could not claim to fully understand.

Finally, the last grain of sand trickled down the hourglass.

The elders had considered many factors in their attempts to anticipate their foe's opening move, but they were all astounded when they met Yao Shen's hollow gaze before he collapsed backwards, like a puppet whose strings had been severed.

No one present could explain what happened, and the two Patriarchs present were equally confounded. However, none present believed that a Soul Emperor could be subdued so easily, and for a majority of them, it was too late to recant their attacks.

With a stomp of his foot, an elder reshaped the earth into sharp spikes and sent them flying in Yao Shen's direction.

Another elder rapidly slashed out with his thin, curved sword, sending a succession of Fire Blades precisely aimed at Yao Shen's chest.

The greatbow user released the solitary arrow he carried, its body constructed entirely of a dense grey metal and easily boasting ten times the thickness of a normal arrow. The tip of the arrow burst into flames, as it whizzed off toward its target.

All these attacks blended together to form the first wave of attacks they had prepared, a mélange of Fire, Earth, Darkness and Wind Qi devastating everything that stood in its path to Yao Shen.

The elders were shocked as their attacks continued unimpeded, Yao Shen's body simply lying upon the ground as if it had been discarded.

When merely five meters separated Yao Shen from certain death, the elders' shock transformed into incredulity. Without their domains, this was the most powerful attack the elders were capable of unleashing. It was as if the wave of devastation they had met a force field or an invisible wall of some sort— the metallic arrow harmlessly bouncing off before it could even get close to harming Yao Shen, the Fire Blades spreading across the seemingly flat surface of the 'wall' before fizzling out and the Earth Spikes simply shattering upon contact.

The attacks had failed in their original purpose, but as the smoke from the aftermath of the attack cleared, a vague silhouette was revealed.

The elder who was closest to Yao Shen faltered in his charge, the sword held in his hands trembling as he craned his neck to make eye contact with the thing protecting Yao Shen.

A ten-foot-tall ghastly, translucent giant towered over the elder, bearing an unmistakable resemblance to Yao Shen— A gentle blue halo outlined the giant's silhouette, giving the impression that the translucent robes that covered its body, an exact replica of the ones Yao Shen wore, were light blue instead.

"Impossible… *Impossible*…" the elder whispered under his breath, instinctively knowing that Yao Shen had chosen to engage in combat directly with his soul. His own Nascent Soul bore resemblance to a mortal infant that rested in his Dantian region, and it had had no ability to assume a physical from— although that gave it superb mobility, any Qi-based attack at the Nascent Soul level could easily shatter his soul. To cultivate to an extent where the soul becomes solid… it was simply unfathomable.

The elder's willpower clamped down on his desire to flee, as he refused to break eye contact with Yao Shen.

The next instant, Yao Shen let out a deafening roar— releasing a concentrated blast of divine sense in all directions, in its most potent, unrestrained form.

The elder had prepared many weaker artifacts that guarded against divine sense attacks, but they all shattered at the same time. He made a conscious effort to shield his soul from the torrent of divine sense that battered against it, but it was like a mortal trying to swim against the tide— a foolishly brave, but ultimately futile effort.

Only two words echoed in his mind before he lost consciousness, two words that carved a deep fear and reverence into his heart:

'Soul Emperor'

24

CONCLUSION

A few minutes earlier…

Yao Shen's robes fluttered in the wind as his gaze fell upon the elders of the Divine Mountain Sect and the Sacred Flame Palace. A small strand of his divine sense focused upon the hourglass, sensing each grain of sand trickle down the slender tube as he took the time to mentally prepare himself.

The comprehensive might of two hegemonic sects of the Azlak Plains lay arrayed against him, the elders exuding an oppressive aura as they readied their weapons for battle. Their sharp, focused gazes tracked his movements with a scorching intensity, staunch determination reflected in their eyes.

However, Yao Shen's expression remained tranquil as he faced down the elders unflinchingly. It was a pity that he had to reveal his trump card so soon, but Yao Shen held no illusions of concealing his secrets from external forces— the Azlak Plains may not have possessed complete records upon the fabled Soul Emperor stage, but the same could not be said for the true power-houses of Ionea. Discarding the mortal body and fighting with the soul was an unfamiliar concept to Yao Shen, since he understood the risks associated with such a maneuver.

Yet, much like Yao Shen's ascension tribulation, his soul was far more potent than it ought to have been at his cultivation stage, even beyond his wildest expectations. While he could not mitigate all the risks involved, he believed the tradeoff to be worth it. He entered a state of absolute focus as the final grain of sand trickled down the funnel, letting go of any lingering inhibitions as he braced himself.

The first thing that he felt was a sensation of profound loss, as his soul rapidly expanded beyond the constraints of his mortal body. A few seconds passed before his form stabilized, the originally imposing elders now appearing frail and insignificant upon being confronted by his towering physique.

The world immediately slowed down in his perception as his control over divine sense reached an unprecedented level, the dissonance between his body and soul no longer limiting his abilities. Yao Shen's indifferent gaze landed upon the volley of attacks headed in his direction, capable of easily evading them but choosing not to— his soul form had a certain heft to it that slowed him down, but he was confident that none of the Nascent Soul level attacks could faze his natural defenses.

His prediction turned out to be correct as the attacks slammed against the exterior of his soul form, fizzling out before they could cause him any real harm. However, Yao Shen's fears materialized into reality as he felt a burst of irritation well up within him that swelled into a burgeoning rage directed toward his attackers— in his soul form, any emotion he felt was magnified multiple times, for while his physical body dulled the true capabilities of his soul, it also formed an equilibrium between the soul and the physical body that allowed him to function without being overwhelmed.

Had it not been for Yao Shen's intricate understanding of emotions as a practitioner of Human Dao and his decades of cultivation experience, the raw, unadulterated anger he felt for the once enemies of the Heavenly Sky Sect might have overwhelmed him. Instead, he *harnessed* the power of that rage, since attempting to fully suppress it was a futile effort— over a century of bitter rivalry along with the frustration, angst and fury it had brought him were released with a mighty roar that served as the carrier for a concentrated blast of divine sense.

He watched with glee as a third of the elders crumpled under the force of his attack, their protective rings, amulets and talismans shattering before their souls slipped into unconsciousness, the power of a Soul Emperor forever imprinted onto their minds. Yao Shen had not attempted to suppress the rage coursing through his soul, for whilst the emotions he felt in this state might be magnified, they still belonged to him— as one who could see and interact with human emotions, he understood the futility of running away from them.

The lofty and overbearing elders of the Divine Mountain Sect and the Sacred Flame Palace that he once feared, then came to acknowledge as equals, were now unable to receive a single blow from him. Perhaps the part of him that belonged to Earth would be unable to understand, but as a cultivator who lived his life in pursuit of the Grand Dao, this was an accomplishment that deserved to be acknowledged.

For let it not be said that Yao Shen was an unfilial disciple— the date of the Modern Sect's establishment would also be recorded in historical records as the day the Heavenly Sky Sect shone the brightest, after decades of stagnation. The day whereupon the Patriarch of the Heavenly Sky Sect alone confronted the entire might of the sacred Divine Mountain Palace and the fearsome Sacred Flame temple on his lonesome and achieved victory!

The historical day when the Patriarch of the Heavenly Sky Sect united the Azlak Plains, establishing all three hegemons under one banner!

This was Yao Shen's pride, and his final tribute to his late master.

A jolt of anticipation ran through Yao Shen's soul, as he realized the full magnitude of what he was about to achieve. He let the magnified emotions influence him, charging forward with renewed vigor.

While the other elders were still reeling from the impact of Yao Shen's divine sense attack, a single pale-faced cultivator dressed in earthen brown robes stepped forward to confront the charging giant.

"*Earth Domain: Divine Mountain,*" Patriarch Kang Long's voice boomed out with an echo, as if his words were spoken in resonance with the very earth itself, slamming both his hands into the ground with a loud bang.

The ground beneath Yao Shen's feet started trembling before a layer of topsoil engulfed him from all directions. He tried to evade, but immediately lost footing as the earth beneath his feet transformed into quicksand. Yao Shen was on the verge of channeling his Wind Qi to escape the encirclement when the topsoil rapidly transmuted into a thick layer of bedrock, entombing him within a thirty-meter-tall mountain.

This was Kang Long's Domain—his will imposing order over the natural law, allowing the Earth to shift between its various forms freely.

Yao Shen watched as another layer of topsoil reinforced the interior of the mountain, before transmuting into bedrock and further thickening the mountain's defenses. The longer he hesitated, the more time Kang Long had to reinforce the mountain's interior until the nigh-impenetrable walls crushed him from both sides.

He laughed.

"Good!" Yao Shen roared, a burst of magnified exhilaration flowing through his soul. "This is how it ought to be!" he proclaimed, the Wind Qi within his soul lake flaring to life. The quicksand was unable to hold him any longer as he careened toward one end of the mountain wall without any intention of decelerating. Instead of utilizing his own Major Dao of Earth or Fire, Yao Shen simply pulled back his fist before slamming it against the harsh bedrock.

The mountain trembled under the sheer force generated from the impact, but ultimately managed to hold. That prompted Yao Shen's laugh to grow even wilder, as another punch rocked the surface of the mountain. His fist penetrated deep within the bedrock, causing a web of cracks to spread across the mountain's surface. The third and final punch shattered the mountain, and by extension, Kang Long's domain.

The bedrock reverted to clumps of Qi-infused soil as it harmlessly rained down upon the ground, but Yao Shen ignored it as his hulking figure snaked forward at Peak-Nascent Soul speed, a step down from his maximum, but enough for his current purposes.

A few moments later, Yao Shen found himself staring down the Patriarch of the Divine Mountain Sect, who was panting heavily after having his domain shattered. His gigantic fist slammed into the chestplate Kang Long was concealing under his vest, a loud bang sound echoing out as the Patriarch of the Divine Mountain Sect was knocked dozens upon dozens of meters away, largely unharmed but unconscious and no longer able to fight.

Another volley of attacks landed upon Yao Shen's soul, a few of the elders having recovered enough to muster a response. The attacks unsurprisingly failed to pierce his soul's defense, eliciting an irritated frown from Yao Shen as his temper started to flare up again.

His figure blurred as he charged toward the elders who had attracted his ire, his imposing frame blitzing forth with surprising agility as he rapidly closed the distance. An aged elder dressed in vibrant red robes stood at the forefront of Yao Shen's ambushers, a sleek metallic spear with a red crystal tip held in combat stance as his gaze fell upon Yao Shen's menacing visage. The elder's grip upon the spear lightly trembled, likely still suffering from the aftermath of Yao Shen's divine sense attack— yet there was no trace of weakness to be found within his firm, unyielding gaze.

There was a momentary lull as Yao Shen drew closer with each passing breath, while the elder conveyed his commands to the five cultivators who had attacked him in unison— two belonging to the Sacred Flame Palace, three to the Divine Mountain Sect. It did not escape Yao Shen how naturally the members of the two rival sects cooperated in face of a greater threat, deferring authority to the most experienced among themselves without any scruples.

The tip of the elder's spear blazed to life, the red crystal that formed the spear-point glowing brighter as it amplified the effects of his Fire Qi. Soon, a searing hot, roiling flame had enveloped the upper haft of the spear, before he kicked off the ground— sending himself careening in Yao Shen's direction with incredible velocity, the spear aimed right for his exposed neck.

The two remaining elders from the Sacred Flame Palace took to the skies, their weapons drawn as they positioned themselves for a pincer attack. One of the elders from the Divine Mountain Sect channeled his Earth Qi before projecting it outward until it had formed an earthen halo around his figure. The ground beneath the elder appeared to shift as it made contact with his halo, the packed soil suddenly exhibiting the viscosity of a liquid as it allowed him to recede into the very earth itself. A few seconds later, the soil reverted to its previous state— leaving behind no traces of the elder's presence.

The remaining two elders from the Divine Mountain Sect did not employ such an ostentatious method, simply drawing their weapons before joining the spear-wielding elder in his charge.

Surprise flashed in Yao Shen's eyes when he saw the elder's choice to directly confront him instead of stalling for time, but he welcomed their decision. A jolt of excitement coursed through him at the thought of the upcoming confrontation, and in his current emotional state, he would not shy away from a challenge.

Yao Shen chose to maintain his current pace, a small smile forming on his lips as he charged headlong into the fray.

The elder remained unfazed at the veritable giant barreling forth in his direction, adamantly continuing on a collision course with Yao Shen— perhaps attributing his recklessness to the instability brought on by his soul form. The vortex of flames originating from the tip of his spear grew wilder as the elder's silhouette arced through the air, hurtling forward at almost Peak-Nascent Soul level speeds. The distance between the two parties rapidly evaporated, until only a few meters separated the elder's spear from making impact.

The elder had invested a majority of his Fire Qi reserves in this attack, and both the density and potency of the flames had been amplified by his Peak-Grade Nascent Soul Artifact— his understanding of the Soul Emperor stage dictated that not even Yao Shen should remain unscathed in face of such a destructive attack. Hence his perplexity, when Yao Shen made no attempt to evade despite only five meters separating the two.

The elder's prideful, dignified expression shifted to one of abject horror when he realized that his momentum had simply *stilled.* For a long second, the elder remained suspended in mid-air, his grip on the spear remaining firm, yet remaining unable to make it budge in the slightest. His gaze slowly inched downwards, his expression paling when he noticed the spectral hand firmly holding the spear in place— the flaming tip merely a meter from piercing Yao Shen's throat, yet unable to take the final step regardless of how much strength he exerted.

The smile on Yao Shen's face grew wider, deriving satisfaction from the elder's horrified expression. He would never attempt such a risky maneuver in his physical body, but in his soul form, his control over divine sense had heightened his perception to such a degree that the elder's attack was simply...

"*Too slow*," Yao Shen softly whispered while the elder was in earshot, before landing a palm strike on the elder's chest that carried a concentrated blast of divine sense, impacting directly against his Nascent Soul. The wide-eyed elder gave Yao Shen a final look of incomprehension as his grip over his spear slipped, sending him tumbling back for tens of li before he lost consciousness.

The two elders from the Divine Mountain Sect who had been trailing behind the Sacred Flame Palace Elder in his frontal assault shared a grim countenance upon witnessing his ferocious attack being neutralized with such ease. However, they were not entirely unprepared for such an outcome, immediately abandoning their charge and instead choosing to flank Yao Shen from both sides. Merely moments after Yao Shen had dispatched the first elder, the two elders stood facing him from diametrically opposite directions.

The elders stomped their feet in unison, releasing a wave of Earth Qi that travelled through the ground and rapidly shaped two concentric domes that sealed Yao Shen within. They had learned their lesson from Yao Shen's fight with Patriarch Kang Long, and understood that he possessed great destructive capabilities— therefore, they continued to expend their Earth Qi, shaping and layering earthen domes, each larger than the previous one, in an effort to contain him.

Yao Shen stood in the center of the dome amidst the darkness, the elder's spear held in his right hand. Seemingly without any reason, Yao Shen hastily sidestepped to the right. A moment later, a sharpened spike fashioned out of hardened, Qi-infused rock whizzed past by him, shattering upon making impact with the dome— the third Elder who had concealed himself underground had finally made his move.

A barrage of earthen spikes erupted from the within the soil in quick succession, the concealed elder no longer holding back after his failed ambush. In Yao Shen's perception, the spears still moved far too slowly to be a threat for his reflexes, and his divine sense managed to pinpoint the elder's location.

Yao Shen's silhouette blurred as he was forced to rapidly evade a seemingly endless onslaught of spikes, giving him little to no opportunity to break through his confinement. Part of him admired the Divine Mountain Sect Elders' combat awareness and synergy, having devised such an effective, albeit ruthless method to suppress him even after their initial ploy went awry.

Be that as it may, Yao Shen's fury rose with every earthen spike he was forced to evade— for to entrap and then whittle down, before dealing the finishing move was a fighting style used to hunt spiritual beasts, not cultivators. To be treated like a spiritual beast, it rankled at his pride— an emotion that shined radiantly even without being amplified multiple times.

"No more," he growled under his breath, his attention falling upon the spear clutched in his right hand. Earlier, he had not deigned to use the spear because it was marked with the elder's divine sense brand— making it little more than an ordinary spear crafted with Nascent Soul Grade materials. Now, though, Yao Shen needed an outlet to vent his fury.

His divine sense unceasingly flooded the brand as he evaded another earthen spike, the manifestation of his soul clashing against the elder's in a battle for supremacy. The elder's divine sense put up a valiant fight, but ultimately could not resist the superiority in cultivation stage. The brand shattered, and Yao Shen immediately replaced it with his own.

Although it was unlikely, he still let out a relieved exhale when he confirmed that the weapon was not primed to self-destruct in the event the brand collapsed. He immediately felt a connection with the sleek metallic artifact, sensing the thrum of Fire Qi nestling within the artifact.

Amusement flickered in Yao Shen's eyes as he effortlessly shattered an earthen spike with a flick of his newly acquired artifact, before drawing upon his Fire Qi reserves and channeling it to the spear-tip.

The artifact functioned as intended, immediately raising the intensity of his flames by a notch. Satisfied by the outcome, Yao Shen did not hesitate any longer— he continuously channeled Fire Qi into the artifact, the intensity of the flame rising with every passing moment. A vortex of blazing inferno had formed at the tip of his spear before the red crystal started flickering, indicating that it had reached the limits of its amplification.

Yao Shen pulled the spear back until it was almost level with his height, before hurling it forward with the entirety of his monstrous strength— the spear artifact left the confines of his grasp, a blur of red light streaking toward the earthen dome with ferocious momentum.

Loud, ear-piercing bangs rang out in quick succession as the flaming spear ruthlessly tore past the thick, earthen-rock structures, the flames alone bringing the rock close to melting point before its metallic body punched through it. Only after piercing the twelfth and final layer of the domes did its momentum begin to flag, carrying on for another hundred meters before the last of the flames flickered out.

Yao Shen's eyes shone with an intense light as he drew upon his copious reserves of Wind Qi, his figure blurring as he shot forth like an arrow released from a taut bowstring. The elder concealed beneath the ground attempted to interfere, but there was a reason why the Wind Element was known for its speed— he could only watch on helplessly as his earthen spears missed by a wide margin, truly caught off guard by Yao Shen's unconventional method to break the encirclement.

Within moments, Yao Shen hurtled past the final dome. He was confronted by the two Elders of the Divine Mountain Sect, who panted heavily as they attempted to muster a defense against his charge. With one glance, he could tell that the elders were on the verge of exhausting their Earth Qi— Yao Shen barely slowed down his pace as he flashed past the elders, striking them with two divine-sense-infused palms that instantly caused them to crumple onto the ground before he took to the skies.

Above him, the two Elders of the Sacred Flame Palace paled as they saw Yao Shen's silhouette rapidly accelerate in their direction, attention split between the ball of concentrated flames they were channeling their Fire Qi into, augmenting and then further compressing the flames with each cycle. In the three-pronged strategy of entrapping, whittling down and dealing the final blow, their role was the latter-most. However, Yao Shen was not supposed to break out of the encirclement in one fluid motion— the original plan was to force him to expend his Qi as he was forced to break through the domes layer by layer.

Of course, the miniature sun that the two elders had manifested had not escaped Yao Shen's perception, but knowing meant little if he hadn't managed to escape. However in its present form, the flames were far too unstable to direct— odds were, they would backlash on the elders themselves.

The panic on the elders' faces grew, stuck between a rock and a hard place, but Yao Shen did not intend to give them time to decide. His figure flashed in front of one of the elders, his massive fist pulled back before slamming against the elder's abdomen and sending him shooting toward the ground. The other elder hurriedly ceased his attempts to stabilize the ball of flame, immediately flying away in the opposite direction.

Yao Shen utilized his Wind Qi to form a thick barrier that buffeted the roiling flames away from him, as the miniature sun rapidly destabilized. Since the attack lacked any direction or control, it had no way to penetrate his defenses— the flames offering little resistance as they were redirected around him. Gouts of flame rained down from the sky in all directions, igniting the land beneath his feet, but for now, Yao Shen's attention remained focused on the fleeing elder.

Despite the head start the elder had, Yao Shen caught up to him within a minute and smashed him out of the skies. After confirming that the elder had been knocked unconscious, he returned to the site of his ascension with a view to conclude the fight.

The moment he landed on the ground, the soil beneath him softened, causing him to sink for a meter before rapidly hardening into solid rock. The elder concealed within the earth was forced to make his move, even though he understood the futility of it— his silhouette resurfaced from within the earth, the saber held in his right hand lunging for Yao Shen's chest.

Yao Shen caught the saber's blow with his left hand, the blade not even a Peak-Nascent Soul Weapon and thus unable to pierce his soul. Without further ado, he knocked the elder out and tossed him aside like a ragdoll, continuing to walk forward.

Twenty li ahead, amidst the burning landscape, a contingent of heavily weakened elders gazed at the approaching Soul Emperor with mixed emotions— awe, shock, begrudging respect and dread, all blending together in a confused entanglement. As if they didn't know what to feel at the display of power that was unfolding in front of them. A third of the elders were still unconscious, while the rest were barely in any condition to fight— Yao Shen could easily finish them off, but he knew that the fight was not over yet.

A man dressed in vivid red robes with golden embroidery stepped forward, his expression placid as he let out a light sigh. "You all shall yield. This duel will be decided between the two of us," Lei Weiyuan, Patriarch of the Sacred Flame Palace commanded, even to those belonging to the Divine Mountain Sect.

Most of the elders had defiant expressions of their faces, but not a single one spoke out against the Patriarch's orders. To yield without fighting was shameful for a cultivator, but to continue fighting a duel where one was vastly outmatched was outright disgraceful— the elders were not hot-blooded youths who could not accept reality for what it was. One of the Patriarchs was unconscious, and the strongest among them had been bested without managing to leave a scratch on Yao Shen's soul.

Their role in this fight was over.

"I yield."

"I yield."

"I yield."

Their voices rang out one after the other, and they soon departed to heal those who had been injured in the battle.

Only Yao Shen and Lei Weiyuan remained on the battlefield.

"Is this your doing?" Yao Shen asked, gesturing at the burning landscape— the ideal condition for a fire cultivator to engage in combat.

"Perhaps," Lei Weiyuan replied, revealing a slight smile.

The world seemed to still for a moment as the two Patriarchs thought back upon their rivalry and the events that led up to this moment, before two domineering voices rang out, roughly at the same time,

"Domain: Sacred Bird, Marayan"
"Domain of Illusory Shadows"

Yao Shen unleashed his domain— imposing his will over the natural law that governed Eliria, proclaiming that the surrounding territory fell under his dominion. Within his domain, Yao Shen was the sovereign— any foreign entity that dared to encroach upon his territory would face suppression from the laws of Wind, Water and Shadow, restricting them from taking flight or tunneling through the ground unless they were able to escape its sphere of influence.

Or so it should have been.

For Yao Shen's claim had just been contested.

The flames burning in the vicinity stilled in abeyance, before flooding toward Lei Weiyuan from every direction, acknowledging his authority over the laws of fire. The moment the flames entered Lei Weiyuan's sphere of influence, they started roiling and shifting until they reshaped into a vague outline of a two-winged bird. With every passing second, the image grew clearer until a majestic bird of prey blossomed into sight, two of its hawkish eyes trained on Lei Weiyuan, while the third eye that rested upon its forehead remained solely focused on Yao Shen. Characterized by long, broad wings, a protruding, curved beak and razor-sharp talons, the flaming bird was an imitation of the Sacred Bird, Marayan— a now-extinct spiritual beast that is still worshipped as one of the guardians of the Sacred Flame Palace.

Soon the sky was dotted with dozens of imitations of the Sacred Bird, Yao Shen's ghastly visage reflected in the birds' third eye as they circled around him with a mighty flap of their wings — the motion so perfect, it was almost lifelike.

Yao Shen had chosen to respond with one of his Patchwork Domains, namely, the Domain of Illusory Shadows. The Minor Dao of Mist, a subset of the Major Dao of Water, engulfed the surrounding land with a curtain of heavy, churning grey mists that obfuscated sight— heading right for Patriarch Lei Weiyuan. The Minor Dao of Water, which referred to an elementary understanding of water manipulation, was employed to rapidly shape Water Qi into humanoid constructs that resembled the dimensions of Yao Shen's physical body. The Minor Dao of Shadow formed the exterior of the water body, coating it in a thin layer of Shadow Qi, and finally, Yao Shen's Major Dao of Wind was unleashed. A moment later, each of the illusory clones dual-wielded two sharp wind blades that were empowered by a sizable portion of Yao Shen's Wind Qi reserves.

The Domain of Illusory Shadows was one of the reasons why Yao Shen's resourcefulness and ingenuity as a cultivator was respected, the original iteration utilizing four Minor Daos to create an effect that was greater than the sum of its parts. Mist obscured sight, serving as the foundation for the domain. Water comprised the clone's interior, known for its regenerative abilities, while Shadow comprised the exterior, acknowledged for its ability to dampen divine sense. The resonance between mist and water meant that the clones could utilize the Mists to regenerate, while Wind, an element Yao Shen was most familiar with, was used to deliver the final blow.

However, the current iteration of his domain was imbalanced. The three Minor Daos struggled to contain the sheer potency of the Major Dao of Wind and Yao Shen's attempt to suppress or outright shatter Lei Weiyuan's Sacred Bird Domain failed. This was the reason why the elders had not unleashed their domains in unison at the very outset of the battle— the weaker ones would simply shatter upon contact, while the rest would inadvertently clash with one another.

Each of Yao Shen's illusory clones flickered to life as a thread of divine sense linked them to himself, splitting up and silently receding within the mists now that a direct confrontation was inevitable.

On one side lay the vulturous flaming birds, patiently waiting for an opportunity to strike. In juxtaposition, the roiling mists drew nearer to Lei Weiyuan with every passing breath— both the Patriarchs waging an invisible battle with an intention to suppress the other's domains, but ultimately failing to gain an upper hand.

Lei Weiyuan chose to be the first to break the deadlock, pressured by Yao Shen's encroachment. Since he had reshaped the divine birds from the aftermath of Yao Shen's duel with the elders, his Fire Qi reserves had largely remained untouched.

Lei Weiyuan approached the limits of his abilities as he frenziedly invested his Fire Qi to elevate the flames of each Sacred Bird to a new realm, their silhouettes warping and destabilizing a few times before he managed to regain control. Now that he had made the decision to finally act, there was no hesitation— the Sacred Birds, which had been stealthily building up reserves of concentrated flame, reared their head in Yao Shen's direction before unleashing a torrent of orange-red flames that ruthlessly tore holes in the cloud of grey mists, instantly vaporizing it upon contact.

The illusory clones had barely left a sound as they weaved through the mists like specters, using the Major Dao of Wind in bursts to amplify their speed. However, the Sacred Bird's flames were spread out enough that a quarter of the illusory clones were caught in the blast radius, attempting to buffet the fiery inferno with their wind blades— a valiant, but ultimately futile effort.

Yao Shen's fury was reignited as he felt his connection with a quarter of his clones being severed, Lei Weiyuan exploiting the weakness in his domain to suppress and weaken his sphere of influence. Yao Shen's response was almost instantaneous, a harsh, whistling sound echoing out as the illusory clones rapidly consumed their reserves of Wind Qi before releasing two arcing wind blades in unison.

The Sacred Birds immediately split off in an attempt to evade the volley of wind blades heading for them, but Lei Weiyuan had not expected Yao Shen's counter to be so swift. The wind blades blurred forward at a blistering pace, instantaneously bisecting a third of the Sacred Birds in half before the residual winds scattered the remaining flames.

Lei Weiyuan's expression turned grim as he felt his sphere of influence weaken, but his initial objective had been met. Yao Shen repeatedly attempted to reform the curtain of mists that concealed his illusory clones, but ultimately, the Minor Dao of Mist had no way of resisting the might of the Major Dao of Fire — the ambient temperature had been raised to a point where his mist cloud was forced to continuously shrink.

A majority of Yao Shen's illusory clones were now exposed, and it was not an opportunity Lei Weiyuan could afford to miss.

The Sacred Birds flapped their wings before breaking out into a dive, careening toward the illusory clones from different angles — reaching the pinnacle of their speed as they headed toward the ground like a flaming meteor. Mists instantly vaporized upon coming into contact with the Sacred Birds, leaving a trail of flames in their wake as they came crashing down.

A few of the Sacred Birds opted for speed over Qi-empowered attacks, attempting to claw the illusory clones' head off, only to be parried by wind blades. Some waited to cover the distance, before discharging a gout of flames at close range. The illusory clones either evaded or chose to directly confront the flames— some succeeding in their attempt to buffet the winds until they directly managed to strike the Sacred Bird, while a few misjudged the timing and perished.

Dozens of battles were fought simultaneously, Lei Weiyuan's fist clenched as he bore the strain of orchestrating a multitude of skirmishes at once. On the other hand, Yao Shen was completely relaxed as he manipulated his illusory clones to scatter one Sacred Bird after the other with almost mechanical precision, barely feeling the strain of controlling them in his soul form.

A few minutes later, over a third of Yao Shen's clones remained standing, while Lei Weiyuan was down to a mere pittance of four Sacred Birds. He panted heavily as his gaze fell upon the small cloud of mists that still remained, Yao Shen still not having chosen to show himself. His Fire Qi reserves were on the verge of exhaustion, his divine sense almost entirely spent, a solemn expression on his face as he analyzed the situation. The aftermath of their battle had left the landscape ablaze, deep incisions carved into the face of the earth by awry wind blades.

Among the myriad reasons for Lei Weiyuan's defeat, one of them had been the versatility of Yao Shen's domain, brought along by the humanoid form he had chosen to adopt for his clones. Yet, there was a reason why Lei Weiyuan had modelled his domain after the guardian beast of his sect— a very important, and fundamental reason.

A domain was the imposition of one's will over the natural law of Eliria, yet there was no necessity upon the form or method one utilized to impose their will. Lei Weiyuan, as a cultivator brought up in the Sacred Flame Palace, had been taught of the Legend of Marayan from a very young age. The fabled spiritual beast once renowned as the Emperor of All Flames had not been seen upon the continent of Ionea for centuries, but the disciples of the Sacred Flame Palace believed that Marayan would return if their sect was ever reduced to the verge of destruction. For there was a very specific aspect of Marayan's fable that gave credence to this belief...

Lei Weiyuan's eyes shone with an intense glint that bordered upon the verge of madness, as he boldly proclaimed five words that left even Yao Shen shocked.

"Domain: Sacred Bird Marayan, Rebirth."

For a moment, it felt as if time itself had been reversed— two streaks of blood leaked from Lei Weiyuan's eyes, his expression rapidly paling as he stretched his control, his dominion over the fire element beyond what should have been possible. The flames scattered in the surrounding landscape immediately responded to his call, a rapidly ballooning sphere of flames forming above him that started to shape itself into a two winged, three eyed bird that eclipsed even Yao Shen's soul form— easily three times the size.

Perhaps Lei Weiyuan's faith would never be rewarded, but his belief certainly was.

The thirty-foot-tall flaming bird caused the observing Sacred Flame Palace elders' breath to seize, their attention mesmerized as they gaped at the awe-inspiring sight— for a moment, it was as if they were transported in time to the pinnacle of the Sacred Flame Palace's existence.

Then the dream ended.

A sigh echoed out behind Lei Weiyuan, as Yao Shen, dressed in satin-white robes, held the tip of his sword at his throat. The cloud of mists that Lei Weiyuan believed Yao Shen to be hiding within scattered, revealing another one of his illusory clones.

"Admirably fought, Brother Lei. But this fight is *over*." Yao Shen's tone was one of solemn respect, as he gazed at the almost fully formed Sacred Bird one last time, before he contested Lei Weiyuan's control with his own understanding of the laws of fire. The flaming bird rapidly warped, before losing its form entirely— one half of the sacred bird forcibly torn away using Yao Shen's Major Dao of Fire.

Lei Weiyuan stood in silence as the flames rained down around him, his hands trembling from over-exerting his abilities before he let out a weary sigh.

"We yield. The duel is yours," The words were announced loudly despite Lei Weiyuan's exhaustion, and for a moment, even Yao Shen couldn't believe what he was hearing.

The duel was over.

He..... had won.

25

FOUNDATION

THE CORE FORMATION guardian of the Divine Mountain Sect who held the peak-quality communication mirror in his hands had an increasingly stupefied expression on his face as he watched Yao Shen tear through his Patriarch's indomitable Divine Mountain Domain with his physical strength alone, a shocking feat that threatened to shatter the guardian's worldview.

He watched as the assault led by the fearsome Elder Yongliang of the Sacred Flame Palace was dispatched with ease, Yao Shen walking out unscathed from the encirclement.

And finally, he watched as the Sacred Bird Marayan was reborn anew, the thirty-foot-tall flaming bird sending waves of terror down his spine. The revelation that Patriarch Lei Weiyuan was capable of such a feat would normally be a grave threat to the Divine Mountain Sect's longevity, but in that moment, the guardian watched on with hope— only to watch Yao Shen ruthlessly tear the Sacred Bird, symbolizing the glory of the Sacred Flame Palace, *in half.*

Panic welled up in the guardian's heart, not having prepared for an outcome where the combined might of the two hegemons of the Azlak Plains…lost. Twenty-two elders and two Patriarchs losing against *one* cultivator, Soul Emperor or not, was not an outcome one could prepare for— not an outcome that should have been possible. The guardian was the son of Elder Junjie, the elder that had harried Yao Shen with attacks from beneath the earth, and thus had almost complete access to the sect records— no such feat had been recorded in the known history of Azlak Plains before.

His instinctive knee-jerk reaction was to shatter the communication mirror— as one deeply loyal to his sect, the very thought of submitting to another filled him with *utter* revulsion, and the oaths had not been sworn yet. *All was not lost.... Not yet.*

A firm hand clamped down his shoulder, startling Guardian Shihong since he hadn't detected any movement in the vicinity. Zhou Hui stood next to him, his expression almost as stunned as the guardian himself, uttering two words that smothered any final thoughts of resistance he held in his heart.

"Keep recording."

Half an hour passed as the elders from both the sects took time to recuperate, some consuming healing pills while others sat down in a meditative posture to replenish their Qi. Yao Shen stood by his lonesome in the center of the devastated clearing, displaying no impatience at the elders' actions— No cultivator enjoyed remaining in a vulnerable position outside the bounds of their sect, especially not those who had managed to cultivate all the way to the coveted Sect Elder position.

Only after all the elders had recovered enough strength to be comfortable in combat did they hesitantly shamble forward in Yao Shen's direction.

The world exploded in color as Yao Shen activated his human sight, despite the elders' attempt to restrain and conceal their emotional state. A dense cloud of uncertainty swirled around the elders, its bleak greyness consuming all other emotions that it encountered in its path, before they had a chance to fully form.

Yao Shen saw a flickering red cloud that represented the emotion 'anger' being consumed by the cloud of grey mists, replaced by the seemingly all-pervasive 'uncertainty' that dominated the landscape. The elder in question was pragmatic enough to understand that as one who broke the deadlock between the three hegemons of the Azlak Plains, Yao Shen had been far too reasonable in his response. A newly ascended Soul Emperor wielding the power of the Esoteric Daos could easily kill two Nascent Soul Patriarchs belonging to rival sects without facing any real repercussions from the righteous path.

But Yao Shen had not gone down the bloody path of suppression through strength, instead choosing to shatter the established status quo.

For one accustomed to anticipating deception and subterfuge with every word, every step and every action their rival took, *kindness* was truly their greatest weakness. The rivalry between righteous path sects seldom devolved into open conflict, but that did not mean it was any less cutthroat. The Azlak Plains may be considered a small territory, but that size was only relative to the rest of Ionea— Natural Treasures, hidden inheritances, spiritual ore veins, rare spiritual herbs were dotted across the land, and each hegemon strived to monopolize the resource before their rivals got a wind of it. However, the existence of spy networks like the Heavenly Sky Sect's Faceless ultimately made most such attempts futile, forcing the three hegemons to devise a solution. This was why disciples fought over resource points in place of the elders, and although killing was frowned upon, many ancient inheritances had methods to render divine sense ineffective— effectively nullifying the ability of the elders to pry within the inheritance grounds.

This was why, even when confronted with Yao Shen's mercy,

none of the elders of the Divine Mountain Sect and the Sacred Flame Palace held any gratitude toward Yao Shen. Each of them held their own theories and rationalizations behind Yao Shen's unprecedented actions, yet the obvious truth continued to elude them— for an action borne out of goodwill and a desire for betterment was no different from irrationality in their calculating, utilitarian mindsets.

All that remained was uncertainty, tinged with a feeling of loss.

While the other elders slowly inched forward in Yao Shen's direction, some feigning injuries while others openly wore their conflicted emotions upon their faces, one man broke away from the pack.

Elder Yongliang walked toward Yao Shen with a poised gait, his head held high as his proud gaze met Yao Shen's. There was no arrogance held within those plain brown eyes, but at the same time, the elder felt no discomfort at his loss, and no shame at his prized spear, which he held in his right hand, having its divine sense brand shattered.

The clouds of uncertainty held no sway over Elder Yongliang as he continued to walk forward until only a few meters separated him from Yao Shen. A vibrant orange cloud had almost entirely enveloped the elder in its embrace, growing larger with every passing second, representing the emotion '*determination.*'

Despite being completely bested in combat, confronted by a force that exceeded the realm of his understanding, the determination in Elder Yongliang's heart burned with the same intensity as the flames he held dominion over.

Yao Shen could not remain unmoved in the face of such staunch determination, in part because Elder Yongliang's resolve was reminiscent of his own. Fate had pitted them as enemies, and while it remained to be seen if they could co-exist as allies, the very possibility alone was quite unprecedented.

"As the defeated in this duel, I, Yongliang Luo, shall honor the conditions set by the victor," he proclaimed, his words spoken boldly without any hesitation. To the elders who were yet to come to terms with their new reality, his words echoed out like the thunderous claps of descending heavenly tribulation— shocking them out of their reverie.

Yao Shen gave him a curt nod before he began reciting the words of the oath. "Yongliang Luo, do you, upon your honor, swear your loyalty to the newly established Modern Sect?"

"I, Yongliang Luo, swear my loyalty to the Modern Sect upon my honor as a cultivator of the righteous path."

"Yongliang Luo. do you, upon your honor, swear not to betray the interests of the newly established Modern Sect unless the Sect by its direct actions, betrays your trust first?"

"I, Yongliang Luo, swear not to betray the interests of the Modern Sect unless I am given reason to believe that the Sect, by its direct actions, has betrayed my trust first."

Yao Shen gave him another nod, shattering the divine sense brand he had left on his spear with a thought.

"Bow before your Patriarch," Yao Shen's voice boomed out with authority, attracting the attention of all the elders in presence, including the ones from the Heavenly Sky Sect.

They watched with bated breath as history itself was being forged in front of their eyes, some elders watching with a faint flicker of hope in their heart— hoping that the prideful Yongliang Luo would refuse to bow, hoping for something, *anything,* to buy them more time.

Unfortunately, their hopes were destined to be shattered.

Yongliang Luo gave Yao Shen a light bow, low enough to be respectful, yet not reverent in the slightest.

"Rise as an Elder of the Modern Sect."

Yongliang Luo complied, his expression inscrutable as he uttered the words, "Grand Patriarch."

"Elder," Yao Shen acknowledged, and Yongliang Luo took his position at his side.

The remaining elders, bound by the terms of the duel that had been witnessed by all three hegemons of the Azlak Plains and the Eastern Righteous Path Alliance, gave up the final embers of resistance that they held in their hearts as they stepped forward, one after the other.

. . . .

"Rise as an Elder of the Modern Sect."

. . . .

"Rise as an Elder of the Modern Sect."

. . . .

"Rise as an Elder of the Modern Sect."

A heavy, oppressive silence blanketed the clearing as the Elders of the Sacred Flame Palace and the Divine Mountain Sect stood behind Yao Shen, their expressions solemn as their gazes gathered upon the only two remaining cultivators that stood opposing Yao Shen.

The Patriarch of the Sacred Flame Palace. Lei Weiyuan.

The Patriarch of the Divine Mountain Sect, Kang Long.

Yao Shen's human sight instinctively shifted to the two Patriarchs. No trace of surprise reflected upon his face when he found himself unable to detect any clouds of emotions surrounding them. Their sharp, intelligent gazes met his own, no longer containing arrogance befitting their position, yet exposing no hint of weakness or subservience either. As Patriarchs, their actions were directly tied to the wellbeing of their sects— making it only natural that they would spare no effort to ensure that their emotional state could not be deduced. .

But Yao Shen did not require his human sight to understand the two Patriarchs' emotions. Instead, he needed only ask himself what he would feel if the same thing happened to him. How he would feel if his foundation, the synthesis of his life's pursuit was laid claim upon by another? The sect where his master, a mighty elder, had taken a gamble upon a non-legacy family disciple with limited talent, now lost, owed loyalty to another.

Regret. Frustration. Anger. Shame.

But not hatred. His own pride would not allow himself to hate the victor of an honorable duel wherein the odds were weighed in his favor. The pride of a Patriarch, both a great strength and an exposed weakness.

Yao Shen's gaze shifted to the elders behind him, the clouds of grey mists representing the emotion 'uncertainty' only grown denser as they watched with apprehension, and he could not help but think how apt the color 'gray' was to describe the relationship between the three hegemons of the Azlak Plains.

Immediately after his ascension, Yao Shen had immediately confronted the two Patriarchs for their sins, which had included the assassination of an elder. Undoubtedly a grave sin, if the truth had ever been so straightforward. The elder in question, Elder Shirong, had climbed his way to the position with the aid of the Zhu family. While both Yao Shen and Elder Shirong were non-legacy family disciples, there had been no solidarity between them— while Yao Shen had attained great power while preserving his honor and dignity, Elder Shirong's personality seemed to grow more belligerent and vengeful with every rank he climbed. After all, not all reacted to power equally— and as long as Elder Shirong's ire was concentrated upon the rivals of the Heavenly Sky Sect, the Zhu family saw no reason to interfere.

Ultimately, Elder Shirong ended up violating one of the unwritten rules of the righteous path— in his grudge with Elder Yongnian of the Divine Mountain Sect, he had slain his nephew, Guardian Huiqing. The Divine Mountain Sect was naturally furious beyond reasoning, and the Sacred Flame Palace saw an opportunity to weaken the Heavenly Sky Sect. A few years later, he was assassinated by an encirclement of four elders from the two sects, and it was rumored that Elder Yongnian himself landed the finishing blow— revenge had taken its time, but it had eventually caught up.

Who was in the right, and who was in the wrong?

From Yao Shen's perspective as Patriarch, the life of a Nascent Soul expert had been traded for a core formation guardian. While there was no love lost between Elder Shirong and him, as Patriarch, he was obligated to demand an answer. Was Elder Shirong the one in the wrong, then? Yao Shen, in the two hundred years he had lived in Eliria, had come to understand that in the world of cultivation, nothing was ever as simple as it seemed. Yao Shen had his suspicions, for whilst power had the ability to corrupt even the purest of hearts, it did not turn the competent incompetent.

There existed certain cultivation techniques that were not demonic in nature, but still frowned upon within the righteous path— increasing the strain on the cultivator's Dantian that continuously allowed them to exhibit power beyond one's threshold and advance through the stages faster at the cost of future potential. Such a technique would never be given to the Zhu family's own, but Elder Shirong was merely an outsider, recruited up from a mortal village after his talent for cultivation was unearthed— much like Yao Shen himself. While these cultivation techniques could not change one's personality entirely, the erosion of one's Dantian in the early stages of cultivation could easily affect a cultivator's emotions, making him more irritable and angry. Over time, this effect would only amplify— while he could not say for certain, it was a plausible explanation.

Then, was Elder Yongnian's decision to kill Elder Shirong in his quest for revenge the correct one? The answer to that lay in another question: was justice only the prerogative of the strong? Had it been any other guardian that died at the hands of Elder Shirong, the Divine Mountain Sect would have settled the matter after receiving reparations from the Heavenly Sky Sect.

Who was in the right, and who was in the wrong?

As Patriarch of the Divine Mountain Sect stepped forward with a resolute expression etched upon his face, Yao Shen realized that despite his understanding of the Esoteric Human Dao, he had no answer to that question. Everything was simply... gray.

Yao Shen dwelled on such complex thoughts no longer as Kang Long approached, his every step sending a pang of regret coursing through the Divine Mountain Sect Elders— for in mere moments, their sect, their home, would exist no longer.

Kang Long stopped a few meters away from Yao Shen, his expression stony and his fist lightly clenched as his gaze fell upon the elders of his sect, now standing at the command of another.

Yao Shen let a moment in silence pass, a sign of respect, to differentiate his oath from the rest of the elders, before he began reciting the words.

"Kang Long, do you, upon your honor, swear your loyalty to the newly established Modern Sect?"

His clenched fist tightened, but ultimately, he did not dishonor the agreement.

"Yes."

The remaining words of the oath of first betrayal were recited, and unsurprisingly, Kang Long once again agreed.

"Bow before your Patriarch," Yao Shen's voice boomed out with aplomb, and with it, the hearts of the Divine Mountain Sect shattered as their Patriarch bowed before another.

"Rise as the Earth Patriarch of the Modern Sect," he declared, and Kang Long complied, before taking his place at his side, half a step behind him.

The same terms of the oath were recited to Patriarch Lei Weiyuan, who betrayed no trace of his true emotions through his body language or expression.

Once again, hearts were shattered as the Patriarch of the Sacred Flame Palace bowed before another.

"Rise as the Flame Patriarch of the Modern Sect," he proclaimed, the intoxicating, heady rush of power imbued within his declaration.

Lei Weiyuan moved to stand at his side, and finally, the formation was complete— Yao Shen stood at the forefront of the congregation, twenty-two elders proficient in multiple Major Daos arrayed behind him. To his left, was his Earth Patriarch, Kang Long, a master of defense and entrapment. To his right, was the Flame Patriarch, Lei Weiyuan, a master of offense and destruction. This represented only two-thirds of the power of the Modern Sect, a force that could no longer be ignored.

Yao Shen finally uttered the words, as the reserve elders along with Zhou Hui and his contingent watched from a distance, the words that the masters of the Azlak Plains believed that they would never hear in their lifespans:

"I, Yao Shen, with the heavens as my witness, hereby declare the Heavenly Sky Sect, Divine Mountain Sect and the Sacred Flame Palace's forces to be united as one under the banner of the Modern Sect, the now undisputed rulers of the Azlak Plains, with the power vested in me as the Grand Patriarch."

26

SKY

ZHOU HUI silently observed as the cultivator whom he had considered a rival not long ago now stood at the helm of a procession that represented the combined forces of the Sacred Flame Palace and the Divine Mountain Sect— a feat that should have been unimaginable in and of itself.

He watched as Lei Weiyuan and Kang Long, both revered cultivators who had stood at the apex of their respective sects, acknowledged their allegiance to another. It was not, however, the exhilarating thrill of victory that greeted him, but rather vexingly, Zhou Hui realized that he shared more in common with the defeated. As the scion of the Hui Family, Lei Weiyuan and Kang Long were both adversaries he had studied thoroughly, designed countermeasures against, and ultimately, if the situation between the three hegemons of the Azlak Plains ever devolved into an open war, prepared to kill. It would not be incorrect to state that Lei Weiyuan and Kang Long had some influence in shaping the cultivator he was today, acting as an external stimulus that constantly pressured him to hone his Dao of the Wind— lest he be left behind, outmatched and deemed unworthy in the pursuit of power that cultivation was.

When Yao Shen had easily crushed the two Patriarchs, he had also, inadvertently, defeated Zhou Hui yet again.

The defeat of ambition.

Bitterness. Resentment. Frustration.

These were the emotions Zhou Hui ought to have felt, *yet...* when his gaze fell upon Yao Shen's satin-white robes that symbolized the dawn of a new era, he found himself unable to muster such small, petty emotions in face of such a grand accomplishment. The unification of the Azlak Plains, fulfilling the unspoken wish of the bygone ancestors of the Heavenly Sky Sect— Zhou Hui realized that, buried deep within his heart, a flicker of excitement had ignited as he witnessed Yao Shen led the procession of Elders. The youthful exuberance he had believed to be all but lost once again flowed through his old bones. For, as long as he had known, Zhou Hui had been the metaphorical 'sky'--- talent, background and inheritance— of these three core pillars that elevated a cultivator in their path to power, he lacked none. As a Peak Nascent Soul Stage cultivator, he had reached the ceiling of the Azlak Plains.

Or so, at least, had he believed— until Yao Shen tore the sky asunder by ascending to the Soul Emperor stage. The revelation had come at a price, for Yao Shen had proven to be a herald of change. However, as Zhou Hui's gaze shifted to the elders of the two sects, he could see it in their eyes... the concealed, yet definite, yearning for power. For all whom were present upon this day had gotten a taste of a Soul Emperor's power, and as influential cultivators, it was engrained in their very nature to desire it for themselves. The prison of belief would no longer able to cage their ambition— for one amongst their own, a vagrant cultivator of the Azlak Plains lacking both talent and background had done what they all believed impossible.

Zhou Hui found his anticipation only growing as he thought back upon Yao Shen's promise to help the legacy families unearth the inheritance left behind by their ancestors. If Yao Shen stood true to his word, would the inheritance be enough to give him the confidence to ascend to the Soul Emperor stage?

The distant, forlorn dream of ascension no longer seemed so implausible, after all.

"Cultivators of the Modern Sect, heed my edict!" Yao Shen's voice sounded out with a regal dignity that it had lacked before, his words carrying the confidence and weight of a monarch.

"Grand Patriarch!" echoed out their reply in unison, from the reserve elders of the Heavenly Sky Sect to the three Patriarchs in attendance— for Yao Shen had truly earned the right to be addressed with such prestige.

"Sky Patriarch, Zhou Hui," Yao Shen addressed first, prompting Zhou Hui to approach the procession of elders.

A few moments later, Zhou Hui stood facing Yao Shen, the two old rivals sharing a moment of silence before Yao Shen passed his edict.

"You shall return to the Sky Division of the Modern Sect along with Elder Jie Tang. Inform the sect of my triumph, and let it be known that the Azlak Plains now stand united under the banner of our sect. The affairs of the sect shall be yours to manage, but so will the responsibility for its safety. Do not let down your guard, and do not underestimate the treachery of the demonic sects," Yao Shen proclaimed.

"Yes, Grand Patriarch," Zhou Hui acknowledged with a light bow, the motion meeting surprisingly little resistance from his own pride, now that he had come to acknowledge Yao Shen as the *cautious* hope of the Azlak Plains. He then took his place at Yao

Shen's side, waiting for the edict to reach its conclusion before he departed.

"Elder Meili Zhu. Elder Zixin Ren." Yao Shen called out two names in succession, not having to wait long for a woman in her mid-thirties and a bald old man with bronzed skin who was grinning from ear to ear to blur forward into his sight.

"Since we are now amongst friends…" Yao Shen began, his words clearly referencing the contingent of defeated elders that stood behind him, "…let us speak freely. Meili?"

"Yes, Grand Patriarch?" The Patriarch of the Zhu Family, her usually gentle, playful voice now strained, carrying an underlying tone of respect that was lacking earlier.

"Do we have an estimate for the Flame and Earth Division's respective treasuries?" Yao Shen did not dance around the topic, choosing to cut directly to the heart of the matter.

A cloud of the emotion 'surprise' wrapped around Meili Zhu as she immediately understood his intentions. Without tarrying, she replied, "As you mentioned, Grand Patriarch, the former Heavenly Sky Sect, Sacred Flame Palace and the Divine Mountain Sect were centuries-old rivals. We have clashed over many resource points over the past decades, and a majority of the resources required for each sect's cultivation are not secret. Given all those factors, as Master of the Skyless Hall, I am confident in giving you an assessment for each sect's respective treasury," Meili Zhu replied, her coy smile returning at the expense of the uncomfortable expressions of the defeated elders. What Meili had conveniently left out was that espionage, namely by the Faceless under her command, had played a major role in her information-gathering activities.

"How confident are you in the accuracy of this estimate?" Yao Shen asked, unsurprised by her response. Given the long history and the rivalry between the three sects, it was only natural that they would extensively monitor their rivals' activities.

"I am certain that there should be no major discrepancies between my estimate and the contents of the treasuries, Grand Patriarch," Meili Zhu replied gracefully, but Yao Shen could clearly sense her amusement as the expressions of the elders further blanched.

"How soon can you procure this estimate?"

"Within a day, Grand Patriarch."

"Very well. Elder Meili, would you be willing to accompany me to the Flame Division of the Modern Sect, provided that I guarantee your safety?"

"It would be an honor, Grand Patriarch."

Yao Shen nodded, satisfied. He clearly sensed the growing discomfort amongst the elders, and decided to address the matter now instead of letting them stew in their discomfort. "Do not worry, Elders. The Modern Sect has no desire to claim what is yours, and neither is it a desire for resources that drives us. Your personal resources, inheritances, techniques, ancestral weapons and any other manner of wealth you possess shall remain your own, entirely untouched. The Sect Treasury shall be managed with my oversight, to ensure that the resources are equitably distributed amongst those who prove themselves worthy. However, be warned— any attempt to siphon wealth from the treasury that is not your own will be met with consequences, and few have the ability to conceal the truth in front of my eyes."

A few relieved looks were exchanged between the elders, as the worst-case scenario for them had just been averted. Having placated the elders for now, Yao Shen's gaze shifted to the Ren Family reserve elder.

"Elder Zixin Ren, will you and your contingent accompany us to the Flame Division of the Modern Sect?" Yao Shen requested more so than commanded, not willing to prod the powder keg any more than absolutely necessary.

Zixin Ren broke out into a delighted laugh before replying

with enthusiasm that was unbecoming his age, "Grand Patriarch, this old man would be delighted to follow you to the depths of the Bloodsoul Forest."

To Zixin Ren and the rest of the reserve elders, the joy of seeing their old rivals be crushed so one-sidedly was alone enough to absolve most of the ill-will brought on from being on opposing sides of the political spectrum. To enter the inner halls of the Sacred Flame Palace, which were forbidden grounds for a cultivator of the Heavenly Sky Sect, as visitors … few things in the world could bring the jaded reserve elders more satisfaction.

Yao Shen gave him a curt nod before he made the final announcement of the day. "Earth Patriarch Kang Long, you may order your elders to return to the sect and wait for our arrival. You shall accompany us, along with Flame Patriarch Lei Weiyuan and the Elders of the Flame Division to the former Sacred Flame Palace, where we shall debate upon the future direction of the Modern Sect."

Things progressed relatively smoothly after Yao Shen's announcement, as the former Divine Mountain Sect elders departed in order to make sure the sect was not susceptible to an attack, while three Patriarchs including Yao Shen, the elders of the former Sacred Flame Palace, Meili Zhu and the reserve elders, headed for the land that once served as the abode of the mythical bird of legend, Marayan.

27

SERIS VILLAGE

THE JOURNEY to the Sacred Flame Palace passed by largely uneventfully as Yao Shen and the contingent of elders made their way through the grassy, open fields of the Azlak Plains. Any spiritual beast in their vicinity would instinctively flee upon sensing the torrential concentration of Qi headed in its direction, the wide swathes of lightly forested land offering little in the way of concealment.

The geographical layout of the Azlak Plains made it more accessible to weaker cultivators who lacked the ability to perceive their surroundings via divine sense, for one could easily spot an approaching spiritual beast far in advance. That, however, did not mean that the region was free of danger— for the more powerful Spiritual Beasts remained sequestered within the depths of the Nayun Forest, rulers of their own bountiful kingdoms that lacked in neither Natural Treasures nor valuable spiritual herbs; also the primary reason why Elvenhold held the Azlak Plains in such high regard.

The Beast Emperors, a title given to Spiritual Beasts that had cultivated all the way to the Nascent Soul level and achieved sapience, retaliation was as cunning as it was brutal— every few decades, the Beast Emperors would cull the weakest amongst their pack by commanding them to charge headlong into the human lands.

Led by Beast Emperors that were on the verge of exhausting their lifespans, the Beast Tide would ravage everything in its path — many mortal villages extinguished in the blink of an eye. Whilst the resources of the Nayun Forest were plentiful, the three hegemons of the Azlak Plains could not allow such a valuable source of wealth to go untapped— resulting in the conflict of interest between the Spiritual Beasts and the Cultivators of the Azlak Plains.

The Gorge of Death, The Labyrinth of the Ancient Chen Clan, the purported inheritance grounds of the legacy families— the Azlak Plains had no dearth of opportunity or danger, though ultimately, the region was vast while the population of cultivators remained tiny in comparison. Though each hegemon had held dreams of expansion, many secrets remained unearthed and sizable sections of the map had grown obsolete with time— for this was a land that had once supported numerous sects and clans, now reduced to a shell of its former glory.

Most cultivators, however, could traverse the Azlak Plains as long as they maintained the due diligence required of a cultivator. For while Spiritual Beasts were a long-standing threat, only the young and the foolish amongst their pack would dare venture alone into the open grasslands of the Azlak Plains, only to be confronted by the bitter truth that the law of the jungle did not apply in face of a group of cultivators that desired its beast core.

The vigilance of patrolling cultivators combined with the value of spiritual beast cores, meat and other byproducts ensured that any wandering beast would be swiftly hunted down by the first sect whose disciple spotted it in the wild. This allowed the mortal villages of Azlak Plains, which were mainly situated near one of the three former hegemons, the subordinate sects and a few near the Grand Sealing Formation, to exist and live their lives out in relative peace.

Yao Shen's eyes gleamed with interest as he spotted one of those very mortal villages ahead, gently stopping mid-flight as he stopped to examine the structure from afar. Sharpened wooden spikes had been dug around the perimeter of the village, the trunk of a young tree cut down and repurposed for each one that jutted out. It only took one glance for Yao Shen to discern that it was the work of mortals, an impassioned, if ineffective attempt at dissuading weaker spiritual beasts from approaching. The smooth, reinforced grey stone wall that traced the elliptical circumference of the village without any chips or breaks in between barring the village entrance formed the second barrier that any invader would have to overcome— far more effective at its intended purpose.

His divine sense swept through the village, easily identifying a little over a thousand villagers as they went about their duties— weary, bedraggled men dressed in overalls returning after having spent the majority of the day toiling in the fields whilst hawkers attempted to attract their attention with their ever-enthusiastic spiels, offering a wide variety of goods that ranged from farming implements and crude mortal weaponry to a small selection of cured meats likely supplied to them by the Sacred Flame Palace. The women of the village had busied themselves in disciplines that were equally important in keeping the small economy of the village functioning— Yao Shen observed as an aged woman deftly knitted together a sweater in preparation for colder weather, her skill acquired through years or perhaps decades of practice. Another more enterprising woman, a young maiden in her early twenties, stir-fried lean cuts of meat in a seasoned wok, much to the delight of the two hungry children that peered at her with mesmerized expressions on their faces, from their seats at the wooden stall's counter. Their parents, on the other hand, could not help but smile lightly at the brother-sister duo and their antics— the meat supplied by the Sacred Flame Palace was likely spiritual beast meat of the lowest grade that had either lost its efficacy with time or due to improper storage, but for mortal villagers, it was a delicacy that they were grateful for, the contented smiles of the mother and father saying as much.

The village spoke of a life of the happiness and contentment brought from a simple life of hard work, but not all was so idealistic in practice. Without any water or earth cultivators within the village, the sanitation practices remained primitive. While even the weakest of cultivators were immune to mundane afflictions, the same could not be said about mortals, who comprised the majority of the human population. And when it came to the village's defenses, they were laughable— no stone wall could stop any real threat, especially not a spiritual beast, whose true threat could not be assessed by cultivation level alone. For the beasts had many treacherous abilities, some boasting sharp claws that could alone rend a cultivator's blade into pieces, while a few others even had the ability to secrete poison that could kill a cultivator instantly.

In actuality, the sole foundation establishment Flame Cultivator that was cultivating in the village elder's residence was the only true defense the mortal village had, his role to alert the sect in case a spiritual beast or demonic sect thwarted the peace of the village before attempting to resist it. Yao Shen encountering this mortal village meant that the Sacred Flame Palace could not be far now, likely within a few dozen li.

"Grand Patriarch, why have we stopped?" Meili Zhu chose to be the one to break the silence, as the impressive congregation of elders behind him waited for his command.

"What is the name of this village?" Yao Shen asked, his question addressed to the cultivators of the Sacred Flame Palace.

"Seris Village, Grand Patriarch," an elder helpfully supplied, his voice betraying his curiosity.

Yao Shen's expression turned thoughtful as he gazed down upon the village from afar, and while the elders present could not see anything of value in the ordinary mortal village, they knew Yao Shen was a practitioner of the Esoteric Human Dao, and its secrets were something that they were all interested in.

"Wait here. There is something that I must do."

There were two mortal villages that Yao Shen could have claimed to have been intimately acquainted with. The first was the village he was born and brought up in, his talent as a cultivator unearthed at the adolescent age of twelve. Back then, he was not Yao Shen, the mighty Soul Emperor and the Master of the Modern Sect, but merely a pre-pubescent boy who had an inkling of talent in manipulating Qi. To leave behind everyone and everything he had ever known in their small, cozy village... and to do so willingly, with the blessing of his parents— such was the allure of standing among the fabled warriors that could shatter mountains and reverse the flow of rivers.

Yao Shen could not help but recall the last time he had visited his birthplace, a hundred years after he had joined the Heavenly Sky Sect as a cultivator of the righteous path. He still remembered the conflicted emotions that he carried in his heart as if it were only yesterday, unsure himself why he had chosen to arrive now, gazing at his village from afar with a wistful expression on his face— for everyone he had ever known in the small village had perished, not to a rogue demonic cultivator or an errant spiritual beast, but instead to an absolute foe both the mortal man and cultivators faced alike: *time*.

Had Yao Shen recovered his memories of Earth back then, he would have understood that he sought closure for a relationship that he never had the privilege of having. A relationship that he had been robbed of.

Cultivation in the Heavenly Sky Sect had given Yao Shen almost no time to pursue other endeavors, for he had been whisked away from the simple life of a mortal villager and introduced to the cutthroat world of cultivation overnight. Though the Heavenly Sky Sect did not outright forbid any disciple from returning home to visit their mortal parents, as an outer sect disciple who lacked both backing and background, he could not have afforded any distractions if he wished to catch up to the arrogant Legacy Disciples and become a Core Disciple one day himself.

It was only later, when Yao Shen involved himself more directly with the administration of the sect did he realize that such an arrangement was intentional. He felt foolish for not having connected the dots earlier, foolish for never having wondered why mortals were not allowed into the Heavenly Sky Sect. Why there was a need at all to distinguish between mortals and cultivators, when they were both human?

The answer lay in one of the few history lessons that were taught to every disciple, regardless of background or upbringing: The Tale of Shan Lin— The cultivator who fell in love with a mortal woman. Though Yao Shen was sure that the tale had been romanticized over time, this was a true story passed down from generation to generation, a warning across time.

Shan Lin was described "as a cultivator of unequalled might, a true hegemon of the righteous path." No details beyond that were given, but for an ancient cultivator to be described as such, if it were not exaggeration— then he was likely stronger, far stronger than Yao Shen himself. On the other hand, Yanmei Tao was described as a headstrong woman with a fiery temper, the woman known for her sharp tongue and her odd choice of profession: a woman blacksmith. Contrastingly, Shan Lin could be described as the embodiment of the original values of the righteous path itself — noble, kind and virtuous—he made no distinction between mortal or cultivator, even believing that the demonic path's twisted and foul cultivators could be reformed, could once again walk the path of righteousness.

Their paths intersected when Shan Lin stopped by her village, selflessly offering to heal every man, woman or child that required his aid. Despite his kindness, the villagers still feared Shan Lin. For back then, there existed no pact to restrict the activities of the demonic path, and the sect system had not been developed yet— for whilst Shan Lin was kind and noble, the others that united under the banner of the righteous path were not necessarily so. The villagers feared that a single misstep, a single errant word that the "lord cultivator" might take as an offense, would result in their doom.

But there was one woman who did not fear Shan Lin.

One woman who did not request anything from Shan Lin.

One woman who saw Shan Lin for what he truly was…just a man, of flesh and blood, who had stood alone for far too long.

Their relationship blossomed, for Shan Lin had finally found a woman that did not have her gaze clouded by awe, a woman that did not care for his unrivalled strength or cultivation. Shan Lin laughed like he had never before, feeling joy and happiness that mere words alone could not describe. However as time passed, the bliss Shan Lin felt slowly came to a grinding halt. For whilst he loved Yanmei and he knew that she loved her back, there was a problem. With every passing year, time exacted its toll without mercy— her originally lush black hair slowly losing its vitality as the strands of grey started gaining prominence. Her smooth, light brown skin having lost its enchanting luster, the wrinkles of age now visible on her still beautiful visage. Her sharp, daring grey eyes that once made him fall in love with her now held a hint of exhaustion that could not be hidden from his senses.

Both of them knew that this day would eventually come. But for Shan Lin, a cultivator who had lived for an unknown number of years... he had not known... not expected it to be so fast. With each passing year, the smile on Shan Lin's face grew more forced, until he stopped smiling altogether. As the day of parting grew nearer, Shan Lin grew more and more desperate. Utilizing the resources of the righteous path, he explored solutions in a multitude of fields ranging from alchemy to even mortal folk cures, whilst the other cultivators of the righteous path started to express worry at his stability.

When Yanmei Tao, the love of his life, lay floating on a bed of water, her skin withered, her face gaunt and pale, her bones brittle — Shan Lin finally snapped. If the righteous path did not have the answer, then he would go to the demonic path. The demons, cunning and cruel as ever, would not miss on such a heaven sent opportunity to sow discord— so they gave Shan Lin what he wanted, without exacting a price.

For the true price lay in the method itself.

The once paragon of the righteous path ended up committing the greatest sin of all, as he slaughtered an entire town of mortals, laying down an evil, tainted blood path formation. Such was Shan Lin's genius in the Dao of Formations, requiring merely a few days of preparation to master such a complex formation.

He saw as the life breathed back into Yanmei's aged body, as she broke one cultivation level after the next. Early Stage Qi-Formation...Early Stage Foundation Establishment... Early Stage Core Formation... With every cultivation level Yanmei broke, the effect of time reversed itself until she was reverted to the state when Shan Lin first met her, a young woman in her early twenties. However, her expression grew increasingly horrified as she got back upon her feet and looked around at the death and devastation Shan Lin had caused.

The half-crazed Shan Lin heaved a sigh of relief as he embraced her, only to notice a disturbance in her vitality.

Surprisingly, Yanmei embraced him back as tightly as she could, whilst Shan Lin's heart sank into the bottom of the abyss.

She uttered three words, three unexpected words that made Shan Lin realize the horror of his own actions, the foolishness of his own decision to trust the demonic path for even one second... and finally, to realize what a monster he had become.

"I forgive you," she said, as two trails of black tears flowed down her cheeks. With it, her core shattered and she immediately reverted back to her aged state, drawing her last breath not long after.

Thus went the tragedy of Shan Lin, who died deep in demonic path territory in his pursuit of vengeance, alone eliminating over a thousand demonic path cultivators before he met his end... and also the reason why righteous path sects encouraged one to sever attachments with the mortal world.

Yao Shen realized that whilst he originally found logic in this rationale, his beliefs had changed after inheriting his memories of Earth. Separating the mortal world from the world of cultivators was not an action borne out of caution, but of cowardice.

To love his mortal parents would be inviting the inevitable pain of separation into his life. A century was a long time for a cultivator, but for mortals, it was their entire lifespan. It would be pain unlike anything Yao Shen had felt before, and yet...

Was it better not to love at all, for fear of the anguish it would bring?

Preposterous!

Yao Shen would choose to love and hurt, rather than choosing not to love at all. Cultivators were men and women who braved swords and spears, the fury of the elements and the wrath of the Heavenly Dao— what was a little pain in face of that?

Yao Shen would not tolerate such foolishness in his vision for the Modern Sect, but change could not happen overnight.

The second time Yao Shen had intimately acquainted himself with a village and its populace was a few years after he had ascended to the Nascent Soul Stage. He wandered the Azlak Plains in search of ways to improve his cultivation, his position as a Sect Elder of a relatively unimportant post allowing him to take extended sabbaticals without causing many issues for the Heavenly Sky Sect.

However, Yao Shen was a much different man back then. His ascension to the Nascent Soul stage had been fraught with peril, and whilst he had succeeded in the end, that did not prevent his insecurities from gnawing at the weaknesses in his psyche. While Yao Shen had always been known for his mental fortitude, that did not mean that he was infallible— for as an elder, his weapon was inferior for his station, his older methods no longer suitable for the Nascent Soul Stage and his talent, lacking. Had he not been so vehemently opposed to accepting the aid of one of the legacy families and thereby indirectly pledging his loyalty, his progression would have been far smoother.

Many months passed by as Yao Shen scoured the Azlak Plains for opportunity, only to be disappointed time after time. That was not to say that his journey bore no fruits at all, for he had encountered Qi Springs that were guarded by Spiritual Beasts which he slew, and occasionally encountered a natural treasure or two. The only problem was, they were far too weak to have an effect at his level, leaving Yao Shen no choice but to report the location of the Qi Springs to the Sect and move on.

Dejected but not disheartened, Yao Shen ultimately made the decision to turn back and return to the sect. For if Nascent Soul resources were so easily found, they would have already been long exhausted and he had a long lifespan ahead. On his return journey to the sect, Yao Shen's divine sense detected a village around twenty li away from his current location.

Contrary to the conclusions the elders or the other Patriarchs might have drawn, Yao Shen's foray into the Human Dao was not motivated by a thirst for power or ambition, but rather, like some of humankind's greatest inventions back on Planet Earth, it came to him through pure accident.

When he gazed at the village from afar, it reminded him of the peaceful and tranquil life he had originally lived. His attempt to get closure at his birthplace had resulted in failure, for Yao Shen had eventually decided against visiting the village. For the Heavenly Sky Sect had made sure that word of his accomplishments had spread to every nook and cranny of the village, part of their subtle propaganda to encourage mortals, for them to *want* to join the sect of purported immortals, instead of fearing the routine clashes with demonic sects and spiritual beasts. For this very reason, his portrait was nigh enshrined in the village's makeshift assembly hall and his mortal parents had lived the lives of kings, showered in mortal gold and expensive luxuries.

He had no heart to visit a village full of sycophants who yearned for his favor, yearned to stand where he stood, without realizing that the grass was not necessarily greener on the other side; especially not for non-legacy disciples.

However, this new village that he had stumbled upon provided him with an opportunity to experience the life that he had been robbed of. Unlike most cultivators, Yao Shen had never held any disdain for mortals— for while it was in the nature of cultivators to seek power and face the might of the heavens, arrogance had never been his calling. It was hard not to be arrogant, for these were existences that danced at the edge of life and death, few experiences able to compare to testing the wrath of the heavens themselves and surviving. He did not blame them, but he could not be like them either.

So Yao Shen seized the opportunity, approaching the Heavenly Sky Sect guardian who was stationed at the village in secret. With his help and his oath to keep Yao Shen's activities secret, they crafted a backstory that would sound believable to the villagers of Nariri Village. He introduced himself to the villagers as a migrant from a neighboring village who had decided to part ways after he lost his wife to sickness, simply a mortal man who wished to start afresh— willing to work hard in exchange for food and shelter.

Since the guardian, who had returned to his post, quickly verified that Yao Shen was who he claimed to be and not some nefarious demonic cultivator in disguise, the village chief accepted him into their community, moved by his story. For a mortal man willing to brave the journey through the Azlak Plains unescorted was either a bold or truly desperate one.

For the next six months, Yao Shen lived the life of a mortal villager. During the day, he toiled in the wheat fields, harvesting the stalks of wheat with his crude sickle at the slow, cumbersome speed of mortals and surprisingly, finding the action cathartic. Had Yao Shen felt the fatigue from his work like the other villagers, perhaps his opinion would be different.

However, through repeating the process day after painstaking day, Yao Shen gained an insight. This entire field of wheat, he could harvest alone in an instant, thresh it and separate the chaff from the grain perfectly. However, it took the combined efforts of ten villagers, even then taking close to a month. And somehow, Yao Shen found that inefficient, obsolete and time-consuming method so much more *meaningful.*

When he first tasted the *Ciapa*, a spiced mortal flatbread that was cooked using the wheat he had harvested by hand at the Uttrala festival, he could not help but swear that it tasted better than the finest cuts of spiritual beast meat he had sampled in his life.

His worldview and perception of mortals gradually started changing, his duties shifting from harvesting to planting new seeds that would require much care to grow into crop that would feed the village. His free time was spent mingling with the villagers, spending his hard-earned coin on new clothes, lean cuts of meat and whatever else attracted his fancy.

Yao Shen came to realize that mortals were no less for not being able to cultivate, only making him wonder what criteria the Heavenly Dao used to separate the worthy from the unworthy, who deserved to be able to cultivate and who did not. If anything, they were greater— for while cultivators often lived reclusive and aloof lives, mortals did not have the luxury of waiting. Their lives were but a blip in the timespans of powerful cultivators like Yao Shen himself, but that did not mean they did not have the same hopes, dreams and ambitions as himself— but even further magnified, spurred on by the finitude of life.

When Yao Shen asked himself the question back then, if he would be happier if he had never awakened his talents as a culti-vator or not… He realized that he had no answer to that question. To live a short life, where happiness and sorrow, joy and despair, love and hatred were magnified endlessly, or to live for far longer, overcoming great challenges and often finding himself alone in the pursuit of the laws of the world, the great secrets of Eliria.

Yao Shen did not have an answer.

And it was in that moment that the world exploded in color. His Human Dao awakened. It would take many years for Yao Shen to understand his new power, and even longer to conceptu-alize his domain into reality.

Perhaps what triggered his awakening was the realization that despite their similar appearances, cultivators and mortals, were so different physiologically that they could be labelled different species, at the heart of it were just... *humans.* No different from each other, no more or less superior than each other, driven by the same conceptualizations of love, hate, desire, sorrow, life, death, regret, anguish and determination. Time could perhaps dilute those emotions, but it could never truly take them away, even if one wanted it to.

After all, they were all merely humans.

And now, as Yao Shen floated above Seris Village, announcing his presence so that his sudden arrival would not alarm the villagers, he had one singular question that he sought an answer to.

One question that he required the answer to, if he were to envision a better future for mortals as he laid down his foundation for the mortal sect. A future where mortals were no longer entirely powerless in face of the whims of cultivators, himself included.

Yao Shen sensed the wary gazes of the villagers, their expressions one of trepidation and caution as they scrutinized the cultivator who calmly hovered above their home, his satin-white robes fluttering with a gentle breeze. For whilst the residents of Seris Village were not entirely unaccustomed to the presence of cultivators, they had always worn either azure-blue, earthen-brown or fiery-red colored robes. Not white. *Never white.*

A group of children that had been play-fighting with wooden swords, fantasizing of one day becoming Qi Cultivators that roamed the Azlak Plains in search of adventure and glory froze when confronted by the object of their envy. The cacophony of the small village market could be heard from afar; the age-old back and forth as men and women alike passionately haggled with mortal shopkeepers, the discordant sound of a hammer striking metal as a young, likely an apprentice blacksmith, applied the finishing touches to a harvesting sickle, and a gaggle of families making conversation over supper— only to be replaced by an abrupt, *deathly* silence.

The womenfolk hurriedly clasped the hands of their children and rushed to their homes, barring their doors with a thick wooden plank while the older children reached for the hatch that was camouflaged beneath either coarse, makeshift carpets or old spiritual beast hide. They scurried in without second thought, following the unofficial protocol that was used for beast tides.

Most of the grown men, however, reached for any blade or even farming implement in the vicinity, as long as it was made of mortal metal. Fear was reflected in their gazes, yet the symbolism behind their actions was equally evident— they did not know who Yao Shen was, or what he wanted from them. But if the unknown foreign cultivator wished to harm their wives or children, he would have to go through them first.

It was not Yao Shen's intention to alarm the peaceful folk of Seris Village and the more well-informed among them ought to have realized that by now— for the demonic path's attacks were always as swift as they were ruthless, their intention to cause as much destruction before the righteous path sects in the vicinity could dispatch reinforcements. A demonic path cultivator would not deign to inform the villagers of his presence, for honor was an entirely unfamiliar concept to them.

But in announcing his presence, he had stumbled upon an uncomfortable reality—one that he, like his predecessors, had always known of, but never been able to address. Depending on one's perspective, the villagers' current plight could be seen as either pitiful or admirable. Pitiful, for the only defense the villagers could muster was a futile show of force, for both the mortal men and Yao Shen alike knew that nothing could stop him if he truly meant harm to their mortal dwellings. Admirable for the very same reason, for while blades and bloodshed could not shake the core tenets of a demonic path cultivator, perhaps such a raw display of bravery in the face of certain death could. Though Yao Shen would not count on it.

It did not require a Soul Emperor to level Seris Village. And neither was a Nascent Soul Grandmaster needed, for that would be akin to using a boulder to hammer in a nail. Merely a single core formation cultivator, or a group of foundation establishment cultivators was enough to reduce this mortal village to naught but ash. Granted, daring to launch an attack so close to the Sacred Flame Palace was not without a high degree of risk, but the demons were nothing if not bold.

"Fear not, denizens of Seris Village. I am Yao Shen, Patriarch of the Heavenly Sky Sect, and I mean you no harm," his voice echoed out, his tone gentle and reassuring.

A cultivator dressed in the colors of the Sacred Flame Palace stepped forward, his scrutinizing gaze falling on Yao Shen before he nodded.

"That is indeed the Patriarch of the Heavenly Sky Sect," he spoke aloud, for all the villagers nearby to hear, including a middle-aged man in his late forties whose worried expression immediately eased upon receiving confirmation. Yao Shen had intentionally addressed himself by his former title, in an effort to avoid any further confusion— for he did not expect the villagers or the Sacred Flame Palace Guardian to have heard of the Modern Sect's establishment this soon.

Surprisingly, the guardian himself did not seem perturbed by Yao Shen's presence deep within Sacred Flame Palace territory. Though he would report this matter to his sect at the earliest opportunity, one of the cardinal principles of the righteous path forbade the disputes of cultivators from stretching onto the mortal world. This was precisely the reason why Yao Shen, like his predecessors, could not make major headways in changing the landscape of mortal infrastructure— for whilst the safety of mortals was the combined responsibility of all major righteous path forces in the region, the deteriorating relationship between the three hegemons of the Azlak Plains prevented any meaningful change from being implemented.

Yao Shen's gaze shifted back to the middle-aged man dressed in a cream-colored tunic and plain white breeches, the cut of his fabric a little finer than the villagers that flocked toward him, his rotund build a mark of wealth and prosperity; for whilst the mortal villagers were all well-fed, between their physically demanding jobs and a limited surplus, few had the privilege of eating and drinking for pleasure instead of sustenance.

Yao Shen watched calmly as the corpulent man instructed a few men around him, the tone of authority in his voice unmistakable. He soon identified the man as Seris Village's chief, as a young man broke off from the growing throng of villagers that were congregating near the chief and the guardian, sprinting toward the center of their settlement.

His destination was made clear as he slowed down his pace, approaching a large metal gong that was placed atop a pedestal. The young man hoisted the wooden mallet that had been leaning upon it, striking the gong thrice— an indication to the remaining villagers that were still in hiding that the threat had passed.

Only after the women and children had begun to trickle out from their hideaways did Yao Shen begin his slow descent, gently landing in front of the village chief.

"L-Lord Cultivator," the village chief stuttered, the air of authority around him instantly evaporating the moment Yao Shen landed; his head was slightly lowered in deference and he did not dare lock eyes with Yao Shen. He took a moment to compose himself, drawing upon his wealth of experience as the chief, before continuing, "What brings your esteemed self to our humble village?"

Yao Shen's expression turned ponderous, unsurprised by the caution the village chief showed him. "Before we discuss the purpose of my visit, there is one thing that I am curious about."

"Please ask, Lord Cultivator," the village chief replied, his tone still cautious but far less tense than before.

"Why did you and the men of the village not flee when you first saw me? Surely you do not believe that mortal steel could harm me?" he asked.

The village chief slightly blanched at the question, his expression turning hesitant as he thought of ways to avoid a direct answer.

"Speak your mind, Village Chief. Upon my honor as Patriarch, you will face no repercussions from the Sacred Flame Palace for speaking your mind," Yao Shen encouraged.

His words had the intended effect, as the village chief hesitated no longer. "It is true, Lord Cultivator. We..." he said, his gaze shifting to the gathering of villagers behind him, ".... did not truly expect to injure you with our blades. Had it been a beast tide, we would have taken shelter under our houses and hoped that the spiritual beasts would pass by us after destroying our village. However, the senses and intelligence of a cultivator such as yourself cannot be fooled— our weapons may be poor in make and our strength feeble, but if we choose to stand our ground, perhaps we may buy enough time for the Sacred Flame Palace's reinforcements to arrive."

Yao Shen fell silent for a moment, unable to imagine how *frustrating* it would be for the villagers of Seris Village— to be attacked by hostiles that wished to harm their families and yet lack the strength to defend their loved ones. Part of him had forgotten the privilege of powerful cultivators, for whilst he had many worries and equally as many concerns, the sheer inability to defend his sect from hostile elements was not one of them.

"I see," Yao Shen replied, his left fist slightly clenched as he tried to imagine the *rage* the villagers of Seris Village must feel at their own inability, at the ruthless world they had been born in, and finally, at the Heavenly Dao, for denying them the ability to protect what they loved.

"Lord Cultivator!" A young, chipper voice interrupted their conversation, both Yao Shen and the village chief's gaze shifting to a young mortal boy that could not be older than twelve, his eyes brimming with curiosity. The boy's mother looked mortified, but her son was far too eager to be interrupted. "Have you come to select disciples?"

Before the mother could move to profusely apologize, Yao Shen walked toward the boy and gave his hair a light, friendly tousle. "No, child, the time has not yet come," he explained, his tone apologetic. The boy's energetic demeanor immediately wilted, his expression turning somewhat sullen.

"However, I have a gift for you," Yao Shen added with a small smile.

"A gift?" he asked, his interest immediately piqued.

Yao Shen's divine sense scoured his spatial ring for a suitable gift, settling on a small dagger that was exceptionally light, an early stage Qi-Refinement blade. The blade itself was useless for Yao Shen or even any of his disciples, his spatial ring having amassed a plethora of odds and ends amassed over the years. But when Yao Shen pulled the small dagger out of his spatial ring, the boy's gaze was immediately captivated.

Its bluish-bronze surface glinted in the sunlight, its sharpness beyond any mortal blade's capabilities. Yao Shen sheathed the blade, handing it to the boy's mother, who immediately understood, bowing low before accepting it.

"The blade shall be yours when you come of age. Until then,

be a filial child to your mother and work hard, in whatever pursuit you end up choosing."

"Thank you, Lord Cultivator." The child bowed, clearly over-joyed at the bestowal. The surrounding villagers watched the young child with awe, some immediately concluding that the child would become a powerful cultivator in the future, while others watched on in jealousy, wishing it were their child that had received the bestowal. However, none would dare to lay their hands on a gift by a cultivator, and the boy's status had been forever elevated within Seris Village.

Yao Shen gave the boy a nod, before he moved to address the villagers.

"As for the purpose of my visit, I must admit that I was merely passing by the region. However, now that I am here, as a practitioner of the Water Dao, while I cannot reverse the effects of aging, I can help stymie it. Water Qi will cleanse your body of impurities, allowing it to heal old wounds and slowly repair the wear and tear of time; if you so will it," Yao Shen offered, much to the surprise of the elders, who carefully observed from a distance. While healers were occasionally dispatched from the sects to heal mortals, it was only limited to those in urgent need. A powerful cultivator such as Yao Shen offering to heal an entire village was almost unheard of.

"Many thanks, Lord Cultivator," the village chief almost shouted in his excitement, offering a deep, respectful bow to Yao Shen.

The villagers behind him echoed that sentiment, each one offering him a bow in deep gratitude.

The village chief's men started organizing the crowd into one singular long line that stretched from one end of Seris Village to the other, while those who did not seek healing were asked to step out of the crowd and stay at a distance.

One by one, the villagers stepped forward to receive healing, and Yao Shen sent a gentle pulse of Water Qi through their bodies that eliminated all impurities it made contact with. The ones who were healed would soon cough out a black, tarry substance, then profusely thank Yao Shen. The elderly mortals now walked with a vigor in their step, their loose skin no longer sagging and their eyes brimming with vitality. Their wrinkles had receded, each elderly man and woman looking almost twenty years younger. It was beyond Yao Shen's ability to give them their youth back, but their confidence? That, he could.

The sickly would no longer be troubled by their poor constitution, and old injuries would no longer trouble the once injured.

As the crowd of people requiring healing dwindled, Yao Shen instinctively knew that he would receive the answer to his question soon.

So he closed his eyes, and when he opened them again, he had activated his human sight.

There were many questions that even Yao Shen, the Soul Emperor of the Azlak Plains, was *afraid* to ask.

After retrieving his memories of the lifetime he had spent on Earth, there were many questions that he dared not dwell upon too deeply, lest they result in the creation of a heart demon.

For one, there was the similarity between Earth and Eliria. He found himself asking if his reincarnation had truly been a mistake, a cosmic miscalculation that resulted in his arrival on the continent of Ionea. Earlier, Yao Shen would discount any other possibility off-handedly, but now... he could not help but wonder if there were greater forces at work.

Was he meant to change Ionea? Eliria itself? The mere idea sounded preposterous, laughable even, for he had received no special boon from the heavens, nothing but the animosity of the Heavenly Dao. Yet, he had ascended to Soul Emperor. And now, he sought to reshape this new world in the image of his old one, albeit better.

Then, there was the existence of humans itself. What were the odds that the same species could be found on two different planets? Eliria had two moons and one sun and the conditions for life were similar. What was the connection between Earth and Eliria?

If there truly was a connection, did that mean there was a way back to his home planet? If given the choice, would *he* choose to go back?

Eliria was cloaked in a fog of mystery, and there were many questions that he would perhaps never receive the answer to.

Yet, there was one among them that he required an answer to, if he wished to involve mortals in his vision for the Modern Sect.

Ionia, and Eliria itself, was an ancient land. Though Yao Shen could not be sure when mortal civilization first sprang up, he would venture a guess that it was as old, if not older, than the first human that walked on Earth.

Yet mortals were merely a footnote in the history of cultivators, there was no mention of sprawling mortal cities that had thrived in the past, no record of historical discoveries or inventions attributed to their name. There was no dearth of legendary figures in the cultivation world, but when it came to mortal heroes, the list was all but empty.

While the humans of Earth had started from nothing, using sharpened rocks to hunt in the early days, then discovering various metals scattered across the Earth and learning to forge them, making sharp blades that could slice through bone and sinew alike. Then came the discovery of gunpowder that was used to create weapons that moved faster than human reflexes could adapt to, and finally, there was the creation of weapons so potent that even Yao Shen had no confidence in surviving them.

Their cities were vast jungles of concrete and metal, their

inventions allowing them to accomplish feats they themselves could not dream of and their trade, prosperous.

Why then, was there such a difference between the mortals of Ionea and the humans of Earth?

As Yao Shen opened his eyes, the final piece of the puzzle finally fit into place— in that moment, he knew he had the answer. A cloud of reverence so thick that it was almost suffocating ensconced the villagers, its silvery-white radiance stinging at his eyes. Every mortal man and woman alike, whether they had been healed by him or not, revered his presence as if… as if… he were a *deity.*

What need was there to cure mortal afflictions when cultivators such as Yao Shen could do it with the tap of his finger?

The answer, naturally, was to strive hard to become a cultivator, until one day they were proficient enough to heal their ailing parents!

What need was there to spend years to develop architecture, when cultivators could raise walls and housing in a matter of days?

How could mere mortals, that required weeks just to harvest wheat, dare to think about raising tall buildings with their meagre strength? No, no such matters were naturally the realm of cultivators.

Why should mortals spend their limited lifespans researching weaponry, to devise counter measures against spiritual beasts, when cultivators could slay them by hand?

If one wished revenge against the spiritual beasts that terrorized their small village, one naturally had to defy the heavens and step upon the path of a mighty cultivator!

Yao Shen realized that the problem the mortals of Ionea faced was not that of ability, intelligence, determination or even skill. For he had seen the determination of the mortal villagers when they had stood their ground against a foreign cultivator, he had firsthand experienced their intelligence and skill when he had lived among them for six months and unlocked his human Dao, and he had no doubts about their ability, for he, too, was once a mortal.

The problem was one of *mindset*.

Yao Shen left the village not long after, having healed the last of the villagers. Having finally received the answer he sought after. He now knew what he must do.

Soon, the vague outline of the Sacred Flame Palace was visible in the distance.

28

FLAME DIVISION

Yᴀᴏ Sʜᴇɴ's divine sense scanned the Sacred Flame Palace from the periphery of his range, taking in the myriad sights and sounds of the unfamiliar sect. For he knew that after today, for better or worse, the Sacred Flame Palace would no longer be the same.

The overarching theme of the sect's architectural layout could be summed up in one word: *bold*. Unlike the Heavenly Sky Sect, there was no translucent bubble that enveloped the perimeter of the sect, giving the false impression that the Sacred Flame Palace did not have any external defenses. Yao Shen, however, knew better— whilst the Heavenly Sky Sect employed a defensive formation to secure its borders, the Sacred Flame Palace, true to the destructive nature of Fire Qi, had chosen an offensive one.

They called it the 'Boundary of Purification,' a grand name befitting its capabilities. Controlled by a true Formation Spirit, it was a runic formation carved beneath the earth. Any foreign cultivator that dared to charge headlong toward the Sacred Flame Palace would be incinerated by scorching-hot flames at the Nascent Soul level, and any projectile attacks would be reduced to dust long before they could strike true at their mark. The true beauty of the formation lay its in versatility, for whilst there were many lacunae within the rule-set it was governed by, the Formation Spirit itself was *sapient* while lacking sentience, and had the ability to override those laws.

Thus, one could not circumvent the Boundary of Purification by holding a Sacred Flame Palace cultivator hostage and walking alongside them in hopes that the formation would not harm its own— such a folly had been committed in the past, and the tragic result had been two deaths instead of one.

The outer sect was clearly visible from afar, the infrastructure reminiscent of a military outpost back on Earth in its shared utilitarian design. The first thing Yao Shen noticed was the lack of an Outer Exchange, for there were no entrepreneurial disciples hawking their wares, be it in the form of spiritual herbs acquired outside the sect, a weapon they had outgrown or even any form of eatables. Each of the major edifices were dyed in contrasting hues of red, and one of them led to a wide, three-story pagoda whose wooden eaves were painted in a mellow terracotta color. Dozens of disciples dined on the first floor of the pagoda, making small talk over their meal, while the higher floors were reserved for guardians and elders.

Although the Sacred Flame Palace looked awe-inspiring from afar, with each different hue of red representing a Minor Dao of fire, Yao Shen could feel the difference in its general atmosphere. Each disciple of the Sacred Flame walked with a *purpose* in their step, at most in small groups of twos and threes, through the clean, neatly organized roads, their expressions cold and their demeanor aloof.

Even the young Qi-Formation disciples were so reserved and focused, one could only imagine why the former Patriarch of the Sacred Flame Palace had been so stubborn, even as he fought a losing battle.

Each member of Yao Shen's contingent was handed a talisman that marked them as a guest of the Sacred Flame Palace, the proverbial keys to the kingdom. Once they were inside the sect, the odds of a conflict diminished significantly, for the odds of hapless disciples being caught in the crossfire was too high. However, all the members of Yao Shen's contingent had made their own defensive preparations, and further insisted that the Sacred Flame Place Elders walk alongside them.

The first one to enter were the three Patriarchs, with Yao Shen activating his Human Dao Domain just in case the Formation Spirit flagged him as an enemy.

His mystical domain immediately drew the attention of the disciples, who watched on with shocked expressions as an outsider took his first steps on the outer sect's territory. Their expressions blanched further when they saw their Patriarch accompany the white-robed man, his expression inscrutable. The hawk-eyed elders who had stayed back to defend the sect watched on with dismay, knowing the outcome had already been set in stone.

Alas, such was the value of oaths in a world without contracts.

Soon, the rest of his contingent arrived, stopping a few steps behind him. Twelve Elders of the Sacred Flame Palace along with the delegation from the Heavenly Sky Sect lay arrayed behind the three Patriarchs, a force so intimidating that it caused the disciples' hearts to beat faster.

Finally, Lei Weiyuan stepped forward, and all eyes were immediately drawn toward him. His hands were clasped behind his back, giving him a dignified bearing and his expression, indecipherable. Yet, the projection of invulnerability was but a façade, for Yao Shen and the elders could see his tightly clenched fist lightly trembling, as Lei Weiyuan recited the terms of the oath slowly, *patiently*, perhaps wishing that his recital would never end.

His every word was like a sharp dagger stabbed deep into the hearts of the Sacred Flame Disciples, for the presence of the Heavenly Sky Sect Patriarch here could only mean one thing.

"... The combined forces of the Sacred Flame Palace and the Divine Mountain Sect were bested in combat by Patriarch Yao Shen of the Heavenly Sky, alone and without any assistance from other cultivators. As per the oath, from henceforth, the Sacred Flame Palace shall be referred to as the Flame Division of the Modern Sect."

The announcement was met with *silence.*

The disciples turned their gazes to the elders, whom they looked upon for wisdom and guidance when the path ahead was enshrouded by mists. The ones they idolized, however, chose to maintain a stoic silence— a few even averting their faces, unable to meet their hopeful, or rather, *desperate* expressions.

This time, it was Yao Shen that stepped forward.

"Hear me, oh disciples, guardians and elders of the Flame Division!" Yao Shen's Qi-empowered voice shook the adrift disciples from their reverie. Their focus reluctantly shifted to the man in white, whose chiseled jawline, straight black hair and surprisingly kind brown eyes did not match the description of the old, ruthless Patriarch of the Heavenly Sky sect they were familiar with. He seemed to be in his mid-thirties by mortal standards, the ascension having knocked a decade off his appearance, but his bearing spoke of one far beyond his age.

"The word 'Modern' is derived from an ancient, *obsolete* language that I daresay not many of you would have heard of. It *represents* but a single concept, *embodies* but a simple notion! What do you think it means?" Yao Shen rhetorically asked, passion now seeping into his voice.

The throng of disciples remained silent, but Yao Shen could feel that his question had piqued the interest of a few curious minds.

"*Progress*!" Yao Shen exclaimed, his voice rousing even those disciples who haplessly gazed at the colors and mosaics of the Sacred Flame Palace around them, once a symbol of their glory, now a painful reminder of the radiant past.

"Never before in history have the three hegemons of the Azlak Plains stood as one cohesive whole. The Era of Turmoil has long since passed, yet we cling on to ancient enmities like fools who cannot see the bigger picture! Our ancestors have long since perished, and their feuds alongside with them. For so long, we have been *weak*! For so long, we have been *divided*! Just how the Demons of the Bloodsoul Forest prefer us to be!"

Yao Shen could feel a burst of anger rise in the crowd at the mention of the demonic sects, as more and more heads turned to gaze in his direction. He may not have the trust of the audience, but their attention, he was starting to get.

"I, Yao Shen, as a cultivator of the righteous path, say, not anymore!" his voice boomed with righteousness. "Divided no longer. Weak no longer. Together, the Modern Sect, the Sect of Progress, shall stand strong and bring prosperity to this land!"

Yao Shen could see that a few younger disciples were moved by the grand ideals he spoke of, but talk alone could not win confidence.

"There is but one core tenet that the Modern Sect stands for, and that is *fairness* above all. I ask you to trust me, Yao Shen, not because I bested your Patriarch and elders in combat. I do not ask you to acknowledge me as your Patriarch, solely because you are bound by the oath and your honor, to do so. I ask you, oh, disciples, guardians and elders of the Flame Division, to trust me because I stand for a cause greater than myself!"

The sound of clapping came, not from the audience, but surprisingly from behind him. Meili Zhu brazenly applauded her own Patriarch, and the contingent from the Heavenly Sky Sect caught on. Zixin Ren seemed to enjoy each second, his claps sounding out more like the beating of war drums. Left with no option, the Elders of the now Flame Division broke out into applause of their own, and the disciples, followed in their footsteps.

Soon, the entire Flame Division applauded for Yao Shen— though he felt no satisfaction from receiving the applause. He knew that Meili was only asserting his rule. The hearts and minds of the Flame Division could not be won in a day, but all things considered, this was not the worst of beginnings.

"For now, the elders, guardians and disciples will return to their duties. Tonight, there shall be a banquet for all, irrespective of station or seniority. All will dine in the same hall— the spiritual wine will not stop flowing and the Sky Division shall send over its finest chefs. The Patriarch of the Flame Division, Lei Weiyuan, shall accompany I, Yao Shen, Grand Patriarch of the Modern Sect, and help me familiarize myself with your esteemed sect."

Yao Shen's brief speech came to an end, though the disciples did not seem to receive the message as they continued standing there, as if they were expecting something else. If they thought that he would humiliate them by ordering them to do menial tasks or disrespect their sect so that they could direct their anger and disappointment toward him, they were sorely mistaken.

"Did you lot not hear the Grand Patriarch? On your way now," Flame Patriarch Lei Weiyuan snapped, his familiar voice immediately rousing the disciples to action. They slowly started dispersing, returning to their tasks with conflicted emotions in their heart.

The guardians went back to their posts, and the elders too started returning to their duties. With even one component missing, the machinery of the sect would stop functioning, and that was not his intention. The Earth Patriarch and the Sky Division's contingent was escorted to guest residences, leaving behind only Yao Shen and Lei Weiyuan.

"What would you like to see first, Grand Patriarch?" Lei Weiyuan asked, his tone more intrigued than bitter.

Yao Shen smiled lightly at the question, before answering, "The Sparring Stage."

29

THE SPARRING STAGE

FLAME PATRIARCH LEI Weiyuan's expression turned curious, his gaze shifting to the disciples that had convened around a lightly elevated platform. White lines had been painted along the perimeter of the makeshift arena, clearly demarcating the confines within which the duel could permissibly take place. The spectators wore sheepish expressions on their faces instead of dejected or conflicted ones, their attention seemingly captivated by the two disciples that stood in the center of the arena.

"As you wish, Grand Patriarch." Lei Weiyuan nodded, and the two cultivators gently took to the sky. Only a few moments later, the two powerful cultivators hovered over the Sparring Stage, the tension in the atmosphere spiking as the wary disciples slowly angled their sight upward, none daring to directly meet Yao Shen's thoughtful brown eyes.

The smile on Yao Shen's face grew slightly as his eyes fell on the two combatants, long having scanned them with his divine sense. The color drained from their faces when they found the terrifying *Soul Emperor's* gaze locked on to them, trembling as they gave the Flame Patriarch beseeching looks, wondering how they had offended Yao Shen.

Yao Shen's hand moved, and the disciples immediately flinched. A burnished metallic spear was withdrawn from his spatial ring.

"Do not be afraid, children," Yao Shen's serene voice echoed out as he balanced the spear in his cupped hands in a clearly noncombative posture. "I was merely intrigued by your duel and wished to add to the wager."

The two disciples immediately sighed out in relief, inadvertently exchanging glances with one another. Surprise was reflected upon their faces, for neither had expected such an outcome.

Of course, Yao Shen was not truly interested in seeing two Qi-Formation disciples spar; a duel at that level was no different than play-fighting in his eyes. Instead, he was intrigued by the disciples *themselves* and what *they* represented. On the left, was the first among them to recover his composure, a young boy that was perhaps fifteen but not over sixteen years of age. His sword glinted under the afternoon sun, its brilliant sharpness accentuated under the golden rays of light. His crimson robes bore an insignia that his foe did not, the strokes of ink spelling out the surname 'Cui.' If there were any doubt remaining, the hushed whispers of the spectators had spoken of a 'Young Master,' upon whom many a young disciple had wagered part of their meagre wealth.

It was unsurprising that even entertainment in the Sacred Flame Palace seemed to revolve around combat, and whilst gambling was not a virtue of the righteous path; the sect administration was wise to allow the disciples *at least* some outlet to blow off steam.

Opposing him was an older opponent, easily two years elder to the Cui Family's young master. His weapon of choice was a scimitar, one that had clearly seen heavy use. Its edge, while not dull, paled in comparison to his adversary's, and its curvature already evincing a light warp.

Yao Shen lightly flicked the spear in his hand, causing it to land just outside the bounds of the Sparring Stage, digging into the soft earth.

"That is a peak foundation establishment level artifact, a reward for the victor from my side." Yao Shen's proclamation caused a buzz of excitement to run through the crowd, some giving the spear covetous glances while others eyed the arena with building anticipation, slightly less intimidated by Yao Shen than they were earlier.

Yao Shen's gaze shifted to a guardian, who seemed baffled by the sequence of events. He sent a message to him via his divine sense, commanding him to commence the duel.

The guardian nodded, seemingly to no one in particular, tightening his grip upon the mallet that was held in his right hand before striking a large beast-skin drum.

A powerful reverberation echoed out as the mallet struck the drum's center; the sound generated by the impact could easily deafen a mortal on the spot. A few seconds passed before the drum was struck again, and this time, the spectators joined in, stomping their feet in unison with the drumbeat. Each subsequent strike that followed was marginally faster than the last, the tempo rising with every passing breath.

Amidst the din, a bead of sweat trickled down Young Master Cui's forehead. His grip on his sword unconsciously tightened and the cultivator found that his pulse was racing, swaying along with the rising tempo of the drumbeats. Not once had his gaze fallen upon Yao Shen's wager, the spear artifact, for the Cui Family did not lack foundation establishment level artifacts. However, his rapid, shallow breaths indicated that he faced a different kind of *pressure,* a burden that his foe was all but oblivious to.

For the one presiding over his duel was not a Core Formation master, nor was he a Nascent Soul grandmaster. He was a Soul

Emperor, and in that moment, it did not matter if Yao Shen was a former enemy of the Sacred Flame Palace. It was an *honor* to have his duel witnessed by Yao Shen, but it was not the thought of earning Yao Shen's favor that drove him. The very reputation of the Cui Family hung in the lurch, like a piercing sword that was dangled over his head. Victory would be rewarded, but defeat? As a member of the legacy families that governed the Sacred Flame Palace, defeat to an outer sect disciple that had been a mortal not too long ago was *not* an acceptable outcome.

"You will win," His great-grandfather's calm voice sounded out in his mind, the absolute certainty in his tone immediately easing the boy's expression. His great-grandfather, a Nascent Soul Elder, had not promised him a great reward for his victory and neither had he offered last-minute guidance to prevent him from losing. It was only three brief words, yet that was all he needed to hear.

For he was Longtian Cui and greatness was not demanded from him. It was expected.

Opposing him, his foe, an outer disciple who went by the name Zhengwei, found his gaze flickering between Young Master Cui and the spear that was only separated from him by a dozen meters.

Though he was not immune to the uncertainty bubbling in his gut, the beating of the drum was also met with a growing anticipation. Today might have been a dark day in the history of the Sacred Flame Palace, but for Zhengwei, the sun seemed to shine a little brighter, its radiance finally reaching the forgotten corners of the world. To him, it did not particularly matter who ruled the Sacred Flame— for whilst he might share a sect with the legacy families, they remained worlds apart. Everything he owned, he had earned, unlike the pompous young master that had drawn a blade against him.

The propaganda of the Sacred Flame Palace had not infected

him, for it had been only a few years since he had arrived at the sect. Indeed, while he had shared naive dreams of becoming an unrivalled cultivator that stood upon the peak of the world, that had soon been washed away by the ground reality of life in the outer sect. The blade he wielded was won from another after a hard-fought duel. The scimitar technique he employed was something he had cobbled together himself, pieced by borrowing from the common sword techniques the other disciples employed— for the instructors seemed content to do the bare minimum, trusting the wheat to separate itself from the chaff. Outer sect disciples were not worthy to receive individual instruction, and most were lucky, even grateful, to receive a few pointers. His success had been met with treachery, from his own brothers and sisters. Once mortals, now cultivators, a group of outer sect disciple attempted to gang up on him, jealous of his rapid progression— that day, Zhengwei had realized that he could trust no one in the wretched continent that Ionea was. He had subdued them at the cost of a broken rib, dishing back twice the punishment he himself had taken— and from then on, none had dared to cross him.

Just like today, he would subdue the Young Master of the Cui Family, and make them realize that he, Zhengwei the nameless, an orphan, a once mortal, was worthy of their attention. The spear glinting in the corner of his vision was a boon that had *literally* fallen from the skies, and if he won, he would enter the sights of the strongest cultivator in the Azlak Plains.

It was at that moment that the drumming reached its crescendo, the two fighters locking sights as their muscles tensed up.

And then it was replaced by a sudden, abrupt silence. The sudden halt of the drumming was intended to disrupt the focus of the combatants, for battles in the cultivator world did not come with a warning. However, its true purpose was to signal the commencement of the duel— Zhengwei was the first to recover, letting out a loud battle cry as he charged forward with a mad intensity in his eyes. Half a second had been lost, the rhythm of his breathing disrupted— even though he knew it was coming, he was not yet skilled enough to avoid it.

Longtian Cui reacted a step later than Zhengwei, choosing to meet the latter in his charge. The spectators held their breaths as the two rising stars of the outer sect charged forward, one with the sword and the other with a scimitar.

The shrill sound of metal clashing against metal ran out, and the thrilled crowd let out loud cheers. Both the disciples had cycled Qi through their body to increase their speed and strength, and in the end, it was Longtian Cui who was forced to take a step back.

Zhengwei's eyes lit up as he saw a golden opportunity, his eyes shining with complete focus. He unleashed a torrent of blows in rapid succession, his sword carrying the weight of his desires. His blows were wild and untamed, like a feral beast of prey that had been unleashed into the wilderness— the wide grin upon his face and his hawkish eyes that tracked his quarry with utmost precision made Zhengwei's scimitar style more reminiscent of a spiritual beast than man, causing Longtian Cui's expression to grow paler as he was forced back step after step, a glimmer of fear reflected in his eyes.

Emboldened, Zhengwei continued to invest more Qi into his blows, determined to give his opponent no chance to launch a counterattack.

"It is a pity," Yao Shen lightly sighed, his right hand moving rapidly as he sketched something upon a scroll that was clipped to a wooden support.

"Too young," Flame Patriarch Lei Weiyuan replied, his voice barely above a whisper.

Longtian Cui attempted to defend, but Zhengwei's scimitar style was too erratic— refined where a simple blow would suffice and oddly straightforward when a skilled opponent would use a maneuver, to gain advantage.

Duels at the Qi-Refinement level could be often one-sided, for disciples at this level had only so many ways to counter. Longtian continued to be pushed back, until merely a few meters separated him from the white line that marked the boundary-line.

At the cusp of victory, Zhengwei could almost taste the glory that awaited him. It was then that his instincts rebelled against that thought. His opponent, who had been heavily panting and seemingly expended, completely transformed. Longtian Cui met Zhengwei's gaze, his expression placid as he, in a display of exquisite skill, switched to a reverse grip with a flick of his wrist.

Zhengwei immediately wished to retreat, but he had already committed to the blow. He watched in shock as Longtian Cui gently caught his blow with the sharp edge of his sword, before relaxing his grip. Zhengwei's scimitar let out an ear-piercing sound as it slid along the edge of the young master's blade, only sheer determination allowing him to pull back his blade before it smashed upon the ground and left him open to attack.

He felt the air being knocked out of his lungs, for whilst he was ready to defend against blade, Longtian Cui unleashed a Qi-empowered kick into his sternum.

Frustration flowed through Zhengwei as he went sliding back for a dozen meters, immediately spitting out a mouthful of blood as he frenziedly tried to spot his foe.

The young master was upon him in seconds, his expression almost serene as his slender blade unleashed a thrust directed toward his abdomen.

"Damn it!" Zhengwei screamed, batting the blade away with his scimitar. But while Zhengwei's scimitar style was untamed, Longtian's was the opposite— methodological and calm, this time, it was Zhengwei who was repeatedly pushed back. Each strike had the same amount of force behind it, but Longtian's sword technique was a thing of beauty; graceful and refined, resembling a master artisan given free rein upon a broad canvas. But most importantly, it was deadly, as Longtian increased the speed of his thrusts and slashes in waves, confronting his foe with a greater challenge each time he got used to his rhythm.

Zhengwei's defense grew desperate, for while his foe's blows were light, they were relentless, never-ending. So far, he had been able to match Longtian's speed, blocking his strikes with gritted teeth, but if he increased his tempo by a notch, he knew the fight would be over.

As he parried a strike while forced to take a step back, he mentally prepared himself, estimating the next strike's trajectory with his superhuman reflexes and repositioning his blade.

He waited to hear the familiar clang of steel against steel, but none came.

His instincts screamed at him, and Zhengwei realized with horror as the blade slipped underneath its own that he had reset the tempo and gone back to the speed he had begun his volley of attacks with. The final blade, the one that would take his life, would also be the slowest one.

Defiance welled up in his heart, and a strong fury at his treacherous opponent caused his left arm to ignite in flames, reaching for his face.

As the blade and the Fire Qi were on the cusp of dealing fatal attacks, Yao Shen unleashed his divine sense.

This time, both the disciples paled as an inviolable force locked down upon their bodies, freezing them to the spot. Their deadly attacks were inches away from each other, but they would never be able to take the final step.

Yao Shen gazed down upon the children, letting out another light sigh. In his eyes, this duel had never been a fight between disciples, but instead, a fight between a representative of the outer sect and the legacy families. It had allowed him to gain much insight into the Sacred Flame Palace's operation, for much could be deciphered from this simple battle.

And ultimately...

"This duel is over!" Yao Shen's voice echoed out loudly, the thrilled spectators letting out cheers as both named were loudly chanted.

"Zhengwei!"

"Young Master Longtian!"

Zhengwei let out a relieved sigh as he gave his opponent a proud look. On the other hand, Longtian Cui gave him the same placid expression, as if the outcome did not concern him. Which was surprising, for while a draw was not the outcome he wanted, for Longtian Cui, it might as well have been a loss.

"The victor is..." the crowd hurriedly silenced themselves as Yao Shen spoke, "... Longtian Cui," his voice rang out.

The crowd immediately broke out in murmurs as Zhengwei's eyes flared up with confusion. He immediately gazed at Longtian, who remained locked in place as he was, his expression unchanged.

A sinking feeling enveloped him as he felt the restriction on his neck ease.

"His leg!" a sharp-eyed spectator pointed out, causing the spectator's murmurs to quell.

Zhengwei slowly tilted his neck, swiveling enough to see that...

... his left leg had crossed the white line.

30

REWARD

YAO SHEN'S expression was tranquil as he applied the finishing touches to his sketch, neatly rolling the papyrus scroll before pocketing it. He gently waved his right hand, causing the Fire Qi that Zhengwei was channeling to instantly flicker out. A wave of immutable force separated the two disciples by a few meters, and then Yao Shen withdrew his divine sense.

The two disciples immediately felt control over their body return to them. Longtian Cui sheathed his sword before clasping his hands behind his back, his bearing the very epitome of composure as he met his defeated foe's gaze.

As Zhengwei felt Yao Shen's restrictions upon his movement loosen, he realized that his hold over his scimitar was lightly trembling, from the sheer *disbelief* he felt at his loss. Even now, he could perfectly recall the burst of exhilaration that flowed through his veins as he pushed the young master of the Cui Family with a scimitar technique that he, a mere Qi-Formation disciple had created. Yet, the reversal came so suddenly, with such swiftness that Zhengwei could barely come to terms with the situation. In mere moments, his chance at obtaining an immensely valuable artifact had been lost, the opportunity seized by one who had no need of it.

Zhengwei could not accept it.

Longtian Cui concealing his abilities was within his prerogative, a stratagem that Zhengwei himself had utilized on multiple occasions. That was not what bothered him. So far, Zhengwei had been operating under the belief that he had accurately assessed his adversary's capabilities, for he had not won duel after duel without knowing how to choose his battles carefully. However, only now did he realize the sheer extent of his error.

Zhengwei's gaze flickered to the throng of spectators that had quieted down their cheers, observing the sympathetic glances a few offered him as if he had somehow been wronged.

'The fools,' Zhengwei thought, sheathing his scimitar with a flick of his wrist. Not once had Longtian Cui's placid expression changed, not even a glint of emotion visible in his *damnable* amber eyes as the Grand Patriarch had announced the name of the victor. That was not the gaze of a cultivator who relied on something as fickle as luck to win his battles. What even was luck, but the envy of the spectators and the rationalization of the defeated?

No, from the moment Zhengwei had stepped on the Sparring Stage, this was the outcome Longwei Cui had envisioned. Longtian Cui's feigned weakness followed by that ruthless counter was all a smokescreen to conceal his real objective— it galled him to admit it, but Zhengwei had never expected his adversary to defeat him by utilizing the very rules of the Sparring Stage itself. Perhaps that was exactly *why* he had chosen to do so.

How frustrating.

He truly could not bring himself to accept it. The feeling of his actions being *manipulated* by his adversary left a bitter taste in his mouth, the humiliation of not realizing his foe's layered ploy until the very end gnawing at his pride.

His right fist was clenched tight, causing Zhengwei to realize that, more than anything, he was angry.

Yao Shen observed the young Zhengwei's tumultuous emotions via his human sight as he began his slow descent. In truth, both Yao Shen and Flame Patriarch had long since analyzed the outcome of this duel, though there had been one surprise along the way. While Zhengwei's scimitar technique was deceptively powerful and its novelty could catch an opponent of lesser skill by surprise, passion could only go so far. His sword blows were too telegraphed under Longtian Cui's observant gaze and his tells fairly easy to identify. As long as one could bear the initial onslaught, Zhengwei's overly complicated sword art would turn out to be his own undoing.

Ultimately, though, Zhengwei's defeat stemmed from a lack of crucial intelligence. He made the same mistake Yao Shen once had, a mistake that many disciples of mortal upbringing ended up making— he saw the young master of the Cui Family as a peer. Longtian Cui had controlled the rhythm of the battle, displayed exceptional combat awareness and had subdued his adversary without revealing any more of his abilities than necessary. That was not the standard exacted from a Qi-Refinement level disciple.

Longtian Cui was not Zhengwei's rival. The scions of Legacy Families were trained in the martial way from the moment they could walk, fed valuable elixirs and pills that could bolster their potential, if only marginally, and receive the tutelage from their family elders, who would contentedly answer any question their scion might pose.

Yao Shen had often wondered where he would be if his master had not acknowledged his determination and taken him as his only disciple. He would no doubt have found his own way to rebel against his fate, like young Zhengwei who had created his own scimitar technique out of a desire to be acknowledged. But would he have reached the same accomplishments he had today? Would he still be Yao Shen, Grand Patriarch of the Modern Sect?

Yao Shen had never been a prodigy, but his determination alone could be considered a talent in and of itself. However, how many outer sect disciples had there been, as or even more talented than him across the generations? How many of them had the privilege of a Nascent Soul Grandmaster accepting them as his disciple?

Zhengwei's fight had moved Yao Shen, for he could imagine himself in the former's shoes. As much as Yao Shen would like to claim that his accomplishments were entirely his own, the debt he owed to his master was far too heavy for that. His grit, determination and willpower allowed him to forge a path where others saw none, but had destiny played its tune a little differently, he might have found himself in Zhengwei's position. Though he had not interacted with the disciple directly, his human sight had allowed him to see the burgeoning cloud of angst and resentment he carried along with him, like a disease that polluted everything around him before he ever got a chance to enjoy it.

Why did a talented disciple of the Sacred Flame Palace feel that way?

What *worth* did talent even have, without the infrastructure to support it?

In that moment Yao Shen's thought crystallized, his objective behind observing the duel between two disciples, one a legacy family disciple and the other an ordinary mortal who had ascended to something greater, met.

Outer Disciples.

Inner Disciples.

Core Disciples.

These distinctions had originally been created to foster competition between disciples, to incentivize them to continually hone their skills and improve their cultivation or face the consequences. For there was no greater nightmare for a cultivator than to be left behind by his peers. *Forgotten. Disregarded.*

They also served a more pragmatic purpose, for no sect or clan, no matter how powerful, could claim to have infinite resources. On the continent of Ionea, strength had always been the yardstick to measure worth, and the segregation of disciples by their performance had not only ensured that the majority of the resources went to the most talented amongst them, the *true* future of the sect; it also pushed disciples who desired the lucrative resources beyond their limits, creating anomalies like Yao Shen who defied both expectation and reason.

However... this archaic system had outlived its usefulness. The Azlak Plains were in decline, and yet, even though Yao Shen was subconsciously aware of the faults with this tiered system, the thought of overhauling it had never crossed his mind. Not until now. Not until he saw a young, talented outer disciple fail to reach his potential, because the outer sect was not considered worthy of the same quality of instruction as the inner sect.

If Yao Shen had learned anything in his decades of experience as Patriarch, it was that change always came with resistance. There were many uncertainties, and whilst it was easy to point out the faults of existing systems, replacing them seldom turned out as rudimentary or simple. Any good leader would hesitate when confronted with a choice that had the potential to change existing societal structures, and regardless of whether the outcome was beneficial or disastrous, history would remember him for it.

Nevertheless, it was time.

Yao Shen alighted upon the Sparring Stage, his presence causing the spectator's cheers to die down as their attention shifted to him. Even Flame Patriarch Lei Weiyuan was curious, still unable to puzzle out Yao Shen's intentions in hosting this inconsequential duel; for whilst there were a few elders that derived contentment from offering guidance and tutelage to disciples, the Grand Patriarch of the Modern Sect had never been one of them.

Yao Shen expanded his divine sense outward, enveloping the spear artifact that was embedded in soft earth before willing it in their general direction. The spear artifact was gently propelled forward, until it came to a pause in front of Longtian Cui, barely separated from him by a half a meter.

Though Zhengwei attempted to conceal it, bitterness flashed in his gaze as he saw the spear artifact hover forward toward his rival, Longtian Cui. Snippets of their battle flashed in his mind as Zhengwei wondered what he could have done differently, scouring through his arsenal of scimitar forms, searching, *hoping* for one that could have turned the tides of the duel... only to circle back to one singular answer.

Zhengwei had trained relentlessly in preparation for this duel, refined his scimitar technique to the limits of his understanding and expended all his strength in the battle. Yet, Longtian Cui stood facing him, not even a scratch to be found upon his crimson robes. The answer was as cruel as it was simple— Zhengwei, as he was right now, could not defeat Longtian Cui, regardless of which of his tactics he employed.

For the first time since he had stepped on the path of cultivation, Zhengwei had encountered an impregnable wall that neither deception nor brute force could surmount. Yao Shen detected the shift in his emotions with his human sight, as the cloud of angst slowly started shifting, forming a small, muted greyish-white cloud that represented the emotion 'resignation.' Part of Zhengwei could not help but start to give in, to simply accept that there was and always would be a gap between a cultivator from a mortal family and a member of an ancient family that had guarded its inheritance from the Era of Turmoil.

"Do you know what the most important aspect of a duel is?" A calm voice rang out in Zhengwei's mind, or rather, more accurately, his soul, that immediately startled him. He was on the verge of panicking, when he remembered that Nascent Soul Cultivators had something called 'divine sense' that they could utilize to transmit messages with.

It did not take him long to deduce who would communicate with him, for none of the Sect Elders had ever shown interest in him, much less use their divine sense to surreptitiously pass messages. He subtly directed his gaze to Yao Shen, who answered his silent query with a brief nod.

Surprise filled Zhengwei as he realized that the Grand Patriarch of the Modern Sect wished to speak with him, his other tumultuous emotions fading for now as he focused upon his words.

"Contrary to what you might believe, it is not martial strength. It may have played a role in your defeat, but it did not decide the outcome. Combat techniques, Weapon Artifacts and even upbringing all play a non-insignificant role, but once again, they alone are insufficient to decide the outcome." A small smile bloomed on Yao Shen's face as he saw the confused expression on Zhengwei's visage.

"Fundamentally, a duel between cultivators is a battle for information. Now, observe your foe's sword arm carefully." Zhengwei's confusion grew even deeper, but he chose to obey his instruction.

"Your reward." Yao Shen spoke aloud this time, his words signaling Longtian Cui to receive the spear.

A bead of sweat trickled down Longtian Cui's forehead as he stretched out both his arms to gingerly receive the spear in an almost reverent posture. The spear landed in Longtian Cui's hands, and he immediately bowed.

"I thank you for this bestowal on behalf of the Cui Family,

Grand Patriarch." Longtian Cui finally allowed him posture to relax as he sincerely thanked Yao Shen.

Zhengwei immediately noticed that Longtian Cui's sleeves were no longer folded, now stretching out to the base of his hand, but besides that, he could not make out any difference.

Yao Shen chose that moment to surreptitiously release a small, almost indetectable burst of Wind Qi that pulled back Longtian Cui's right sleeve for a few moments.

Zhengwei took a sharp breath, a mix of shock and disbelief reflected in his eyes as he caught a glimpse of Longtian Cui's sword arm, which was bruised so heavily that the skin had turned a deep purplish-black. It was nothing that the healers of the Cui Family could not fix but... not once in the battle had Zhengwei suspected that his opponent was injured so grievously. How could he even hold his sword with his arm in that condition? How had he not noticed? How much pain was he fighting through?

"We all see the world through our own paradigms, child," Yao Shen's voice once again sounded out in Zhengwei's mind. "The scions of legacy families project a veil of invulnerability when confronted with the outside world, for whilst they are offered many advantages by virtue of their birth, there is also a price that must be paid— *weakness* is not an emotion they are allowed to exhibit, and *defeat* is not an outcome they can accept. Only when you see beyond your biases and prejudices can you pierce the veil, and come to the realization that your foe is made of the same flesh, bone and blood that you are."

The words echoed in Zhengwei's mind, and for a brief moment, he set aside his dislike for the legacy families, set aside his prejudices against Longtian Cui and briefly allowed himself to forget the unfair treatment the outer sect had meted out to him. Zhengwei knew himself well enough to know that he could never truly allow himself to forget his biases, for anger was the fuel he ignited to progress rapidly in his cultivation.

But…

For that brief moment, Zhengwei allowed himself to feel admiration for Longtian Cui and his resolve.

"You fought well. Both of you." Yao Shen's loud voice shook Zhengwei out of his reverie. Longtian Cui moved to bow, and Zhengwei mirrored his movements. Their gazes crossed paths as they bowed, and Zhengwei realized that there was no *mockery* concealed in his eyes, his expression lacking the condescension he'd always imagined there would be. All Zhengwei found was two inquisitive eyes that seemed to be driven by a thirst for knowledge instead of the vile, selfish gaze he had expected.

Longtian Cui began to walk off the stage and Zhengwei moved to do the same, when Yao Shen called out, "Wait."

Zhengwei turned around, only to see Yao Shen toss what looked to be a papyrus scroll in his direction. The very same papyrus scroll Yao Shen had been sketching on during the duel.

He was already immensely grateful for Yao Shen's instruction, but he only seemed puzzled as he caught the scroll.

Without being prompted, Zhengwei unfurled the scroll as his curiosity got the better of him.

A few moments passed as he studied the series of drawings, all depicting a robed cultivator wielding a scimitar conducting varying series of strikes and following a different footwork each time.

Zhengwei's hands started trembling as he clutched the papyrus scroll in his hands as if it were more valuable than his life, recognition flashing in his eyes.

This was his scimitar technique, its original twelve forms expanded to a stupefying thirty-six scimitar forms, refined to an *astonishing* degree, so much so that it took him a few moments to recognize it.

"Tha—" Zhengwei tried to croak out a word of gratitude, but his voice failed him. His heartbeat accelerated as his mind tried to puzzle out if what he was seeing was real, or some sort of cruel jest, while his eyes felt a warmth that almost felt alien after years of maintaining a stony facade.

Zhengwei bowed deeply, this time with complete sincerity, as he finally managed to stutter out the words, "T-Thank you."

Two trails of warm tears trickled down his cheeks, seeping into the papyrus scroll but unable to cause any damage to the ink.

After seeing Yao Shen nod, Zhengwei hurried off the Sparring Stage, fearing that he would not be able to control his emotions any longer.

Zhengwei the nameless, born to parents whose names he could not remember, had forgotten what it felt like to experience kindness.

He would cry in his personal quarters not long after the duel, and later that day, Longtian Cui would offer to spar with him on a regular basis in the Cui Family residence.

This time, Zhengwei would accept.

31

BANQUET

UNBEKNOWNST TO ZHENGWEI, the papyrus scroll he had received from Yao Shen served a secondary purpose. A communication talisman had been skillfully embedded upon the scroll's rear, for it would have been a pity not to have given young Zhengwei a method to contact him. He had displayed ample of the quality that Yao Shen valued most in a disciple, namely, *resolve* and whilst the inadequate tutelage the Sacred Flame Palace offered had limited his potential, it would do so no longer.

The final three forms of the scimitar technique Yao Shen had refined were a test, their difficulty and complexity far outpacing the preceding ones.

As Patriarch, it was Yao Shen's duty to plan two steps ahead of the sect elders, who often prioritized short-term gain over long-term sustenance. He could only do so by tapping into the unrealized potential of the coming generation— whilst Yao Shen had no intention of accepting any more disciples presently, the same might not hold true a decade from now.

Perhaps Zhengwei would surprise him. Nevertheless, he would not be the only disciple whose future Yao Shen would decide to invest in.

. . .

Yao Shen and Lei Weiyuan departed not long after the duel's conclusion, coming to a stop before the inner sect's entrance.

The inner sect was shrouded by a fairly impressive concealment formation that weaved thin strips of Shadow and Darkness Qi into a domed lattice that served to dampen and restrict divine sense probes.

Lei Weiyuan took the lead and Yao Shen followed, holding on to the talisman that marked him as a guest in the eyes of the Formation Spirit. Whilst Yao Shen didn't fear betrayal, he found it prudent not to grant the Sacred Flame Palace any easy avenue to do so. He activated his Human Dao Domain before taking forth a step into the darkness behind Lei Weiyuan, who had already blinked out of his sight.

The first thing Yao Shen felt was the noticeable spike in temperature, a roiling wave of hot air impacting against his skin that alone made the inner sect inhabitable for any mortal. Bright light shone in his eyes, but it did not obscure his vision in the slightest.

Though Yao Shen had received extensive intelligence relating to the inner sect's layout, this was the first time he had personally witnessed it for himself.

And it was glorious.

A statue of the Sacred Bird, Marayan, towered over the surrounding edifices, clearly visible from even the furthest corners of the inner sect. Aptly positioned in the heart of the small town, the likeness of the Sacred Bird was brought to life with vibrant hues of red, further accentuated by flecks of gold dotted over its majestic wings; three brilliant spiritual gemstones that had been carved to perfection had been slotted into the three-eyed Sacred Bird's eye sockets, shining with an ethereal silver luminescence.

While the statue alone was a sight to behold, Yao Shen knew that it served a far greater purpose; for it served as the Formation Spirit's dwelling. Five canals originated from the statue's base, stretching out until they were on the verge of intersecting with the concealment formation before angling downwards, until they were seemingly subsumed by the packed earth beneath. The canals divided the city into equally as many portions, for it was not water that flowed through it, but rather, a continuous stream of liquid flames that swept forward through the obsidian canals, raising the ambient Fire Qi in the atmosphere by several degrees.

He could now understand why Lei Weiyuan believed in the legend of Marayan, for this was a sight enough to inspire reverence in those exposed to the teachings of the Sacred Flame from a young age.

A second, more concentrated boundary of purification was concealed beneath his feet, the reward that awaited anyone foolish enough to attempt to sneak in the inner sect. The liquid flames supplied by the canal were utilized to ensure that the two boundaries of purification remained functional at all times and to adjust the Ambient Qi density accordingly. Some found the formation to be wasteful and a tad too luxurious, but whilst that might be true, Yao Shen found the formation to be the quintessential work of a Flame Cultivator— for what greater deterrent could there be than a scorching hot wall of flames burning invaders to ash?

Yao Shen finally withdrew his Human Dao Domain as he stepped outside the boundary of purification's reach, following Lei Weiyuan as they came up on what looked to be a residential area.

Lei Weiyuan led Yao Shen through a broad, stone-tiled road. The housing in the inner sect displayed a much greater degree of individuality in comparison to the outer sect, a few particularly impressive pagodas nestled in walled enclosures catching his attention, their color schemes ranging from spirited scarlet and orange to more mellow, yet equally arresting greys and whites. There were also single-story houses that were clumped together in groups of four, centered around a small courtyard and wide, elongated dojos that were arrayed together in the northeastern part of the residential area, likely the residences of disciples.

Flame Patriarch Lei Weiyuan came to a stop before a relatively smaller, yet no less impressive three-story pagoda painted in an auspicious vermillion with gold and silver embellishments.

A quick divine sense scan revealed that the rest of his contingent had already arrived and were likely awaiting his presence.

Yao Shen and Lei Weiyuan spent the next thirty minutes going over minor details of the banquet, informing the latter that he would be attending personally. Meili Zhu graciously played the part of the host, serving the two Patriarchs warm tea that was soaked in Sona root and crushed Ecium flowers— strong but not overpowering, the tea left behind a spicy aftertaste that crushed any hint of drowsiness or fatigue Yao Shen might have felt at the long day. A true delicacy, though that had more to do with the skill of the brewer than the ingredients involved.

After Lei Weiyuan departed, Meili Zhu informed him that the finest chefs from the Sky Division had been dispatched, carrying a larder full of delicacies in their spiritual rings. That was good; showing magnanimity at this stage would hopefully allay fears of being mistreated under his command.

The estimate Yao Shen had requested would be arriving tomorrow morning, in the early hours after dawn. Inspecting the treasuries before then would serve no purpose besides aggravating the cultivators of the Sacred Flame, thus Yao Shen chose to spend the next few hours peacefully cultivating within the confines of his room.

Not long after, it was time for the banquet.

. . .

The banquet was to be held in the outer sect, but the three-story tall dining hall was not equipped to host such a magnitude of patrons. The sect guardians Lei Weiyuan had entrusted with the task of organizing the banquet acted with haste, mobilizing the disciples while they scoured the outer sect for an alternative.

Ultimately, it was decided that the training field was the most apt, and perhaps the only venue sizable enough to host the entire strength of the Sacred Flame Palace. Hundreds of disciples swept the field, clearing it of weights, static targets, blunt weapons, training dummies and other random paraphernalia that had found its way to the training field over the years.

The dry, cracked earth beneath the disciples' feet now looked far more conspicuous after the land was stripped off all the equipment that it had amassed over the years. The Boundary of Purification running beneath the Sacred Flame Palace meant that any moisture in the soil would instantly evaporate, leading to desertification within the Sacred Flame Palace and its immediate vicinity.

Plush carpets were rolled out by disciples in groups of ones and twos, superhuman speed and agility allowing them to cover the entire region in a matter of minutes. Long wooden tables were brought from the dining hall, and when those alone would not suffice, procured from other halls. Within an hour, five rows of long tables running parallel to each other, stretched out from one end of the training field to the other. At the head of the arrangement, a particularly eye-catching amber-colored table with golden embellishments rested upon a dais, placed horizontally to allow an eagle's eye view of the entire banquet.

All this was accomplished in an hour's time, displaying the frightening efficiency of cultivators when directed to mundane tasks.

.   .   .

It would be an understatement to say that large-scale celebrations were uncommon amongst cultivator sects. Usually, the further a cultivator advanced on the path to power, the more they would lose touch with their mortal side— time no longer held the same meaning for them, and those who could not keep up with their cultivation pace would ultimately become but a memory, for time did not operate on the same scale for those separated by stages of cultivation.

Any elder of the Sacred Flame Palace had likely seen companions, lovers and even family snatched away by time, while they remained relatively untouched by its influence.

Thus, it was no wonder that powerful cultivators lived rather solitary, reserved lives and those traits were passed down to disciples who looked up to them as role models, leading to the creation of an extremely rigid society. Only they did not know of and could not understand, the pain and loss the 'aloof' facade that powerful cultivators projected concealed.

When Yao Shen arrived at the banquet, he could not help but be surprised at the sheer number of disciples in attendance. Cultivators usually did not amass in such large gatherings unless they were mobilizing for large-scale combat, and the Azlak Plains had not seen war for centuries now.

Such a large gathering reminded Yao Shen of state fairs back on Earth, as old, pleasant memories bubbled up to the forefront of his consciousness— he remembered the seemingly endless throng of people that were dressed in colorful outfits, small children running around with gleeful expressions without a care in the world and the plethora of sweet and savory delights whose pervasive aroma was a persistent accompaniment to the state fair experience.

Earth had invented many festivals that had originally served different purposes, but over time, had evolved to become celebrations of life. Mortals on Ionea too had their own harvest festivals, one of which Yao Shen had himself attended before when he was in disguise, but the cultivators had none.

Flame Patriarch Lei Weiyuan and Earth Patriarch Kang Long took their seats on his either side before the elders began to fill in the remaining seats on the amber long table.

The murmuring of the disciples died down with his arrival, their attention slowly shifting to him. In that moment, he was the sole focus of the gazes of thousands of disciples and hundreds of guardians— some watching him with caution and suspicion, some others with trepidation and even fear, while a few looked on with veiled anger and even resentment.

Yao Shen took a sip of spiritual wine from his goblet, the strong, fruity liquid rushing down his throat and providing a small burst of vitality, before he stood up to address the Sacred Flame Palace.

"Disciples and Guardians of the Flame Division," his Qi-empowered voice echoed forth, loud enough that even those seated at the very end of the training field could hear him clearly.

Yao Shen saw a few disciples wince at being addressed as the 'Flame Division,' but it was necessary to reinforce his authority.

"The history of the Azlak Plain is a long and contentious one..." Yao Shen's words were spoken with a gravitas that befitted his station. "...and I do not expect mere words alone to move your hearts, the same way, if our positions were reversed, I would not put my faith in one aligned against my sect not too long ago."

This time, there was a far stronger reaction from the audience — one of surprise, even astonishment, for no one present had expected Yao Shen to address the elephant in the room directly.

"The past, *our* past, is part of what defines us as a cultivator. It is both what unites us, as members of the righteous path, and what divides us, by the color of our robes. Each of us carries our own pasts, replete with our cherished memories, our accomplishments and our triumphs... but... let us not forget our missteps, our failures and our regrets, as much as some of us may wish to. Tonight, cultivators of the Flame Division, I ask a favor of you," Yao Shen's words might not have been enough to move the crowd, but it did make them fall into an introspective silence.

Yao Shen had not attempted to imbue his words with emotions to accentuate the speech's impact, partly because influencing such a large crowd was beyond his abilities. In truth, though, even if he had the capability to do so, he wouldn't.

Simply because he didn't need to.

"On this night, let our pasts not be the *only* thing that defines us. For the river of time flows in one direction, and that is forward. The ideal past will forever remain an ideal, but the future is something we can yet shape. Let this day be a celebration, as on this day, the cultivators of the Azlak Plains stand together as one, united whole..." Yao Shen paused, raising the goblet of wine aloft with his right hand.

"On that note, I raise a toast to Flame Patriarch Lei Weiyuan and to the future prosperity of the Flame Division. Let the banquet commence!"

His words served as the signal, as dozens of disciples dressed in azure robes exited a row of tents, each of them carrying large platters laden with cuts of spiritual beast meat, half a dozen different types of flatbreads, a few different offerings of curries, broths, soups and more. Immediately behind them were disciples in fiery red robes that offered a different selection of dishes.

That night, spiritual wine was offered to disciples who could normally never afford it. The taps did not stop flowing, and the Heavenly Sky Sect had provided what seemed to be a never-ending supply of spiritual beast meat.

Many disciples recalled releasing sighs of relief that night, sighs they themselves didn't realize they were holding. A reprieve from the grueling routines they followed released months of tension, and that night, many uptight cultivators who would normally be considered antagonistic and irate smiled and even laughed, drunk on spiritual wine.

That night, despite the banquet being thrown by one they considered an enemy, the disciples of the Flame Division slept a little easier.

32

THE SOLARIS KEEP

THE NEXT MORNING, Yao Shen received word from Meili Zhu that the estimates he had requested had arrived, along with ten guardians from the Heavenly Sky Sect that would be assisting in the 'auditing process.'

He had two major concerns that he hoped to address on his second day in the Sacred Flame Palace, though it would only be the first step in what would likely be a long, challenging journey.

The first concern was a question of ideology and a part of the answer that he sought lay in the memories he had inherited from his previous life— for the humans of Earth had evolved their own conflicting jurisprudence across their long and bloody history that clashed together to form cohesive systems of governance. However, the major distinction between Earth and Eliria meant that Yao Shen could not directly implement those systems, for the two worlds had very different conceptualizations of '*power*.'

Eliria, or more specifically, cultivators, would never embrace an elected ruler that did not have the martial strength to support his claim. Yao Shen could, of course, try and enforce such systems, but the only outcome that would lead to would be the creation of an empire that would be founded on the basis of his strength, and consequentially, collapse not long after his demise.

No, he could not *directly* implement such a system, but he could borrow doctrines from it.

Yao Shen did not need to create different institutions or branches to achieve a cohesive system of governance, for the three factions of the Modern Sect were united only in name. The Sky, Earth and Flame divisions would unwittingly achieve a system of checks and balances, for they could be trusted to keep a close eye on the other divisions and ensure that resources were being directed to their intended purposes instead of being consumed by a smog of corruption, nepotism and greed, as had been the case with Yanyue.

After all, they had done so for centuries without requiring any additional incentives; and Yao Shen did not expect that to change overnight.

As for his second concern, he would address that in a joint conclave with the other two Patriarchs and the elders present.

An hour after daybreak, Yao Shen, along with Meili Zhu and the ten guardians, were led to a new section of the inner sect. Special bridges constructed out of some variant of fire-resistant timber served to facilitate transport over the blazing canals, at least for those who yet lacked the ability to take flight.

Yao Shen found the inner sect, or more specifically, the Formation Spirit rather fascinating as he made his way across the bridge; part of him wondering if there was any way to reorient the Spirit's core directives to, say, cover a larger territory. Neither the Sky Division nor the Earth Division had a Formation Spirit of their own, making Yao Shen's knowledge on the topic painfully incomplete.

His musings were interrupted as the administrative district

came into view. The first thing Yao Shen noticed, or rather sensed, were the furtive glances that landed upon his person the moment he stepped inside the territory.

There were far fewer buildings in the administrative district, though conversely, each of them was characterized by unique architectural choices and some structures even seemed to be designed with specialized purposes in mind. An expansive, stepped ziggurat-like structure particularly caught Yao Shen's attention, a thick plume of smoke rising from a chimney on topmost layer— the Sacred Forge made a particularly impressive first impression, situated at the eastern end of the district.

Every few minutes, a patrol of sect guardians would pass by them, and Yao Shen could tell that their progress through the city was being tracked. The streets were clean, immaculately so, while the district itself seemed to be sparsely populated. Besides a few disciples that avoided his group like a plague and the patrolling guardians, there seemed to be no one.

They were first guided to a broad-set ivory tower, where a pinprick of their blood and a small fragment of their divine sense was taken to mark them as a member of the Sacred Flame Palace in the eyes of the Formation Spirit. All in all, the entire process took an hour, and they now had access to both the outer sect and the inner sect, having been given a clearance at the elder level.

Having fulfilled the prerequisites, they were finally escorted to their intended destination.

The Solaris Keep was a building that seemed to defy the architectural norms of both Earth and Eliria, if it could even be called such. A perfect cube nestled in the heart of the administrative district, the lack of any window openings or apertures to allow fresh air in giving it a rather disconcerting first impression. Lines upon lines of runic inscriptions were inscribed upon every inch of the Solaris Keep's exterior, and Yao Shen could clearly sense the Fire Qi that pulsated through them and he knew the purpose they served.

Immediately after the Era of Turmoil, the objectives of every major sect, at least among those that had survived, had shifted to rebuilding their defenses, and more importantly, finding measures to deter conflict. The Solaris Keep was merely a remnant of those measures, a deterrence true to its name— Yao Shen could, with some difficulty, breach the defenses of the Flame Division, but recovering resources from the keep would be an impossibility.

Not because the defenses of the keep were impenetrable, no; for there existed a far simpler solution. True to its name, the Solaris Keep would burn with the brilliance of the sun at the drop of a hat— a Nascent Soul resource did not necessarily have the resilience of a cultivator at the Nascent Soul level. In fact, most high-level resources did not have particularly strong defenses.

The philosophy of the Flame Division was a simple, yet domineering one— if they could not have the resources accumulated across generations, then no one could.

Patriarch Lei Weiyuan waited for them at the entrance of the Solaris Keep, his hands clasped behind his back as he pondered upon the odd fractals engraved upon the surface of two staggeringly large double doors that covered an entire face of the perfect cube that the keep was.

The two Patriarchs exchanged cordial greetings, though Yao Shen could tell that Lei Weiyuan's expression was a little strained.

Nevertheless, there was no trouble as Lei Weiyuan gave a verbal command to open the gates.

A loud rumble echoed out, the ground beneath them beginning to lightly quake as the double doors parted open slightly, just enough to allow a grown man to pass through.

There was nothing but darkness on the other side, but Patriarch Lei Weiyuan didn't hesitate as he stepped inside, disappearing from sight the moment he was completely through.

After activating his Human Dao Domain, Yao Shen followed, stepping into territory that was completely unknown to the Heavenly Sky Sect— for only elders were allowed inside the Solaris Keep, its secrets privy to only them.

It was indeed a risk, but Yao Shen did not believe that the Solaris Keep had the ability to subvert his Human Dao Domain. For if it had, then it also had the ability to subdue the entire Heavenly Sky Sect decades, or even centuries ago.

So he went, into the darkness.

Were it not for Yao Shen's divine sense, he would not be able to make out the seemingly endless flight of steps that lay before him that stretched deep underground. Thankfully, the guardians who had been chosen to accompany Yao Shen for the auditing process had been informed in advance to carry non-flammable light sources with them.

The heavy, tense breaths let out by the guardians and the footfall of their group upon the mottled stone steps were the only sounds exchanged for the next hour, as they continued to descend into the depths of Eliria. The guardians were understandably nervous, for if things were to go awry, they were the group least likely to survive, but they tried to combat their fear with excitement.

Another fifteen minutes passed before Patriarch Lei Weiyuan finally came to a stop before a far smaller door that was carved into solid bedrock.

"Extinguish your light sources," the Flame Patriarch instructed, and only when the last guardian had done so did he give the command to open the door.

A warm orange glow seeped through as the door slowly

swung open to reveal an awe-inspiring sight. The first layer of the Solaris Keep stretched for as far as the mortal eye could see, its design more reminiscent of an arcane library than a mere treasury or reserve.

The northwestern section of the keep was dominated by an extensive collection of artifacts, whose purposes ranged from relaying information and increasing movement speed to outright weapons of war— a collection of both conventional and non-conventional implements that were designed for combat. Most were stored behind simple crystal cases, while a few select artifacts had to be kept sealed behind runic inscriptions, likely the ones that possessed an artifact spirit. There was one thing however, that they all shared in common; for information pertaining to each artifact was recorded on a metal plaque that was affixed on the displays.

The capabilities and limitations of the artifact, where and how it was acquired, the year of acquisition and any other relevant information was penned down with painstaking detail.

Natural Treasures placed in receptacles that preserved their vigor, large crates of spiritual ore organized by their purity and potency, taels of refined metals stacked on top of each other in the form of ingots that would later be utilized to forge weapon artifacts, an entire section dedicated to by-products acquired from spiritual beasts, like their horns, antlers, fangs, venom sacs and of course, beast cores, that could be used to forge various kinds of artifacts.

Such a display of wealth could move even Yao Shen, whose gaze flickered to a collection of scrolls, beast-hide tomes and dusty journals that looked like they had seen better days, let alone conniving elders like Meili Zhu or the guardians.

"Impressive," Patriarch Kang Long of the Earth Division, who Yao Shen had insisted accompany them, remarked— echoing a sentiment shared by most, if not all, present.

Meili Zhu used her divine sense to convey a message, confirming what Yao Shen had begun to suspect— whilst not all of the wealth of the Flame Division could be concentrated on this one floor, especially since Spiritual Plants, Alchemical Pills and other treasures that were not suitable or necessary to be stored below ground were likely kept separately, it already exceeded their estimates. Yao Shen wasn't surprised, for Meili Zhu's cunning and the Faceless' existence could only fill the information gap by so much.

That spoke to the Flame Patriarch's earnestness, though the truly priceless treasures were likely already in the possession of the legacy families or hidden away well in advance.

Which was fine, for now. Pushing beyond a reasonable limit would benefit no one and Yao Shen had no intention to commemorate his rule by sowing the seeds of insurrection.

"Patriarch Lei Weiyuan, I thought only elders were allowed in the Solaris Keep," Meili Zhu's sickly-sweet voice rang out, a hint of surprise echoing in her words. She was undoubtedly referring to the aged cultivators that clearly did not reach the Nascent Soul level, taking care of mundane tasks like cleaning display cases and organizing newly acquired resources in the correct sections of the keep, at least at first glance. They numbered in the dozens, which would normally be a significant vulnerability.

"The Gatekeepers," Lei Weiyuan replied. "Every decade or two, cultivators who have given up on their ascension are chosen to maintain the upkeep of the Solaris Keep. Their character and loyalty to the sect is above reproach, for the Gatekeepers are either nearing or approaching the end of their natural lifespans, and they are to live the rest of their lives in the keep. In return, the sect offers a great remuneration to their descendants, far beyond what an average guardian can hope to earn in their lives."

"Their loyalty to the sect is commendable," Yao Shen remarked, looking at the aged cultivators with a newfound respect. Cultivators they might be, but it took more than a desire for wealth to live out their twilight years devoid of the warmth of the sun, hunkered down in a repository of unimaginable wealth yet unable to spend even a single fraction of it. Whether that loyalty was to their descendants or to the Flame Division made little difference.

"Indeed," Lei Weiyuan tersely replied, allowing a hint of regret to seep into his voice.

Neither Yao Shen nor Lei Weiyuan looked at the Gatekeepers with pity, for a cultivator did not offer pity to the strong of will.

The former wished to change many things, but even he did not yet dare dream of a world without sacrifice.

Mayhap, though, this particular sacrifice was no longer required. The Gatekeeper's existence was primarily to guard against espionage, but with the three sects united under one banner, their existence became rather redundant.

But if he simply ended the system, he would dishonor their sacrifice, their dream of a better, more prosperous future for their descendants. And Yao Shen knew that Lei Weiyuan would always keep one Gatekeeper stationed within the sect, for it would be foolish to let go of the greatest bargaining chip he had over Yao Shen— the Solaris Keep could not be forcibly taken, as long as there remained at least one man stationed within.

He had no intention to seize the resources of the keep, though he would be lying if the thought did not cross his mind for a second— his old self, the mind of a calculating, shrewd Patriarch, had mellowed with his awakening, but he was still the same man. The Gatekeepers had lived a full life and now they deserved to spend what little remained of it with their children and grand-children.

Yao Shen internally nodded, having made up his mind.

"How do you keep a record of the keep's assets?" Yao Shen asked,

A small smile made his way to the stoic Patriarch's face, as he hollered at one of the Gatekeepers to bring him '*the artifact.*'

A portly old cultivator with a genial smile walked over with a bulging sheaf of papyrus that was held together by a thin wire spiraled over multiple times to serve as a binder that seemed woefully inadequate.

"Honorable Patriarchs." The cultivator bowed gracefully, his face devoid of any reproach as he held the papyrus logbook forward.

"Thank you, Yunru."

"It is a pleasure to be of service, as always." He bowed, the smile never leaving his face as he took his leave. Yao Shen had utilized his human sight to glance at the man's departing silhouette, and he found nothing but the elusive golden cloud of contentment. It was not that his concerns for the Gatekeepers were misfounded, but as Yao Shen had found through years of observing both mortals and cultivators, some people managed to find inner peace regardless of what hand fate dealt them— to simply be happy with how the world was, how their life had been and to desire no more. A simple enough concept, yet one Yao Shen doubted he would attain in this lifetime. His desire for change, after all, was the very antithesis of contentment.

His expression turned into a perplexed frown, for the sheaf of papyrus in Lei Weiyuan's hand was quite simply blank.

"Log," the Flame Patriarch stated out loud, surprising the bystanders.

Words began to blossom on the topmost sheet of papyrus, before the logbook rapidly started flicking through pages at an astonishing speed. Soon, there was only one solitary sheet remaining as the writing began to taper off a quarter of the way through.

Upon taking a closer look, it was revealed that a record of

every item in the keep was written down in the artifact, along with its categorization and the date it was acquired.

"Cease," Lei Weiyuan muttered, and the writing instantly disappeared.

Next, he withdrew a piece of charcoal from his storage space and wrote down upon it.

'Spiritual Ore'

Yao Shen watched on curiously as a response was scrawled back by the artifact.

'Grade?'

'Nascent Soul'

'Purity?'

'Low'

The topmost sheet of papyrus tore itself out from the binder with a burst of Wind Qi, before it began to hover away toward the east.

"What a fascinating artifact." Yao Shen's eyes had already lit up with surprise, and even more so, shock as he immediately understood the artifact's purpose. It reminded Yao Shen of Earth and its capabilities, even though the effect was very rudimentary and limited in comparison. His shock stemmed from the fact that few would expend time in designing a utility-based artifact such as this one, especially their militant ancestors.

"As you all have likely guessed, the sheet of papyrus will show us to our desired item. It does help in managing the keep, but this artifact has too many limitations," Lei Weiyuan explained, dampening some of Yao Shen's initial excitement.

"The artifact spirit?" Yao Shen asked, guessing at the root of the problem.

"It is unresponsive and the artifact was designed to work with the metal plaques that are affixed to each item. We ran out a decade ago, and since then, we have been forced to rely on manual records."

Yao Shen almost clicked his tongue at that, his disappointment obvious. Though if the artifact really was that useful, the Flame Division would have already utilized it across the sect. As for creating an artifact spirit, that was an art none of the forces in the Azlak Plains possessed, so replicating it was also a lost cause.

"Very well," Yao Shen muttered before shifting his attention. "Guardians?"

"Yes, Patriarch," they echoed in unison, with slightly too much enthusiasm.

"For now, make one copy of the logbook and the manual records each, and verify them to the greatest extent feasible. "

"Yes, Patriarch!" they bellowed in unison, and soon split away with their respective tasks. Some spoke to the gatekeepers and enlisted their aid, but those were all logistical matters Yao Shen need not be concerned with.

Only Yao Shen, the two Patriarchs, and Meili Zhu remained, watching the guardians and the Gatekeepers work in tandem with each other.

"I have made a decision."

He felt the two Patriarchs' attention shift to him, their expression one of interest as they awaited his decision. They would not yet recognize the significance of his subsequent words, but Yao Shen intended for *that* moment, *that* decision, to be a pivotal one— a defining mandate that would set the tone for the rest of his time as Grand Patriarch.

"A day ago, the Flame Division was presented with a choice." Yao Shen's voice was soft and tranquil, his hands clasped behind his back as he simply took in the grandeur of the Solaris Keep. "A choice between honor and deceit. A decision that could very well decide the fate of the Flame Division for the coming decades, if not centuries."

Patriarch Lei Weiyuan remained calm, seemingly unmoved by Yao Shen's words; however, Yao Shen noticed a brief disturbance in the Earth Patriarch's usually unreadable emotions.

"Our honor was once what united us as members of the righteous path. Not as a sword that hangs above our heads and neither as a constant need, rather, a constant desire to maintain and uphold the reputation of ourselves and the families we represent. We are far weaker than our ancestors in martial strength… and it is easy to blame lost inheritances and forgotten knowledge for our ineptitude." Yao Shen had an almost melancholic smile on his face as memories of his past… his missteps, flashed through his mind.

"But we often choose to forget that it was not all that separated us from our ancestors. When the radiance of the sun was obscured by dark clouds, the greenery of the grass concealed in an eerie, thick blanket of fog and it felt like all was lost… It was **honor** that gave strength to their blade, cutting down the demons concealed in the mists. For the knowledge that the path they walked down was the correct one, the righteous one, was enough to blow back the clouds of despair, to allow the warmth of the sun to once again bless Ionea's land…

"…The Flame Division has honored me, Yao Shen, by its display of sincerity. It has honored the spirit of the Modern Sect, by choosing to believe that the Azlak Plains are capable of progress." Yao Shen did not actually believe that Lei Weiyuan was even close to fully convinced, if he was at all, but that did not change fact. The Flame Patriarch had ample opportunity to skim, or outright conceal a significant portion of the treasury's wealth and Meili Zhu would have been none the wiser. His display of strength, undoubtedly, was the greatest factor in Lei Weiyuan's compliance, but a small part of him wanted to believe that, deep down, *somewhere,* the Flame Patriarch wished to see his perhaps naive, definitely over-ambitious vision for the Modern Sect blossom into reality.

"I refuse to meet honor with avarice. Confronted with such wealth..." Yao Shen gestured at the sprawling keep before him. "...even the most virtuous of souls would be swayed by temptation. Thus, I have devised a solution."

Meili Zhu's expression turned somewhat pensive upon hearing Yao Shen's words, but the other two Patriarchs listened closely, wondering if his grandiose speech had any substance behind it.

"The wealth of the three divisions belongs to the Modern Sect. However, the Modern Sect itself exists to serve the interests of its divisions, which includes, as some of us often forget, even the weakest among the outer disciples. Therefore, it is only natural that *each* sect's treasury should be managed and supervised by representatives from all three major divisions." Yao Shen concluded his explanation, a small smile forming on his face.

Meili Zhu's eyes glinted with clear surprise, which shifted to confusion for a few seconds before settling on clarity.

"*Each* division?" Lei Weiyuan asked, putting clear emphasis on the word 'each' as if he could not believe it.

"Namely, the Sky, Earth and Flame Divisions of the Modern Sect, our three major divisions," Yao Shen retorted, the smile not leaving his face. "From henceforth, a clear record will be kept pertaining to each treasury's assets and elders will not simply be allowed to withdraw wealth or resources without notifying a representative from each sect first. If any elder is found to be siphoning resources for their personal gain, then they will be required to compensate the Modern Sect with two times the value of the stolen resources. After the treasury's losses are recompensed, the remaining wealth shall be awarded to the division that reported the transgression." Yao Shen's words were spoken with an air of finality, and for a moment, the two Patriarchs fell into silence, slowly digesting the information.

His ploy was an open one, borrowing from Earth's jurisprudence. Instead of creating different institutions of governance, he would simply use human nature to create internal checks and balances. The three divisions did not consider themselves to be a cohesive whole, and it was in their best interests to ensure that no one division progressed too far ahead of the other two.

The three divisions would now be inclined to monitor each other's treasuries with the vigilance of a bird of prey, waiting, *watching,* until their rival made a mistake. Not only would this cause a grievous loss of face to the elder that was outed as a disgraceful pilferer, but it would also place them in Yao Shen's good graces. The additional resources were just a bonus, for the loss of face alone was far graver a consequence— a gap that could not be bridged by wealth or martial strength.

Yao Shen, powerful as he might be, was just one man. He could fight off demonic cultivators and spiritual beasts, but corruption, ironically, could not be stymied through his efforts alone.

The only real question was if the elders' love for wealth and resources trumped their desire to see the other division suffer a significant loss.

"Will a division's treasury only be utilized for the benefit of that specific treasury?" Patriarch Kang Long finally spoke, his words measured and cautious. Yao Shen had been known for many things, but a seasoned politician had not been one of them — thus, it was quite surprising to see him fashion such a ruthless trap, one that they could not help but willingly walk into.

"For the most part, yes," Yao Shen replied calmly. "There will be certain joint projects that will require contribution from all three divisions, but be assured that the benefits will also be shared equitably. And of course, the divisions will be allowed, and even encouraged, to freely exchange resources between them. We must not forget that we are now one family, and the needs of our fellow family members must be considered in good faith."

"I see," Patriarch Kang Long replied, the tension in his voice fading. That was as fair an answer as he could have hoped for, and at least it did not seem that it was Yao Shen's intention to plunder their resources. "Thank you, Grand Patriarch," he added in a far lower tone, so much so that if Yao Shen were not a cultivator, he wouldn't have been able to hear it.

Meili Zhu's expression had paled slightly, but she did not interfere in a conversation between the three Patriarchs. She could, but it would only expose her uneasiness at the decision. For if one did not covet what did not belong to them, they had nothing to fear from Yao Shen's decision.

Not long after, Meili Zhu and Patriarch Kang Long excused themselves— likely to inform their respective sects of Yao Shen's decision, and perhaps, for their elders to stop engaging in any such activities.

The guardians continued their task relentlessly, though Yao Shen suspected that it would yet take them a few weeks before they were done compiling and verifying all the relevant information.

Yao Shen finally took the opportunity to ask the question that had been simmering in the back of his mind for quite some time now.

He knew that Lei Weiyuan would not be naive enough to expose all his Gatekeepers in a place where Yao Shen could kill them nigh instantaneously. There had to be at least one hiding somewhere, ready to send the command to incinerate the Solaris Keep at a moment's notice.

His divine sense could not detect any hidden rooms or passageways, barring a passageway that led deeper into Eliria's depths. The conclusion was obvious; there were most definitely more layers to the Solaris Keep, though he doubted any would be as expansive or as affluent as this one.

Naturally, his curiosity led him to push his divine sense deeper down the passageway, only to be met with genuine surprise. Had Yao Shen been even a second late in recalling his divine sense, the portion he extended would have been shattered in half.

The divine sense of a Soul Emperor, *shattered.*

"You may choose not to answer, if you wish, but what lies beneath this layer?" he asked, already having a vague idea of the answer. For anything else would not make much sense.

Patriarch Lei Weiyuan seemed to have expected that question, transmitting his reply directly with his own divine sense.

"*Interesting.* Would you be willing to lead the way?"

Patriarch Lei Weiyuan took a few seconds to think about it, and then simply shrugged.

"Why not."

33

ORIGIN TREASURE

SOME THOUGHT of the Heavenly Dao, the mighty heavens, as an existence akin to a deity. Others respected the heavens, for it was heaven's tribulation that judged if a cultivator was worthy of ascension or not. That respect may have been born out of fear, for most would find it prudent not to slight a being that had the ability to decide their fate. A few, like Yao Shen, refused to bow under heaven's mandate.

But if there was one matter upon which all three groups would find themselves reaching an agreement upon, it was the Heavenly Dao's inclination to present the denizens of Eliria with trials and tribulations.

A cultivator's inheritance, in elementary terms, was a communion between the past and the present, a method for a dying cultivator to pass on the culmination of a lifetime's study, be that in the form of a martial technique, a forging method, an alchemical pill or even an ancestral weapon. Of course, these were only one type of inheritances, albeit the most valuable type as well. There were other inheritances that had little to do with one's own understanding of the Dao, simply resources or knowledge that a cultivators wished to pass on to his descendants.

Some inheritances required the inheritor to possess the ancestor's bloodline, but Ionea's past was a rather perilous one. One would wonder why beings that tended to be as self-absorbed as cultivators would leave behind inheritances at all, but the reason behind it was rather banal— A powerful cultivator may have the ability to cheat time, but they were not timeless existences.

Thus, in a compromise between their pride and a desire to live on, if only in the form of their created techniques, they would leave behind inheritances that one could access only after a series of trials that measured the quality the deceased ancestor valued the most. Flame Cultivators tended to value strength above all, thus Yao Shen would not be particularly surprised if he encountered a vicious beast in the inheritance trial of a Flame Cultivator.

However, this led to an interesting conundrum. What happened if an inheritance trial lay unclaimed for decades, if not centuries? What happened if an inheritance trial lay dormant from the Era of Turmoil? Only the inheritance trial of a remarkably powerful cultivator could stay intact for thousands of years, leaving the rest unguarded.

Normally, the answer would be simple— the lucky cultivator who stumbled upon the unguarded inheritance would claim it.

However, the Heavenly Dao could not allow a Qi-Refinement Cultivator to easily obtain a supreme treasure. Or at least, that was the leading hypothesis. If one wished to claim the knowledge of the ancients, they had to prove themselves worthy of it,

Thus, the Heavenly Dao would allow the artifact spirit or divine sense embedded within the artifact to absorb a sliver of Heavenly Qi, reinforcing its defenses to a frightening degree and preserving the inheritance within, even enhancing it in some rare cases.

This led to the creation of Origin treasures, one of which Yao Shen presently stood before.

. . .

"These are what remains of the inheritances the Sacred Fla—" Patriarch Lei Weiyuan lightly coughed, taking a breather to correct himself, before continuing, "... inheritances the Flame Division had acquired in the aftermath of the Era of Turmoil. The records indicate that originally there were dozens, if not more, of such inheritances, but either they were successfully unsealed or the contents of the inheritance were lost in the process."

"Why do only these remain?"

"I suspect it to be a combination of a bloodline lock and a tricky self-destruct mechanism, though they transformed into Origin Treasures far before my time."

"So you are speculating?"

"Yes," Patriarch Lei Weiyuan replied, quite truthfully. "Though the contents of the inheritances ought to be quite valuable, considering that my ancestors were not willing to part with it."

"What about the Amadori? Did you reach out to them?"

Patriarch Lei Weiyuan let out a wry chuckle at that. The Amadori Clan belonged to neither the righteous nor the demonic path. There were a few factions on Ionea that could truly claim to be free of influence from either side, and each of those had proved their might beyond reproach. Though, perhaps, "clan" was a misnomer—- anyone who met the Amadori Clan's strict criteria and passed their trial could take up the surname "Amadori," but in doing so, they would renounce any previous ties they held with the two paths.

The reason why they were so feared was because they specialized in unsealing Origin Treasures, implying that each member of the clan possessed frightening control over their Qi and divine sense, but that was not all. Who knew what manner of potent artifacts, forgotten techniques and Domain Concepts had they amassed across the centuries?

Their true strength was unknown to the Azlak Plains, but what the Azlak Plains knew was already enough to know that the Amadori were not a foe they could afford to make.

"I did," Lei Weiyuan bitterly replied. "They wanted everything found within the Origin Treasures, and offered to compensate us with Natural Treasures and if the find was valuable enough, even Pseudo Soul Emperor treasures."

Thankfully, the Amadori did not take refusal as an offense. They simply did not need to. Origin Treasures were incredibly potent, naturally meaning that the risk involved in unlocking them was incredibly high. Trading an elder's life for an unknown reward was not a worthwhile gamble.

In Earth's terminology, the Amadori ran what was essentially a monopoly.

"Why didn't you accept?" Yao Shen asked. The Heavenly Sky Sect possessed its own Origin Treasures, but Yao Shen's predecessors had traded them to the Amadori, and were generously compensated for the same. Back then, they hadn't been of particular interest to him, and Yao Shen would likely have done the same— it was trading dead weight for a far more tangible benefit.

"Perhaps, it is because I am a Flame Cultivator, but as you are well aware, my kind can be… *stubborn*. A trade where the opposing party is willing to easily offer such lucrative resources is no trade at all, it is a robbery. My ancestors preserved these Origin Treasures for a reason, and I will not be the one to trade them away."

"A bold decision. Shall we see if it paid off?" Yao Shen asked, his tone carrying an almost unfamiliar emotion, one that he hadn't felt in a long time.

The distinctive thrill that could only be brought on by the unknown.

. . .

"Are you certain about this?" Yao Shen asked the Flame Patriarch, a rather perplexed expression on his face.

"Grand Patriarch Yao Shen," Lei Weiyuan's tone conveyed the seriousness of the matter, the tension in his voice all but palpable, "would I be correct in assuming that you are familiar with the Sky Division's records upon the Amadori?"

Yao Shen had studied the records decades ago, not long after he assumed the mantle of Patriarch, but his near perfect memory allowed him to recall its contents in a matter of seconds.

"Yes."

"Is there any record of the techniques the Amadori employed to unseal the Origin Treasure? Failing that, is there even a passing description of their methods?"

Yao Shen's eyes widened, as he once again parsed through the contents of the record in his mind. The record only contained a log of the resources the Sky Division had obtained from trading with the Amadori, but there was not even a passing mention of how they had managed to unseal the Origin Treasures in the first place. There was little else cultivators feared more than the unknown, and there was little more they sought out than to demystify it. He could not believe that the ancestors of the Sky Division were not interested in the Amadori's methods... then why?

Yao Shen locked eyes with Lei Weiyuan, seeking an answer. In truth, part of him wondered how he missed it, but as a newly appointed Patriarch back then, a distant, secretive faction wasn't exactly high on his priority list.

"The Amadori Clan does not allow outsiders to pry upon their methods," Patriarch Lei Weiyuan explained, but his answer alone was not enough to satisfy Yao Shen's curiosity. "Strength determines many aspects of life on Ionea, Grand Patriarch Yao Shen. But from my understanding, based upon the ancestral records my family has left behind, Origin Treasures are an enigma that defy traditional norms. Though a supremely powerful cultivator could simply endure the backlash of the origin treasure and force it open, he is as likely to destroy its contents in the process. Or at least, that is the strongest conjecture I can offer you."

"So the reason you do not want a share of the spoils is..." Yao Shen trailed off, his expression hardening.

"Make no mistake, Grand Patriarch Yao Shen. If you wished to eliminate me, you could do so now. If you acquire another treasure, it does not significantly affect that reality. Feuding over something I could not obtain in the first place does not serve my interests." Patriarch Lei Weiyuan's eyes shone with a steely glint, his implication obvious.

"The knowledge," Yao Shen muttered aloud.

"Is far more valuable than any artifact you may find," Lei Weiyuan completed his sentence.

"What makes you think I have the slightest chance at success?"

"Admittedly, the thought did not strike me at first. The second layer has been abandoned for decades, for only the senior most elders are allowed to venture this deep into the Solaris Keep and they have little interest in an unobtainable treasure."

Patriarch Lei Weiyuan took a deep breath to calm his unsettled nerves before continuing, "Only when I saw that you were unperturbed at the sight of an Origin Treasure did it click in my mind. Had you been an ordinary Soul Emperor, your reaction ought to have been one of *fear or caution*. However, your methods are... bizarre and unpredictable and you are likely the closest the Flame Division will ever come to unlocking this mystery."

Yao Shen processed the new information he had been given, realizing that there was still too much he didn't know about Ionea. Even Patriarch Lei Weiyuan was far more well-informed than him, and these lapses in intelligence were a flaw Yao Shen had to correct before they proved fatal.

"Why tell me this?" Yao Shen asked, his eyes narrowing. Lei Weiyuan was no friend of Yao Shen, and if he had withheld this information and let him succeed in unsealing an Origin Treasure... From what he now knew of the Amadori, they would come after him. For evidently, there was more to their methods than divine sense and Qi control, and they would go to lengths to protect their secrets.

What lengths, was the real question.

Patriarch Lei Weiyuan shook his head. "The Amadori Clan is not limited by the pact. Though they do not confront either path, if slighted, I fear they would rather level the entire Flame Division rather than risk the creation of a faction that could mimic their achievements."

"I suspect that is not all," Yao Shen retorted calmly.

"Grand Patriarch Yao Shen, you said it yourself; The Azlak Plains have been in decline for centuries now and I find myself at the end of the road. My chances of ascending to Soul Emperor are implausible, at best. We must adapt, and we must adapt fast if we are not to be swallowed by the inevitable change of tides. I am not as ambitious a man as you are, Grand Patriarch, but the flames of passion yet burn in my heart," Patriarch Lei Weiyuan replied, his eyes shining with the intensity of a Flame Cultivator.

"You would risk alerting the Amadori Clan?" Yao Shen's words were communicated via divine sense, for some things should not be said aloud.

"The creation of the Modern Sect has already offended the conservative forces among the righteous path, who especially despise coups. The demonic path will quake in fear at the idea of old righteous path sects setting aside their differences and banding together, and whilst the pact will prevent the situation from devolving into an all-out war, they *will* find ways to retaliate.

Insignificant the Azlak Plains may be, but it is the idea that cannot be allowed to spread. You play with fire already, Yao Shen, and if you fail, it is not you alone who will burn," Patriarch Lei Weiyuan's words echoed in Yao Shen's mind and the gravity of his statement was such that Yao Shen did not object when he dropped the honorifics.

Confronted with the truth, Yao Shen could not deny it. Change could not exist without risk, and the risk was not something that only he bore.

"How much do the Amadori know?"

"They know that I have at least one Origin Treasure in my possession, but that is the extent of their knowledge. In their eyes, I am probably a country bumpkin holding on to it purely for sentimental reasons and….perhaps they are not far from the truth."

"The elders?"

"The number of elders that know about the Origin Treasures, I can count on one hand. They are old and rigid in their thinking, and provided I take certain measures, will not suspect anything."

"I still do not think that the Amadori alone can monopolize the knowledge pertaining to Origin Treasures," Yao Shen replied after much thought.

"Perhaps not, but if other factions know how to do so, they do not advertise it, and they likely have the strength to defend themselves against the Amadori Clan. We do not."

"If I succeed, the contents of the Origin Treasure will be mine. In exchange, I will provide you with a comprehensive account of the unsealing process, but you will not share it without my permission. If I suspect you have, I will kill you. In return, I will inform you before I share this information with a third party. Is that agreement acceptable to you?" Yao Shen asked Patriarch Lei Weiyuan via his divine sense.

The latter seemed completely unperturbed with the death threat, no longer concealing the excitement in his gaze. These were the only Origin Treasures that the Flame Division possessed, but how many such existed across the Azlak Plains? How many such Origin Treasures existed across the entirety of Ionea?

"I accept."

Yao Shen did not say anything for a few seconds, knowing that he was venturing into completely unfamiliar territory. If he accepted, he would have a closer tie with Patriarch Lei Weiyuan as a result of their shared secret. It was a risk, but that knowledge would implicate Lei Weiyuan as much as it would do him, and he at least had the power to defend himself. And in all honesty, there had always been the possibility of a hegemonic power coming after him to extract the secrets of Human Dao. The Origin Treasure might be one possible source that could allow him to resist, to fight against forces far stronger than him.

There were only two options before him— either kill Lei Weiyuan here and now, and gamble if he could identify the Gatekeeper that possessed the 'killswitch' before he blew the Solaris Keep to dust or simply accept the proposal. The former would mean destroying the foundation for the Modern Sect, so it wasn't much of an option at all.

Yao Shen chose to accept.

Now came the real test.

Yao Shen stood before a reinforced obsidian door, cycling Qi through his body in preparation for his first true challenge after reaching the Soul Emperor stage. His Human Dao Domain had already been activated, silhouettes of mortal farmers harvesting illusory stalks of wheat scattered across the broad stone hallway that comprised the second layer of the Solaris Keep.

"Are you sure these defenses will suffice?" Yao Shen's tone was tinged with dubiousness as he placed his hand upon the obsidian door's surface in order to get a measure of its defenses.

The Five Origin Treasures in possession of the Sacred Flame Palace each had their own 'containment wards' that seemed to be forged out of pure obsidian— undoubtedly the work of a skilled Flame Cultivator, however, that alone was not enough to provide much reassurance.

If these Origin Treasures had truly survived from the Era of Turmoil, their strength could not be measured by banal scales like cultivation stage or artifact rank.

"Do not worry, Grand Patriarch Yao Shen. These containment wards were left behind by my ancestors. Even if the Flame Division were to be reduced to ash on the morrow, these wards will survive."

Yao Shen raised an eyebrow at that statement.

"Obsidian, in itself, is not a particularly valuable material. For Flame Cultivators, its true value lies in its proximity to our element and its ability to withstand heat. Runic engravings cover the interior layer of the containment wards, accentuating the material's desirable properties like its heat resistance, and conversely, downplaying or outright eliminating undesirable properties like the rock's brittle nature," Lei Weiyuan explained, answering the unspoken question.

"If the rune-script is so effective, why not utilize it in a defensive formation?" Yao Shen asked.

Patriarch Lei Weiyuan shook his head wryly. "We can only decipher basic rune forms. There are entire sections of the script whose purpose we cannot comprehend, their complexity such that even mimicking them is pointless. All we can do is maintain the small-scale formation and hope that someone capable of deciphering them is born one day."

Yao Shen nodded in understanding.

"Very well. Is there anything else I must know before making my attempt?"

Lei Weiyuan seemed to take a moment to think about it before responding, "I would not attempt to breach the Origin Treasure's defenses by tunneling underground. Not only is the Origin Treasure likely to have countermeasures for such a ploy, but... this is pure speculation on my part... it is an extension of heaven's will and therefore..." Lei Weiyuan left the last part unsaid, his face paling slightly at the thought of a heavenly tribulation being brought down upon the Flame Division.

Yao Shen's expression turned serious at Lei Weiyuan's implication. Based on his understanding of the Heavenly Dao, it was certainly capable of such a measure if scorned.

"I did not expect it to be that simple, either way," Yao Shen gave Patriarch Lei Weiyuan a nod before applying strength to the obsidian door. It slowly swung open, and he slipped inside.

A piercing silver glow illuminated the small room, making the rune-script upon the uneven obsidian walls legible to even mortal eyes. However, Yao Shen did not spare the complex script even a glance, his attention captivated by a metallic strongbox that rested upon a stone dais at the opposite end of the room.

The ambient Qi in the air swirled around the strongbox, releasing a light thrum of *power* that was audible only to the ears of a cultivator. Yao Shen did not know if the original inheritance had been sealed in such a form or if the Heavenly Dao had reshaped it after it became an Origin Treasure, but it took only one glance at it for him to know that no attack he was capable of could pierce its defenses.

The silver metal comprising the strongbox's exterior had been steeped in such a magnitude of Qi that Yao Shen could barely distinguish it from a Qi-Construct.

Nevertheless, he took a step forward. Followed by another.

There was no response from the Origin Treasure.

Only when he had reached the halfway mark did the Origin Treasure finally respond.

Yao Shen's reflexes went haywire as they screamed at him to

evade, but the time-lag between the fluctuation in the ambient Qi and the attack was far shorter than he had expected.

His Wind Qi flared to life, as Yao Shen swerved to the left as fast as his reflexes allowed. A beam of concentrated Light Qi shot out from the Origin Treasure, its radiance so strong that it stung his eyes.

His eyes narrowed in shock as the Patriarch of the Modern Sect realized that his right arm was gone, *vaporized*.

Fear, true fear, welled up in his heart as he hurriedly retreated. He was not a stranger to the emotion, but even his ascension had not been *this* ruthless. Surprisingly, though, there was no follow-up attack, even though Yao Shen would be hard-pressed to evade it in his present condition.

"Interesting," Yao Shen muttered aloud, channeling his Earth Qi and forming a small rock in his hand. First, he tossed it a few meters in front of him. The Origin Treasure remained inert. Next, he tossed another rock directly at the Origin Treasure at a curved angle. A beam of light shot out from the origin treasure, inciner-ating it once again at the halfway mark.

To rest his hypothesis, Yao Shen stretched a thin thread of divine sense forward. His goal was the small opening in the center of the strongbox that was too circular to pass as a conventional keyhole. This time, he got a bit further than the halfway mark, but he had chosen to approach from the sides before he winced out loud, his divine sense shattering.

That confirmed it.

The strongbox possessed what Yao Shen mentally termed as a 'sphere of perception.' The Origin Treasure would only retaliate when he trespassed into the spherical layer of divine sense, and only when he survived its onslaught and passed through the restrictive layer would his own divine sense function outside his body.

Or at least Yao Shen hoped it would.

He charged again, this time holding nothing back. Yao Shen blazed forth with the wind aiding his cause, his movement completely erratic and patternless. He evaded the first beam of light, followed by a second and a third, his attempt to confound the Origin Treasure working surprisingly well so far.

Until the Origin Treasure released five beams of light simultaneously and Yao Shen, who had accelerated so much that he would never be able to slow down in time, could only watch on helplessly for a few moments before he was vaporized instantly.

"I died," he spoke after one of the silhouettes outside the containment ward morphed into his likeness.

Patriarch Lei Weiyuan attempted to hide the surprise he felt at Yao Shen's blunt statement, but failed to do so. The cultivator who had subdued the entire Flame Division had only managed to last a minute against an Origin Treasure?

How terrifying.

"What was it like?"

Staying true to his word, Yao Shen spent the next ten minutes narrating his first attempt, which Lei Weiyuan meticulously noted down.

"It would not be nearly as difficult if the Origin Treasure could be located to an open field. The small containment ward makes evasion far more difficult than it ought to be."

"Why do you suspect the 'keyhole' to be a part of the solution?" Lei Weiyuan mused aloud.

"I don't see any other reason for the Origin Treasure to restrict my divine sense otherwise. Besides, if all it took to access it was speed, then the Amadori would not be nearly as respected."

"I see."

A day passed, and during that time, Yao Shen 'died' another four times. He had informed the delegation from the Sky Division that he was studying rune-script, for there were another seven empty concealment wards that had likely housed other inheritances or volatile artifacts at some point in time, now utilized for his 'study.'

As far as excuses went, it wasn't the greatest one, for Yao Shen had never really displayed an inclination or strong interest in the formation path. However, compared to his other shifts in his personality, it was far less noticeable. So much so, that he doubted that even Meili Zhu, with her keen senses, would suspect anything.

After all, one did not simply challenge the monopoly of an ancient clan on a whim, like Yao Shen was currently attempting to do.

He would select a few scrolls and tomes from the Solaris Keep at random, as long as they vaguely had something to do with runes or formations, before venturing back into the second layer to further give credence to the ruse.

Once he was finished replenishing his reserves of Human Qi, Yao Shen was ready to tackle the Origin Treasure again.

He had cobbled together a makeshift movement technique, spending hours between each death to meditate upon his shortcomings and find a way to mitigate them.

The end result was a movement technique that required that he dedicate too much of his concentration to be useful in a real battle. The one time he had attempted to fly over to the Origin Treasure, eight rays of Light Qi had viciously pulverized him and it was safe to say that Yao Shen did not desire a repeat of that experience.

So this movement technique would be limited to the ground, which actually played to his advantages.

Yao Shen stepped inside the containment ward, and the moment his foot landed upon ordinary stone tiles, they began to partially liquefy, until they had transformed into quicksand. The ground was the only part of the room that wasn't layered with obsidian, and Yao Shen was thankful for it.

The reason why this technique was so tricky was because he was utilizing his Earth Qi to transform rock into quicksand only with the small surface area his feet was making contact with. If he tried to turn the entire floor into quicksand and destabilize the second layer, the artifact would instantly kill him. He knew, for the one time he had tried, or rather, attempted to try, he felt an unmistakably vast presence weighing down upon him, upon his soul— the Heavenly Qi that was concealed within the artifact making its presence known.

Thankfully, this clever compromise did not prompt any such retaliation. Running or even diving away from the Light Qi attacks, even with the wind at his back, had proven to be too slow. So Yao Shen, utilizing his knowledge from Earth, sought to eliminate the friction generated from his feet making contact with the ground as much as he could. If a surface without friction existed, an object would simply slide forever, to the lowest point. While he could not create such a surface, he could borrow from its concept.

Wind Qi would guide his movement, and instead of running, he would slide across the floor's surface like a marionette controlled by another. The only question remained if his reaction time was fast enough.

Yao Shen propelled himself forward toward the Origin Treasure. The first beam of Light Qi shot out not long after and Yao Shen swerved to the left, missing it by a little more than a hair's breadth. The next thirty seconds passed as Yao Shen's silhouette rapidly blurred, weaving through the beams of Light Qi with a maniacal fervor.

His heart hammered in his chest, his senses stretched to their absolute limits as his surroundings faded into the background, leaving behind only the anticipation and fear brought on by the next incoming beam of light.

A beam of light punched through the side of his torso, causing a burst of warm blood to pour out. But the wound wasn't fatal, and Yao Shen could sense that the onslaught would not last much longer.

He willed himself forward, fighting through the pain and…

The attacks stopped.

Yao Shen cauterized his wound, standing ten meters away from the artifact. Even he seemed surprised that he had succeeded, which was a testament to the nightmarish difficulty involved in even getting to this point.

This close to his goal, Yao Shen didn't dare to hastily approach the Origin Treasure. Instead, he decided to test his hypothesis.

He extended his divine sense a meter ahead of his body and simply waited.

It didn't shatter.

Almost completely convinced now, Yao Shen directed his thread of divine sense into the small circular opening, guessing that it was the proverbial key to the lock.

Yao Shen's eyes lit up as he knew he had made the correct gamble.

Information flowed into Yao Shen's mind through his divine sense, more in the form of *instinct* over *language.*

Before him lay a solitary archway, the only opening in what seemed to be an impenetrable wall of foreign divine sense, its density far surpassing his capabilities to pierce through. The archway's diameter was identical to the circular keyhole, however, its semi-circular structure meant that he would have to shrink his divine sense's thickness by almost half.

Sweat trickled down his forehead as he slowly siphoned off excess divine sense, his attention devoted to thinning down the thread of divine sense he had slipped inside the Origin Treasure.

A minute passed before he believed himself to be ready. Yao Shen's eyes flashed with determination as he willed the thread forward, his curiosity demanding he know what lay ahead.

The moment his divine sense passed through the first archway, he felt a presence weigh down on the thread. It did not hinder its movements, the intention more to inform Yao Shen that he had crossed the point of no return. He could no longer siphon off divine sense without the archway closing down upon the thread, eliciting a grimace out of him.

He now understood what attribute the Origin Treasure wished to test, namely, divine sense control. For before him, there were now two archways in place of one, albeit having halved in diameter.

He couldn't siphon off any more divine sense and there was no room to wriggle another thread through the first archway, leaving behind only one possible solution.

He had to split the thread of divine sense into two smaller strands and pass through the two archways simultaneously.

Yao Shen held his right arm forward to help him visualize the process, and if one were watching closely, they would realize that his hand was trembling from the strain. After his ascension to Soul Emperor, the strength of Yao Shen's soul had ballooned rapidly whilst he lacked the proper technique and method to harness or even control its potency.

The fact that his soul far exceeded the realm of an early-stage Soul Emperor did not help his cause.

Thus, it would be no exaggeration to say that divine sense control was amongst his greatest weaknesses, even though Yao Shen did not yet fully understand its significance.

His head throbbed from the exertion, a long, trying hour

passing before Yao Shen finally managed to split the thread into two perfectly circular strands. This was exactly the level of difficulty he had expected from an inheritance that had survived from the Era of Turmoil, but even Yao Shen's face dropped when he saw what his reward for passing the second stage was.

This time, there were four archways.

Pressing himself beyond this point was futile, more likely to damage his own soul in the process.

Letting out a weary sigh, Yao Shen retracted his divine sense and gave the Origin Treasure a withering look. A blend of curiosity and mild frustration drove him forward, as he decided to experiment a little.

Yao Shen simply meant to force the Origin Treasure open with physical strength alone, but the moment his hand landed upon the surface of the Origin Treasure, a Light Qi attack that Yao Shen could only describe as a 'solar flare' vaporized him without the slightest possibility of resistance, the heat he felt in that millisecond beyond what any Flame Cultivator he had ever met was capable of.

Lei Weiyuan patiently recorded down every word that Yao Shen uttered, occasionally interjecting to seek clarification or ask a question.

"...to conclude, rather ironically, if you were in my stead when it came to the actual 'unlocking' process, there would be far greater odds of success. In fact, I wouldn't be surprised if you outright succeeded," Yao Shen concluded his explanation with a rather wistful sigh. To be so close and yet so far away, the Heavenly Dao was truly a fickle mistress.

"But I would have died a hundred deaths before reaching that point," Lei Weiyuan remarked with some humor in his voice, shaking his head. "At the very least, we have established the basic process of unlocking an Origin Treasure. This knowledge alone is easily worth a Pseudo Soul Emperor artifact. It also..." Lei Weiyuan paused, locking eyes with Yao Shen before he concluded the sentence, "...tells us that the Amadori Clan is far more powerful than our estimations."

Yao Shen grimly nodded at that assessment.

"How much longer can we stay down here without drawing suspicion?" Yao Shen asked, unperturbed by the findings. The die had already been cast the moment the two Patriarchs delved into the secrets of Origin Treasures. Now, there was nothing else to be done but move forward.

"I would not risk spending more than a week down here," Lei Weiyuan replied after giving it serious thought. To mortals, that might seem like a long time to seclude oneself in study, but for cultivators who could spend years, or even decades in seclusion, it was far too brief a time for Yao Shen to derive anything of value from the 'rune-script,' which was his cover story.

"A week? That will have to be enough."

The second Origin Treasure was easier to deal with, at least in the initial phase. Whilst 'Light' was not an Esoteric Dao, very few cultivators were able to cultivate it to the Major Dao stage. The reason was its volatility; the element equally likely to liquefy one's own internal organs as it was the enemy's. Only those with a natural-born affinity for the element could cultivate it to higher stages without prohibitive risk, and Light Cultivators were known to guard the purity of their bloodline quite vehemently, making the likelihood drop even further.

Thus, Yao Shen was rather relieved when the Origin Treasure utilized Shadow Qi, a known quantity, to assail him.

The concept behind the attack was similar to Lei Weiyuan's domain. Shadow blades, spears and arrows homed in on Yao Shen from multiple directions, able to reorient themselves and sweep in for a subsequent attack upon missing their target. Thankfully, the individual attacks were far slower than beams of Light Qi, and Yao Shen was able to retaliate, even shatter a few shadow spears that came too close for comfort. Coupled with the new movement technique he had created for evasion in cramped quarters, Yao Shen managed to close in on the Origin Treasure.

It had only taken one 'death' and besides a long gash running across his back, a surface level wound, Yao Shen was more or less in one piece.

Part of him was relieved that the mechanism for clearing the first phase hadn't changed, meaning that the information he had recorded earlier held real value, but at the same time, Yao Shen was desperately hoping that it had a different trial for him.

Trepidation filled his heart as he threaded his divine sense forward. An inky black strongbox rested upon an identical stone dais that was seemingly absorbing all light in a one-meter radius, shrouding itself in a cloak of shadows. It was only Yao Shen's divine sense that allowed him to make out its features in the darkness, for the strongbox was just a splotch of pure darkness in an already dimly lit room otherwise.

His divine sense snaked forward, hoping against hope that he would be able to unlock the mechanism this time.

Once again, information flowed through Yao Shen's mind. His confidence rose, but he did not allow himself to slip into conceit.

Even if the Origin Treasure hadn't hinted at the solution, it wasn't a particularly challenging one to reach. He had felt this sensation before, when he had shattered the divine sense brand on Elder Yongliang's spear and replaced it with his own, a battle dictated by one's soul strength, visualization technique and willpower.

An artifact, at its core, was designed to be bound to a cultivator. However, there was a limit to the amount of divine sense an artifact could hold, a physical law beyond which there was simply no room left for further encroachment. The same way if an empty bucket were to be filled to the brim with water, the water in itself would not harm the structural integrity of the bucket, divine sense in and of itself could not damage an artifact.

However, the water in the bucket could be evaporated, and then replaced the same way if one coveted ownership over another cultivator's artifact, they had to destroy their divine sense brand and replace it with their own.

The strength of one's soul did give a cultivator an indelible advantage, however, visualization techniques, which were essentially the crystallization of one's willpower were what dictated victory or defeat when confronted with a foe that possessed similar soul strength.

Elder Yongliang's divine sense brand was visualized in the form of a phalanx of spears that clashed against a solitary, radiant sword, which was Yao Shen's visualization technique. It also reflected the difference in their ideologies, for whilst Elder Yongliang was a 'product' of his legacy family, his tutelage and his own determination, Yao Shen had seen himself as a lonesome cultivator whose merit and self-worth were determined by the strength of his blade for far too long.

Yao Shen took a moment to compose himself, before willing his divine sense forth in the shape of a radiant sword that would slay all those that dared stand in his path. It was a domineering visualization technique that hurtled forth without hesitation, ready to confront the unknown.

The retaliation was almost instant.

Yao Shen gasped in surprise.

The soul strength was identical to his own, undoubtedly a machination of the Heavenly Dao. That, however, was not the surprising part.

Were it any other cultivator, he would describe the scene as if the stars in the sky were hurtling down toward Ionea. Yao Shen, however, knew that the phenomenon had a term— a *meteor shower.*

His sword hurriedly attempted to evade, destroying a few meteors in the process. His radiant sword dwarfed any individual meteor in size, but that wasn't much of an advantage when thousands of meteors were raining down toward it, the scene as captivating as it was shocking.

Yao Shen dodged, swerved and retaliated as much as he could, but soon, the scratches in his sword turned into cracks and chips before the sword cracked altogether.

Blood dribbled down Yao Shen's chin as he stood in awe of the most powerful visualization technique he had ever witnessed, questions running through his mind.

Three days passed in the blink of an eye, and during that time, Yao Shen challenged the Origin Treasure three more times. Victory at this point was an impossibility, for he had been mistaken— it was not his ability to shatter divine sense brands that was in question, but his visualization technique.

He hoped to derive some insight from the Origin Treasure, to meditate upon it and steal its secrets. However, despite his efforts, all he could manage was a shoddy imitation… he knew he lacked something crucial, but he couldn't put his finger on what.

Finally, Yao Shen gave up, knowing that he wouldn't derive anything from the Origin Treasure in the short term.

His luck further took a downturn when Yao Shen attempted to unlock the third and fourth Origin Treasures. Though perhaps 'attempted' was too strong a word.

Yao Shen's Human Dao Domain essentially made his physical body invulnerable as long as he kept his domain active, but the same protection did not extend to his soul. He did not truly die and resurrect himself, his methods were nowhere near that profound.

The soul, his soul, possessed its own defense mechanism. Just like a spiritual beast could instinctively sense danger, when Yao Shen entered the containment ward, his soul started to send warning signals with such intensity that he immediately retreated, without even attempting to unlock the Origin Treasures.

His face had been pale as a ghost, for Yao Shen knew what the warning meant.

Certain, no, *instant* death.

Of course, he chose to withhold that bit of information from Lei Weiyuan, instead claiming that the two treasures were at the Soul Paragon level.

That left one last, final treasure that would decide if the risk of offending the Amadori had been worth it.

He stepped inside.

The final encounter went differently than Yao Shen expected.

The Origin Treasure was the least remarkable of the four he had laid his eyes on, though two of them had been mere glimpses. A mottled, unassuming grey metal strongbox lay upon a stone dais, much like the other five.

When Yao Shen approached it, thankfully, there was no flurry of attacks this time. He noticed a fluctuation of Earth Qi, and in the next few seconds, an Earthen Rock Golem was shaped from the dirt, stone and sediment that lay beneath them.

Surprisingly, the fight in itself wasn't a particularly challenging one. Yao Shen had feared a cave-in when the Rock Golem's mighty fist struck the obsidian wall, but thankfully, the runes flared to life and prevented such an outcome. The strength contained behind those fists was easily enough to kill Yao Shen in one shot, but with his new movement technique, which he had begun to call 'Earthen Weave,' he danced around the Golem, leaving long gashes across its body with his sword.

Normally, he wouldn't be able to damage such a construct easily, for it was clearly at the Soul Emperor level. However, Yao Shen had reached the Major Dao stage in Earth Cultivation, allowing him to disrupt the Golem's natural regeneration and amplify the effects of his attacks.

A mindless puppet ultimately could not contend with the cunning of a cultivator, as Yao Shen drove his sword through the Golem's rock eyes, causing it to crumple onto the ground with a final whimper. His own Earth Qi prevented it from piecing itself back together, and he calmly walked past it.

The fight could have been much simpler if Yao Shen used his offensive domains, but he did not dare drop the protection of his Human Dao Domain.

For if he had learned anything, it was to *never, under any circumstance,* underestimate what an Origin Treasure was capable of.

The moment of truth drew nearer as Yao Shen willed his divine sense forward for the last time.

A loud click rang out in the concealment ward, and he immediately pedaled backwards, suspecting a trap.

He detected a massive fluctuation in Earth Qi the next second, but no attack followed.

Yao Shen's facial expression changed, from caution to absolute joy as he realized that the Origin Treasure, rather, the strongbox that contained it had swung open, releasing all the residual Qi it had amassed over the centuries.

Within seconds, the Earth Qi in the room had reached saturation, and the spot had become a haven for Earth Cultivators.

Yao Shen had done it.

He had unlocked his first Origin Treasure.

Within the Origin Treasure lay an ancient, mottled grey bell that was roughly the size of his palm and three withered scrolls that had degraded beyond recognition.

Though Yao Shen suspected that the treasure was of much inferior quality to the other four Origin Treasures, in that moment, it didn't matter.

For he knew, from the moment he laid eyes on it—

It was a Soul Emperor Level Artifact.

34

SOUL EMPEROR ARTIFACT

Y<small>AO</small> S<small>HEN</small> carefully examined the mottled gray bell that lay inert in the palm of his hand. Though the artifact's physical weight was negligible, his hand trembled under a different kind of pressure as it weighed down upon his *soul* instead.

He drew solace from the fact that there was no foreign divine sense brand imprinted upon the ancient bell, which made the task ahead significantly less challenging. Nevertheless, from his experimentation so far Yao Shen knew that there was one final hurdle that he had to cross before he could claim the bell artifact as his own.

Time seemed to stretch on endlessly as he fought to overcome the bell's resistance to his divine sense, forced to continuously apply pressure or risk losing his entire progress thus far.

Two grueling days passed by before Yao Shen saw the proverbial light at the end of the tunnel. It would have likely taken longer, but rather ironically, it was his prior attempts at unlocking the Shadow Origin Treasure and repeatedly contesting himself against the '*meteor shower*' divine sense brand that had made the task less trying. Though his divine sense brand was no more powerful than before, it had gained an additional degree of refinement and flexibility that aided in his cause.

Yao Shen let out a defiant roar as he pressed his brand forward, aiming to conquer the bell artifact in its entirety. A final burst of resistance from the artifact attempted to hinder his cause, but he would not falter this close to his goal.

He had surmounted the Origin Treasure's combat trial.

He had proved himself worthy of this artifact.

He was Yao Shen, Patriarch of the Modern Sect, and he would be denied no longer.

A light chime rang out as he felt the last of the bell's resistance sputter out, his Brand coalescing in the form of a radiant sword that lay nestled comfortably within the bell's clapper.

He reeled a few steps backward as an influx of knowledge flowed through his mind, the additional strain causing his Human Dao Domain to flicker in and out of existence. Though the scrolls Yao Shen found within Origin Treasure were too damaged to be of any use, the artifact still had the ability to communicate its purpose through instinct.

Yao Shen's eyes widened in surprise as he roughly translated the sensations and instinctual reactions he felt into merely two words. His voice was barely a whisper as he spoke,"....*Refine... Soul*."

There was also something more, something far more... *potent* that the artifact was capable of, but the sensation cut off before it could form into a coherent message.

Yao Shen did not resist as he felt the strength drain out of his legs, falling backwards onto the ground. His Human Dao Domain collapsed seconds later, a reminder that his domain, as clever as it might be, was a far cry from true invulnerability, if such a thing even existed in the first place.

Then he began to laugh in jubilation.

After eliminating the possibilities, Yao Shen had reached a

singular conclusion. One that even a man as composed as himself took a few seconds to digest. The artifact Yao Shen had obtained from the Origin Treasure belonged to an arcane path that few in the Azlak Plains could claim to understand, namely, *Soul Cultivation.*

Unfortunately, this was neither the time nor the place to test his newly acquired artifact. Not to mention, Yao Shen had already resolved not to divulge its existence to a single soul unless absolutely necessary. Lei Weiyuan would naturally suspect the truth, for the Heavenly Dao, as ruthless as it might be, followed its own twisted notion of 'fairness' rigorously. Yao Shen's reward could not be limited to tattered, illegible scrolls, no matter how much the Heavenly Dao disliked him and his Human Dao.

However, so what?

As long as Lei Weiyuan did not know the specifics of the artifact Yao Shen had acquired, he had no way to prove anything to the Amadori, if they were ever to fall out. Not that he could, without sharing in the consequences.

If anything, this short excursion had managed to serve an unintentional purpose by drawing Lei Weiyuan closer to his camp. Both parties had benefitted from the arrangement and both parties now risked offending a greater power that neither one could afford to. Shared secrets did not bind as well as shared blood, but the present situation was more beneficial to Yao Shen compared to the shaky foundations their professional relationship was based on before.

Now, before leaving the containment ward, he had one last problem to solve.

First, Yao Shen attempted to store his bell artifact in his spatial ring, albeit very slowly. He winced when his spatial ring started to quiver under the pressure, unable to withstand the pressure exerted by a bona fide Soul Emperor level artifact. If he continued to force it through, the spatial pocket would likely shatter and its contents, forever lost.

When that line of inquiry failed, Yao Shen only saw one reasonable solution. Once an artifact was branded with divine sense, it became an extension of the soul, in a manner of speaking. Whilst Nascent Soul Cultivators did not have souls that were corporeal enough to support physical artifacts, the same could not be said about Soul Emperors— since the bell artifact was an extension of his soul, Yao Shen could naturally store it in his soul lake.

He did not wish utilize this option for he did not fully understand the artifact's capabilities, but at the same time, carrying the artifact on his person was an even worse option.

Resolving to be cautious and ready to react to any irregularities, Yao Shen placed the bell artifact within his soul lake, stilling the waves in that region.

The final hurdle crossed, Yao Shen swung the containment ward's door wide open and stepped out.

"Grand Patriarch!" Lei Weiyuan's tone did not bother to conceal the surprise he felt at seeing Yao Shen walk out unscathed.

A fair conclusion, given his domain had failed.

"It is done," Yao Shen stated with an unnerving calm, as if he had not just flipped an age-old convention upon its head.

Lei Weiyuan's eyes shot open in shock, his gaze wandering past Yao Shen and into the containment ward, which had been partially left open— upon the stone dais, where he knew the Origin Treasure ought to be kept.

He involuntarily flinched when the realization crept up on him. The Origin Treasure was... gone.

Yao Shen, too, had been surprised to see the strongbox

missing when he woke up from his meditative trance two days later, but it did not take him long to figure out what had happened. The metal that comprised the strongbox had been so heavily steeped in Qi that it dissolved not long after he had unsealed it, likely converted into topsoil. Only three illegible scrolls remained, with large chunks of papyrus decayed beyond repair and some parts missing entirely. What little writing remained was smudged so badly, it was impossible to recover the original characters.

"Those scrolls…." Lei Weiyuan muttered aloud.

"Unfortunately, they are damaged beyond repair. You may examine them if you wish to do so, but do not touch them," Yao Shen offered, mainly because he knew Lei Weiyuan would receive nothing of value from the scrolls.

"Why is the Qi density so high?" Lei Weiyuan asked as he gingerly approached the scrolls.

"A byproduct of the unsealing process, I suppose. Who knows how long the Origin Treasure has been accumulating Earth Qi for."

"I see," he replied, but his attention was partially taken up by the damaged scrolls.

"Is this the reward for unlocking the Origin Treasure?" Lei Weiyuan shook his head, no longer bothering to examine the scrolls.

Yao Shen just offered him a simple nod in response.

Tactfully, Lei Weiyuan chose not to delve upon that topic further, choosing to shift his focus to the unlocking process.

Honoring their agreement, Yao Shen truthfully explained the process from the beginning to the end, only omitting the part where he acquired the bell artifact.

Six days had passed since he had stepped foot upon the second layer of the Solaris Keep, short enough that there should be no suspicion, yet still longer than he would have preferred.

Both cultivators returned aboveground, each of them walking out having gained something beyond their wildest expectations.

The containment ward was sealed to make sure that the Earth Qi did not leak out. Yao Shen would return, for such a high density of Earth Qi could benefit his cultivation, another unexpected gain from his actions.

Meili Zhu did politely inquire for the reason behind his absence, but she had no reason to suspect anything. His newfound interest in rune-script would make sense too after what he had planned came to fruition.

For tomorrow, sharp at noon, Yao Shen planned to hold a joint conclave where he would reveal the next phase of his plans.

The Mortal Capital, All Haven.

35

CONCLAVE

Yao Shen had not allowed himself to reveal any outward sign of weakness during his excursion with Patriarch Lei Weiyuan, but now, in the privacy of his quarters, he sighed wearily before slumping against a plush divan's cushioned side.

His soul still ached lightly from repeatedly forming divine sense brands in short succession, and few, if anyone at all, knew the toll his Human Dao Domain left upon his mind. There was indeed a reason why Yao Shen opted to take a break each time he 'died' during the unsealing process, the mystique behind its inner mechanisms less… *impressive* then one might assume.

He closed his eyes and allowed himself to fall into a state of meditative rest, giving his soul time to recover from the exertion.

His rest turned out to be more short-lived than he had hoped, the first rays of sunlight cascading through the windowpane, gently rousing him awake. A bleary-eyed Yao Shen blinked away the exhaustion he felt, cycling Water Qi through his body for a burst of rejuvenation.

Before they parted yesterday, he had already informed Lei Weiyuan to make arrangements for the conclave. In a few hours from now, a guardian would lead them to the chosen premises, likely to be the Flame Patriarch's residence itself.

Yao Shen withdrew a few sheets of papyrus and a sharpened piece of charcoal from his spatial ring before he began to sketch out schematics with unnerving precision.

After all, he had preparations to make.

It was, in fact, Flame Patriarch Lei Weiyuan who had arrived personally to escort the contingent from the Sky Division.

His personage was not required for such a trivial task, but Yao Shen took it as an acknowledgement of their improved relationship.

And his arrival made things more convenient, for he was in no mood to slowly walk through the streets of the administrative district out of consideration for the guardian escorting them.

They took to the skies at Yao Shen's behest, reducing an hour's walk to a matter of minutes, as they directly alighted upon the sixth floor of a grandiose pagoda, easily the most imposing structure in the residential district.

It may have been a far cry from his own Silveni's Heirloom, but not every sect could boast a Soul Emperor Level Construct as their Patriarch's residence.

A strong aroma of tea leaves suffused the well-lit room, an ornate teapot resting upon a short-legged table the source of the redolent fragrance. It reminded Yao Shen of the first rains of the monsoon season back on Earth, the petrichor emanating from the wet grass rejuvenating and soothing to his soul— as if Mother Nature herself were expressing her love for the world.

Plush cushions were placed equidistantly on either side of the table, the elders from the Sacred Flame Palace who were considered qualified to attend this meeting already seated in a cross-legged position.

Yao Shen took his seat in the center, and the two Patriarchs sat opposite him. The remaining contingent from the Sky Division seated themselves on Yao Shen's side, paying no particular heed to the order.

Silence permeated in the room as the venerable members in attendance waited for tea to be served. Yao Shen took a moment to examine a vivid mural that was painted directly upon a wall, covering its entire length. It depicted the blurry silhouette of a cultivator dressed in crimson robes, wielding a flaming sickle that stretched on for double the height of a mortal man, arrayed against what seemed to be an entire legion of cultivators dressed in deathly black robes.

At first glance, it seemed to be the depiction of an over-exaggerated tale, but the choice of weapon gave him some pause. A sickle was extremely unwieldy in actual combat and across his years, Yao Shen had barely seen any cultivator of note utilizing it, even for experimentation.

His momentary distraction ended as a young girl entered the room, wearing a simple green kimono and ceremonial sandals. She held a tray in her hands that held glazed clay cups that had been recently heated, placing them before each of the elders with practiced motions. Then, she reached for the teapot before pouring tea with blurring motions, filling each cup to the three-fourth mark before moving to the next.

The reason behind her haste soon became evident, as the moment the lukewarm tea made contact with the cup, it began to rapidly froth and bubble up. What was scalding hot for mortals could only be considered warm for cultivators, so Yao Shen reached for the cup after scanning it for poison with his divine sense.

The art of True Poison brewing was supposed to be lost to time, but after unsealing his first Origin Treasure, he did not have the same level of confidence in what 'most cultivators' believed to be true. Either way, caution did not hurt.

Yao Shen took one long sip from his cup, a flicker of surprise flashing in his eyes. He took another sip. It was as if liquid silk flowed into his gullet, words alone seemingly insufficient to describe how preternaturally smooth the tea was. Warmth spread throughout his body, his breathing suddenly feeling *cleaner*, *lighter*, as if a weight had been lifted off his chest. The world, or at least his perception of it seemed more... optimistic, brighter in a sense.

For a moment, it was as if the sins of a lifetime of cultivation had washed away, leaving behind only purity.

It was a facade, but one he allowed to influence himself. If only for a little while.

Then the sensation faded, seemingly receding as quick as it had begun influencing him. Yao Shen realized that his cup was empty as the magical sensation left him.

"What is this tea called?" Yao Shen asked, his tone one of appreciation.

"Cloud Tea, Grand Patriarch," one of the elders replied.

A light chuckle escaped him before he replied, "A fitting name, indeed. Good tea."

His words seemed to act as a signal, as the contingent from the Sky Division offered their compliments as well. Even the Earth Patriarch, Kang Long, seemed to be impressed by the Cloud Tea.

The Flame Division had not held back in its hospitality.

Now that the pleasantries were over, gazes slowly began to shift to Yao Shen, waiting for him to speak.

"On this day, representatives from the Sky Division, namely myself and Elder Meili Zhu, the Flame Division, namely Patriarch Lei Weiyuan and the Elders of the Flame Division and finally, from the Earth Division, Patriarch Kang Long, are all present. I would like to commence today's proceedings with a Dao Discourse."

A Dao Discourse was a clash of ideals, where one's status and qualifications held no meaning, only the weight behind their words. The cultivators present exchanged confused glances at Yao Shen's proclamation. On one hand, Dao Discourses could be immensely beneficial to weaker cultivators, who could compete with their comprehension of the Dao— giving them the chance to learn from their opponent.

However, at the Nascent Soul Level, one did not simply trade secrets so easily, especially when the relationship between the three divisions was so tenuous.

Lei Weiyuan was the only one who remained unperturbed, having gained a deeper understanding of Yao Shen's methods and goals.

"Grand Patriarch Yao Shen, what Dao shall serve as the topic for the discourse?"

Yao Shen gave the Flame Patriarch a searching glance before a sly smile made its way to his face.

"Human Dao."

The Flame Division Elders exchanged confused glances, seemingly hoping to find some modicum of surety in their fellow colleagues' countenances. Truthfully speaking, the contingent from the Sky Division was faring no better, but they had gained some manner of resistance to their Grand Patriarch's tendency to subvert expectations by this point, thus choosing to maintain silent, stoic expressions instead.

Tradition dictated that the one who proposed the Dao Discourse share his knowledge first, thus passing on the responsibility to present Yao Shen with questions to the attending elders and Patriarchs. However, none present knew enough about the

Esoteric Dao to make purposeful inquiries; and to ask frivolous questions would be to lose face.

Before the silence could transition into discomfiture, he decided to intervene, offering, "I would like to make a proposal."

"Please, go ahead, Grand Patriarch," Earth Patriarch Kang Long was quick to reply, his inflection betraying the relief he felt.

Yao Shen gave a grateful nod in his direction before continuing, "My Dao is an Esoteric one and consequently, I do not expect the venerable attendees to be well-versed in its specifics. Thus, I wish to begin with a thought experiment."

"A thought...experiment?" Meili Zhu slowly enunciated the words aloud, hoping to demystify its meaning. Both words existed in Liwan, the language that was predominantly used by cultivators and mortals alike in Ionea, though admittedly, the translation for the word 'experiment' was rather inexact.

"A thought experiment is a..." Yao Shen paused, searching for a description that would capture the intrigue of his fellow cultivators, "... tool that Human Dao Cultivators employ to further our understanding, in a manner of speaking."

A wave of surprise reverberated through the hall before the cultivators in attendance shifted their full attention to Yao Shen, their gazes solemn. Whilst one could not hope to decipher the secrets of an Esoteric Dao through a second-hand experience, it was still unheard of for a practitioner to give out such knowledge. They did not completely believe Yao Shen's claims, but they *would* listen with the utmost care.

Since there were no objections even after a minute had passed, he continued, "Very well. Close your eyes."

The cultivators complied without protesting, for it was not eyes alone through which they could perceive the world.

"For a moment, I wish for you to visualize your daily lives in each of your respective divisions." Yao Shen's tone was calming and gentle as he imbued the emotions 'tranquility' and 'peace' into his words using his Human Dao. His influence was immediately noticed by the cultivators, but they did not fight it — it was nothing their willpower couldn't immediately overcome.

"Suddenly, your senses detect a loud explosion, one you place within the sect." Yao Shen's inflection turned overbearingly loud and raucous, a sharp juxtaposition in face of the calm he had projected earlier. The emotions 'shock' and 'surprise' were imbued into his words, painting a disturbing atmosphere.

The elders, of course, were unmoved, but his efforts served well to paint a vivid image in their mind's eye.

"You rush out of your abode, weapon artifact in hand. Your sight confirms the grim picture your divine sense had painted. An army of demonic path cultivators lays arrayed before you, their numbers beyond your wildest expectations—" Yao Shen was about to continue, but one of the elders interrupted him.

"Which sect does the army belong to, Grand Patriarch?" the elder asked, a tinge of hatred audible within his voice. The hatred wasn't directed toward him, but seemed to be the general hatred of the man toward the demonic path.

"That is irrelevant," Yao Shen replied, not at all bothered by the man's question. This was a Dao Discourse, after all. "A thought experiment deals in suppositions, not fact. You may visualize whichever demonic sect that comes to mind."

The elder replied with a nod, signaling that his questioning had concluded.

Yao Shen continued onward, "There is no time to prepare, nor to think. This attack was a well-prepared one, for your worst fear has come to life. That explosion has destroyed your sect's protective formation. You hurtle forward toward the enemy, for you are a prideful righteous path cultivator and you do not flee in face of cowardly demons. That is your sacred duty. That is your path. That is your *Dao Heart*."

A few impassioned nods and grunts were exchanged as the cultivators affirmed Yao Shen's words.

"The elders and Patriarchs, together, manage to hold back all the Nascent Soul and Soul Emperor cultivators that belong to the demonic path, averting the worst of the crisis. However, with the protective formation gone, thousands of weaker cultivators rush into the city."

"A grave crisis," another elder murmured under his breath, but his words did not escape him.

"A grave crisis indeed. Weaker these cultivators might be, but that is only by our standards. In the face of our sect guardians and disciples, these cultivators are far more terrifying than even facing us!" Yao Shen intoned, his words imbued with 'horror,' an emotion that he had recently confronting when attempting to unlock Origin Treasures.

"Blood Cultivators, if given the time, have the terrible ability to transform a light wound into a fatal one. The Dark Elves will scythe through a cultivator of similar rank effortlessly, their natural reflexes and speed beyond our human body's raw capabilities at lower ranks. And if there is a Soul Cultivator among their ranks, he will kill dozens, if not more, with a single attack. The Azlak Plains has not faced such an attack since the pact came into existence, however, the aim of this thought experiment is to pose to you, all well-respected, some revered members of the Modern Sect— what will the disciples do in the face of such an attack? What will the guardians do? Will they stand and fight? Will they surrender to the demonic path? Will they run?"

"Naturally, the cultivators of the Luo Family will face the enemy, no matter how dire the situation may seem to be!" Elder Yongliang, the Flame Division Elder whose spear he had briefly stolen, exclaimed. "Our legacy dates back to the Era of Turmoil, and our ancestors fought and survived a war far fiercer than anything the present era can offer. We survived then and we will do the same now.

The fiery elder seemed offended at the notion that his family would retreat in the face of overwhelming odds, and perhaps his reaction was a justified one. He merely sought to defend his family's reputation.

"That may be true, Elder Yongliang. However, that was not my question. I asked you all," Yao Shen paused to gesture at the attendees, "what the disciples and guardians would do in face of such an attack. Your families, as powerful as they may be, are a minority when compared to the entire population of the sect. A fact that many of you seem to have forgotten." Yao Shen's voice turned sharp toward the end. "Most of them share a background similar to mine, recruited from one mortal village or the other, a displaced or perhaps unwanted orphan and the occasional late-bloomer seeking a more adventurous life."

This time, it was Earth Patriarch Kang Long who rose to counter Yao Shen's discourse, "Grand Patriarch Yao Shen, it is only natural for the cultivators of our Modern Sect, be it a new disciple or a member of the legacy families, to rise and fight against a demonic path incursion. The legends speak of the demonic path's cunning and shrewdness— if the situation is devolved to the point of all-out war, the odds of any disciple successfully escaping are negligible to none. Even if they did, a bounty with their name would be sent out to all righteous path sects, as it has been for every traitor who defected to the demons for centuries. As for surrender… Death would be a far preferable outcome to that."

Yao Shen let out a chuckle at his statement. The Dao Discourse was finally getting interesting.

"Patriarch Kang Long, you have been mingling with power so long that you have forgotten what it feels like to be weak. Let me present you with a question."

"Go ahead," Patriarch Kang Long replied, his brows furrowed in concentration.

"Patriarch Kang Long, why do you cultivate?" Yao Shen asked, his voice brimming with an intense curiosity.

After some thought, he replied, "There is no one singular reason I can give in answer to that question. My cultivation exists to defend the Earth Division from threats, and for that cause, I am willing to give my life. I also cultivate to honor the ancestors of the Long Family and to uphold the will of the righteous path. I cultivate to protect the ones I care about from harm."

"An astute answer. Patriarch Kang Long, another question. Do you fear death?" Yao Shen asked, his question drawing more than a few raised eyebrows, some even wondering if it was his attention to insult the Earth Patriarch's face.

"A cultivator that does not fear death is no cultivator at all, Grand Patriarch. One cannot pry upon the secrets of the Grand Dao without first pondering upon the value of one's own existence," Patriarch Lei Weiyuan replied with composure.

Now that was an impressive answer.

"You are partially correct, Patriarch Kang Long. You are also, however, partially incorrect," he replied.

That caught Kang Long's attention.

"You see, Patriarch Kang Long, you fear death because you value your own life. But you are not truly *afraid* of death."

"I do not understand," the Earth Patriarch replied, wondering if this was truly how Yao Shen developed his Human Dao.

"The mortal farmer grows grain to feed his village. The mortal potter sells his wares in exchange for grain so he can provide for his wife and offspring. But why does the cultivator cultivate? Why do you, Kang Long, venture deep into the Nayun Forest to hunt powerful spiritual beasts, risking your life? Why do you boldly face the wrath of the heavens, step after step, in the pursuit of cultivation?"

"I..." the Earth Patriarch began to respond, only to face the realization that he had no answer to give.

"The legacy of your ancestors. The burden and the responsibility of your sect. The desire to rejuvenate the glory of the Azlak Plains. The selfish desire to see what lies at the highest echelons of power. Or, more simply, the desire to live longer. These are your anchors, Kang Long. These are what make you something greater than the sum of your parts. Something more than 'just' yourself. Now tell me, what anchors does a disciple, who had been a mortal merely a few years ago, have to offer?" Yao Shen's voice was strained as he looked Kang Long in the eye. For once, he was struggling to contain his own emotions.

"*Anchors...*" The word rolled off Kang Long's tongue, his tone ponderous. What anchors did a mortal child whisked away to a world of cultivators have? Why did he cultivate? The more he thought about it, the more his expression seemed to scrunch up.

"I don't know," he replied after a while.

Yao Shen mirthfully laughed for a good minute before shaking his head. "Patriarch Kang Long, you were born a prodigy. Privileged. Protected. I do not blame you for your failure to answer. But, surely, you understand when the demonic path attacks, mere *platitudes* will not be sufficient to win the war! The demonic path is vicious and barbaric in their methods, but they are also far stronger at the weaker stages of cultivation. You think the fear of death will suffice as an anchor? *Laughable!* Your defense is unrivalled in the Azlak Plains, Kang Long. Perhaps that has made you forget that the ***fear of death does not give one the courage to stand!***"

"Then, Grand Patriarch, what anchor does such a cultivator possess?" Meili Zhu's pacifying voice gently sounded out, the only one brave enough to speak. The other cultivators, even including the Flame Patriarch, seemed stunned into inaction as they meditated upon Yao Shen's shocking words.

Yao Shen's eyes seem to fall a little, their original brightness dimmed by a fleeting sorrow as he softly spoke, "That which you take from them. *Mortal friends. Mortal Family. A home.*"

Silence befell the hall.

"Some onlookers may think my actions whimsical," Yao Shen finally spoke, banishing the cloud of silence that was suffocating the room. "But those present today, as respected elders and my fellow Patriarchs, know better. A Patriarch does not make a move without tethering the interests of his sect to his action." Yao Shen's words were spoken with a sincerity to them. From the insipid reactions of the other cultivators, that assumption seemed to be a given.

Yao Shen had been a known quantity for decades, and a rising star of the Heavenly Sky Sect for much longer than that— it was far easier to believe that his actions now were part of a long-running ploy rather than his personality changing overnight.

"When I first arrived at the Flame Division, Patriarch Lei Weiyuan graciously offered me a tour of the sect. Most, if not all, of you are aware that I first chose to visit the Sparring Stage. A rather vexing choice, wouldn't you agree?" Yao Shen asked rhetorically.

"The reason is quite elementary. Once, I, too, was a disciple of the outer sect. Having seen through that paradigm, I know that it is the quickest way for a glory-seeking disciple to achieve fame and renown," Yao Shen elaborated.

"There, I found exactly what I was seeking," he said. "A young outer sect disciple facing a scion of the legacy families."

"In his right hand, he brandished a dull blade whose edge was marred down by the ravages of time. In his mind, the blade techniques offered by the Flame Division were not enough, so he fashioned his own technique by borrowing inspiration from a dozen others. In his heart, he carried the bitterness and resentment of a dying old man, instead of the spark and vitality of youth." Yao Shen shook his head before continuing, "My intention is not to blame the Flame Division. Patriarch Kang Long, I asked you what your anchors were," Yao Shen gazed at him.

He nodded back.

"So it is only apt that I reveal my own. The reason I cultivate, the reason I became the former Patriarch of the Sky Division, is partly due to the kindness my master offered me by taking me as his disciple. Whether it was cultivation resources or techniques he had pioneered through years, perhaps decades of experimentation, he held nothing back. His will to see the Sky Division prosper passed down on to me, so I strived to assume the mantle of Patriarch. Soon, I had disciples to teach, duties to fulfill and my own sect to protect from the machinations of the demons, and for that reason, I could not stop in my pursuit of strength. Even if that risked losing it all," Yao Shen's tone was calm, relaxed, as if he saw a greater truth the others in the room could not yet comprehend.

"But what do they have? What reason do they have to fight, but fear? Hopelessness? Despair? I do not blame the Flame Division, for I am certain that this is not an isolated case. No, I blame us all, for in our avarice, we have forgotten what it means to be *righteous*. I blame myself the most, for I chose to overlook these issues when I lacked the strength to enforce the change," Yao Shen's tone remained placid, concealing the self-deprecation he felt in that moment.

He had never claimed to be a saint, but that did not mean that he could not acknowledge his past inaction.

"Then, Grand Patriarch..." Meili Zhu spoke up, her tone thoughtful. "What do you propose?"

All eyes landed on Yao Shen.

Yao Shen inwardly smiled, thanking Meili Zhu for her astuteness.

He withdrew a solitary sheet of papyrus from his spatial ring, placing it upon the table. It was a map of the Azlak Plains. The West was dominated by the behemoth that Nayun Forest was, the North occupied by the Labyrinth of the Ancient Chen Clan, the furthest reaches of the South concealing the enigma that they aptly named the 'Gorge of Death.' The Eastern border was protected by the Grand Sealing Formation, dotted by a few mortal villages that were situated at the eastern corner of the Azlak Plains.

Many such villages were situated in the central region of the Azlak Plains, which comprised the territory of the three hegemonic sects.

"Would any of you like to point out the simplest way to defend the territory of the Modern Sect?" Yao Shen asked, the previous gravitas in his voice replaced by a growing enthusiasm.

The elders exchanged nervous glances.

Yao Shen chuckled.

"Of course, you all already know what it is," Yao Shen said, a piece of sharpened charcoal held in his hand.

"Yet, it has taken us hundreds of years of conflict and the birth of a Soul Emperor for me to do this," Yao Shen's voice spiked, his words echoing with power.

Charcoal brushed against papyrus as Yao Shen extended a line from the Sky Division to the Flame Division that was relatively situated toward the northeast. Using the Flame Division as a vertex, Yao Shen stretched out another line upward, connecting the Flame Division to the Earth Division. Finally, a final stroke of charcoal slashed downwards, connecting the Earth Division to the Sky Division. Using the three divisions as vertices, a triangular perimeter was formed.

"This is the reason why I united the three divisions," Yao Shen revealed to a slightly shaken audience.

"But, Grand Patriarch, there is no way we can possibly oversee such a large territory," one of the elders protested.

"That is indeed one of the challenges," Yao Shen replied, having expected the rebuttal. "It is true that we cannot afford a large-scale protective formation on this scale. However, we do not necessarily need one. Each of the divisions have their own robust defenses, so for our purposes, a large-scale detection formation would be far more efficient and cost-effective."

"But... why?" the elder asked, and many around him echoed that statement. Why take such measures if there was nothing to protect in the center? They knew Yao Shen's real purpose would be revealed soon.

"I wish to build a city. A city unlike no other on Ionea, no, dare I say, all of Eliria itself. A city that defies all cultural and social norms, a city that will *unite* the Modern Sect. A city that the cultivators of the three divisions will fight for, one they will defend to their dying breath— and they will do so with a smile on their faces. I call it, **The Mortal Capital, All Haven**."

His words received exactly the reaction one would expect from a group of cultivators. Confusion. Skepticism. Mistrust.

Yao Shen withdrew a sheaf of papyrus from his spatial ring, slamming it on the desk.

"A city where mortals and cultivators will be considered equal," Yao Shen said, as he plucked out a sheet of papyrus from the sheaf and placed it in the center of the table.

"This is the first innovation. I call it an 'Apartment'."

Murmurs and whispers were exchanged as the elders peered closer to get a look. A detailed blueprint was intricately sketched out upon the sheet of papyrus, delineating a ten-story-tall architectural construct that was supported by cylindrical earthen pillars that stretched deep underground. A cross-section of the first floor sketched out the floor plan, which would be mirrored by every story above it.

Yao Shen had designed for there to be four flats on each floor, each one possessing three bedrooms, one living room, one 'bathroom' and one balcony that would be under the owner's sole prerogative to utilize and enjoy. Of course, he deserved no credit for the design— with his soul being as powerful as it was, it only took him a few minutes of meditation to recall all he knew about architectural design, and he'd ended up recreating a smaller version of the apartment complex he used to live in.

Notably, though, Yao Shen had made marked deviations from the layout he'd remembered, beyond architectural approximations or errors that stemmed from insufficient knowledge. Modern plumbing was something that was simply beyond Yao Shen's ability to recreate, as he lacked both the skillset and the necessary sciences to come even close to aping the end-result of thousands of years of human engineering.

The good thing, though, was that Yao Shen didn't have to.

The Dao of Formations, or *Runic Formations,* if one were to use a more technical term, were considered a rather vexing branch of study. In fact, 'Dao' was a misnomer when it came to the study of formations, for whilst anyone could study and recreate formations, one could not cultivate it in the traditional sense. However, the more Daos a formation master grasped, the deeper his formations would grow in both depth and complexity— provided that the formation master was talented enough.

That made the study of *Runic Formations* invaluable, yet the three hegemonic sects of the Azlak Plains didn't have a single true formation master they could call upon in times of crisis.

The problem, unsurprisingly, stemmed from a lack of knowledge.

Basic rune-script was something that even the weakest of cultivators could learn and something that many stronger cultivators, like Yao Shen, believed to be a necessary part of a cultivator's arsenal— for it was the only real means of judging the danger posed by a foreign formation that they could encounter in one of their explorations.

However, not even Qi-Formation disciples held much interest toward the *true* Dao of Formations, to utilize rune-script to create powerful defensive and offensive formations.

Their decision would be a wise one, for *basic rune-script* seemed to be the building blocks of a greater whole, a fragmented language that the cultivators of the *Azlak Plains* lacked the knowledge to piece together. Not only was it inefficient, the effect produced by *basic rune-script* was also far weaker than what a cultivator, with the same input of Qi, could manage.

Greater rune-script, on the other hand, could create a containment ward that could block the backlash of Soul Emperor level attacks, like the one sealing Origin Treasures in the Solaris Keep.

However…what was considered weak and insignificant by cultivators could become a boon for mortals.

If any disciple was asked to envision a formation, the first thing that would come to their mind would be a connected, circular formation, like the Flame Division's boundary of purification. Yao Shen, in his blueprint, had disregarded those conventions— yes, a connected formation did amplify its power, but… *'intensity'* was not the variable that Yao Shen sought.

On the ground floor of Yao Shen's apartment, a simple artifact fashioned specifically to house a 'divine sense brand' would be placed, buried a meter below the ground floor. The one immutable advantage of *basic rune-script* was that one did not require an understanding of the corresponding Dao. One did not require an understanding of the Dao of Light to utilize the basic light rune, but it was seldom considered from that angle— the world of cultivation was one that directed its efforts to honing martial strength, allowing auxiliary applications of combat-oriented discoveries to fall though their narrow sieve.

Though Yao Shen had found himself wondering what the intention of *rune-script's* original creator was, in creating a path to power that tore away some of the restrictions of one's path and Dao affinity. He doubted someone that prodigious would fail to consider the change it could bring to mortals' lives, but not once had Yao Shen heard mention of a famous mortal city in the recorded history of the Sky Division.

Though that, perhaps, was one mystery he had no hope of solving. Nevertheless, he was grateful for its existence.

Each flat would have basic runes engraved within the blueprint. Yao Shen had noted the ones he considered the highest priority. 'Light' runes were naturally at the forefront, for he much preferred the soft, illuminating glow brought by the rune over other alternatives. A 'Purification' rune, originating from Water Dao, for waste disposal— the closest Yao Shen could get to a functioning toilet, albeit it would work slightly differently. A simple 'Water' rune, for a functioning water supply. A 'Heat' rune for cooking and heating water for bathing. A 'Cooling' rune for emulating the effect of refrigeration, though Yao Shen wasn't quite sure how well that would work yet. There were even more runes, though Yao Shen was already aware that he wasn't the greatest at rune-script— some of the elders here could do much better, and he would enlist their help, but right now, he just needed a proof of concept.

Where Yao Shen had struggled was the 'connection' part. A traditional formation was engraved in a circular or at best an ovular shape for a reason— one rune flowed into the next and *greater rune-script* was often utilized in these formations, forming one unbroken connection that made sure there was no leakage.

Had Yao Shen not inherited his past life's memories, the idea would never have struck him.

Patriarch Lei Weiyuan, while unleashing his domain, utilized strands of divine sense to control multiple flaming birds that gave incredible versatility at the Nascent Soul level. However, what if he was asked to keep his domain active for an entire day? For an entire week? Even if his Qi didn't run out, his divine sense strands could not withstand channeling Qi at that level for more than a day, not without damaging his soul.

However, Yao Shen did not intend to channel Soul Emperor, or even Nascent Soul level flames. In fact, the Qi the runes could output was so tiny compared to his reserves, that the runes could not really bring any real harm to a mortal, unless they held their hand next to a 'heat' rune or did something equally negligent.

Using a Soul Emperor's divine sense to channel Qi into *basic rune-script.* The idea was so overkill that it would sound preposterous to any elder— after all, why would someone at the peak of the cultivation world bow down and dedicate even a second of his time for mortals?

Preposterous, indeed.

What was a divine sense brand, boiled down to its core?

A divine sense brand was a small portion of a cultivator's soul that was embedded with his will. That was the reason why when he'd tried to forcefully brand Elder Yongliang's spear, he was met with fierce resistance. The same way, when he was trying to unlock the Origin Treasure, the guarding divine sense brand had destroyed his own. Because the owner of the divine sense had left behind an instruction to destroy any invader that dared encroach upon its terrain.

The idea behind the artifact was simple— His divine sense brand, not the radiant sword that he normally used, but a far more benign one, would utilize any and all spiritual ore placed within to channel Qi into the runes, the formation resembling the outstretched branches of an ancient tree, with the chest artifact as its trunk, powering an entire apartment building.

Basic rune-script was inefficient, but the cost involved in powering one building would be so insignificant that a core-formation rank chunk of spiritual ore could power it for decades, if not centuries. The strain on his divine sense would be even lesser, so miniscule that Yao Shen wouldn't be surprised if it existed for the rest of his lifespan.

Unfortunately, Yao Shen lacked the ability to 'code' his divine sense, lacking the ability to give it multiple sets of instructions to react to different scenarios, but even an insignificant portion of his soul was powerful enough to memorize one additional command over a Nascent Soul Cultivator's—tapping twice in rapid succession upon the rune's surface would send the command to begin channeling, and repeating that motion would signal the divine sense brand to stop.

Even tapping through a stick would work, so the mortals did not have any reason to be injured in the process— it was the closest he could come to a button.

The best part?

This entire process would only require Yao Shen to visit each apartment building he constructed once, and it would function on its own for the next few centuries.

His whole blueprint maybe crude, one could even describe it as a cobbled mishmash of ideas but...

It would work.

Yao Shen was certain of it.

And this was only the first of his blueprints.

"Grand Patriarch Yao Shen... this..." Meili Zhu fought to keep the surprise out of her tone, her shocked gaze betraying her cause as she took in the implications of the blueprint Yao Shen had procured.

It was not that his formation's ingenuity alone could change the landscape of Ionea, but rather… even the elders could not claim to live in such luxury. Sure, one of their disciples or attendants would fetch them hot water if they wished to partake in a traditional bath instead of utilizing a touch of Water Qi to cleanse themselves, but this was… *decadent.*

More so, Meili Zhu's astonishment stemmed from the certitude that Yao Shen was the one who had presented the blueprint. As the master of the Faceless, Meili Zhu would be remiss in her duties if she could not claim to have a read upon her own Patriarch's character. Her own political interests aside, Yao Shen was a cultivator whose resolve could move mountains and sunder seas; his dedication to the Grand Dao and his tenacity in repeatedly testing his own limits in an effort to advance to the next cultivation realm were, quite frankly, traits that she admired.

However, Yao Shen was no patron of the arts, not a man that had the patience or time to develop something as mundane as *housing plans.* Yet, the schematics placed before her were the world of a grandmaster artisan whose vision and creativity left the old Matriarch of the Zhu Family at a loss for words. She could appreciate the finer details, the defiance of traditional architectural styles spurring on a few novel ideas of her own.

Yao Shen chose to remain silent, giving the elders a few moments to peruse his design before reaching for another blueprint. A businessman in his previous life, Yao Shen was well-versed in the art of negotiation, knowing the value of the element of surprise. Even astute cultivators who had lived for centuries would be a little perturbed upon being badgered with surprise after surprise, which was precisely what he was going for.

The next blueprint laid out a rough outline of the Mortal Capital, All Haven. Dozens of small squares represented individual apartment buildings that were placed at a small distance from each other, resulting in a front-facing U-shaped formation. The exact number of the apartment buildings required would have to be calculated after an accurate census of the Azlak Plains' mortal population. The space created in the middle would be filled with scenic parks, a few play areas for children and even two or three common-use swimming pools— the 'heat' rune for controlling temperature, the 'water' rune for a continuous supply and the 'purification' rune for sanitary purposes.

Paved roads would connect the apartment complex to the commercial district, which was comprised of a blend of small shops and larger outlets. The district as a whole would play an important role, but Yao Shen had yet to reveal his entire plans.

The next landmark was the 'Martial School,' represented by a large rectangular block that was alone a quarter of the commercial district's size. Every child would be taught basic martial combat theory, close quarter combat and would even be allowed to spar with mock wooden swords. The education provided entirely free of cost. Yao Shen intended for a few core formation cultivators to oversee the mortal children's training. He had a feeling that aged cultivators with no hope of advancing to the next stage would be particularly amenable to the task, especially if they hailed from a mortal background.

He plucked the Martial School's blueprint out and smacked it on the table with aplomb. There was no great profundity in the design, Yao Shen choosing to mimic the common facilities provided to outer sect disciples, a wide dojo sufficient to house mortal children and shield them from the elements whilst they trained.

The murmurs had exploded to open conversation by this point, one of the elders even opting to question Yao Shen directly.

"Grand Patriarch, I am greatly impressed by these... *designs*," he began, opening with a pacifying statement. "But is there any merit in teaching the martial way to… mortal children? Would it not be instilling a false hope, an illusion that they are actually capable of resisting the great dangers that lurk both within and beyond our lands?"

"You raise a fair question," Yao Shen remarked, partly accepting the merit in the criticism. "The first reason is elementary. It is to bridge the gap. Break the status quo. End the unseen resentment. The simple truth of the matter is, the Azlak Plains have reached a point where they can no longer afford to refuse even the most talentless of cultivators. The so-called subsidiary sects are subsidiary in name only and the only reason they exist is to boost the prestige of joining one of the three hegemonic sects. My presence does not change that equation, for I am neither omnipresent nor indefatigable— if we are ever driven to war, there will be a Soul Emperor on the other side to match my presence." He spoke the words that no one present in the room wished to be vocalized, yet none refuted.

"If we are not in a position to refuse those with the ability to cultivate, then I shall see to it that they receive the proper training and guidance from a young age. Decades have passed, and with every iteration, the legacy families' strength wanes. Let this even the field. Let your scions compete with trained and driven disciples, instead of confused and unwilling ones and I promise you, your worries will fade away." Yao Shen's voice echoed with an air of finality, his decision made.

"I… understand," the elder replied, a slight twinge of uneasiness in his tone. Perhaps that was what he feared— his family's scions being overshadowed by a group of mortals.

"The second reason is a matter of morale. There are powers in this world, powers beyond our belief and conception, that could perhaps defeat us with the same ease a cultivator can a mortal. That, however, does not dissuade our ambition… if anything, it *feeds* it. Defying inevitability, defying fate, while it may be ultimately be futile for some, there are few feelings in the world as empowering."

"I had not thought of the matter from that paradigm. I thank you for enlightening me, Grand Patriarch," the elder politely replied, more out of formality than genuine respect.

The elders were only beginning to wrap their heads around the implications of Yao Shen's blueprints, when he placed another sheet of papyrus upon the table, his expression conveying a hint of solemnity.

All eyes slowly inched toward the new blueprint, the elders hosting a range of emotions that varied from trepidation to wariness, wariness to skepticism and skepticism to a burning curiosity. Most 'innovations' and 'new creations' presented to the elders by their disciples and even guardians usually turned out to be vapid baubles, but after a long time, they found their imaginations being stimulated by a fellow peers' avant-garde creations.

The two blueprints Yao Shen had presented up until now utilized existing mechanisms and societal constructs, building upon them from a completely novel direction to create something unique. The 'Martial School' he intended to build, whilst surprising, was not entirely revolutionary. From the paradigm of the elders, it could be interpreted as training a pool of future cultivators instead of a class of mortals.

The traditionalists would perhaps find fault in his 'Apartment Complex' and 'Commercial District,' but mortals living in luxury was ultimately something cultivators from the legacy families did not care much about, as long as the quota of future disciples applying to their respective sects remained the same.

But Yao Shen's third true blueprint was truly *groundbreaking,* in the sense that it aimed to throw in upheaval one of the core tenets of cultivator society, a societal construct that had been rooted in their minds for decades upon decades, centuries upon centuries.

Meili Zhu was the first to react, the composure draining away from her face as she audibly gasped.

Patriarch Lei Weiyuan gave Yao Shen a searching look, his usually dignified expression appearing quite befuddled.

Patriarch Kang Long chose to maintain a stoic silence, seemingly waiting for others to react first.

The other elders were visibly strained as they held back their tongue, unsure if they could afford to attract the ire of their newly crowned Patriarch.

The source of the turmoil, namely, the blueprint, was deceptively innocuous. Yao Shen had once again shamelessly borrowed *'inspiration'* from his memories of Earth. He had delineated an entire college campus, albeit a greatly simplified one— three imposing buildings were sketched out in detail, each one boasting a width that far exceeded any individual apartment building by multiple times. There were only five stories in each building, but each floor had four lecture halls with stepped seating that were individually capable of seating three hundred students with ease.

The same *runic formation* that powered the apartment buildings would be employed in the construction of each of the buildings, albeit with a few minor modifications. Yao Shen had also gone as far as to create single and double story buildings within the college campus that would enhance the students' experience, such as a simple gym, a debate hall and a mess, where the students could get refreshments and/or food anytime they wanted.

That, however, was not what had elicited such a strong reaction from the elders. No, what had truly drawn their shock, and perhaps, ire, was the working title Yao Shen had chosen for the structure, namely: *The Mortal College of Spycraft and Warfare.*

"As I mentioned earlier, the founding ideal behind the Mortal Capital, All Haven, was equality between mortals and cultivators.

Many of you, I suspect, did not believe in the veracity of that statement. After all, how could cultivators like yourself, against whom only a chosen few can stand in the entirety of the Azlak Plains, envision a system where all cultivators were equal, let alone cultivators and mortals?"' Yao Shen asked rhetorically.

"Well, I suppose that depends upon your definition of the word, '*equality*'. If any society could truly achieve true equality, it would be indistinguishable from a utopia. I, Yao Shen, unfortunately do not have the power to give every mortal the ability to cultivate. Neither do I have the ability to ensure every cultivator, regardless of talent, is given an equal opportunity to ascend to the Nascent Soul level. Does that mean equality is a fundamentally impossible goal?" Yao Shen's tone was thoughtful, as he mused the topic aloud.

"No, of course not." Yao Shen shook his head lightly before continuing, " I cannot change the very heavenly laws that govern our realm. So, I asked myself... what is it that I *can* change? When implementing societal reforms on such a large scale, it is naturally essential to think about the possible consequences one's actions might have. To provide mortals with such luxury would be to take away purpose from them and to be purposeless is to wither. Those that wish to farm and engage in animal husbandry will, of course, be allowed to, with aid from cultivators, but that alone would not suffice. So, the only direction I saw was to direct them toward an even greater purpose!" Yao Shen's impassioned words rang out with clarity of purpose, even though the truth remained veiled behind a thick curtain of fog for the elders.

"In All Haven, both mortals and cultivators will be given an *equal* opportunity to defend their city, their land and all that they hold precious. Children aged seven and above will be taught the basics of combat in the 'Martial School' until the age of fourteen. Those children that develop the ability to cultivate will be sent to one of the three main divisions, based on the orientation of their Spiritual Roots— on the promise that they are allowed to return to the Mortal Capital at least once a month. However, what of the hopeful children that wish to serve their land? The ones ruthlessly denied by the heavens for no fault of their own?"

"You mean…" Meili Zhu whispered under her breath, even though she had likely reached the truth a little earlier.

"They shall be extended the opportunity to join '*The Mortal College of Spycraft and Warfare,*' where their minds will be honed in place of swords, wit in place of Qi and shrewdness over combat technique." Yao Shen's gaze shifted to the roof, or rather, what lay beyond it, a confident smile resting on his visage.

"Grand Patriarch, this is… both *unrealistic and unreasonable.*" One of the elders finally raised a voice of protest as he finished reading through the notes Yao Shen had scrawled next to the schematics, detailing the college's purpose.

"Indeed, I cannot possibly fathom what purpose a mortal combing through our combat techniques and historical texts could possibly serve," Elder Yongliang added, his voice more perplexed than offended.

Meili Zhu remained silent.

Patriarch Lei Weiyuan finally spoke, "Grand Patriarch… I must admit that even I am a little lost as to your true intention. If you could elaborate…"

"Very well. These blueprints… whose mind do you think is the architect behind them?" Yao Shen asked, struggling to wipe a grin off his face.

That question seemed to catch the elders a little off guard. It wasn't as if they hadn't considered the question, but up until that point, they were more concerned with the content rather than the designer.

"It seems that one of the Elders of the Sky Division has been concealing their talents quite deeply," one of the elders offered, his choice the obvious one. Perhaps it was one of the elders that hailed from a mortal background.

"As much as I would like to wish otherwise, it is not one of ours," Meili Zhu was quick to interject, her tone sounding rather vexed. "Many of these designs have a very non-linear approach that is entirely foreign to our own historical styles. It is clever, fresh and unique, so much so that if I were inclined to make a guess, I would suggest a cultivator that hails from beyond the Azlak Plains." Meili Zhu finally explained her line of reasoning, and Yao Shen was slightly surprised at the breadth of her knowledge pertaining to matters outside of cultivation.

That caught the other elders' attention. Was that the reason behind Yao Shen's eccentric moves and his sudden spike in power? Was he backed by a foreign power?

"A reasonable guess," Yao Shen replied, "but unfortunately, it is not correct. Let me rephrase it— who, or rather, which demographic is likely to benefit the most from these changes?" Yao Shen asked, unable to hold back his grin any longer.

Eyes widened in shock. Sharp breaths were inhaled. Light gasps exchanged.

"A mortal designed all this?" Meili Zhu finally asked, unable to believe the words being spoken by her own lips.

"A group of mortals, but yes. Or do you think I designed it?" Yao Shen let out a chuckle at the latter half of his statement. Before anyone could doubt his words, he added, "I swear upon my honor as a cultivator, that it was truly a group of mortals that were responsible for these designs."

Yao Shen's words were like thunderclaps in the ears of the cultivators, the sheer disbelief roiling off them so intense that one could think the elders were actually.... *offended* at that idea alone.

Despite his newly acquired memories, Yao Shen was still a man that took oaths with the utmost of gravitas. If anything, Earth's achievements were even greater, for they had no powerful cultivators to look to in times of turmoil. He could not take any credit for the architectural designs and Yao Shen was quite certain that if he were to explain *Runic Formations* to a group of scientists, they could chalk out a far more efficient formation.

That, of course, wasn't to say that Yao Shen was belittling his accomplishments. Only he knew the complexity involved in pioneering or rather, rediscovering an ancient, lost Dao, an accomplishment that few people across both worlds might be able to mimic. He was simply capable of acknowledging his own limits, as one who had studied the Dao of Formations for a relatively shorter time.

"But, Grand Patriarch, these formations.... how could a mortal—" an elder blurted out, instinctively reacting to the assault on his worldview.

"Elder." Yao Shen's voice cut him off, his eyes twinkling with mischievousness. "Surely, one does not require the ability to cultivate just to jot down a theoretical formation? As long as I sufficiently describe the extent of my capabilities, and as you all know, the range, capability and meaning of individual *basic-runes* is common knowledge..."

Patriarch Lei Weiyuan finally interjected, letting out a deep sigh, "It seems... that we have underestimated the capability and determination of mortals. However, while all these accomplishments are indeed commendable, any one of us would be able to reach the same conclusion in a far shorter timespan."

"You raise a fair point, Patriarch Lei; one to which I have no direct rebuttal to offer. What I propose here is not only unheard of, but also likely sounds absurd, to many of the venerable cultivators present today. Nevertheless, I must ask you to take a step back and consider the situation from a different perspective. Us cultivators, we number in the thousands, whilst the mortals' population is measured in the tens of thousands. Our souls allow us powerful and at the higher stages, near perfect memory, which

allows us to 'solve' a particular problem or fact situation *'faster.'*
However, let us take a field of study that has long eluded us,
namely, *Greater Rune-script.* Do you see the issue here?" Yao
Shen calmly asked.

Lei Weiyuan took a long minute to think before replying,
"There are two aspects to *Greater Rune-script* that must be solved
to wield its power, namely, the *language* aspect and the *Dao*
aspect. There have been multiple attempts across the years to
decipher the *language* portion, the prevailing theory that the true
meaning of *Greater Rune-script* will reveal what aspect of a
Major Dao to channel into it while forging the rune."

"And?" Yao Shen questioned.

"They have all failed," he replied, immediately understanding
the point Yao Shen was trying to make.

"As cultivators, we seize power in defiance of the will of the
heavens. Thus, it is only natural that we choose to be stoic when
confronted with great challenges; forgetting that not *all* challenges are ours to solve. It is ironic, that the ones most suited to
decipher the secrets of *Greater Rune-script* are seated in this very
room, yet it is also us, who have their attention split between our
cultivation, managing our families, our sect duties and teaching
our disciples. I ask you, truly— a thousand minds uniting together
to crack one problem, or a solitary mind with perfect memory,
whom is more likely to reach a solution?" Yao Shen pointed out
the greatest flaw in cultivator society, their pride, both the element
that let them stand unfazed in face of unfavorable odds, yet also
the invisible shackles that had been holding them back from truly
progressing all these years.

That stubborn, parochial refusal to ask for help.

No longer.

"Will that... is that... truly possible?" Meili Zhu asked, her
tone somewhat emotionally charged. As the Master of the Faceless, while prying away at the arcane mysteries of the past didn't

exactly fall within her duties, that did not mean that she did not yearn for them.

"The *'Mortal College of Spycraft and Warfare'* will receive a compilation of our historical texts, basic cultivation techniques, the intelligence we have on the demonic path sects, a primer on our capabilities... we will give them an information clearance at the core-formation level, so even if there is a leak, it cannot cause us any significant harm. Their primary focus will be to hone their minds into a weapon, delving into methods, tactics and even uncovered ancient knowledge that can enhance our combat capabilities. As students of history, they will understand how rare it is for a mortal to be given an opportunity to play such a significant role in cultivator warfare, and how blessed they are to be able to live in the city of All Haven. They will be given the requisite motivation, training and knowledge to excel, but only time will be able to tell what the fruits of their efforts will be," Yao Shen explained, planning to jot down everything he remembered of espionage, warfare, combat, geopolitics, negotiation, strategy and deception in one book, that would serve as the guidebook for the 'college' students.

His view was colored by the fact that he had seen humans of Earth utilize this same educational strategy to great effect, and truly did not see any reason why the same success could not translate over to the mortals of Ionea. That did not mean that they were guaranteed to succeed, only that Yao Shen did not expect abject failure.

"For a little time and a pittance in resources, we might achieve the most unexpected of results. Truly, what do we have to lose?"

Well, their pride, for one.

Yao Shen, of course, knew and understood that. Perhaps the other righteous path sects would ridicule them for it. Perhaps they would become a laughingstock among the other races as well.

But Yao Shen was not concerned with their opinion.

The more bizarre and eccentric they saw him as, the weaker they saw him as, all the better.

There were no interjections or further rebuttals against his proposal, so Yao Shen moved on to the final matter in his agenda, namely his plans for the 'Commercial District.'

There would, naturally, be individuals that did not develop the ability to cultivate, and yet, also were not interested in spycraft or research. Besides farming, animal husbandry, pottery and other such endeavors, they would also be allowed to apply for jobs in the Commercial District, even given the opportunity to own stores if they had a competent proposal.

The Commercial District's importance could not be understated, for Yao Shen intended for it to be a bridge between the cultivator and the mortal world.

The main draw would be an 'Auction House' that, for the first time in history, would be open to every righteous path cultivator that belonged to the Azlak Plains, whether they be from the Flame, Sky or Earth Division, or one of the subordinate sects. The auction would be held once a month, under the scrutiny of a Nascent Soul Cultivator. Not only would it employ lots of mortals and require mortals and cultivators to work together, but he hoped that it the curious disciples and guardians would also be drawn to the other attractions of the 'Commercial District'.

Yao Shen had planned for there to be eateries, shops selling hand-crafted trinkets, artworks and even live music performances. There would also be hairdressers, perfume shops and if he could find a way, even confectionaries. He was glad that he'd credited an anonymous group of mortals for the design; otherwise, he would be unsure how to present it to his audience. Overall, Yao Shen hoped that the Commercial District would become a retreat where cultivators, both legacy family and mortal origin ones, could forget their worries, stresses and burdens for a few hours and simply enjoy themselves while stimulating the mortal economy.

It was the least controversial of his proposals, a few of the elders even seemingly interested in the Auction House— the combined pool of three sects having an easy outlet to dispose of unwanted or little understood artifacts and resources could make for some interesting finds, after all.

Since there were no queries and mostly expressions of interest, that marked the end of the Conclave.

The elders hurried out one after the other, having received much information that they would have to meditate upon before deciding their own course of action in these tumultuous times.

Yao Shen intended for construction to begin in a month.

36

THE AUCTION HOUSE

YAO SHEN CHOSE to defer his visit to the Divine Mountain Sect by a few days, more out of necessity than choice upon being inundated with requests seeking his audience. Some he had expected, *predicted,* even while others came as a surprise to him. After the initial shock and consequently, a brief period of inertia, the elders reverted to what they knew best— *leveraging benefits.*

For the tide of change had come, far *faster t*han any of them had foreseen and it threatened to erode the common conceptions, the very elementary tenets of cultivator society. The future was uncertain and tumultuous, but it was also *exciting*, even if the majority of the elders would never admit it.

The Auction House, it seemed, had an even greater impact than he had intended for. The legacy families liked to project an impression of a united front before outsiders, but as Patriarch, Yao Shen had learned to see through that facade, glimpsing at the internal rivalries and occasional disputes. After all, each family had their own needs, desires, and most importantly, *greed* that needed fulfilling— they would subject them to the Zhu Family's guidance for the greater good and overall stability of their power base, but remained fiercely protective of their family secrets, like the Yi Family's alchemical recipes — the ultimate goal to vie for supremacy and become the one family that stood above all.

Up until now, the legacy families hadn't particularly prioritized their various small businesses much, the problem stemming from the lack of a market. The Qi Formation and Foundation Establishment Cultivators were largely supported by the sect but more chronically, the three hegemonic sects couldn't freely trade with each other. Certain non-essential specialties that were unique to one of the three sects could be traded for equally valuable resources from the other two sects, but ultimately, the core secrets, such as Zhiquang Yi's False Core Pill that allowed a Core Formation Cultivator to survive even after failing their heavenly tribulation, couldn't be traded at any cost. Even the items and resources that were sold had to be traded via the sect's treasury instead of the coffers of the legacy families— a rule that was strictly followed, lest one be branded a traitor.

Now, though, with Yao Shen at the helm of the Modern Sect, there was no real reason left for the three divisions to fear themselves being surpassed by one another. The three divisions that had throttled each other's growth and progress for so long could now enter a period where resources, cultivation manuals and even ideas flowed freely, no longer shackled by lines on a map, politics and generational hatred finally losing its grasp over the Azlak Plains.

There was, of course, a major flaw in this idea. One that the Auction House, unbeknownst to even Yao Shen until now, had inadvertently ended up solving. Merely being free to trade did not mean that revered elders or even guardians of a division would be comfortable in conducting trade on formerly enemy territory.

The Auction House was situated in the Mortal Capital, All Haven— a neutral territory shared by all three divisions. Not only would elders and guardians be able to freely visit the city as per their convenience, but it also gave them plausible deniability if the tides ever shifted and their actions were brought into question. One could only imagine the value of a nexus that would facilitate trade between the three divisions, especially since it was ratified by Yao Shen himself.

The elders had seen this eventuality even before Yao Shen, making him wonder what other unexpected benefits, or perhaps, even unintended consequences his decisions might bring as the morality and jurisprudence of Earth interacted with Ionea. He supposed, when it came to political acumen, he was still a little behind the shrewd elders; but when they had proposed to fund the initial setup of the Auction House in exchange for special benefits, like being allowed to view the auctioned items in an advanced screening along with a share in the revenue, it became quite obvious.

Elder Liuxian Xun of the Flame Division made a rather amiable first impression, his light-brown hair curtained in a tidy comb, intelligent grey eyes meeting Yao Shen's own, a natural smile resting on his face that projected a disarming atmosphere as he reached for a cup of warm tea that had been placed before him. In the world of cultivators, that usually meant that Liuxian Xun was not to be trusted, not easily at least—it was generally wise to be wary of the seemingly warm and affable cultivators, for that usually meant that they wanted something of importance from you; even if you yourself weren't aware of its value yet.

Of course, those precepts only applied to regular cultivators, for he was Grand Patriarch and everyone wanted something of him.

Liuxian Xun was technically Yao Shen's junior now, since he both outclassed him in cultivation rank and age, the tall man two, maybe three decades younger than him. As a mid-stage Nascent

Soul Cultivator at that age, he was neither exceptionally talented nor mediocre, though perhaps he should be commended for coming that far whilst specializing in the Dao of the Shadow whilst hailing from a family of Fire Dao Cultivators. It happened, once in a while, that a scion of the legacy families would not inherit any talent in the element that was supposed to run in their bloodline, forcing them to eke out their own path.

While the Sky Division was somewhat unique, specializing in multiple paths, the other two divisions only had a select few families that specialized in Daos outside Earth and Fire, mostly focusing on Water Qi for its invaluable ability to heal.

Perhaps it had to do with the nature of the Wind, for it was one of the rare few elements which had the ability to amplify other Daos, such as using wind to carry forth a torrent of flame or propelling earthen spears and rocks on the back of concentrated bursts of wind. Either way, the ancestors of the Sky Division had been wise to diversify, as the records and general knowledge left by them allowed him a slightly easier time on his path.

"Elder Liuxian, I am, naturally, honored by your willingness to contribute to the Auction House," Yao Shen replied, after having mulled over the man's proposal.

"Grand Patriarch," Liuxian Xun replied, dipping his head lower as a mark of respect.

He lacked the hubris and rigidity of the older elders, a point that Yao Shen supposed went in his favor. Perhaps that was what gave him the confidence to approach Yao Shen when Yao Shen had not agreed to the offers the four elders preceding him had extended, rather generous offers at that.

"And I am sure you are aware of the other elders' proposals," Yao Shen continued.

"Indeed," Liuxian Xun replied, his voice retaining composure, unfazed by the implication.

"After much deliberation, I have reached a solution that I believe will be acceptable to all the interested parties," Yao Shen's expression did not betray the momentary twinge of uncertainty he felt as he placed his handwritten notes upon the table.

The Auction House was part of a longer-term strategy, one that wasn't so readily apparent on the surface. However, the sudden interest of the elders hadn't been factored into this equation. Yao Shen had done the calculations, and ultimately decided that revealing this part of his strategy would bring him the maximum number of benefits later on.

The notes he'd given Liuxian Xun borrowed another concept from Earth, albeit one that was greatly simplified and modified to actually work in Ionea's landscape.

He'd divided the Auction House's ownership into hundred 'shares,' namely talismans imbued with a negligible portion of his divine sense that would certify their authenticity. The concept was rudimentary enough that it only took Liuxian Xun a moment to grasp its essence, similar to the profit-sharing agreements they used, except 'shares' seemed to be intended for a larger investor base.

The key point to note here was that its authenticity was backed by the most powerful cultivator in the Azlak Plains, instead of being based upon notions of honor or a mutual fear. That difference had far greater implications than one might imagine— under the previous system, no one Patriarch had the strength to back such a boisterous proclamation.

What confused him, though, was the distribution. Twenty shares were allocated to each of the divisions, namely, to the new Patriarchs— Zhou Hui, Kang Long and Lei Weiyuan. They would then be responsible for conducting a fair internal auction within the Sky, Earth and Flame Divisions, selling each share to the highest bidder. The wealth raised would be utilized to buy resources wholesale from individual sellers and legacy families alike, hire staff comprised of both mortals and cultivators and, of course, conduct the auctions.

Dividends will be paid to the shareholders from the profit after setting out wealth for operational expenses, depending upon the number of shares in an individual's possession. The real addendum, though, was that Yao Shen had personally promised to honor the shareholder receiving their dues, even going as far as to clarify that even if a legacy family could not produce any more Nascent Soul Cultivators, their descendants would still receive the aforementioned dividend on time.

Considering Yao Shen, as a Soul Emperor, would outlive them all… it was an extremely tempting proposal.

But there was one factor that confused Liuxian Xun. Twenty shares would go to Yao Shen, and considering his assets didn't even equal a few legacy families, he wouldn't be paying anything. That was acceptable to Liuxian Xun, well, not like he was in a great position to argue, but even then… twenty percent was a fairly insignificant sum when Yao Shen could claim a monopoly.

"Grand Patriarch Yao Shen, you have mentioned that there will be a hundred of these… 'shares' in circulation. But in summation, the total distributed shares only add up to eighty," Liuxian Xun looked almost disturbed as he went through the notes for a second time, making sure his eyes hadn't betrayed his cause. Surely Yao Shen wouldn't make such a simple mistake.

"The Azlak Plains…" Yao Shen began, immediately causing Liuxian Xun to stop scouring through the notes and pay attention to his words, "… is an effectively cordoned off territory. The Grand Sealing Formation prohibits access to the sea, thereby giving us no opportunity to map sea-routes and conduct trade. The Nayun Forest, on the other hand, is both a shield and a cage — the cultivators powerful enough to force their way through wouldn't deign to trade with us, while Core-Formation and Nascent Soul Cultivators who might be interested aren't powerful enough to make the journey. The first is an absolute, while the second cannot be changed in the short-term. That leaves only one trading partner that we can secure in the immediate future."

Realization dawned upon Liuxian Xun, but his voice was tinged with confusion as he replied, "But the True Elves have been rebuffing our requests to engage in trade for centuries now."

"Indeed. However, it matters not what the state of our internal politics is. To the True Elves, we went from mere tenants on their purported land to claimants. We went from a divided land to a united one— a force comprised of dozens of Nascent Soul Cultivators, led by an Esoteric Dao Soul Emperor. Moreover, a force with no direct ties to any other righteous path sect. Is that a force they can truly choose to ignore? The True Elves prefer stoicism, yes, but that does not mean that they are foolish."

"You plan to give them the remaining shares?" Liuxian Xun questioned.

"Not *give*. I plan to *extend* an expression of goodwill. Giving them a stake in the Auction House... it does not take much reading between the lines to decipher my intent. And you can only imagine the uproar if Elven goods flowed through our Auction House. After all, it is not that the Elves do not trade with other species, though it has been centuries since they broke off ties with the righteous path." Yao Shen explicated his plan out loud.

"But, Patriarch Shen, the Elves can even choose to ignore the demands of the Western Righteous Path Alliance. What are we in comparison?" Liuxian Xun protested, sidelining his doubts on why Yao Shen was divulging this information to him in the first place.

Yao Shen laughed.

"What are we you ask?" he answered, an easy-going smile now resting upon his face, as if the world danced upon the palm of his hand. "Why, I thought that should have been obvious by this point. We are naturally *better*, of course."

Liuxian remained seated, completely stumped by the response.

'Better…?" he mused in his thoughts, trying to puzzle out Yao Shen's meaning.

"Have you ever seen another cultivator sect even *attempt* to dedicate so much effort to the wellbeing of mortals? Has any Patriarch before me even acknowledged, let alone attempted to heal the unseen divide between cultivators from mortal and legacy origin? I say this not to pat myself on the back, but to point out that from the perspective of the Elves, we have turned a new leaf. Or more accurately, if they still cannot bring themselves to trust us, they will never trust another human again."

"That is improbable… but, admittedly, possible." A brief flicker of admiration flashed in Liuxian Xun's eyes as he calculated the likelihood of that possibility.

"If they refuse, then so be it. Though it will take some time, I, Yao Shen, still have other moves that I can consider to achieve similar results," Yao Shen exaggerated, but only by a little. If he managed to unlock the other Origin Treasures, the possibilities were really as limitless as the stars. Secret weapon-forging techniques, a forgotten pill recipe— he just needed one such unique item to draw the attention of the righteous path sects, albeit the Elves were still the most ideal option, considering their patronage would automatically grant them protection.

"I see. But… why tell me this, Patriarch Shen?" Liuxian Xun finally asked the question that had been burning at his insides for so long.

"Of the five elders I met today, you were the only one that was truly receptive to my ideas pertaining to All Haven's future. The other elders are quite eloquent at feigning interest, but a Human Dao Cultivator's perception is not so easily thwarted. Not that I fault them for chasing benefits... but they ultimately lack the flexibility that I am seeking. The information I have shared with you shall be revealed to the other elders of the three sects in a day's time by their respective Patriarchs. Until then, you may do with it as you will,"

Liuxian Xun seemed stunned by that response for a long minute, as he digested the implications of those words. Kindness, whilst not unheard of, might as well be a foreign concept among cultivators at their level. Of course, Yao Shen was, most likely, motivated by other factors, but that did not change the base truth — this was an opportunity for the Xun Family and, he supposed, also a test from Yao Shen.

He could, after all, do a great many things with the information he'd been given— chief among them being informing his closest allies. He *could.* However, not only would he fail the test Yao Shen had extended, but also, he would be placing the interest of other legacy families before his own.

Accepting this favor meant that Liuxian Xun could secretly act before the other elders, getting a day's head start to liquidate his wealth for the action. Normally, if it was just a matter of the three hegemonic sects, his interest would definitely be strong but... not to this extent.

The mere possibility of Elven trade completely changed the equation.

It would make the Auction House a monolith whose reach extended beyond their small region, to the point where he could imagine powerful cultivators making the journey from afar.

Even though it was possible that Yao Shen would, one day, ask recompense for this favor, it was still one he could not refuse.

"Many thanks, Grand Patriarch," Liuxian Xun offered, his head bowing a little lower this time.

With that, their discussion came to an end, Yao Shen's course of action finalized.

Later in that day, the two Patriarchs and Meili Zhu had quite vigorous reactions when he divulged the entirety of his plan. They were each handed twenty shares and naturally would be responsible for the auction, well, besides Meili Zhu, who would have the shares sent back to the Sky Division and would be allowed to participate in the auction through a proxy.

The Patriarchs themselves were not disallowed from participating in the auctions, whether through proxies or otherwise— It was their own political considerations that dictated that they hold the auction in a manner that could be perceived as fair, so Yao Shen wasn't worried there unless the Patriarchs were suddenly willing to alienate their own allies.

The succeeding three days were the liveliest the three divisions had been in years, if not decades. The internal auctions had sparked a buzz among the upper echelons of cultivator society, a thrum of cautious excitement echoing out despite an attempt to maintain secrecy pertaining to the matter. From the reports Yao Shen had received from his third disciple, Xiaoli, who had his own methods of sourcing knowledge, it was as if the usually calm and tranquil inner sect had woken up from a long slumber— prominent elders that were thought to be in closed door cultivation could be seen brusquely walking from one residence to the next while inner sect disciples scurried around with rather flustered expressions, carrying sealed messages without being aware of their contents.

The venerable Elder Han, the only elder that had been present at Yao Shen's ascension to Soul Emperor, was the recipient of one such sealed scroll. He, as an Elder of the Sky Division, was naturally informed about the upcoming auction and understood its significance. However, his own cultivation had been partially funded by the Zhu Family and although he had paid off his debts, he was one of the poorest elders when it came to his assets.

Even the blade he used was on loan from the Sky Division's treasury, a broad longsword artifact that did not mesh well with his fighting style or his domain, which was primarily centered around the Major Dao of the Wind, along with a few Minor Daos blended in to serve auxiliary purposes.

As a cultivator, he was keenly aware of his own shortcomings — where Yao Shen had lacked talent, Elder Han's demeanor was not the most suited to a cultivator's lifestyle. In his youth, he had not known the importance of carving his own path, instead choosing to accept the Zhu Family's help at the first sign of hitting a roadblock. That had made his path smoother than most cultivators, but it had also made him weak, it had made him *reliant* and even beholden to the Zhu Family's interests until he paid his debts off.

He still remembered the first time he stepped into the Zhu Family's residence, the ostentatious displays and excessively lavish ornaments leaving him almost breathless, the opulence a far cry from his humble outer sect quarters. That, however, was not his most vivid memory of the Zhu Family's Estate— he recalled stepping into Meili Zhu's chambers for the first time as if it were yesterday, the Matriarch of the Zhu family merely an early-stage Nascent Soul Cultivator back then. But his gaze went not to the beautiful cultivator, but the exquisite blade that was displayed upon a wooden stand, placed behind her chair.

"Do you like it?" the cunning woman had asked. "If you cultivate hard and listen to your elders, perhaps that blade will be yours one day." She had whispered the sweet words of temptation into his ears.

The blade had an imposing presence that *demanded* his attention, and for a long moment, he was mesmerized. Its single, curved silver edge stretched across its patterned metallic body, the forging technique employed in crafting the blade resembling a flowing tide crashing against the coast, in all its chaotic glory.

In hindsight, if he had known more about cultivator society, Elder Han would have known that such an effect could only have been created by a Nascent Soul level blade— one that would definitely not be stored so lackadaisically. It had been bait that Meili Zhu had specifically tailored for him, knowing his enthusiasm for swords.

A few years ago, he'd offered to purchase it from the Zhu Family. It was merely an Early Nascent Soul Stage artifact, definitely valuable to someone like Elder Han, but it was only one of many for the Zhu Family. The artifact had been sitting unused in a storage room for decades now, but Meili Zhu had refused to sell it.

Or rather, she had refused to take resources in exchange for the blade.

Instead, she wanted a few favors from him. Elder Han had already experienced the dull vistas and overcast skies that road led down to firsthand, the feeling of being indebted to one as scheming as Meili Zhu was akin to being trapped in the web of a *Slavarn,* a spiritual beast with six thin, jointed appendages for legs, which was known for its ability to spin large swathes of fine webs coated in a natural immobilizing agent. Coming into contact with one swathe of webbing wouldn't immediately render you immobile, but that was the terrifying part— once you stepped into a *Slavarn's* territory, you no longer knew which direction to go in, the webbing too fine to be perceived by anything but the most acute of senses. To be trapped in its web without knowing how broad a net the unseen webbing had cast, to have the taste in one's mouth turn into bitter ash and to witness one's touch render the world into greyscale.

That was how they had made him feel. However, without him even realizing, the subconscious unease and respect associated with the Zhu Family had begun to fade since Yao Shen's meteoric rise. On the scale of the Modern Sect, they were just one legacy family out of dozens. The terrifying Matriarch of the Zhu Family no longer looked so intimidating when contrasted with the veritable monster that Yao Shen was. Slowly but surely, Elder Han was stepping out of the shadow Meili Zhu and the Zhu Family had cast upon him, reclaiming the person that he once was.

Which was why, when he unfurled the scroll delivered to him by a guardian, his reaction was one of anger instead of pleasant surprise.

Humiliation, even.

The Nascent Soul Blade *Zhenyue,* the blade that Elder Han had repeatedly requested to purchase for a generous sum of Nascent Soul grade Spiritual Ore along with precious Spiritual plants and beast byproducts that he had amassed over the years, only to be unceremoniously refused... Now, the Zhu Family wanted to sell it to him, for seven-tenths of the spiritual ore he'd originally offered.

How arrogant!

Arrogant it was... but the Zhu Family knew him well. They knew how possessive he was of his wealth, as one who had to go to such great lengths to obtain it. Patriarch Zhou Hui had set the auction's bidding to be solely limited to Nascent Soul Spiritual Ore of any purity, the de facto currency of the cultivator world. A resource constantly being utilized by elders, the Sect Formations, rearing Spiritual Plants and Natural Treasures... making it hard to procure on a short notice.

If Elder Han bought Zhenyue now, he would be signing away whatever negligible chance he had at purchasing shares in the auction. But he didn't care much for them to begin with— sacrificing the majority of his wealth for one share would be incredibly frivolous.

Normally, Elder Han would have accepted the offer, mayhap even been grateful for it.

Now, though, the illusion was broken. The Zhu Family had financed his cultivation, true. They had given him cultivation resources in the form of elixirs, pills and spiritual ore but never the truly valuable secrets of the Zhu Family. They had given him enough to do well, but never to *prosper.* Elder Han's role was to sit upon the Council of Elders and ratify what the Zhu Family wanted him to ratify, not to outshine the master.

'Not anymore,' Elder Han thought as he scrawled down his reply on a fresh scroll before handing it over to the disciple who was waiting outside his residence.

He had offered them five-tenths of the original offer he'd made years ago, further negotiating down for another two-tenths. That was, at least what he believed to be their bottom line.

It was a bold move. A little reckless. A response that met arrogance with arrogance.

It was very unlike Elder Han.

Yet, why did it feel so fitting?

Why did it feel like breaking free from invisible webs that had been constricting him for so long?

The reply had come swiftly, and it had been about what Elder Han expected. In their strongly worded response, the Zhu Family wished to remind him of their contribution to his growth and how highly he was valued by them. They also *'advised'* him to remember who his allies were and to not chase short-term gains while sacrificing the bigger picture.

All in all, it was a thinly veiled threat that would have swayed Elder Han on most days.

Today, however, was not most days.

A few hours later, Elder Han walked out of the Zhu Family residence with a sleek new blade sheathed in a scabbard that hung from his waist. He had a feeling, though, that he had won back far more than a mere sword, even if it was one he'd dreamed of owning since his childhood years.

This was only one of the many instances of frenzied trades that took place between elders across the three divisions.

There was always the possibility of collusion or bid manipulation, but ultimately, Yao Shen wasn't too concerned about that. At the end of the day, the ability to create a guaranteed revenue stream for their descendants that would exist long after they were gone was too much a draw for them to hold back. This was even before the possibility of the True Elves participating was factored in.

Rather anti-climatically, at least for the disciples that were caught up in this wave of frenetic excitement, the internal auction was conducted behind closed doors.

A guardian from the Earth Division had delivered the shares back to his sect, and Yao Shen had been rather curious if there would be any untoward developments there. He had considered extending an option to defer the auction to Patriarch Kang Long but had ultimately decided against it.

He preferred for the hubbub surrounding the bidding to peter out by the time he arrived at the Earth Division and more importantly, Yao Shen believed that his presence there would only further exacerbate tensions unnecessarily.

Ultimately, though, if there was any internal turmoil within the Earth Division, he was not made aware of it. So far, he had been equitable in his treatment of the three divisions, a point that he hoped that Patriarch Kang Long had conveyed to his Council. Delegating responsibility to Kang Long was also an extension of good faith and a clever move on his part— powerful cultivators tended to value their prestige and Kang Long would naturally wish to maintain his pride and reputation. As long as the sect machinery continued to function smoothly, Yao Shen had no reason to interfere; in fact, he only had incentive to grant more autonomy.

If he had wanted to install a puppet regime, there were much more... efficient ways of achieving that objective. But Yao Shen carried with him the history of an entire other world and he knew the kind of measures he would have to take to maintain and enforce his rule— it would subvert everything he had set out to achieve.

Yao Shen firmly believed that the concept of 'freedom,' or more specifically, 'freedom of will,' was inextricably linked with the esoteric Human Dao. Up until now, he did not have a verifiable method to prove his hypothesis, but the creation of the Mortal Capital, All Haven, would finally give him tangible proof.

Human Dao, or rather, the Dao of Sapience did not quite perceive the concept of 'freedom' in the same way a mortal or cultivator would, or rather, it was not aware of the concept at all. His deduction originated from a simple question, one that Yao Shen had asked himself not long after discovering his esoteric power— '*When is sapience most exercised?*'.

Sapience was not a moralistic concept, as was evidenced by the long and bloody history he'd evidenced back upon Earth. It did not possess conceptions of 'good' and 'evil', 'right' or 'wrong' and 'moral' or 'immoral'. Yet, seemingly in contravention of the aforementioned observation, it required freedom of will to truly flourish.

When mortals, an entire subset of Ionea's population that has been considered insignificant and whose opinions have been deemed insubstantial for so long that they have forgotten what it was to have a voice are given the freedom to become who they want in society, say what they wish to without fear of retribution and offered an education if they wish to chase those avenues— ideas will clash against ideas, conflicting beliefs providing the insight necessary to spark the creation of new ideas; most good, some terrible and a few perhaps, atrocious.

Ultimately, though, the resultant society would allow humans to impose their will upon the fabric of the world to the fullest, to exert the potential of their sapient minds and souls to the greatest extent possible— *that* was why Yao Shen believed that it was only elementary for Human Dao to gravitate toward freedom.

For that same reason, Yao Shen did not wish to disturb the existing status quo of the three divisions unless they left him no choice.

To the other elders, All Haven might have seemed like a vanity project, or at best, a way to appease the True Elves— but not only were his intentions genuine, the Mortal Capital might serve as a way to deepen his understanding of the Human Dao.

The Internal Auctions themselves far surpassed Yao Shen's expectations when it came to the revenue collection— it seemed that he had still underestimated the multiplicative effect of hinting at the True Elves' possible future involvement combined with introducing the concept of long-term investments to the Azlak Plains. There were a few surprises, a small glimpse at the true wealth of certain legacy families — in the Sky Division, the Zhu Family managed to secure a whopping *seven* shares, leveraging their connections and calling upon old favors to raise an incredible amount of funds for a day's time. In the Flame Division, the Xun Family, which had long thought to be declining after their most talented scion failed to inherit talent in the Dao of Fire, in an unexpected reversal, managed to secure five shares, equaling Patriarch Lei Weiyuan's haul.

In contrast, the bidding in the Earth Division was far more subdued, the collections being approximately around what he had anticipated. There was a reason why Yao Shen was comfortable delaying his visit— for whilst fire was an element of destruction, earth was one of creation. A flame may burn brightly and boisterously for one moment of unparalleled glory, however, it fizzles out while the mountain *endures*.

One's element did not decide a cultivator's nature, but Yao Shen would be remiss to claim that it did not influence it. The highest number of shares a legacy family had managed to secure was three, though there were two such families. The rest had a more '*wait and see*' approach— if Yao Shen's gambles really paid off, then there would be other opportunities in the future. Right now, the potential reward was high, but the risk was equally high — they were not willing to squander resources in an atmosphere of such uncertainty, though each family had tried to get at least a single share.

The resources would be delivered to his residence via spatial ring and Yao Shen once again intended to invite representatives from the three divisions to create more checks and balances and to assuage any worries that he would siphon off the funds to further his own cultivation.

Of course, he hadn't been sitting empty-handed the last two days. He had spent his time further refining his designs and marking out shortcomings that he wasn't sure how to best deal with. He had already sent the blueprints back to the Sky Division through Meili Zhu, with a message for Zhou Hui to allocate the tasks to the suitable elders.

With the internal auctions completed, Yao Shen spent the next day conversing with a few elders that were responsible for managing and maintaining the Flame Division's offensive formation. Though the elders were uncomfortable in discussing the specifics of the Formation's inner workings, he still managed to have a very fruitful session upon *Runic Formations* and by the end of it, the elders agreed to improve upon his blueprints.

That had been the final task holding him back. Before settling on one design, Yao Shen wanted an improved version of his blueprints from all three sects, from which he could extrapolate the ideal design— cutting down on the shortcomings of each proposal and only carrying forward their strong points. Of course, getting it perfect on his first try was unrealistic, albeit this way, most of the kinks in his original design would be ironed out. One had to adhere to high standards if they were seeking out the patronage of the Elves, after all.

Now, it was time to visit the Earth Division and finally see for himself what the *Divine Mountain* concealed.

37

THE DIVINE MOUNTAIN

YAO SHEN'S eyelids were shut as he trailed across the sky, using nothing but his divine sense to guide him forth. He allowed the winds to crash against his person, his long hair wildly fluttering at the natural Dao's whims. The landscape beneath his feet was a constantly moving scenery, the individual details flitting past him as he blazed forward at the bona fide speed of a Soul Emperor.

His contingent had long since given up trying to keep pace with him, allowing Yao Shen to truly stretch his wings for the first time since his ascension. The gulf was even larger they had presumed, for despite the utmost of efforts, all the two peak-stage Patriarchs had managed was to keep Yao Shen in the periphery of their gazes.

The preceding fortnight had been one of politicking and scheming, unlocking ancient secrets that only led to greater mysteries and confronting the realization that he presided upon the Modern Sect seated upon a throne of cards, perhaps only separated by a single misstep from folding down and crashing upon itself. The True Elves, the Amadori, the demonic path and the other righteous path sects all swirled around him and if Yao Shen did not exhibit the proper caution required to navigate these tumultuous waters, he would find himself trapped in the center of the vortex.

It felt quite freeing to let go of those tensions and take to the skies, the sensation almost as thrilling as the first time he'd done so. It had been over a century since Yao Shen was a youthful Foundation Establishment Cultivator, his two legs shakily planted upon the flat of a flying sword that his master had procured for him. A blend of fear and exhilaration wrought upon his soul, as he continually shifted his footing in small increments, teetering over the blade's edge by the smallest of margins.

To channel his Qi into the blade and have its effect amplified by the flying sword's own reserves, maneuvering his body to control the direction and fluctuating his Qi input to control speed — the mechanics of flight as a weaker cultivator were, quite ironically, more complex than a Soul Emperors'. His master trailed ahead of him, a curtain of wind roiling and shifting around him, shielding him from the elements. Back then, his master's slightly hunched back could bear the weight of the world in his mind's eye, his aspirations limited to one day matching the senior cultivator's stature as a Nascent Soul Cultivator.

As long as his master's silhouette was still in sight, the young Yao Shen knew that he would come to no harm even if he lost his footing. Though for him, that was never an option— disappointing the cultivator that had given him so much, and yet, asked for so little in return; he would much rather prefer oblivion if the alternative was embarrassing his master. Not that he would be reprimanded for it... In hindsight, it was not the ideal disciple that his master saw in him, no, there were yet disciples more qualified than him even among those that hailed from mortal backgrounds; rather, the son he'd never sired.

So he'd persevered and persevered until the sword beneath his feet was replaced by thin air, his ephemeral soul turned tangible, until he became the mighty cultivator Yao Shen, Master of the Esoteric Human Dao.

Only…the *one* person he had something to prove to was no longer standing by his side when the time came.

There were few things in life that perfectly met one's expectations. Disappointment was commonplace and seldomly, one could have their presumptions shattered; reality exceeding the prison of one's expectations. As Yao Shen hovered above the Earth Division, though, he was at a loss for words— its grandeur was truly a sight to behold, its sheer *presence* permeating across the land. He had thought that the Sky Division's spies had exaggerated, that the elders that had been invited to the Earth Division back when ties between the sects were a touch more amenable, had been embellishing tales to echo their own fearlessness.

The Divine Mountain was a monolithic structure that arose from the depths of the earth, an anomaly in the otherwise grassy plains and forested lands that comprised the Azlak Plains. Towering over the surrounding landscape, the Divine Mountain cast a long, serrated shadow that shrouded everything in its wake in darkness; giving the impression of a vast serpentine beast's crooked fang as opposed to holiness or divinity.

Its surface oscillated between hues of dark-brown and black, every inch comprised entirely of bedrock pulled directly from the earth. The Divine Mountain was truly the most overt display of *raw* power he had seen, for contrary to what many disciples might believe, it was not a naturally formed structure. Two rings of *Greater rune-script* ensconced the base of the mountain, forming complete circular formations that that thrummed with power.

The sun-facing side of the mountain was where the outer sect was situated, in a clever architectural choice. Instead of carving directly upon the man-made mountain's surface when confronted by the inevitable need to expand beyond the boundaries of the inner sect, the Earth Cultivators had chosen to terraform the land instead— raising steppes of soft, fertile earth in a series of terraces or rather, levels, that were connected to the face of the mountain. Each level got progressively smaller in surface area, until the fourth and final step that led to the true entrance of the Divine Mountain. A long flight of narrow stone stairs led directly from ground level to the to the uppermost layer, the entire structure resembling the architectural layout of a ziggurat, albeit one that had been affixed to the side of a mountain.

A secondary formation guarded the outer sect's border, but the Earth Division's true defense would always be the formation embedded into the Divine Mountain itself. One glance at it and Yao Shen could tell that even he was not capable of punching through the rocky outcropping and jagged edges protruding from the mountain, not even *close.*

This had been a concern for the Sky Division of the past, but it worked in favor of the Modern Sect of the present. The expertise and aid of the Earth Division would be invaluable in constructing the Mortal Capital, All Haven and he looked forward to consulting their Elders upon this matter.

Roughly ten minutes later, the rest of his contingent finally caught up to him.

38

SHADOW AND YANYUE

Yanyue's sat in a meditative posture, her eyes shut and her brows furrowed in concentration. Gently clasped between the palms of her hands was the Xue Family's Heart-Cleansing Sea Pearl, a gentle azure glow emanating out of it.

Yanyue cycled the pure Water Qi through her body, each successful cycle adding an additional building block to her rapidly stabilizing 'foundation structure.' It also made her shudder in delight, as years of impurities amassed across her cultivation journey were purified, making her skin smoother, her body cleaner and her visage free of blemishes.

Finally, her eyes shot open.

"E-Elder Sister Shadow?" Yanyue stuttered out upon being confronted by Shadow calmly standing in front of her. "H-How long have you been standing there?" she asked. As much as Yanyue appreciated her elder sister's 'pure' personality, her ability to skulk among the shadows without letting out the slightest sound was one thing she could live without.

"Half an hour," Shadow replied, her expressionless yet beautiful violet eyes staring back into Yanyue's own.

"Uh...erm, why didn't you rouse me earlier?" Yanyue argued,

a light blush coloring her cheeks. To have the strongest core formation disciple in the Sky Division wait upon her was an honor, but it was one she hadn't asked for.

"You were cultivating," Shadow deadpanned rather matter-of-factly.

"I... never mind. So what did you need me for, Senior Sister?" Yanyue asked, trying to mask her meek nature behind a veneer of confidence. She had long since realized that she had to be direct and commanding whilst addressing her elder sister, even when it made her squirm on the inside; otherwise, the intent behind her words would just flit past.

Shadow outstretched her hand, a natural grace in her movements as she offered her a lift. Yanyue accepted her gesture, able to feel the raw, wiry strength contained in her senior sister's deceptively lithe body as she was pulled back onto her feet.

"Let's go," Shadow let go of her hand before turning around and walking in the opposite direction.

Yanyue fought down the instinct to ask *where* they were going, knowing that she was unlikely to receive an answer. Instead, she tried to think of what might have prompted this sudden intervention, knowing how much her senior sister cared for her.

Oh.

Yanyue realized that she had spent the last two weeks secluding herself in cultivation, not stepping out of Silveni's Heirloom even once. From a sustenance perspective, Yanyue had everything she needed to live in the tower, but that was not the real reason why she had ensconced herself in the safety of her fellow disciples.

Her Honorary Master, Yao Shen, was still out of the sect on official duties. With his absence, she had fallen back to her tendency to seclude herself and avoid trouble. Dongmei Xue, the object of her fears and anxieties, still resided in the very same sect as her; still very much alive and in her prime. While an outright attack was unlikely and just Yanyue's trauma exaggerating, there were other ways Dongmei could make trouble for her— like laying out a trap that would sully her reputation and force her master to abandon her.

As Yanyue walked through the streets of the inner sect, she noticed the surreptitious glances and curious looks the other disciples gave her, but none lingered for too long when Shadow swiveled her head in their direction with uncanny accuracy.

She hadn't realized that they had arrived at their destination until her senior sister, who was walking ahead of her, stopped. In a moment of clumsiness, she ended up bumping into Shadow's back, which definitely did the job of snapping her out of her reverie.

"Look," Shadow pointed out, unconcerned by her misstep.

Yanyue blinked away the embarrassment she felt, stepping to the side and looked in the direction her senior sister was pointing in.

An ancient tree rose to the heavens, it's mottled trunk a mélange of dull grey and radiant white mixed in with splotches of silver; the ethereal splendor only accentuated by the mark of centuries, if not millennia. It towered over the Sky Division like a mighty giant, its expansive canopy shielding them from all that dare attack from the sky. Magnificent three-pronged silver leaves dotted the branches, their numbers as vast as the stars in the sky.

Yanyue had witnessed this scenery from afar many a times before, but never dared approach it, never this close. This was the domain of core formation cultivators that were practitioners of the Dao of the Wind, a right that disciples had to prove themselves in battle for. Only twenty cultivators were allowed to cultivate under the Sky Tree at a time, to give the Ancient Tree enough time to recover its Qi— this was an absolute rule, for each Sky Division Disciple had a certain innate respect for its magnificence, for one that provided without asking for anything in return.

"Come," Shadow grabbed Yanyue's arm and began to walk forward.

"Senior Sister, this isn't appropriate," Yanyue protested softly, but there was no weight behind her words— like every disciple of the Sky Division, she too desired to experience the Sky Tree from up close.

Anticipation blossomed in her heart, replacing her anxieties and assuaging her fears for now as they went closer and closer.

In the blink of an eye, they were standing next to the tree.

Shadow sat down. A fidgeting Yanyue followed in her footsteps, mentally doing her best to ignore the other disciples who were giving them searching glances.

Pat, pat.

Yanyue's gaze shifted to the sound, noticing that Shadow was patting her lap. A blush colored her cheeks as she understood her meaning, still not sure what Shadow wanted to achieve.

But she complied, trusting her elder sister with her wellbeing as she lay on her lap, the blush on her face only getting heavier.

"Close your eyes," Shadow asked, her tone not betraying her emotions as always.

That suggestion, Yanyue found amenable— she really didn't want to see the other disciples giving leering glances at her, or worse, mocking her.

"Do you hear it?" Shadow asked, her tone, in a rare change of form, turning softer.

Hear… what?

Yanyue focused at her hearing, unsure what her senior sister meant. Searching, she did not find the other cultivators making the snide comments that her mind was projecting, and for a long moment, she thought that her senior sister was making fun of her, that this was some elaborate, cruel joke… until…

She heard.

The wind. It was the wind. It whistled and hummed, it rustled and howled, it *roared,* it *sighed;* somehow all at once. Somehow, when the dissonant sounds were combined, it resulted in a melody so beautiful, so *divine,* that her vocal cords had no hope of replicating it, not in ten years, not in a hundred.

It was the melody of the wind, and it was the most beautiful thing she had experienced in her life.

A tear rolled down her cheeks, so moving was the performance.

"When I was new to the sect," Shadow began, the soft touch of her finger wiping away the tear. "I used to cry a lot," she whispered, her voice so low that only Yanyue could hear her words.

"Each time I cried, Master took me to rest under the Sky Tree's canopy," Shadow whispered. "And each time, I stopped crying."

If Yanyue were to open her eyes in that moment, she would see a small smile resting on Shadow's visage, before it flitted away.

"I hope it brings peace to your heart like it did mine, Junior Sister."

39

THE EARTH DIVISION

YAO SHEN calmly observed as the massive stone disk guarding the entrance to the Earth Division's inner sect rolled back into position after the last of his contingent stepped inside the cave entrance. Runes flared to life upon its surface as the stone disk seamlessly melded with the Divine Mountain, now indistinguishable from its bedrock hewn interior. Worry flashed upon one of the Flame Division Elder's visage, but Yao Shen was unconcerned as he directed Patriarch Kang Long to lead the way.

Of course, Yao Shen did not reproach the elder for his wariness— a closed off environment entombed by tons of igneous rock on all sides was a nightmare for a Flame Cultivator and the ideal environment for an Earth Cultivator to engage in combat. Were it not for his understanding of the Major Dao of the Earth, even Yao Shen would be hesitant to step inside the Divine Mountain. Even though his prowess in the Dao of Earth might not equal Patriarch Kang Long, his reserves far exceeded, even dwarfed them by a significant margin— enough to supersede the fear of any ambushes, though Yao Shen found the possibility unlikely.

The first oddity that Yao Shen noticed was in the air— instead of the stale, damp heaviness he'd come to expect from venturing underground, he was greeted by a pleasant warm breeze that was evocative of spring's first gust, blowing back the bitter cold of the winter as it heralded the season of growth and renewal. A cloud of silence hung over the wide, well-illuminated passage, disturbed only by the sound of their own footfall echoing out— their dreary journey lasting for twenty long minutes, winding past bends and forks in the path until they could hear the distant murmur of civilization. Turning a final bend, a warm light shone upon them, signaling that their underground excursion had come to an end.

The tunnel they had traversed across spilled out into a vast cavern and Yao Shen was only the second after Kang Long to see what lay beneath them. A fleet of amber in a sea of glittering gold, the inner sect was a magnificent vista, its resplendent beauty only amplified by sunlight cascading from the sky. Yao Shen's gaze naturally shifted upwards, unsurprised to see greater rune-script carved a little below the mountain's sealed peak, concentric circles spiraling downwards until about the halfway point. These formations hadn't been visible from the Divine Mountain's exterior, but the fresh air had to come from somewhere if the Earth Division had sealed all the other entrances.

A layer of soft sand carpeted the hard bedrock that was concealed beneath it, the reddish-yellow granules shimmering as sunlight washed over them. An intimidating fortress lay nestled in the heart of the inner sect, its immediate surroundings barren, making it an anomaly in the otherwise tightly packed town. The amber fortress overlooked the rest of the town, comfortably seated above a large motte— it possessed no crenellations or bastions that one would expect from a medieval era fortress, the T-shaped structure instead enveloped by hundreds, if not thousands of stone lances that jutted out menacingly. Even the large earthen mound the fortress was situated on could be utilized by the Earth Cultivators within to aid in their defense, the only visible entrance a portcullis that seemed to be cast of blackened bone that, even from afar, exuded an oppressive, chilling aura.

The Serenity Mountainhold might sound like a peculiar name for a structure that was so offensively inclined, but like most historical landmarks, its present iteration concealed a tale of mystery and intrigue. Two centuries ago, a rogue demonic path cultivator had successfully infiltrated the Earth Division utilizing some forbidden techniques, laying low until the Patriarch and most of the elders had left the sect. The Serenity Mountainhold's purpose remained much the same to this day, serving as the Patriarch's residence, the treasury and the armory all in one— but it also used to be an assembly area for inner sect disciples, a place to freely discuss pointers, and once every fortnight, listen to the Patriarch's Dao sermons.

It had been a bloody night, that one; as the demon tore through the defenses, disarming, if not killing all that stood in his path. Many disciples, and at least a guardian and one elder had lost their lives as he tore through the feeble defenses left behind— for never had the Masters of the Earth thought that the incursion they had been preparing for would come from within.

To this day, the Earth Division had remained silent on what was stolen from them, though when the then Patriarch had heard, he was furious enough to storm the Nayun Forest in hopes of recovering it— an effort that ultimately proved to be futile.

"How magnificent," Yao Shen complimented in a moment of pure appreciation for the town's beauty. There was something romantic about living in the heart of a mountain, conveying a devotion to the Dao that Wind and Flame Cultivators could not replicate. For Earth Qi was not just a Dao, not just a power to be harnessed— Spiritual Qi played an essential role in the growth of plants, but it could not dictate it. The same way that one could water a plant, make sure it got plenty of sunlight, and back on

Earth, even sprinkle pesticides; but the ultimate decision as to whether it lived or died would still fall on Mother Earth.

Part of the reason Yao Shen had chosen the Dao of Earth to be improved to the Major Dao stage as a boon was because he had always believed that it masked a far greater Dao, a superior truth that few, if any at all, could glimpse upon in their lifetimes. A truth that involved how ecosystems linked the smallest and most insignificant of organisms to the survival of mighty creatures, the potential for life to evolve and even thrive in conditions considered hostile and unlivable a few millennia ago— back on his home planet, he had always wondered if there was a greater force at work that slowly, meticulously perfected biomes and here, on Eliria, he knew that realization to be true.

"The Earth Division is honored by your generous words," Patriarch Kang Long replied, his temperament a little more relaxed now that he found himself back in familiar territory. "Would you like to explore first, or shall we head to your accommodations?"

"Hm, I suppose it has been a long day. Let us disperse for the day, take some time to stretch our legs and approach matters with a fresh mind tomorrow."

"Very well, Grand Patriarch."

40

EARTH WELLSPRING

THE NEXT FEW days fell into a rhythm of productivity, as Yao Shen rapidly ticked off tasks on his checklist. The tour of the Earth Division provided for a good change from the tedium of politics, though little captured Yao Shen's interest besides the Earth Wellspring and the sealed cave systems. The former was a rather ingenious way of improving one's fine control over the earth element, though the degree of complexity involved in the process limited its effectiveness to Nascent Soul Cultivators and higher.

Originally, the Earth Wellspring was intended for weaker disciples that required assistance in honing their control. The concept was simple enough in theory— a small shaft was dug into the earth, its circumference lined with a commonly found metal. The base of the well wasn't lined with stone or brick as one might expect from a mortal one, but instead, the earth was intentionally polluted with small shards of metal, chunks of decaying animal hide and powdered glass. The disciples were required to exert their innate ability to manipulate earth, sifting through the debris and detritus until they managed to reform the soft earth into solid rock. In the beginning, it was a rather elementary task, but as more and more of earth was reformed and excavated, the original ten-meter-deep shaft now extended for over thirty meters, heavily contaminated with debris for another fifteen meters.

Had it not been for the elder responsible for decommissioning the Earth Wellspring choosing to experiment with it instead, its effectiveness in aiding Nascent Soul Cultivators would have gone unnoticed. There was a certain prejudice in the cultivator world, an inclination to search for arcane means when mundane ones would suffice.

Yao Shen had spent longer on the Earth Wellspring than perhaps was considered dignified, his first attempt only yielding a small pebble even smaller than the palm of his hand. It took him an hour to finally form a decent-sized, if mishappen chunk of rock. Of course, if Yao Shen utilized his divine sense, it would be a feat accomplished in seconds and he did not need such intricate control of the earth in his current combat style, simply able to use his Earth Qi to form and shape rock as he willed. However, it served as a good benchmark as he urged Patriarch Kang Long to attempt it.

The Earth Patriarch rose to the challenge magnificently, forming a perfectly even brick of solid rock in half the time Yao Shen had taken. Though he had expected the gulf to be wide, it was still humbling to be confronted with the realization that the other two Patriarchs were *bona fide* prodigies. He would revisit the wellspring when he had time, but unfortunately, that was a commodity he was in dire shortage of these days.

The sealed cave systems, on the other hand, were of even greater interest to him. Out of courtesy to their hosts, Yao Shen had not directly requested access to the cave system— based on the intelligence he had access to, he knew that it was a sore subject for the Earth Division. Something had gone *terribly* wrong in the sealed cave systems, or they were using that excuse as a pretext to conceal a greater truth— either way, disciples and guardians were strictly forbidden from venturing inside and the other elders had not shown much interest either if the *Faceless'* reports were to be believed.

Regardless, Yao Shen was destined to sneak into the cave systems, if for no other reason than to experiment with his bell artifact in a place without prying eyes. Anything of value should have been long extracted from within the caves and he doubted that a creature powerful enough to slay him rested beneath the Divine Mountain— if so, Patriarch Kang Long would have personally offered to escort him to his doom.

How curious indeed.

Another banquet was hosted in his name, giving Yao Shen the opportunity to deliver a rousing speech addressed to the disciples. He no longer spoke of grand ambitions or lofty goals the Modern Sect *would* accomplish somewhere in the distant future, instead choosing to focus upon the present— upon the Mortal Capital, *All Haven.* Yao Shen divulged his plans with fervor, informing disciples that not only would they be able to meet their mortal parents without any of the associated dogma that pervaded in cultivator society, but they would also be allowed to intermingle with disciples from other disciplines on a regular basis without fear of reproachment.

The only way to cure inherited hatred was to give the opposing parties an opportunity to interact with each other in a neutral setting. To talk and to listen, to hear and to understand and to ultimately come to the realization that the other side was only human— mistakes were made; however, they were made on both sides. Perhaps a side was more to blame than the others, but because of how easy it was to carry that intergenerational hatred and fury in their hearts, neither the mortal man nor the cultivator could be held accountable for the sins of their ancestors.

The path would not be an easy one and there would be challenges to the realization of his vision.

But Yao Shen was ready to welcome them with open arms.

There could be no change without detractors, no revolution without pain... but the cost of righteousness was no excuse to succumb to inertia. Would the world, regardless of if it were Earth or Eliria, not be a pitiful place if not a single soul was willing to fight for what they cherished, to stand up for what they believed was right?

Thankfully, the hatred between the three hegemonic sects was mainly rooted in the past decisions and as a result of their contradictory interests. All it required was a little understanding, a modicum of empathy and a healthy dose of shared self-interest, and Yao Shen truly believed that the Modern Sect could stand strong as a single element in face of outside threats.

After the banquet, Yao Shen had to deal with matters pertaining to the treasury, which he ended up delegating to Meili Zhu under oversight of Flame Division Elders and Patriarch Kang Long. The protocols he intended to follow were the same as the ones followed for Solaris Keep, accounting for the assets of the keep and making sure that there were representatives from each division maintaining oversight and serving as checks and balances for each other, so it proceeded without a hitch.

In the meantime, he invited some of the elders he'd conversed with during the banquet, the ones that had displayed a penchant for *rune-scripting* and a willingness to be forthright with that knowledge. Yao Shen had naturally been interested in the *Greater rune script* that both guarded and made the Divine Mountain a pleasant place for habitation and had posed the same question to the elders he had asked of others. Though they genuinely did not have an answer to his question, the inquisitive nature of powerful cultivators meant that they had a plethora of theories and estimates that they were willing to debate in his presence. The Earth Division Cultivators in general had an amiable and receptive attitude, which Yao Shen had come to greatly appreciate.

Of course, the general lackadaisical approach to rune-scripting in the Azlak Plains might have made the conversation equally cathartic for the elders, who kept attempting to improve their knowledge in the hopes of one day understanding the *greater rune* formations that they maintained.

In the end, they agreed to help him refine his designs for All Haven, especially considering that each of them had purchased at least a single share in the Mortal Capital.

It was only on his fifth day in the Earth Division did Yao Shen see an opportunity to slip away for the sealed cave systems.

41

BELL ARTIFACT

IT HAD BEEN a long while since Yao Shen had to resort to sneaking around, especially within the confines of the Azlak Plains. The only person that he had informed of his whereabouts was Meili Zhu, as her assistance had been instrumental in conceiving this scheme. Even now, the depths of her intelligence gathering ability surprised him as he perused the map she had procured for him.

The direct path to the sealed cave systems was too exposed and well-guarded for him to waltz through, so he was forced to take a more... imaginative route. Tunnelling through thick bedrock had proved to be more Qi-intensive than he had initially estimated, draining even his vast reserves. Then, Yao Shen had to disassemble and reform a series of cave walls and do so while ensuring that the noise pollution was kept to a minimum, hopping from one passageway to the next until he reached his destination.

Two Core-Formation guardians were stationed outside the main entrance to the cave systems, their expressions stoic and their body language conveying readiness, like an arrow pulled taut, waiting to be fired. Yao Shen felt like a mischievous Qi-

Formation disciple once again as he conceived a plan to sneak past the guards.

It all happened in a matter of seconds, as Yao Shen 'zapped' the guard on the left with a gentle burst of his divine sense, enough to discombobulate him without causing any lasting harm. Using his Shadow Qi, he swept past the guard's side. The passageway was too narrow for him not to brush past the guard as he moved past him, but Yao Shen was hoping that he was too disoriented to notice.

He eavesdropped on the guard's conversation with his divine sense, just to make sure that his cover wasn't blown. The momentary lapse in concentration was written off as Qi exhaustion, much to his relief. Having his presence discovered would inevitably strain the relations with the Earth Division, an outcome that Yao Shen preferred to avoid.

The solitude of walking through the cave tunnels would be an intimidating and lonesome prospect for most, but with his divine sense stretching ahead and mapping the cave system's layout, he didn't expect any surprises. In fact, it was a welcome change from being the center of attention, as he found himself becoming more and more often these days.

He was surprised at the sheer breadth of the cave systems as he descended deeper into the recesses of the earth, past dead-ends, galleries and wide chambers that splintered into smaller tunnels and rifts. Even after an hour of racing down the passageways whilst simultaneously mapping more routes in his mind's eye, there seemed to be no end in sight.

Yao Shen chose a small chamber for his purposes, specifically one that led to a dead-end. Nothing besides solid rock lay on the other side and he could sense no living beings in the range of his divine sense. That was precaution enough.

He gingerly withdrew the bell artifact from within his soul lake, allowing it to rest upon the palm of his hand as he seated himself in a cross-legged, meditative posture. Next, he pinched the bell artifact between his index finger and thumb, cautiously observing its mottled surface.

He spent a whole minute visualizing his soul, sensing the nigh-imperceptible undulations that ran across its surface as he rapidly cycled through thoughts, an indication that the soul was not the static existence most Nascent Soul Elders considered it to be— they simply weren't capable of perceiving it in its entirety.

Then, Yao Shen jerked his wrist with a rather sudden motion, causing the bell artifact to ring out.

A ripple blossomed outward with the bell artifact as its epicenter, striking directly at his soul without any forewarning. Yao Shen's physical body slammed backwards onto the floor, only his soul form remaining seated, desperately hanging onto the bell artifact. Yao Shen felt trapped in the grasp of a titanic beast, an overwhelming force crushing at his soul from all directions. The sensation was akin to being trampled by dozens of elephants, the strength so immense that resistance was futile; one could only endure.

"You..." Yao Shen roared, straining to keep the vulnerability out of his voice. Memories flashed through his mind one after the other, a blend of his experiences in Earth and Eliria. He had lived an entire mortal life, loved, sired children and left an entire world behind to come to the continent of Ionea. A cosmic accident or an invisible hand, mattered not— if there was no purpose behind his reincarnation, then he would make one. In fact, he already had.

"... have not..." Even now, he refused to let go of the bell arti-fact, instead planting his right foot onto the floor.

"... earned the right..." Yao Shen's body was shuddering at this point, the strain so immense that it appeared as if his soul was going to shatter in the next moment. Nevertheless, he slammed his left foot upon the ground, his eyes glimmering with intensity. This was the reason he had been appointed Patriarch— resolve was his anointed crucible, one that the heavens and he himself had spared no opportunity to push the limits of. Each time it got the opportunity, the heavenly tribulation tried to break his will and each time...

"...*to kill me!*" Yao Shen let out a mighty, triumphant roar as he rose to his full height, the bell pinched between his fingers now seeming puny in front of his towering soul form.

In the next instant, the ripple refining his soul ceased.

Yao Shen's soul form immediately snapped back to his body, the bell falling from his grasp and clattering onto the floor.

"Agh," he groaned, clutching at his forehead. A splitting headache tore away at his mind, but Yao Shen ignored it, choosing to inspect his soul first.

His eyes widened in genuine surprise, the headache all but forgotten.

"This..." he muttered aloud, pacing around in the chamber.

"Is this the power of soul cultivation?" Yao Shen asked himself, his expression looking a little lost for a change.

It had to be tested.

42

THE KEY

YAO SHEN WILLED his Earth Qi, and it responded. Before his eyes, a Golem was shaped from the very earth beneath his feet, taking on humanoid features as it came into being, a near-perfect replica of Yao Shen's own physical body. He then stretched his right arm forward, releasing strands of divine sense that latched onto the Golem's body. His fingers began to flex, twist and writhe, as a divine sense thread running from each of his phalanges connected to a different part of the Golem's body, resulting in a very unusual puppeteering style.

The Golem began to cycle through a bare-handed martial technique, throwing a flurry of hooks and jabs with an occasional elbow mixed in. It was one of the more brutal fighting styles he'd learned as a disciple, which also made it trickier to execute perfectly. As time went on, the construct's choppy fighting style saw rapid improvement, its movements gaining a fluidity that could only come from mastery.

Then the Golem stopped. It stood with its feet planted onto the ground, rendered inert as Yao Shen had withdrawn his divine sense threads.

"Not enough. Not yet," he muttered under his breath as he

walked toward the Golem. It might have seemed impressive at first glance, but Yao Shen was subconsciously relying on his ability to manipulate the earth in conjunction with his divine sense, rendering the exercise pointless.

Two hours passed as Yao Shen delicately sculpted ball joints onto the Golem, giving it functional arms, legs and finger joints. Once he stopped influencing it with his Earth Qi, it folded upon itself and crumpled onto the ground.

"Good," Yao Shen thought to himself, satisfied by the results.

He withdrew a spare sword from his spatial ring and flicked it, causing it to land near the Golem's feet.

Once again, divine sense threads stretched out, this time from both his hands. The Golem groggily got back onto its feet, its first footsteps a little unsteady as Yao Shen got the hang of controlling it without tapping into his earth-manipulation abilities. It withdrew the embedded sword from the earth, gripping the sword with both hands and holding it near the waist level. It felt odd to grasp a sword through a proxy, the lack of tactility requiring a few minutes to adapt to.

The first movements were slow and strained as the Golem transitioned from one basic sword form to the next, from a series of thrusts to a succession of strong, overhead blows then finally bloomed into a more balanced sword form, blending the two into a truly deadly art. As Yao Shen increased the tempo, the sword went flying out of the Golem's hand, biting into the cave walls.

"Almost," he remarked, not at all disappointed with the outcome.

Three hours later, Yao Shen felt like a grandmaster conductor orchestrating the performance of a lifetime, his fingers rapidly twisting and flexing as he lost himself in composing, his symphony the Golem's sword dance. The construct lunged, the construct feinted, it slashed, it cut and even executed a few sweeps, growing increasingly graceful in its movements with every subsequent strike.

After ascending to Soul Emperor, Yao Shen's greatest weakness had been his own inability to control his soul's output, its sheer potency too great for him to manage without years, perhaps decades of practice. This exercise had only confirmed what he had suspected the true purpose of Soul Cultivation, and consequently, his artifact was— when that ripple had struck him, it had caused his soul to fold upon itself.

Though the change was slight, he had most definitely noticed that his soul had shrunk, even whilst its mass remained the same. It had been *compressed,* and just one session was enough to significantly improve his control.

What were the upper limits of refining his soul?

At what point would it begin to harm him instead of improving his control?

What was the second ability the bell artifact concealed, but refused to reveal to him?

The answers to those questions would only be discovered with time, but as Yao Shen finally stopped manipulating the Golem, a smile made its way to his face.

"This is the key," he whispered as his eyes gleamed with anticipation. Not only would the bell artifact help him advance as a Soul Emperor, but it was also the key to unlocking the Origin Treasure that tested divine sense control and possibly, the other ones as well.

Delighted though he might be, his heart wanting to experiment further, he knew he could not. *Soul Cultivation* was an arcane technique that could not be taken lightly. Had he dropped the bell artifact while its effect was reverberating across his soul, even Yao Shen did not know what consequences that would entail.

Even now, it was only willpower that kept the splitting

headache and overwhelming exhaustion at bay. The effects may have been a net positive, but it was not something he could repeat in the short term; intending to give it at least a month as he observed his soul for lingering effects before subjecting himself to Soul Cultivation again.

The more tempting a power was, the more wary one should be of it— the demonic path had many cruel methods that could allow a cultivator to directly jump a rank, enticing many with such seemingly logic-defying methods. What they tended to omit was that one would die not long after conducting such a blood ritual, sometimes in as short as a day or a week, but never more than a year. And the reaper would not allow them to go silently; their deaths would be agonizingly painful ones right until their dying breath.

Overall, he was satisfied by his new artifact's capabilities and chose to return back to his residence. Meili Zhu had recommended that he arrive before daybreak, leaving him with little under an hour to be there.

In the end, he found nothing of value in the sealed cave systems, not even the slightest inkling of danger. The caves were empty, deserted and devoid of any and all natural resources. Which raised the question...

Why were the cave systems sealed to begin with?

43

A GESTURE, AN UNRAVELLING

IT WAS a little past noon when Yao Shen awoke from his slumber. Apparently, he had underestimated the toll *Soul Cultivation* would exact on him, the last few hours a complete void in his memory. True slumber was a phenomenon that he hadn't experienced in decades, if not close to a century. To sleep, to dream and to submit himself to a realm he held no power over was, rather ironically, a veritable nightmare for any powerful cultivator— he supposed that he could only be grateful that his reputation held back others from entering his quarters unannounced.

"Huh," Yao Shen muttered, realizing that even his near-perfect memory could not recall the specifics of his dream, only disconcerting snippets and fragmented emotions. Even in Eliria, it seemed that the world of dreams and nightmares seemed as inscrutable as ever, beyond both science and the perception of one's soul.

He groggily got back onto his feet, stretching his body more out of reminiscence than sore muscles. To think that in another lifetime he had made a livelihood of trade in a relatively peaceful society. In all honesty, he still struggled to accept that reality on some days, as he gazed into the burnished metal mirror, finding his reflection fearlessly staring right back at him. These days, only his reflection seemed to have the audacity to lock eyes with him until he was forced to yield.

The solitude of standing at the apex didn't bother him, but he supposed that there was one aspect Yao Shen had been ignoring. Had it been one of the other Patriarchs in his place that had ascended to Soul Emperor, they would likely be assessing their future options after quelling dissent in the Azlak Plains, the more violent option that Yao Shen had forgone. That option would naturally pertain to the region they planned to shift to, the sect they wished to seek harbor under.

A Soul Emperor was a resource worth vying for and Yao Shen was not oblivious to the knowledge that the Eastern Righteous Path sects would send their envoys to recruit him, their advent likely to be accompanied by honeyed words, grand promises, and of course one or two veiled threats. Mayhap the other races too would send an envoy to approach the proceedings in the name of maintaining balance, their real purpose to gauge his personality and temperament and report back to their respective leaders.

Turning them down would not be easy, for it would mean refusing the culmination of knowledge, the reward for *two centuries* of cultivation. Even negotiating for the path to the Soul Paragon stage might not be off the table and to refuse...it was possible that Yao Shen would never stumble upon the correct method of ascension in his lifetime.

"Hilarious." Yao Shen chuckled, averting his gaze from the mirror and walking over to the balcony. As a disciple, he had always found his master's desire to work for the betterment of the sect a futile, baseless effort. He had always felt that the sect did not deserve his master's grace, that the politicking, backstabbing elders had not earned his master's kindness. How ironic it was, that when the time came... Yao Shen had chosen the same path, even after far surpassing his master and even if it meant turning down the easy path to Soul Paragon.

He supposed that the more one tried to extricate oneself from the person they were raised to become, the more they were inevitably drawn to it.

Thankfully, it was not in the nature of ancient sects to make haste in matters. With lifespans as long as theirs, time simply did not possess the same weight, the same urgency that possessed mortals back on Earth; driving them to make every waking moment count. That gave him a year to accomplish as much as he could before he was subject to their haughty gazes and self-serving ploys.

As Yao Shen took in the sweeping vista from his third-story balcony, an errant thought bloomed into an idea. Instead of taking a reactive approach, why not be proactive instead?

An Inauguration Ceremony for the Modern Sect, to be held in one Earth year's time from the date of his ascension would be a fitting way to welcome the envoys; concealing a deeper significance at the same time. It was a bold declaration to the Eastern Righteous Path sects and a political gambit— for what ruler did not seek legitimacy? Yao Shen was claiming the three hegemonic sects of the Azlak Plains for himself and if the Eastern Righteous Path sects accepted the invitation, they would be giving their tacit approval. He also planned to extend an invitation to the True Elves, for the Mortal Capital, *All Haven* would reach completion by then— it would be the most opportune time to offer them the shares in hopes of securing their patronage.

The brilliance of his scheme lay in the finer details, for he required only one Eastern Righteous Path sect to attend his Inauguration Ceremony to legitimize it. If the Eastern Hegemons were united, or if Yao Shen had overestimated his own importance, his opening scheme would unravel before it even got off the ground. However, if even one of the sects were interested in recruiting him, or at least drawing him to their side as an ally, then they would do him the favor of honoring his sovereignty. Could the others afford to watch from the sidelines whilst their neighboring sect added another formidable military power to their repertoire?

His resolve set, Yao Shen set out from his guest residence in search of Meili Zhu, hoping to enlist her help in delivering the invitations. The sooner they were sent, the more at ease he would feel— he had no wish to field offers from powerful envoys whilst there were so many internal matters that needed his resolution, not to mention the ammunition the foreign dignitaries' presence would provide to his critics.

As Yao Shen walked through the sandy lanes of the inner sect, he could not help but take a moment to admire the architecture that bore some resemblances to Mesopotamian styles, like the use of cuneiforms as signboards for various buildings, the ziggurat-like structure that comprised the outer sect and the generous use of robust columns that reinforced the larger buildings. That was where the similarities ended, as each personal residence had vivid reliefs carved across their surface, one depicting an expansive battle scene, another portraying waves viciously crashing against a large boulder— it was as if each house had a story to tell, a moral to share and a Dao to expound upon. One only had to be willing to listen.

His meeting with Meili Zhu had been a brief yet fruitful one, as she had agreed to have his invitations delivered, most likely through the employ of the Faceless. His debt to the Zhu Family was accruing, yet the Zhu Family Patriarch had yet to ask for the smallest favor in return. It had not escaped him that the Zhu Family had won the bid for seven shares, the highest by far in the *Sky Division*. The truth of the matter was, Meili Zhu was getting on in years, having lived for over three long centuries. Though she had decades yet ahead of her, it was only natural that she would start prioritizing the welfare of her descendants over political wrangling and infighting.

That left Yao Shen conflicted, if he were to be honest. Meili Zhu's past actions, while in the purported best interests of the Sky Division, were not something that Yao Shen could bring himself to condone. Even now, he was almost certain that her amicable front was motivated by her own self-interests, but who was he to cast judgment upon the last wishes of a decorated cultivator that had defended the Sky Division's interests from before he was even born?

Yao Shen would be the first to admit that the past held actions that he wasn't proud of. Moments that he regretted. Mistakes that he wished to take back. Did that mean that he was incapable of change?

No.

Earth's morality would never translate perfectly to Eliria's, that he understood— the same way that a leader like himself held value only in an imperfect world, a world where existed no exact scale that let one weigh their sins against their virtues.

A debt was a debt, a promise was a promise— Yao Shen would not hold the Zhu Family's past against them, and naturally, he would honor the assurance that came along with the sale of 'Shares,' up until his dying breath. For his reputation and the weight of his word hinged on that assurance, if nothing else.

But he would be watching.

In an effort to clear his thoughts, Yao Shen turned his gaze to his surroundings, wanting to take in more of the sect he would soon need to depart from.

His footfall came to an abrupt halt.

Yao Shen's gaze shifted to a young disciple that had seemingly just stepped outside her accommodations. He began to walk over toward her, much to her surprise. Her leaf green hair was neatly braided into a ponytail, the earthen brown robes suiting the modest first impression she gave off well. A short sword was neatly sheathed at her waist and her cultivation seemed quite impressive for her age.

"Please do not be alarmed, child." Yao Shen had a light smile upon his face, his hands clasped behind his back to give a disarming impression. "I merely wished to ask you a question, if I may."

The girl reacted well after the initial stupor, a light flash of determination flashing in her eyes.

She lightly curtsied, seemingly unsure how else to respond to her new Patriarch, before replying, "It would be my honor, Grand Patriarch."

"That..." Yao Shen paused, searching for the apt word. "...gesture you did just now, could you repeat it?"

The young disciple gave Yao Shen a perplexed look, but hurriedly moved to comply. She reached for the ground, palming a fist full of sand in her small, dainty hands, cupped outwards like a monk begging for alms. First she held the first full of sand near her heart, then she raised it above her head, slowly letting the sand fall over her, an expression of reverence upon her face.

"What meaning does this custom have?" Yao Shen asked, straining to keep the edge out of his voice as he found himself on the cusp of realization.

"The Divine Mountain shields us from the elements, from the wrath of those who wish us harm and from the evil spiritual beasts that feed on the flesh of cultivators. This ritual is merely a small gesture of gratitude to him, who selflessly nourishes and protects us without asking for nothing in return," the girl replied, her tone one of genuine gratitude if not reverence.

This. This was what had been bothering him all this while.

"Thank you, child. You may go."

The *Divine Mountain* was an outright vexing name for a *culti-*

vator-made construct. The young girl earlier genuinely seemed to believe that it was a naturally formed mountain that she resided in, a fallacy that the Earth Division seemed all too happy to perpetuate.

But from the beginning, that *name* didn't sit right with him. The Flame Division worshipped the Sacred Beast, Marayan, yes — but it was a *beast* and not a cultivator. It was the very basic tenets of traversing the path of ascension— a cultivator could love another cultivator, could respect them with all his heart, but if they truly wished to continue seeking the path to the Grand Dao, they could never *revere* another cultivator the way one revered a *divinity*.

For to revere another cultivator with such intensity was to create a heart demon— for it was akin to admitting that one would never equal, much less surpass their accomplishments in this lifetime.

When he saw the girl doing that gesture, his subconsciousness had been prickled, as if there was something there that he wasn't seeing.

That gesture, the way she reverently reached for the sand and let it fall over her, as if it were a blessing from the divine...

It immediately caused him to circle back to his original question.

Why were the cave systems sealed to begin with?

What if it was not the cultivator-made mountain that custom, likely passed down from generation to generation, was supposed to revere, but rather the land upon which it was built?

What if the land itself was divine?

Yao Shen's expression was calm as he slowly walked back to his residence. His theory, after all, was only a theory— and a pretty shaky one at that.

Another week passed, as he forced himself to forget about the sealed cave systems and focus on the task at hand.

The design of the Mortal Capital was now being debated on a near-daily basis, as Yao Shen accounted for the feedback and improvements trickling in from the 'specialists' of the three Divisions, allowing him to further refine his designs to an astonishing degree. There were also debates over resource allocation, accompanied by a further round of hubbub when Yao Shen revealed that he had sent an invitation to the Eastern Righteous Path sects along with the non-human hegemons, to the Modern Sect's Inauguration Ceremony.

Whether they liked it or not, their small corner of Ionea would become the center of attention when Envoys from the Eastern Powers, Dwarves and True Elves would all gather in one location. From the perspective of the elders that had a significant stake in the Auction House, it was almost too good to be true, while others found themselves wondering if Yao Shen was biting off more than he could chew and the possibility of their actions resulting in increased interest from the demonic path, which, in all honesty, were valid concerns.

It was only late in the night, on the eighth day, when Meili Zhu gave him the go-ahead. He supposed that her spies had been working to confirm whether his previous visit had gone unnoticed and if the coast was clear.

Little had changed since his last visit to the sealed cave systems, except this time, there were a different pair of guards on duty. This was likely the reason why Meili Zhu had recommended that he wait— the same trick twice, and it would no longer be passed off as Qi Exhaustion or a trick of the mind.

Sneaking past the guards, he once again found himself ensconced in the darkness of the cave systems.

Good. That would serve his purposes well.

On his first excursion, Yao Shen's objective had been to find a secluded spot to test out his bell artifact, so he had indiscriminately utilized his divine sense. Now, though, he did the exact opposite.

Retracting his divine sense until he couldn't perceive anything beyond a meter of his immediate vicinity, Yao Shen felt a sense of vulnerability wash over him that felt… almost *refreshing*. He submitted himself to the ebbs and flows of the cave tunnels, using nothing but his natural ability to perceive the earth as a Major Dao Cultivator in the element. If his divine sense had failed him, then he would scour the cave walls for irregularities, unnatural protrusions, false cave-ins. Only his instinct as a master of the earth element could assist him here, or at least he suspected so.

Yao Shen progressively increased his movement speed every ten minutes as he got more accustomed to relying on his senses. An hour later, he had sped past dozens of tunnels, galleries and the occasional chamber, encountering many forked passageways and three rifts that disappointingly, led to nothing but stalagmites that lay in wait to impale any foolhardy enough to fall through.

Five hours passed as Yao Shen followed his instinct, trusting it to lead him deeper into the cave. He had to be hundreds of feet below ground level at this point, but he kept going, kept searching, kept *sensing* for that spark that would prove that his half-baked theories were more than just delusions.

Yao Shen trusted his gut feeling, for it had been honed across two centuries of trials and tribulations. That did not necessarily mean that he'd arrived at the truth, but there was definitely more to the story that the Earth Division did not want see.

Abruptly, he tripped over an errant rocky protrusion in his path.

He offered no resistance as he was sent skidding forwards due to the downward sloping tunnel, his face brutally slamming against the ground multiple times. The reason why he'd gone inert without warning was because his focus was elsewhere— at the very periphery of his senses, Yao Shen had detected a faint glimmer of an unfamiliar sensation. It possessed an otherworldly *chilliness* that seemed to want to dissuade him from approaching it, causing a pang of fear to churn in his gut. His senses seemed to be of the belief that a single touch, a lone whiff of that sensation would cause the chill to permeate down to his bones, a phenomenon that would haunt him for the remainder of his life.

And then it disappeared from his perception, as if it had never been there to begin with.

Yao Shen's eyes shot open, his expression brimming with intensity as the wind coalesced around him, getting him back upon his feet. His gaze shifted north-eastwards, and without further ado, his silhouette blurred in that direction. The sensation along with its likely corresponding location was already imprinted onto his mind as he rocketed forth.

Out of an abundance of caution, Yao Shen activated his Human Dao Domain as he drew closer, positioning one of the farmer-silhouettes as far away as he could while still being able to maintain his domain.

"I've got you now," Yao Shen whispered as he skidded to a halt, finding himself in a cave gallery. Sandwiched between two jagged cave walls whose mottled surface was painted with a light smattering of moss, he followed along the narrow, straight path cautiously, a blend of trepidation and the curiosity of discovery bubbling in his gut. Minutes passed as he meditated upon the sensation he had felt, his footsteps determined to trace it down to its origin.

Yao Shen paused.

"Huh," he muttered in confusion, finding himself staring down the end of the cave gallery, the rocky walls converging to form solid earth.

How...?

Yao Shen felt chills run down his spine, his divine sense

exploding outward while he shifted to a defensive stance. His farmer-silhouettes waited outside the cave gallery, so even if something were to ambush him, escape shouldn't be a tricky prospect.

Nothing. Nothing at all.

There was no living organism besides him in the entire cave sub-section he found himself in, let alone this one gallery.

Cautiously, Yao Shen pressed his palm against the rocky dead-end.

A minute later, he scowled.

Besides densely packed soil, rock and debris, he found nothing of note. He tried again, this time with his divine sense instead, but the result remained the same regardless of how far he stretched his perception.

As a Soul Emperor, Yao Shen was very sensitive to the passage of time— not yet enough to pinpoint the phenomenon that he was experiencing, but enough to know that something was terribly wrong here. The only reason why he hadn't retreated was because up until now, his soul had yet to detect even the slightest hint of danger.

His expression solemn, he withdrew a small hourglass from his spatial ring, flipping it over and observing the small granules of sand trickling down its waist. Going a step further, he ensconced the hourglass with his divine sense, to ensure that any tampering in its flow would not go unnoticed.

Then Yao Shen began to walk toward the mouth of the cave gallery, his focus razor sharp and determined to fight off any external influences.

Again.

He found himself at the cave entrance, staring at the route he'd taken to originally arrive at the cave gallery.

There was no panic in his gaze as he raised the hourglass to his eye level, watching as the last of the sand was funneled to the bottom part of the hourglass. Apparently, five minutes had passed, but he only remembered a minute, maybe a minute and a half of it.

"What game are you playing at?" Yao Shen whispered, unsure himself who the question was directed to.

Instead of attempting to try and traverse the cave galley again, Yao Shen sat down on the spot and adopted a meditative posture. He drew two parallel lines onto the rocky floor with his Earth Qi, intended to be proportional to the cave gallery that took him five minutes to traverse. Then he closed his eyes, his right index finger resting at the entrance of the 'tunnel' he had drawn.

Yao Shen released a single strand of divine sense, willing it forward in a zig-zag pattern— as if it were bouncing off the walls while building forward momentum. At the same time, Yao Shen traced the trajectory of the divine sense strand with his mind's eye, simultaneously using his finger to engrave its path onto the ground. He felt in complete sync with his surroundings, his focus directed to charting his divine sense's course, hoping to find a clue in that direction.

Two minutes later, Yao Shen opened his eyes.

His finger had reached the end of the drawn tunnel half a second after his divine sense had. In his mind, his divine sense had followed a uniform path, turning roughly at a ninety-degree angle each time it encountered the cave walls. The result should have been a series of roughly equal-sized and inverted triangles, but the engraving on the ground told a different story.

He had followed a zig-zag pattern for the initial phase, but the moment he began to approach the middle part of the tunnel, the pattern completely changed. An elongated triangle was the end result, one that completely ignored the entire middle section of the cave, or at least its right side, before the pattern reinstated itself.

"How truly fascinating," Yao Shen muttered aloud in near

stupefaction. He didn't know what manner of artifact or construct was capable of rendering an entire section of land invisible to divine sense, physical sight and almost earth sense as well, but it clearly existed and… it was powerful enough to confuse the senses of a Soul Emperor.

Now that he knew it existed, though, the gig was up.

Yao Shen got back onto his feet, taking a minute to measure his pulse against the hourglass. That gave him a good approximation of time, or rather, how many heartbeats comprised a minute.

One… two… three…

His focus was so honed in that moment that every heartbeat rang in his ears, the sound of his slow breathing clearly audible in the eerie silence of the cave systems. A Soul Emperor did not appreciate his perception being tampered with and Yao Shen was no exception— there were other, more violent ways of getting around this restriction, but he had not forgotten that his original objective was reconnaissance.

The hundredth heartbeat struck, but Yao Shen kept walking. That meant a minute had passed.

He kept going until the hundred and fiftieth heartbeat rang out in his ears, coming to a sudden halt.

The resistance was immediate.

His brain and soul seemed to be working in tandem as they tried to convince him that there was nothing of note in that direction. A vista so mundane lay toward his right, that deigning to glance at it would be an affront to his venerable personage. Nothing but a rocky cave wall, one of thousands he'd encountered on his way to this unremarkable cave gallery.

A sense of lethargy had enveloped him, dulling his mind, weighing down upon his soul; the sensation akin to being submerged neck-deep in a viscous liquid. As long as Yao Shen just kept walking instead of fighting against that sensation, he would find himself on the other side, unharmed. Perhaps the reason why the psychological suggestion was so powerful in the first place was because it only compelled him to ignore a portion of the cave gallery, instead of guiding him to do something that would harm himself or surroundings.

"You..." Yao Shen's tone was audibly strained, the suggestive powers of this artifact far more potent than he had first imagined it to be. So much so that... despite his best efforts, he was struggling to fight back against its influence. " ...*Dare?*" he snarled as he was forced to take a step forward.

Yao Shen's hands blurred, reaching for his soul and plucking out a small, mottled bell from his Soul Lake. Without hesitation, without even giving himself time to brace for its impact, he rang it.

He was able to hold on to the bell artifact for ten long seconds before he let it slip from his grasp, its *soul-refining* effect clashing with the *psychological suggestio*n influencing his soul. Yao Shen was violently jolted out of his reverie as he felt the lethargy that had taken hold over him rapidly recede, his eyes once again brimming with vigor.

The next instant, a hacking cough echoed out in the cave gallery as Yao Shen spat out a mouthful of blood. That was the price he had to pay for interrupting the *soul-refining* process midway.

"Worth it." Yao Shen grinned, a bloodied grin that was more terrifying than ecstatic. His Human Dao Domain was still active, so he simply dispelled his current 'self.' One of the farmer-silhouettes reformed into his spitting image, calmly walking down the cave gallery until he stood before the bell artifact. The damage to his soul had unfortunately carried over, but it had been minimal—having much to do with his extraordinary soul.

Retrieving the bell artifact, Yao Shen's gaze shifted to the right side of the cave gallery.

Before him rested a relatively broad alcove that was carved

into the cave wall, a sizable depression that Yao Shen had evidently walked past twice, without detecting anything amiss. The culprit behind his plight was revealed, as Yao Shen took in the complex rune that stretched across the curvature of the alcove, a faint crack running across its surface that indicated its inertness.

He had never seen a single rune, even amongst *Greater Runes,* display this level of complexity— truly making him suspect the antiquity of these defenses and more importantly, the secret that they guarded.

Yao Shen kept maintaining his Human Dao Domain as his palm landed upon the alcove's surface.

"Now, what are you hiding?" he muttered under his breath, once again subject to that chilly sensation. His Earth Qi flared to life, rapidly separating the tightly packed rock blocking his path.

A minute later, an entrance had been tunneled through, a burst of aquamarine light flooding through the opening.

He gasped.

44

THE FINAL QUESTION

THERE WAS a final question that had been eluding him, tantalizingly sitting just outside his grasp. The most effective of deceptions had a tendency to conceal themselves a little outside the realm of rationality, beyond the threshold of what most perceived as logical or even *possible*.

So Yao Shen asked himself the question.

What would practitioners of the earth consider worthy of their veneration?

The answer had been staring him in the face all this while.

What race did every human earth cultivator wish to surpass?

What race was endowed with a natural ability to manipulate the earth?

A bead of sweat ran down Yao Shen's forehead, trickling past his eyes and falling onto the rocky cavern floor with a light splash, disturbing the tranquil stillness of the vast chamber that spilled out before him.

"*Dwarven... Lumenite,*" he uttered haltingly, the disbelief in his tone echoed out by the chamber, as if in mockery of his surprise.

The Ore of Light. The most volatile metal in existence. A possession that the Dwarves had never once traded to the outside world in its raw form, the only known mine nestled in the heart of the *Dwarven Mountain Range,* guarded by a third step cultivator. It was said that the artifacts and constructs traded by Dwarves to the outside world contained only trace amounts of forged Lumenite, but even that was enough to surpass anything the Azlak Plains were capable of replicating.

A weaker-willed cultivator would be rendered into a stupor upon being confronted with such a sight, but Yao Shen possessed the wherewithal to slowly inch backwards, refraining from any sudden movements. The chamber's walls were encrusted by the aquamarine crystal ore, its protruding edges forming a brilliant kaleidoscope of ocean blue and sea green— Yao Shen could feel the thrum of Qi pulsating within the crystalline ore, struggling to imagine the sheer energy that it had amassed after what seemed like centuries, if not millenniums of dormancy.

On the other hand, the concealed chamber's soil displayed an interesting phenomenon— using his earth sense, Yao Shen could tell that it had been sapped of all minerals and nutrients, robbed of the ability to facilitate life; leaving behind only a blackened, seemingly charred husk of what once was an amalgamation of fertile soil and rock.

Yao Shen, however, was too focused on his retreat to notice the finer details— the chamber stretched on for at least one li in length, which was roughly a kilometer in Earth's terminology. If this volume of *Dwarven Lumenite* was destabilized... then Soul Emperor or not, he would not be able to survive the backlash and Yao Shen would not be surprised if the Earth Division was replaced by a steaming crater.

One of the most coveted resources in the world lay before him, yet all he could do was slowly retreat.

His expression gradually turned somber, as the consequences of this discovery pierced through his muddled thoughts.

This was a.... declaration of war.

If the truth of this matter ever got out, it would not just be the Dwarves that would come knocking at his doorsteps. An entire, untapped reserve of *Lumenite,* one of the primary reasons for Dwarven dominance in the hands of a force not yet powerful enough to guard it... it was basic geopolitics. Anyone who coveted the metal, had incentive to prevent the Dwarves from skyrocketing in strength or simply wanted a sample to study its strengths and weaknesses would turn the Azlak Plains into their proxy battlefield, jeopardizing *everything* that Yao Shen had been working toward.

He knew enough about the mindset of hegemons to know that cutting off the Earth Division would change nothing and only invite further suspicion— the boundaries and divisions made by the weak held little meaning for them. Besides, if there was one untouched mine in the region, who could be sure that there wouldn't be others?

Yao Shen had only just stepped outside the chamber when his eyes flashed with a sharp glint. His right hand shot out, glowing with an earthen light as it intercepted a spike fashioned out of solid bedrock heading right for his abdomen.

"Kang Long," Yao Shen snarled, the fury in his voice palpable as he clenched his fist hard, causing the earthen spike to shatter into hundreds of small pieces. The ambush held no real weight, most likely because a serious attack would risk destabilizing the lumenite. But that was not where his rage stemmed from. "*What have you done?*" he asked, the question poised more to his position as Patriarch of the Earth Division than his actions as an individual.

Kang Long slowly stepped outside the shadows, his demeanor

unflappably calm as he walked with his hands clasped behind his back. "If it were anyone else that had made this discovery, and by anyone I truly do mean *anyone,* I would have been forced to kill them," his voice echoed with gravitas in the cave gallery, as he kept walking forward unconcerned of retaliation. "But I cannot kill you. At most, I can disturb the lumenite and blow us both to dust, but that would defeat the whole purpose of it," Kang Long let out a weary sigh as he came to a stop a dozen or so meters before Yao Shen.

"I suppose I have failed my greatest responsibility as Patriarch, then." Kang Long withdrew an ornate brush and a small inkpot from his Spatial Ring, but Yao Shen did not flinch at all. He already had a solid approximation of the sheer magnitude of volatile Qi trapped within the ore and knew that the consequences would be cataclysmic if it were to be purposely set off.

Kang Long could not threaten him with that card.

"Will you let me repair the *Greater Concealment* rune whilst you pose your questions?" he asked, expression relaxed, as if he knew that Yao Shen would not refuse his request. Or rather, he *couldn't.*

"Fine," Yao Shen replied with some hesitance in his tone. "If you try anything, know that I will not stay my blade," he added, his expression stoic.

A minute passed in silence as Kang Long began to apply the first touches to the rune, his brush imbued with Qi and an ink that seemed to be an infusion of spiritual plant and beast blood.

"You know, I never expected this moment to arrive during my tenure as Patriarch, but now that it has... I find it oddly relieving." Kang Long painted a long stroke across the rune's surface, letting him observe as the long gash running across its surface began to reknit itself.

"I will give you one chance to relay the truth. The selfishness of the Divine Mountain Sect has placed the entire Azlak region in grave danger, so don't blame me for being ruthless if you insist on deceiving me," Yao Shen warned.

"One day, we must all answer for the sins of our ancestors, I suppose," Kang Long replied. "You are correct, of course. The truth implicates us all equally, so it is only just for you to know the entire tale, from its inception. Be forewarned, though, for it is only my perception of the truth that I am capable of retelling."

"That will suffice," Yao Shen replied, still unsure how he felt of the events progressing in this manner. Would he have been better off not knowing? Perhaps. Now that Pandora's box had been unsealed, though, there was no resealing it.

"Contrary to what many believe, contrary to what even most Elders of the Divine Mountain Sect believe, our sect did not originate in the Azlak Plains," Kang Long began with a bombshell revelation.

Yao Shen chose to remain silent.

"Our beginnings came from about the last place you'd expect. A clan fleeing pursuit, from whom, I do not know. And I suspect that after three millennia, it matters not. After a century of hiding, in the aftermath of the Era of Turmoil, an ancestor of mine sought to create stability for his descendants. The Azlak Plains had a poor concentration of Spiritual Qi and limited resources, but there was plenty of unclaimed land for war-weary cultivators to start a new life with," Kang Long slowly explained, his tone almost sounding regretful.

"I do not know if it was the work of a guiding hand, a stroke of fortune or simply an accident, but my ancestor and his fellow brethren discovered, or perhaps, chanced upon the cave system you find yourself in today. They were operating under the mistaken assumption that they had chanced upon an ancient dwarven inheritance, though they did find it rather bizarre that it would be situated in the middle of nowhere, as we both know, cultivators tend not to look too deeply into reversals of fate." Kang Long paused to paint another line across the healing rune.

"What they found was beyond their imagination. A half-finished armor set forged entirely out of *Dwarven Lumenite*. An armor, that even in its incomplete state, was worth a hundred times more than their greatest possession. What they *didn't* expect was a Dwarf Lord returning with a fresh haul of Lumenite, only to find his defenses dismantled and his cavern invaded. A fight ensued. A tragedy followed," Kang Long let out a weary sigh, as he applied the final brushstroke. "Powerful as the Dwarf Lord was, he was on his lonesome, returning after a strenuous excursion. Neither side could allow the other to escape after the battle began. Four cultivators died before the Dwarf Lord was finally felled."

"What of the Dwarven Mountains? Do they know of this matter?" Yao Shen finally interjected, finding it unlikely but still finding himself compelled to ask.

"My ancestor only found out more about the Dwarf Lord after his demise. His name was *Vondar the Eccentric* and he had been exiled from the Dwarven Mountain Range."

"Why?"

"The Dwarves are of the belief that *lumenite* is a metal whose existence is rooted in Dwarven Ritual. That, due to their devotion to the Earth and the Mountain, the earth had blessed them with a metal native to their kind. Vondar challenged that belief, before, when he was known as *Vondar the Scholar*— one of the greatest to exist in dwarven history. He claimed that he could build an artifact that could track lumenite ore deposits and convinced his fellow scholars of the possibility."

"It failed?" Yao Shen offered.

"Indeed, even after a decade of efforts and countless resources from the then Dwarven Emperor, his research yielded no results.

The Dwarf who was once seen as a scholar and a prodigy was labelled a fraud who rebuked Dwarven values. He was exiled."

"So they never bothered figuring out what happened to him. What a tragic waste of his genius," Yao Shen commiserated.

"If they had, they would have discovered that he had been right all along. The armor Vondar the Eccentric was forging was for his triumphant return to the mountain, the return that never was."

"What happened afterwards?" Yao Shen asked.

"My ancestors personally had cave systems sealed upon being confronted with the horror of their own actions and the fear of Dwarven retribution that haunted them. To conceal their crime from ever seeing the light of day, the Divine Mountain Sect was founded upon the very land that held the entrance to the sealed cave systems. The detection artifact along with any artifact or construct that held Vondar's divine sense Imprint exploded. His notes were preserved, but their complexity far exceeded my ancestor's realm of understanding. The armor was either lost or stolen over a millennium ago, but details on that matter are both scarce and before my time."

"This is indeed a riveting tale, Patriarch Kang Long. But surely you do not expect me to take your words at face value, especially when you claim that all of the Dwarven artifacts were *conveniently* lost and what was preserved holds no actionable value.

"I suppose not." Patriarch Kang Long let out a defeated sigh. "Yao Shen, with this secret exposed...the fate of the Divine Mountain Sect rests in your hands. If I had any confidence in killing you, I would already have attacked. If trading my life for yours would be a viable outcome, I would do so without hesitation. With those two options ruled out, I can only point out that I never claimed that *all* the artifacts were lost," Kang Long explicated.

"You mean…" Yao Shen's eyes widened in shock, truly not having expected this turn of events. Even if Kang Long had claimed to have lost all the artifacts, Yao Shen could truly not rule out that possibility. Three millennia was a long, long time even for a cultivator and the time period after the Era of Turmoil had seen many desperate rogue cultivators, fragmented remnants of sects and vengeance-fueled cultivators seeking resources. The cultivators of that era had little to lose and everything to gain; even the Sky Division had lost much of its ancient knowledge and resources to those frequent raids.

"With the information in your possession, you could approach the Dwarves and seek amnesty in exchange for the location of the mine. I know you can see through my intentions as I see through yours, Yao Shen. So let me be the one to tell you that my intentions are not pure— if I show you the remnant artifacts and let you take possession of them, you shall be an accomplice merely by not reporting to the Dwarves."

"And in doing so, I would lose control of the Modern Sect, subjugate the Azlak Plains to a foreign, non-human power that would tear it apart in search for this mythical ore and invite raids from the demonic path. In doing so, I would destroy everything that I stand for," Yao Shen replied as he slowly walked over to Kang Long, resting the palm of his hand upon his shoulder.

"You underestimate me, Kang Long. You underestimate my resolve. You underestimate how far I am willing to go to manifest my ambitions into reality. This…" Yao Shen's free hand gestured to the almost completely repaired rune stretching across the resealed entrance. "… might allow the Azlak Plains to rise beyond your greatest imagination. However, that is not its true significance," Yao Shen's voice lowered as he continued, "Tell me, Kang Long, why did your ancestors choose to seal the cave?"

"Because they were afraid," Kang Long replied and Yao Shen noticed how his posture tensed as he said those words aloud.

"They were afraid and exhausted, survivors of an era whose horrors we can only imagine. But what are we? What is the Azlak Plains of today? Consumed by the inertia of endless politicking and meaningless infighting, we have been gnawing at each other for a pittance of resources, fueling our own decline. This *ore* is not significant on its own, but rather, it is a shared secret that allows us to rise to the greatest heights and fall to the lowest of lows as one," Yao Shen let go of his shoulder, his expression losing solemnity.

"If it is a shared secret, if it is the threat of mutual destruction of our land that allows us to finally set aside our differences and move together toward the future as one, then so be it," Yao Shen smiled, despite the increasingly uncertain future he was hurtling toward.

Patriarch Kang Long began to walk toward the cave galley's exit, in an effort to hide the thrum of his beating heart, the light tremble of his hands.

He was… inspired? Him? The Stoic Patriarch of the Divine Mountain Sect renowned for his impenetrable defense swayed by the words of another leader? How… ridiculous.

Yao Shen silently walked behind him.

"Patriarch Yao Shen, will you be willing to answer a question of mine?"

"Please, Patriarch," Yao Shen replied politely.

"What do you hope to achieve with the Modern Sect? What ambition drives you so, that you are willing to risk the wrath of the children of the earth? I seek not empty promises and vague platitudes, but the unadulterated truth," Kang Long asked, his words echoed from the heart.

"The truth?" Yao Shen muttered aloud, as the relaxedly walked toward the exit of the sealed cave systems. "Very well," he replied, taking a deep breath before he willed those words into speech.

"I wish to create a version of Ionea where the *darkness* of the Era of Turmoil can never resurface."

The latter half of the sentence, Yao Shen thought was better off left unsaid.

"First Ionea, then the world."

Modern Patriarch will continue in Book Two!

THANK YOU FOR READING MODERN PATRIARCH

WE HOPE you enjoyed it as much as we enjoyed bringing it to you. We just wanted to take a moment to encourage you to review the book. Follow this link: Modern Patriarch to be directed to the book's Amazon product page to leave your review.

Every review helps further the author's reach and, ultimately, helps them continue writing fantastic books for us all to enjoy.

———

Also in series:
Modern Patriarch
Modern Patriarch 2

Check out the entire series here! (Tap or scan)

———

Want to discuss our books with other readers and even the authors? Join our Discord server today and be a part of the Aethon community.

Facebook | Instagram | Twitter | Website

You can also join our non-spam mailing list by visiting www.subscribepage.com/AethonReadersGroup and never miss out on future releases. You'll also receive three full books completely Free as our thanks to you.

Looking for more great books?

Join Dirk and his genius Goose companion in their relentless pursuit of the perfect run. Dirk was America's golden boy. Olympic golds, Wheaties box — the works. That was ten years ago. Turns out going to prison is terrible for sponsorships. Now, he's alone, a felony on his record, and bitter at the world. Enter the Tower of Conflict. Just what a man needs to get out of a rut — the end of the world and a Tower to Climb. Aided by his talking goose animal companion, magical cape, and the Goddess of Fate herself, Dirk is primed to take this Tower by storm. He was always more of a lone wolf, but when the competing alien races start smacking humanity around the Tower, he'll be forced to lean on his teammates, unlock new magic, and broker reluctant alliances. Because if he doesn't, humanity is doomed... *Welcome to the Tower, Climbers. Try not to die on the first day!* **Don't miss this hilarious new LitRPG Apocalypse featuring a sometimes loveable and oftern muderhobo-ey MC, a know-it-all goose companion, honking good humor, a detailed System, time-loop magic, and more. It's perfect for fans of *Dungeon Crawler Carl*, *Towers of Heaven*, and *Tower Climber*.**

Get Darling of Fate Now!

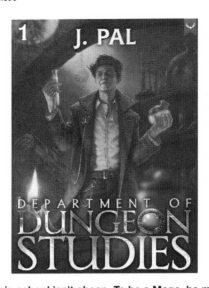

Magic school isn't cheap. To be a Mage, he must work smart and learn fast. Fate dealt Nox the Alchemist unfavorable cards, but he has learnt to compensate for his shortcomings with scholarly pursuits, tenacity, and sheer grit. Fortunately, for him Woodson University and their scouts are always seeking individuals with his work ethic. The Department of Dungeon Studies sees the value of the mind and its ability to overcome all limitations. After all, they stripped the divine of their titles. The department turned gods into Dungeon Lords and their domains into Dungeons. Now, the department can teach Nox how to use magic to stand strong in a broken world. It will give him the tools to achieve his ambitions and his limitations will force him to the forefront of arcane discovery. Unfortunately, more immediate challenges await Nox, too. He lacks the means to pay the university's ridiculous tuition. Only alchemy and smart business deals will earn him the hundreds of gold coins he needs. **Join Nox on his journey from Novice to Archmage in this Arcane Academy LitRPG series from J Pal, bestselling author of *The Houndsman* and *They Called Me Mad*. It features a unique magic system which involves cultivating a solar system in one's core, Detailed spell crafting and alchemy, Dungeon diving, arcane archery,a magic university setting and so much more.**

Get Department of Dungeon Studies Now!

————

For all our LitRPG books, visit our website.

ABOUT THE AUTHOR

Since he was a child, Daoist Enigma always enjoyed getting lost in worlds other than his own. Fantastical, exuberant worlds where the only limits were set by one's own imagination. As an adult, he decided to embark upon a journey of creating a world that he could truly call his own. Through the trials and tribulations that followed, he is delighted to present to you his first series, Modern Patriarch, with many more to come!

You can find him on Patreon : https://www.patreon.com/daoistenigma

and Royal Road: https://www.royalroad.com/profile/183221/fictions

Made in the USA
Las Vegas, NV
23 August 2024

94317130R00254